FRENCH QUARTER

STELLA CAMERON

FRENCH QUARTER

KENSINGTON BOOKS
http://www.kensingtonbooks.com

KENSINGTON BOOKS are published by

Kensington Publishing Corp.
850 Third Avenue
New York, NY 10022

Library of Congress Card Catalog Number: 97-076039
ISBN 1-57566-312-0

First Printing: September, 1998
10 9 8 7 6 5 4 3 2 1

Printed in the United States of America

For Jerry, the love of my life

Portrait of a Scoundrel

A scoundrel, a vicious man,
he goes with a leer on his lips,
winking his eye, shuffling his foot,
beckoning with his finger.

Deceit in his heart, always scheming evil,
he sows dissention.

Disaster will overtake him sharply for this,
suddenly, irretrievably, his fall will come.

Proverbs 6:12–15

One

The towel settled over the man's face, his shoulders, his chest. A big towel, Jack Charbonnet thought, and damp. It made a white death mask of Errol Petrie's features, a shroud for his body on the stark tiled floor.

Jack watched the scene framed by the partially open door into the bathroom.

He took several more steps into the bedroom and reached the foot of the empty bed. He heard the beat of his own heart, but felt nothing. Nothing.

An urge to shout imploded. If he shut his eyes and opened them again, he'd see more clearly, and Celina Payne wouldn't be standing over Errol.

Bamboo ceiling fans turned slowly, clicked on their rods, their long, discolored cords swinging in the humid air. When Jack had entered the courtyard of the Royal Street house, another day was heating up in the Quarter. The warm breeze brought snatches of noise, and the scent of gardenias and old beer past the arched grillwork gate that closed off the yard.

Only minutes earlier he had walked through the streets, annoyed at Errol for insisting on a meeting before nine in the morning, when he knew Jack took his daughter to school every day, and wasn't available until later.

None of that mattered now. Errol's message must have come in while Jack was explaining to his mother-in-law that he couldn't bring Amelia to her for the weekend. That had been after midnight. Then he'd turned off the ringer so he wouldn't hear if she called again. And he hadn't checked for messages until he got up. If he had listened before he went to sleep, he'd have called Errol back. . . .

Celina made a noise, a faint, choking sniff. He noticed she wore a loose yellow bathrobe, and that her short, red-brown curls shone in the yellow overhead light. Her feet were bare. Disjointed parts of a picture he didn't want to see.

Closing his eyes wasn't going to make this go away. "Celina?" His voice grated obscenely in the still morning gloom behind closed shutters in the bedroom.

She choked again, and spun around. Her face shocked him afresh. Bloodless, the skin might be fused to bone, and her dark blue eyes were vast and unblinking. She looked at him without recognition and caught hold of the doorjamb.

"Good God!" Jack said. The numb sensation in his limbs dissolved. He trembled inside, but adrenaline pumped through him and he strode to throw the bathroom door wide open.

"Errol," Celina muttered. "Errol."

Jack faced the bathroom. The footed porcelain tub came into full view. Pools of water puddled into dips in the uneven white-tiled floor where the boards underneath had warped.

He smelled what he should have smelled before: liquor. He'd brought the remembered scent of gardenias muddled with beer into the house with him, then been vaguely aware of Celina's incongruously innocent lemony fragrance. The pungent odor of bourbon hadn't registered.

His stomach constricted, and this time he did glance at Celina. She continued to grasp the doorjamb. Her eyes were squeezed shut, and she moaned.

Errol knew better than to take a drink—didn't he?

Jack looked down at an outflung hand and forearm.

Below the white towel, Errol's long, muscular body was naked.

Naked but for a brilliant green rubber ring on his flaccid penis.

Celina gave a thin, broken cry. "Not Errol. He's got so much to give, so much to do. We need him."

Crouching, Jack used a finger and thumb to lift the towel until he could see Errol Petrie's face, his sky-blue eyes wide open and glazed in death.

Celina cried out and stumbled to the foot of the bed. She clung to a mahogany post.

"What happened here?" His heart beat harder and sweat stuck his shirt to his back.

Her mouth opened and closed, without a sound now, as if she fought unsuccessfully for air.

"Speak to me." Death, even violent death, had touched him before, but it hadn't hardened him to the horror. "Celina, say somethin'." The urge to shout had returned. He controlled it.

"Why are you here?" she asked at last, in barely more than a whisper.

"What the—" He bit back an expletive. "Errol called me late last night. He asked me to come first thing this mornin'. Not that it matters a damn why I'm here. Where's the aid car? How long ago did you call the aid car?"

She shook her head.

"Tell me."

She said, "It's too late. He's dead. He's so cold, Jack."

He knew she was right, but he knelt and put an ear to his old friend's chest and listened.

"I knew his heart wasn't good," Celina said. "He must have been in the tub when the pain started. But he wasn't supposed to die. He's too young to die. Dreams—"

"Dreams isn't the issue right now," he said, and didn't care how sharply. "The foundation will land on its feet. I'll see to that. You still haven't told me what I want to know. How long has he been . . . How long, Celina? And what happened that would cause him to have a heart attack?" He was sure he already knew, but he wanted to hear it from the fair lady's lips. He'd warned Errol to get rid of his so-called assistant, but he wouldn't listen.

She had pressed her lips together and looked fixedly across the room. He followed the direction of her gaze and got up.

A tangle of clothing lay on the blue and green silk rug near an antique sea chest that had been in Errol's family for more than a hundred years. Jack walked closer.

Celina made another strangled noise. He didn't turn back. The clothing was underwear, a woman's skimpy black silk bra and panties, garter belt and stockings. To the left, between the bed and the bathroom, there was something else black. A long piece of silk, like a narrow scarf. Another scarf caught his eye—still tied to one of the posts at the head of the bed. A glove made of shiny black fur poked from beneath a rumpled pillow.

Fury pumped the blood through his veins. He turned on Celina Payne, ex–Miss Louisiana, the woman he had feared for months was spending more time with Errol than either of them would confess. "I warned him to stay away from you. I told him you were bad news for a man like him."

"And you were wrong," she shot back. "He already had a bad heart. That wasn't my fault."

He pointed to the heap on the carpet. "What do you think it would do to New Orleans's favorite charity if a picture of this room made its way onto the front page of some rag?"

"What he did with his own time should be his business."

He laughed and felt his throat tighten. "You'd like that, wouldn't you? If anything grubby could be brushed under the rug just so you could continue to be the Dreams Girl? You and your parents got plenty out of Errol's nonprofit organization, and you want to keep on gatherin' the goodies. And all in the name of makin' the dreams of dyin' children come true."

The speed with which she moved caught him off guard. She flew at him and he barely stopped them both from falling. Her fists threw a frenzy of ineffectual punches at his body and head. He flinched, but captured her wrists and shook her.

At once she stood still. The anger in her eyes fled, replaced by . . . resolve? Resolve, and intense dislike for him. Not that there had ever been any doubt about their mutual distrust.

"The police have to be called," he told her.

"The aid car has to be called," she said without inflection. Her soft voice reeked of old New Orleans society, the kind of old New Orleans society that couldn't be bought. "The aid people will call the police," she added.

Suddenly she was so cool. He released her and put some distance between them. "You seem to have this all worked out."

"Someone has to. If you think about it, you'll see I'm going to do what has to be done."

He looked back at Errol, then at the floor.

"You made your point very well, Jack. The last thing we can afford is mud on the reputation of Dreams. So we're going to help each other make sure that doesn't happen."

Two

Celina heard the coldness in her own voice and bowed her head. One thing she'd always been proud of was her ability to appear calm under pressure. Mama wasn't "steady," Daddy had always warned. For her parents' sake it was up to Celina to be real steady. Evidently she'd perfected her act very well. Too bad she felt as if she were disintegrating inside.

Jack Charbonnet gave her one of his unfathomable stares. "You didn't even bother to get Antoine."

When he was outside, Antoine was the Royal Street gardener. When he was inside, he filled whatever position was necessary. "He doesn't live here. It's early."

"Not that early. He was working on the banana trees in the court-yard when I arrived. When did Errol collapse?"

"It was seven or so when I found him."

"It's after nine now. Antoine gets here before seven, doesn't he?"

What was he trying to say, to ask? "I didn't go for Antoine because I didn't think about it. That's all I can tell you."

"That man has worked for Errol for years. He loves him. You knew that."

"I didn't think to get him," she repeated. Jack Charbonnet wouldn't batter her into losing control.

He turned on his heel and returned to crouch over Errol. Celina's legs wobbled and she sank to sit on the floor. Errol ran Dreams as a tight ship. Every penny they took in from auctions and other fund-raisers went to terminally ill children and their families, to funding services to those children, and minimally for the support of Errol and his staff of two: Celina and Antoine. Rooms on the other side of the second-story apartment—antique stores occupied the ground floor on Royal Street—rent-free rooms were a good part of Celina's compensation.

Jack Charbonnet didn't approve of her living there. She knew because she'd overheard him telling Errol as much. Today she'd seen how he assessed what she wore, and she remembered his voice when he said, "Sure, your private lives are separate. And you didn't hire her as the Dreams Girl to wring donations out of horny old men— rich, horny old men, because she's beautiful and sexy? She'll bring trouble, Errol. Get rid of her."

"Errol," she whispered, and touched a fingertip to the tumble of green sheets and green and gold spread spilling over the side of the bed. She'd chosen them for him to replace his threadbare linens. "Oh, Errol." Her dear friend, her best friend, the one she could rely on to listen, to smile, and to help when she needed help. He'd told Jack he was wrong about her, and warned him not to raise the subject again.

Errol was dead.

Yesterday he'd told her she looked tired and given her this morning off. She had been in bed when calls began switching through from his lines to her phone, and she came to see if he was all right.

Celina shuddered. How long had she stood there, looking down at him?

She had panicked, almost fainted, then refused to believe he wouldn't come to and smile at her.

What was the sickly smell in the room? The fans moved sluggishly through heavy air.

Errol's blond hair, turning gray at the temples, was clearly visible to the left of Jack's lowered knee. Celina didn't think Jack was looking at Errol, but that he had covered his own face with his right hand.

She heard his long, slow exhalation, then he stood up and said, "Why did you put the towel over his face?" without turning to her.

"I don't know." She felt ill, but she was calmer now. "How do you know why you do things when you do them?"

"Most people have an idea." He swept up the towel.

She drove her fingers into her hair. "Most people don't find their best friend dead on the bathroom floor with"—she waved her hands— "like that—like he is. I couldn't bear that he was so vulnerable. His eyes. He looked so shocked."

"Your best friend?" Jack turned around and walked slowly into the bedroom. He still held the towel. "Curious thing to call your boss. I'm going to ask you again. What went on here?"

He stood so close, she had to crane her neck to see his face. "That's where I found him—how I found him. I don't know what happened."

According to talk, Jack's roots were Cajun on his father's side, and they showed in his thick, black hair which he wore short, and in a lean face that never appeared completely clean shaven. His eyes were that hazel color, perhaps more green than hazel, and could hold an unblinking intensity Celina found uncomfortable. A tall man, his broad-shouldered body was muscular but slender, and he moved with deceptively languid grace. They said he was dangerous, but the reasons were never clear. A man to fear, she'd been warned by her mother, but Bitsy Payne feared most people whom she didn't consider her social equal.

"You didn't expect me this mornin', did you?" he asked in his deep, slow tones. His drawl wasn't as strong as some, but it was enough to be another reminder that Jack Charbonnet's family tree was very different from Celina's. He made her too aware of being female, had done so from the first time they met. She didn't recall another man having the same, or even a similar impact on her.

"No. Jack, Errol—"

"You didn't call for help because you were tryin' to decide what to do next."

He managed to make every sentence sound like an accusation. "I was trying to make sense out of this," she told him.

"Shouldn't have been tough. Unless you didn't know Errol's father died of a heart attack at fifty. His uncle was fifty-two. Errol ignored it, but he'd already been told he was high risk." He glanced at the pile of women's underwear she'd seen on the floor earlier. "I thought he had himself under better—Never mind. If I had to go on a hunch, I'd say he died because somethin' was too much for him." His eyes narrowed and he looked her over slowly enough to make her even more edgy.

She averted her face. "I knew about his heart. But I can't believe he's dead. I just can't believe it."

"Regardless of what you can believe, we'd better get back to the plan you were working on before I got here."

Celina held quite still for a moment before looking up at his face again. "Plan?"

"The one you said I'm goin' to help you with. That's the one you started on when you decided not to call for help when he died."

"I wasn't with him when he died."

"So you say."

Her head hurt. "So it was. I wish I had been there when he collapsed. Perhaps I could have helped him."

He strolled to pick up the underwear. Very deliberately he held each piece aloft.

Celina blushed. A pair of black panties that were nothing more than a small triangle and some strings, and a transparent black bra with lace stitched around holes cut out where a woman's nipples would be. The stockings had lace at the tops but were torn. The garter belt was another abbreviated collection of elastic covered with gathered silk. Jack threw the black scraps on the bed.

She got to her feet. "I'm going to have to leave this room. I can't bear it here any longer."

He went around her and closed the door. "I understand your feelin' that way, *chère*. I feel the same way, but you and I aren't goin' anywhere without some really careful thought, remember? There's too much tied up in Dreams to allow it all to slip away now."

Goose bumps ran along her skin. "So you are worried about the foundation losing money."

"Money doesn't have a thing to do with this. Everything he was working for depends on people being willin' to hitch their wagons to Dreams with absolute assurance that the last thing they'll be faced with is scandal."

She crossed her arms. "I know all about what makes the foundation click. I know it from every angle. You invested in Dreams. Errol told me you did. A lot of money."

"Sure I did. At the time . . . No, you don't have to know any more about my part in everythin'. You're an employee, an employee I didn't want hired, let alone set up in an adjoining room to Errol's."

"I'm not in an—"

"Figuratively speaking," he said, blinking slowly. "All you have to do to get here is walk through a few rooms. I figure we're in this together, *chère,* so I'm going to say things I wouldn't say otherwise. Errol was a recoverin' addict."

Did he think she'd worked side by side with Errol for almost two years and known him for years before that without being aware of the demons he'd fought?

"He came through a long, dark tunnel. That was his description, not mine. But he made it through—almost." His unflinching gaze moved beyond her again. "Dammit, he tried to get past it. He surely did try."

Celina had always assumed Jack knew Errol's secrets, but evidently

Jack had no notion she might know them, too. "He must have been in the bath and felt ill. There's water all over. He made it out and collapsed."

"It could have happened that way," Jack said. "It probably did. He was a charismatic man. Women always fell for him. That's what made it so hard on him."

"Don't." She couldn't stand to hear it all aired, all of the past Errol had managed to bury. "He was a good man, the best."

"He was a recoverin' alcoholic."

"Member of a large club, according to what I hear," Celina said, thinking of her own stepfather.

"The stuff was more poisonous to him than to most of the other members. He was told he had what amounted to an allergy. It scared him. But he fell off the wagon this time."

She'd smelled liquor of some kind. "You don't know he was the one—"

"The one doing the drinking? Rather than the lady who owns those?" He pointed to the clothing on the bed. "Okay. Let's say you weren't the one he had fun and games with before he died. He didn't need you flauntin' yourself in front of him seven days a week. Turnin' him on so he might be more vulnerable."

"Flaunting?" Even the word stunned her. She spread her arms. "Have you ever seen me flaunt myself?"

He looked her over from head to foot and gave a short laugh. His all-seeing stare brought a rush of heat. Her own intense response shook her. He said, "Do you get to be Miss Louisiana without flauntin' yourself?"

She winced. "You weren't talking about a beauty pageant six years ago. You were suggesting I've been trying to attract Errol in a sexual way right here and now."

"Haven't you?" He bent forward from the waist and studied his feet as if seeing his shoes for the first time. "You think you're hard on the eye dressed in a thin robe like that? Or dressed in any old thing at all?"

"Why don't you say what's really on your mind? Yes, Errol was a recovering alcoholic. He was also a recovering sex addict."

Jack's head snapped up. "How the hell did you know that?"

"He told me. Back at the beginning when he hired me he told me and said if I had any concerns about that he'd understand." The amazement in Jack Charbonnet's fine eyes gave Celina satisfaction. "His father was a friend of my parents'. I knew Errol from when I was a little kid. When he got married, I was the flower girl. Natalie was a bitch. He never should have married her."

Jack's sudden, sharp laugh wasn't what she'd expected, and she smiled involuntarily.

"He never told me all that—about bein' acquainted with you before. I was at the wedding too. I don't remember the flower girl. I didn't know you had that kind of shared history."

"You never bothered to find out."

Jack ran a hand around his neck. He said, "We've got to make decisions and act. Errol's death is tragedy enough. What good would it do if his name got tainted by whatever went on here?"

She shook her head.

"It's not important," he told her. "As you said, what a man chooses to do in the privacy of his own home is his own business—as long as he does it with consenting adults, and by the look of what I've seen so far, the lady he was with was very adult."

Tears filmed her eyes. She nodded.

"We're going to clean up anything that didn't belong to Errol, then raise the alarm. Errol asked me to come over, but he was out when I got here. Or that's what I thought. You came along—ready to go to work—and we shot the breeze for a while. We waited. Then we got suspicious and came looking. And *voilà*. Does that work for you?"

"You must have made up a lot of stories. You're good at it."

"As a matter of fact, I've got at least one fan who thinks I am. But this is a simple story. It's even got elements of truth in it."

She began to tremble again. "Then what?"

"They come and deal with . . . They come and take care of things."

"I didn't mean that. I meant afterward. Dreams."

"It'll go on," Jack said as if speaking through his teeth. "After he lost his boy, he behaved like he was givin' up. Then he came up with the idea for Dreams and it kept him going. It became his life and it does so much good."

She wanted to turn on him, to tell him that she knew he wasn't the kind of man who stayed awake nights worrying about sick children, that she knew Errol had been paying back the big loan he'd got from Jack back at the beginning. And the payback had been with big interest attached. Jack wanted to be sure his investment continued to pay off.

"I'll be in the bathroom," Jack said. "The bedroom's all yours. Nothing gets left behind unless it belongs to Errol. Got that?"

Oh, yes, sir. She gathered the handful of black silk and held it at arm's length. "What am I supposed to do with it?"

"Grow up," Jack said, but his voice was even. "Use your head and start looking around."

He went into the bathroom again. Celina didn't want to look, but couldn't stop herself. He made a ball of the towel and dropped it, then made a visual search of the space.

"How—" Celina swallowed. "How long ago do you think he died?"

"I'm not a pathologist." He bent over Errol's body.

Celina saw what he was doing and did look away. How could the act of touching a dead man's penis be at once so personal yet so impersonal?

She picked up a long, black scarf from the floor and untied another from the head of the bed. The fur glove was almost hidden by a pillow. Celina took a tissue from the pocket of her robe and used it as a barrier between her fingers and the thing that disgusted her. She dropped the glove among the heap of silk.

A bottle of bourbon had rolled under the bed. Fortunately it had been capped. The room was stuffy and foul smelling. "Should I open a window?" she called.

"No," Jack said, so close behind her she jumped and spun around. "We're going to admit they'll find our fingerprints all over this place, but you don't open windows in someone else's bedroom, not if you're only supposed to be trying to find them."

"Where should I put all this stuff?" Celina asked, not wanting to as much as touch it.

"In your apartment."

She gazed at him. "I don't want it there."

"What you do with it later is your business. That's where it will have to go for now." He picked up the phone beside Errol's bed and dialed the emergency number. Then he said, "Medical emergency. Heart attack. I'm not sure, but I think so. I understand. I'll stay on the line. Someone will be waiting for you down below." He held an open hand toward Celina, and in the palm rested the awful green rubber ring she'd seen.

When she backed away, he frowned and motioned her to come to him. She did so and he pushed the ring among the other things she held while he gave the Royal Street address to whoever was on the phone.

He hung up and said, "Go. Now. Get dressed fast and come right back. They'll be here."

"You've forgotten something," she said. "Whoever these things belong to. What if she comes forward and says what really happened here?"

"Go," Jack said. "She's not going to say anything."

"How can you be so sure?"

He looked her directly in the eye. "I'm sure."

Three

Miss Payne could move fast, he'd give her that. Jack had heard the approach of sirens, and now feet clattered on the stairs from the courtyard. Only minutes had passed, but Celina had already sped to her rooms and back, and managed to exchange her robe for a loose white linen dress. She was still frantically buckling flat brown sandals.

Jack heard Antoine say, "He this way. Lordy, I don't know what the matter," and shot a warning glance at Celina before going to fling the bedroom door open. He was confronted by medics. They passed Antoine in the hall and hurried through the bedroom to the bathroom, carrying steel cases of equipment and a portable gurney.

"Mr. Petrie?" Antoine said. "What the matter, him? He sick? Mr. Charbonnet? Miss Celina?"

Celina went to Antoine and threaded her hands around one of his massively muscular arms. "We need you," she told him. "It's bad, Antoine, very bad."

"Lordy, lordy," Antoine muttered, wiping his spare hand over his sweating face. A giant of a man, his tightly curled hair had turned gray, and each flash of very white, gold-edged teeth chopped his dark, finely featured face in two.

"Thank you for showing the medics up," Jack told him, feeling the depth of the man's distress.

Antoine said, "I gotta go to Mr. Petrie, me."

"Not now," Celina said. "We have to allow the medics to do their job."

Jack studied her face. Either she was concerned for Antoine or the lady could act.

"Mr. Charbonnet," the man said, "you tell me what happen?"

"You know Mr. Petrie didn't have a good heart," Jack said.

Antoine waggled his head. "He dead. You sayin' he dead, him."

More sirens sounded, quickly growing closer. Jack met Celina's very blue eyes again. He saw a question there and raised his brows. If they hoped to salvage as much as possible here, she had to keep her cool.

Two cops appeared behind Antoine. One said, "Excuse us, podner," and they made their way into the bedroom. Jack glanced behind him at the activity inside the bathroom. The medics worked over Errol's body. When he turned back, Jack saw that Antoine cried silently and made no attempt to hide the tears.

One of the policemen left the bathroom. "Might be better if you three gave me your names, then took a seat in another room," he said, flipping to a clean page in his notebook. "We'll start with you." He pointed his pen at Antoine.

By the time each of them had complied, another siren sounded and rapidly zeroed in. It cut off outside the building.

Within moments, loud male tones rose above other, more quietly spoken men's voices. "I am going up there. If you want to stop me, you're going to have to shoot me in the back. Right there between my shoulder blades. Just make sure you give me a chance to take off my shirt first. It's linen and cost a bomb, I can tell you."

Jack felt an urge to laugh at what he recognized as Dwayne LeChat's dramatic declaration.

Compact, with blond curls still wet from the shower, Dwayne wore denim shorts and a flowing white poet's shirt. He tore into the bedroom a few steps ahead of two more members of the New Orleans Police Department. Beneath a perfect tan, his round face was almost as white as his shirt. He pushed Antoine aside and started for the group in the bathroom, but stopped. "I knew it," he muttered. He glanced at Celina and said, "Is he dead?"

"We're afraid he may be," Jack said quickly. Celina's eyes darted to his and away again. He'd have to keep on top of things or she'd give them away. "Why don't you go into the parlor, Dwayne? Errol would want you here. He thought of you as family."

Dwayne chewed the knuckles of his left hand. "You're talking about him in the past tense already. You think he's dead for sure. Oh, my God. How?" He turned to Celina. "How did it happen, darling? He's—oh, I don't care, I refuse to speak of Errol in past tense. He's the gentlest of creatures. He *abhors* violence. No one would deliberately hurt him."

Jack stared at Dwayne, then shook his head slightly when a policeman, his cap pushed back from his sweating brow, asked, "What makes you think Mr. Petrie was deliberately hurt, Dwayne?"

"He's as fit as a fiddle, Mulligan," Dwayne snapped, his intelligent brown eyes sharp. "You gentlemen of the law are a trifle too quick for your own good—unless some law-abiding citizen needs you to actually *think* about something. Then your tiny little minds crawl—in reverse. I want to see Errol."

"I don't think that's a good idea at the moment," Officer Mulligan said.

Dwayne gave him a pitying look and went toward the bathroom anyway. As owner of a drag club on Bourbon, he was on at least a last-name basis with most city cops. No one knew if LeChat was really Dwayne's last name. Jack liked the guy. He was rarely serious, but he was a man who made a faithful friend.

"I'll go and wait in the parlor," Celina said, holding his gaze. She seemed to want him to get the message that she was in control. "I'll take Antoine with me."

"I should wait outside," Antoine said, his expression desolate.

"You'll wait with me," Celina said firmly. "I need you, and Mr. Petrie needs you to be here too."

A sudden, uncontrolled burst of sobs froze them all. Jack turned around in time to see Dwayne stagger backward, his hands pressed to his stomach. Mulligan caught him by the arm and led him to the others, saying quite gently, "I think this is too much for you, Dwayne. Why not give yourself a break and go sit in the parlor? Have a drink."

"My God!" Dwayne pulled away from the policeman as if he were afraid of being hurt. "He *is* dead. They're going to take him away and cut him up. They'll take his insides out and paw him and poke him and make their nasty, sterile little notes. And they won't know anything about who he was. You can't open a man's body and find *him* inside. Errol Petrie isn't in there anymore."

Jack pinched the bridge of his nose. He wasn't good at shows of emotion.

"Go sit down, Dwayne," Mulligan repeated. "Maybe you could take him, sir," he said to Jack.

With a nod, Jack took Dwayne firmly by the elbow and guided him from the bedroom and along the corridor to the parlor. Once inside, he steered the other man into a daffodil-yellow armchair and poured him a brandy.

Celina came to stand in the middle of the room. Antoine hovered awkwardly to one side. Both declined a drink with a shake of the head.

Jack heard more footsteps in the hallway but didn't bother to find out who else was descending on this house of death.

Celina touched his sleeve hesitantly and immediately dropped her hand. He wanted to take that hand in both of his and press her palm to his cheek. He wished they were alone. He'd wished that on a number of previous occasions, but never as desperately as now. Wanting her was suicidal, and even allowing the thoughts he'd had about her to surface at a time like this was bizarre.

Without warning, Antoine bowed his head and wept. His body jerked with each racking sob, and Dwayne leaped up from the chair to mutter to himself and pace.

Agitated, Celina said, "Stop them, please," and clapped her hands over her ears. "This is too much."

He agreed, but couldn't allow himself to give in to an urge to yell for calm. "You'll be able to leave soon," he told her, not at all convinced he was right. "The police will have some questions to ask, but then they won't keep you."

"I won't be going anywhere." She sat on the couch that matched the daffodil-yellow chair, crossed her legs, and twitched her skirts around her knees in an unconsciously provocative gesture.

Jack's glance at her legs wasn't so much unconscious as inevitable. They said her legs had bought her the Miss Louisiana title. Jack didn't believe any woman got to be Miss anything that a lot of people coveted on the strength of their legs, or any other thing God had given them. Not a pair of long, long legs, or a pair of deceptively innocent navy-blue eyes—or a mouth many would consider too big.

Or did they?

Taken a piece at a time, Celina Payne might not be spectacular. Put all those pieces together and she was physically irresistible— except to Jack Charbonnet.

Antoine's sobbing subsided and Dwayne threw himself back into the chair.

Jack cast about for something other than Celina to hold his attention. He ran his gaze up the high white walls to gold crown moldings, a still life in oils that hung over the fireplace, and vowed to improve his timing when it came to admiring the female of the species. Thanks to Celina's redecorating talents, and Errol's indulgence of her influence over him, the room was tastefully beautiful.

When she spoke again, he realized she'd expected him to respond to her last statement. "I take it you don't have a problem with that, Jack," she said. "I'll be staying here for the present anyway. I'll have a lot of work to do to keep things running."

She'd have a lot of work to do? Jack studied her again and decided he might not enjoy some of the battles that lay ahead. On the other hand, they might not be all bad. . . .

"I'm glad to hear you say that," he told her, taking some pleasure in the surprise on her face. "Your help is going to be needed, I'm sure. Errol told me many times that you kept him on the straight and narrow around here."

A rap sounded on the open door and a man with an official air but dressed in rumpled plainclothes stood there. "Detective O'Leary," he said. "NOPD. I'm going to ask all of you to remain here, please. I'll be asking each of you to speak with me alone. Nothing to worry about. Just formality at this point."

Jack straightened up and pushed his hands into his pockets. "Sure. I'll be glad to do anything I can, but couldn't you let Miss Payne take a rest first? She's had a terrible shock, Officer."

"Detective," O'Leary corrected. "And haven't you had a shock too, sir? Under the circumstances, it might be as well if Miss Payne hung in here until we've spoken with her. Just procedure. I'm sure you all understand. Did you turn the victim over, Mr. Charbonnet?"

"Over?"

"You didn't?"

"Why would I?"

"No reason. I was just asking."

Why didn't the man come out with whatever he was almost saying? Jack walked to the door. "I'd be glad to be questioned first," he said. "But how about you tell us all what's on your mind?"

"Nothing definite to tell until the autopsy's been performed."

Antoine said, "Lordy, lordy," and shook his head repeatedly.

Celina wrapped her arms tightly about her middle and blinked back tears.

"You're not suggesting"—Dwayne rose from his chair—"that is, Errol had a heart attack, didn't he?"

"He may have," Detective O'Leary said. "The medical examiner will tell us if he did. And if he had one, the examiner will tell us when he had it—before or after."

The detective enjoyed his little games. Jack didn't. "I'll bite," he said. "Before or after what?"

"Before or after what probably killed him."

His chin jutting, Dwayne walked toward the detective. "What kind of a goddamn comment is that, O'Leary? You don't have a heart attack *after* you're dead, do you?"

O'Leary took out a smashed pack of cigarettes, lit up, and squinted from Dwayne to Jack to Celina and back to Jack. He exhaled slowly and said, "I guess Dwayne's got a point there, huh?"

Four

Celina didn't want to be alone with Jack Charbonnet. He either looked at her and apparently didn't see her at all, or he looked and saw too much. At the moment, he stared at her, stared at her face, then her body—all the way to her feet and back.

The questioning was over until they were called again. Antoine was showing the police through the areas at the back of the courtyard that were used primarily for storage. Errol's rooms were taped off and the police continued to examine and photograph the scene.

Jack shifted his attention. "There's a crowd in the street," he said. He stood to one side of the window to peer down. "As soon as the ghouls go away, I'd like you to let me take you somewhere for a good meal. You look as if you need one."

She stopped herself from giving a sarcastic response. "Dwayne should be back with coffee soon," she said instead. Dwayne had insisted on kitchen duty and informed Celina that he didn't need or want her help.

"Coffee isn't going to be enough," Jack said. "For either of us."

She didn't answer. Much as she wished it were otherwise, she knew this man was only being polite. He had never approved of her, never approved of Errol hiring her. Most of all, as he'd already mentioned several times that morning, he absolutely disapproved of her living there.

"Do you think Errol was murdered?" she asked.

Jack wandered away from the window with a faraway look in his eyes. "I think the police are moving in that direction. But they've got to be wrong. I'm convinced of that."

"If they aren't," she persisted, "we destroyed the evidence at a crime scene."

"I know."

"Should we go and tell them what we did?"

"For God's sake, no. Please do as you originally said you would—when you were dealin' with all of this so calmly. Keep your mouth shut."

A flush shot into her cheeks at his tone. He sounded so angry.

Without looking at her, he said, "He called me late last night. I was on the phone, so he left a message on my voice mail. Damn, why didn't I check to see if anyone had called?"

She didn't feel like soothing his feelings. "We do what we do."

That earned her a flicker of green eyes in her direction. "Yeah. I suppose we do."

"It wouldn't have made any difference." She didn't do the cruel thrust well.

"It might have. When we find out how . . . We don't know when he died yet, do we?"

The man had a way of tossing even a small kindness back. "No," she said.

The clip of high heels on wood silenced them both.

"Celina?" Her mother's voice echoed from the hall. "Where are you? It's your mama."

Jack flopped into a chair. "Exactly what we need," he said. "Some additional drama."

"You're talking about my mother," Celina said while her heart sank at the prospect of what was about to come. "In here, Mama," she called. "We're in the parlor."

"You sound as enthusiastic as I feel," Jack murmured. "Can we hope she won't get hysterical on us?"

Celina spared him a glare and rose as her mother entered the room.

"There you are, Celina," Mama said. "So much fuss. Police, TV people, cameras—and such a crowd. How people do love to gawk if they think they're goin' to see something awful. I actually had to sneak into the courtyard and hope I wasn't noticed. Then a policeman tried to stop me from coming up here! I ask you—stop me from visitin' my own daughter!"

"What are you doing here, Mama? I told you last night that I'd call you later today."

"We argued last night," Bitsy Payne said, tears filling her eyes. "I just could not stand another minute knowing you were not happy with your mama."

"Not now, Mama. Please." Celina hated to look at Jack. Her mother had a way of embarrassing her whenever they were together in front of other people.

"Mornin', Mrs. Payne," Jack said. He'd risen from the chair. "Can we expect your husband too?"

"Neville's under the weather." Bitsy didn't as much as spare Jack a direct glance. "Your daddy's in bed, Celina. I've unplugged the television. I can hope he doesn't watch the news."

"So you know what's happened?" At least there was no need to say it all out loud again.

"I imagine all of New Orleans is gossipin' about it." Bitsy's brunette hair curved to frame her carefully made-up face. Her penciled brows arched high, and there was a lack of mobility in her youthful features that Celina knew was due partly to a surgeon's knife.

Bitsy did look at Jack then, and her expression flattened. "Celina, I have always told you to be very careful who you get involved with. We aren't used to this sort of person." She continued to glare at Jack.

"This kind of person?" he murmured.

"Neville and I know all about you," Bitsy told him. "So do all of our friends. You may think that because it was your father who was a notorious gangster, you can pretend you have nothing to do with that sort of thing."

Gangster? Celina digested the word, all the time watching Jack. His expression had closed, closed but for the derision in his eyes.

"Is it true that Errol was murdered?" Bitsy's strident voice dropped to conspiratorial tones. "Right here, and with you in the house?"

"Nice of you to mention our friend's death," Jack said. "We think he died early this morning. At this point we're waiting for the medical examiner's opinion. Until he says otherwise, we're assuming Errol had a heart attack."

"Oh!" Bitsy fished in her tiny pale-blue handbag for a lace-edged handkerchief and dabbed at the corners of her eyes. "Dear Errol. Always such a gentleman. And so kind to you, Celina. Not that Wilson seems to like him very much. I can't understand why."

At the mention of Wilson Lamar's name, Celina made fists at her waist. She felt her eyelids twitch and a cold shiver made a ladder of her spine. Lamar was a successful lawyer, and a hopeful in the next Louisiana senate race. He was also a hanger-on to the senior Paynes' social connections.

"Rather cuddle alligators," Jack said clearly.

"What?" Celina turned to him. "What did you say?"

"I was just decidin' what would be most distasteful to me. The company of some people, or of alligators. The gators won."

"What people?" Bitsy asked, sounding deeply suspicious.

Jack ignored her question.

"This is beyond all," Bitsy complained when Jack showed no sign of responding. "I don't know what you can be thinking of, Celina. Here alone with *him*. What if your name and his are . . . well, mentioned together in the papers? You know your daddy doesn't like talk. Our friends . . . well, there's surely never been any talk attached to the name of Payne."

Embarrassment became an agony. Celina wondered just how much Jack knew about the arrangement between her parents and Dreams for the use of their Garden District home. They were paid, not only for allowing their house to be used as an auction venue, but for encouraging some of their well-connected friends and acquaintances to attend—and to buy. Mama and Daddy got a percentage of the profit for every sale made on their premises to someone they'd invited.

Leading with a shoulder, Dwayne pushed open the door and entered with a tray of mugs. "Coffee LeChat," he announced, and turned. When he saw Bitsy, he frowned, but said, "Mornin'."

Bitsy muttered, "Pervert," not quite softly enough.

"I'll come over to the house later," Celina said rapidly. "There's a lot going on here, Mama. Not nice things. You go home to Daddy and I'll be along later."

"Don't you tell me what I should do, young lady." Bitsy pointed at Jack. "See the way he looks at me? How dare he. Just because he knows I know what he is and he hates me for it. His kind are dangerous, Celina. Jealous and desperate. You don't know because you've led a sheltered life. But they'll do anything to try to be accepted in our world."

Desperation stole most of Celina's breath. *"Mama,"* she pleaded.

"I told Errol he shouldn't be mixed up with a man like that."

"Jack Charbonnet is a gentleman," Dwayne LeChat said softly, and set down the tray—also softly. "You, lady, are a fool and a snob—forgive me, Celina."

"Well," Bitsy said, but her voice shook. "How dare you, you *pervert*. I want you out of here today, Celina, but not before we settle our affairs to our satisfaction. Do I make myself clear?"

"Please be quiet, Mama. Jack will be responsible for overseeing Dreams now."

Bitsy snorted. "Errol wouldn't have allowed *that*. And don't you be sucked in by a handsome face and smooth talk. They're a certain kind, my girl, Cajun trash tryin' to use money to buy respect. No background. They say his mother was never married to his father anyway—and she was half his age."

Jack took a step toward the Payne woman and felt rather than saw Dwayne move. The other man rested a hand on his shoulder and said, "Let it go, Jack. She's not worth your anger."

He looked into Bitsy's spiteful brown eyes and saw other brown eyes, these a contrast to long, blond hair. The hair had fanned wide on the surface of the pool, and the eyes had stared unseeingly upward. His mother's naked white body atop a blue air mattress, bobbed on the surface, her legs obscenely splayed. Blood from the gaping wound across her neck stained the water.

His father, or what was left of him, was pinned with metal nut picks to a wooden trellis on the wall outside open doors to the master suite. Racked by his own agony, he watched his wife tortured, raped, and killed before his throat was also cut. Even if they hadn't dealt the final, killing slash, Pierre Charbonnet wouldn't have wanted to live with either the memory of his beloved wife's death, or with what Win Giavanelli's men had already done to him.

"Jack?"

Evidently his mother had tried to persuade his father to turn his back on the Giavanelli family, and crime, and he had finally made a suicidal move to do what she wanted. If he'd been only an associate he might have got away with it, but not as a made man, not as one of Win Giavanelli's most trusted captains.

"Jack, what is it?"

He heard Celina talking to him. Her voice came from a great distance. "Yeah." It had been a long time since he'd seen the images so clearly. They'd haunted him from his tenth year through his adolescence, until the day he'd made up his mind what he had to do. Then he'd put them aside, but not forgotten them.

Jack had never stopped wanting vengeance, and he was getting closer to his goal.

Win Giavanelli, still the family boss, had given the order for his parents' assassination. He was going to die for that. Jack had expected to see him dead a long time ago, but he'd also learned that if he hoped to be unscathed afterward, he had to be patient.

"Celina," Jack heard Bitsy Payne say. "You do know he's got connections to the mob, don't you? Look. He's staring at me. I heard his mother was killed by the mob. The man she was living with was murdered too. Not that he didn't deserve it. He was a very rich criminal."

"You are talkin' about my parents, Mrs. Payne," Jack said when he could make his voice work. "Pierre and Mary Charbonnet? They were murdered when I was ten years old."

"Oh, Jack," Celina murmured, and the horror on her face showed she hadn't known.

"I didn't know about your parents," Dwayne said. "My sympathies, Jack. Bad luck. Of course, if you'd had my parents, you'd have been glad if someone decided—"

"Thanks, Dwayne," Jack said quickly.

"There was a lot of money," Bitsy said, and Jack eyed her, fascinated, wondering just how far she would go. "And there are plenty of people who wonder what happened to it."

He had his answer. "Are you talkin' about my parents' estate now, Mrs. Payne?" he asked, and if she had any sense, the soft pitch of his voice would have made her very nervous. "Because if you are, there's no mystery. I was the sole beneficiary, which seems unremarkable to me."

"Blood money," she muttered. "Drug money. Payoffs."

She didn't have any sense. Ah, well. "Blood money? I wouldn't know anything about that. Or payoffs. But I do have to set you straight on the drugs, ma'am. Hard for a man to get rich on those. Cosa Nostra has a very strict code of ethics. Good family ethics. If a brother deals in drugs—he's dead. Insults against the family? Same sentence."

Bitsy Payne backed toward the door. "Neville will wonder where I am," she said faintly. "Come along, Celina."

"I have to stay until the police say I can go," Celina said. "But I'll call you a cab."

Bitsy showed no sign of budging.

"Wait a few minutes and I'll walk you out," Dwayne said. "If we get questioned by the press, just say, 'No comment.' I'll tell them you and I are old friends. We came to give our condolences together because we're a comfort to each other."

Bitsy said, "Call me a cab, Celina."

Five

Naked on top of the rumpled bed, Wilson Lamar stretched and yawned and slapped his flat belly while he smiled down at the only body he revered—his own.

"Aren't you just a teensy bit wiggly, Wilson?" Sally Lamar asked her husband, watching him in her dressing table mirror.

Wilson was always partly erect—something else that brought him pleasure. It used to bring Sally pleasure before he'd lost interest in making love to her.

Brushing her long, dark red hair slowly, she caught his blue eyes in the mirror and smiled at him. "Just a teensy bit?" she murmured. "This is going to be a long, busy day. Let's give each other something to remember while we get ready to charm the people tonight. Some encouragement?"

"We've slept the morning away. Where's the remote? I'm going to miss the one o'clock news."

Sally knew enough to make sure her smile didn't slip. "On the table beside you, hon." The bastard. He was nothing without her. "They're putting those darling white lights in the trees, Wilson. I think I'm going to ask for more along the galleries. What d'you think of that, lover?"

If Wilson thought about anything at all at that moment, it was Wilson. Everything he ever did was calculated to the greater glory of Wilson Lamar, and the senate race he expected to win. He didn't answer her question, but then, she hadn't expected him to do so.

The fine silk nightgown Sally wore was white, with thin straps that didn't want to stay on her shoulders. Only her breasts stopped the garment from succumbing to gravity. She got up to stand in front of the French doors she'd already opened, clasped her hands behind her head, and arched her back, taking pleasure in a warm breeze that passed over her body.

"Get away from there, Sally," Wilson said. "How many times have I told you not to advertise your wares to the world?"

"Why, Wilson, you do care," she said, and walked onto the gallery, catching up a robe as she went. She hummed, and played a game she liked. Inside her head she created a little roulette wheel and gave it a spin. Her white ball bounced around and the wheel slowed. "Red is yes, and black is no," she chanted quietly. "Red, I do, and black, I don't. Red, I get what I want, and black, well, I guess I'm not in the mood for black today. We'll have to see what we can find at the party tonight." She wouldn't have any problem finding a willing playmate to pass a little time with.

She pulled on the robe and leaned on the gallery railing. The beautiful old double-galleried house was on the southern edge of the Garden District and had belonged to Sally's parents. Her mother had died first and her father remarried but,—good for Daddy, and good for Sally—when he died, the hopeful young widow discovered it was to Sally not her that the house had been left. The house and almost everything else wealthy Claude Dufour owned. After all, Sally's lawyer had pointed out when the widow complained, Sally's mother had been Claude's bankroll, and it was only appropriate that Sally should inherit.

"Mornin', Mrs. Lamar," Opi called up from the front steps to the house. Caterers, florists, and sundry other people preparing for the evening's event scurried in and out from vans parked in the driveway.

"Mornin'," Sally replied to Opi. He had been with her family for more years than she had, and she'd long ago forgotten exactly what he did except that nothing happened in the house that Opi didn't orchestrate. Rotund, bald, and the color of milky coffee, either he'd advanced in the household at a very early age, or he was an old man. Hard to be sure.

"Well, I'll be," Sally whispered to herself. She'd have pulled back inside if it wasn't already too late—if that upstart boy hadn't already seen her. He stood under a tree, watching as if he'd been waiting for her to appear.

She didn't even know his name. He was a new member of the household staff. Not that she had any idea what he did. Yesterday he'd sauntered past her, his sweet ass tight inside jeans washed so thin, she could see the shadow between his cheeks.

First she'd followed him through the oaks until she had a chance to speak to him alone. Then she'd taken him to the old gazebo, and it had all been so much fun—until he turned rough. He'd scared her and she'd told him to get lost, but there he was, smiling up at her.

Tonight there would be a big fund-raiser for Wilson's campaign. The old house and its sumptuous gardens would ring with music and laughter, and the clink of fine crystal and china. Deals would be made. For a "small" consideration, Wilson would remember his friends who helped him get to the senate. Already the pot was gratifyingly huge, but it had to be a great deal larger. And Sally would be the gracious hostess, the bestower of sisterly confidences on rich women, suggestive winks on rich old men, and, as the hour grew late and the company became drunker, sly crotch squeezes on rich men who were not too old.

But that was tonight.

Sally deliberately ignored the boy—she didn't even know his name—and studied the men at work threading lights among live oaks draped with Spanish moss. She glanced behind her and saw Wilson propped on one elbow, his expression rapt as he watched the only god he worshipped almost as much as himself, and money—the media.

She turned to the gardens once more. He was still there, and he was looking right back at her. Standing in the shade of one of the oaks closest to the house, he sank his hands into the pockets of his jeans and stared up at Mrs. Sally Lamar. Insolent boy. He'd pushed her down, ripped her underwear. Oh, he'd been good—good enough for her to want more—but there was something about him that made alarms sound in her head. Besides, she was thirty-six. This sun-tanned, hard-muscled, eager-to-be friend might be twenty-one or two, or a little more. Or he might not. A tall, dark-haired, dark-eyed, beautiful young thing. Possibly a dangerous young thing. She would ignore him.

His finger, pointed at her, mesmerized Sally. He kept right on pointing and strolled from the shade into the light.

Heading for the house. He was heading for the house!

When he reached the bottom of the front steps, he sent her a knowing look and folded his arms. He nodded toward the entrance, then disappeared beneath her, through the front door.

Sally felt the beat of her heart in her throat. She went back into the bedroom, keeping her steps slow. Wilson continued to stare at the TV screen that all but covered a wall, and acknowledged her presence only by letting out an exasperated breath and shifting irritably when she walked in front of him and out of the room. She closed the door quietly behind her.

From the balcony that ran around the second story there was an unobstructed view of a central hall. Tessellated black and white marble tiles, walls hung with dark red brocaded silk, white stone urns overflowing with hothouse flowers already put in place by the florists—a small gold-draped dais where a harpist would serenade arriving guests. Daddy would have approved. Sally approved of it, but she didn't have time to admire her taste while the sinuous, fluid-limbed man approached the stairs with the kind of nonchalance that belonged only to the foolish or the self-confident. Everyone was too busy working to notice when he climbed upward, one large hand on the gilded banister. His light denim shirt was unbuttoned to the waist, showing plenty of black curly hair on his chest.

And the way those soft jeans dipped and bulged over his crotch.

Heat and cold chased across her skin. She had to get rid of him. He was young, and wild, and could be difficult to control. Control was Sally's thing. She always controlled the men she chose to play with.

This time she'd control the boy too. She'd show him who was in charge, enjoy him, and make sure he didn't come near her again unless she did the approaching and the asking.

One of Opi's Jelly Roll Morton tapes burst to life from the dining room. Sally snapped her fingers to "Black Bottom Stomp" and turned her back on the man who climbed the stairs. Sashaying to the music, she made her way into one of the guest bedrooms. She dropped her robe at the entrance to the bathroom and began to hum and clap. There were always plenty of big, fluffy towels in every bathroom. Sally pulled two from a cupboard and hung them on a rack near the shower before turning on the water.

Yes, this time her strong, young lover would learn about being used, and he'd want her again so badly that he wouldn't dare to put another foot wrong.

The bedroom door slammed shut.

Sally boogied, her bare feet beating a rhythmic tattoo on the cool, deep-water-green tile.

He entered the bathroom, hovered by the door, watching her. Then he locked them in.

His eyes were dark, but dark blue, not brown, and maybe she'd misjudged his age.

"How old are you?" she asked softly.

"Old enough, me." His liquid voice was deep, the cadence heavily Cajun. "You?" he asked.

"Old enough, me too," she said, making herself laugh. He was too sure of himself. "Where did you get all that chutzpah so soon? Come on, how old? Twenty?"

He raised his chin. "Twenty-three. That too young? Or too old? I show you it's just right, lady."

Sally danced toward him and locked her wrists behind his neck. "You aren't going anywhere until I say so, and I don't say so. I call the moves around here. Dance with me, baby. Show me how you can move."

He swallowed, and his neck jerked sharply, and a thrill ran down her spine. He talked a great story, but the big boy was a bit nervous this time. Sally kept one hand behind his neck and used the other to play with the hair on his chest. She stood on her toes and ran her tongue along his square jaw and into his ear. He made a moaning sound low in his throat.

"You're going to make love to me," she whispered. "And afterward you're going to go away and you'll never do what you did out there again. No one saw you—at least, I don't think so. But you will never risk arousing my husband's suspicions. Next time, you wait for me to send for you."

He shivered, actually shivered.

"Now let's get close," she said. "You can do anything you want. And I'll do anything you want. And you'll do *everything* I want. Do we have a deal?"

"Maybe."

Sally stood absolutely still. "Maybe?"

"You want somethin' I got. What you want I don't give away— not unless I'm offerin'."

She slapped him hard across the face. She didn't get a chance to hit him again.

He grasped her wrist, spun her around, and pushed her arm just far enough up her back to make her bite down a scream. The face Sally saw above her own in the mirror was very confident. He smiled at her, a tight, downturned smile, and his eyes narrowed against steam from the beating shower.

Placing his mouth on her left ear, he said, "Probably we should make no loud noise, no?" and eased the pressure on her arm. He slid his free hand around her waist and splayed his darkly tanned fingers over her belly. "You should be polite, you. Thank the guest for comin'.

Ask him if he got everythin' he want. Maybe he say yes." He rested his mouth on the side of her neck but never lost eye contact in the mirror.

She had judged him right the first time. Dangerous. He could cause a lot of trouble. The "boy" had shivered with excitement at the promise of a chance to dominate a woman who should have been beyond his reach.

"What you say, *Mrs.* Lamar?"

Sally placed a hand on top of his on her stomach and smiled at him. "Tell me your name." She dipped her head slightly, let the smile slip away slowly. The little touches that went into seduction came naturally.

"You love sex," he said baldly. He bared very white teeth and sank them lightly into her shoulder. "Perhaps you love sex almost as much as Ben."

"Ben." Not a name she would have expected. Perhaps the white ball had landed on black after all. Despite the steam, she began to feel cold. "You've been gone from your work a long time. They'll wonder where you are."

"I work for myself, me." He spread his legs, pressed her bottom into his pelvis. "Aquariums. You remember the new aquariums Mr. Lamar order? Today I stock them. Nobody watchin' me. Nobody know if I leave for a while."

She considered and discarded the notion of threatening him with an accusation of unprovoked attack. At least until she was safely away from him. "You are very handsome, Ben. But you know that, don't you?" Her mouth was so dry. "I'm sorry if I offended you by thinking you'd want me."

"I do want you. You're lots of woman. Yesterday was very good. Any man want you. But I don't like to be told what I want."

"I'm sorry."

"No, you not sorry, you are frightened of me. I like that too. Fear bring respect, and a man is not a man if a woman he fuck don't respect him."

Sally's legs weakened, but she locked her knees and stood firm. Damn Wilson for ignoring her all the time. This was his fault, but if he ever found out, he would probably laugh and say she'd got what she deserved. Wilson wouldn't find out; nobody would. Her dear husband never came looking for her; if he did, he might have walked in on her with a man long before then.

She wished he would walk in now.

"You like this?" Ben asked, stroking downward between her legs and making the thin silk gown instantly wet. "Tell me how you like?"

Sally grew warm again, then hot. What the hell. She could handle a twenty-three-year-old with a big head. "I like it a lot, Ben. But I want you to tell me what you like. I thought you were going to tell me."

"I like it here, in this house. I get sick of aquariums."

Horrified at what he might be suggesting, she covered his probing hand. "What do you mean?"

He trapped her tightly against the green marble counter. His penis might as well have been naked—she could feel its hard outline and its pressure on the small of her back. Her breathing grew shallow and her breasts stung.

"This what I mean," he said quietly. "I want you give me a job, you. The pool. I look after the pool, maybe—and other things."

He began to terrify her. "I'm not sure—"

"You sure." Releasing her arm, he cupped her breasts and pinched her nipples between his fingers. "No man better than Ben. And all yours. Whenever you want, you come to me."

"*Live* here?" she asked. "Is that what you mean, you want to live here?"

"No." He laughed. "I got my own place. Like my own place. I show it to you and you come when you like."

Then why did he want a job here?

"And I be here to give you surprises when you bored, yes?"

No, she wanted to shout, but he was tightly wound, a steel coil of energy inside, and she'd be a fool to risk unleashing the cold rage he'd already shown himself capable of.

The pressure on her back became a rhythmic bumping. He darted his tongue in and out of her ear and bared her breasts. "Great tits," he said, scraping the edges of his thumbnails over them until she tossed her head restlessly. She burned from her breastbone to her knees, and throbbed heavily where her labia swelled.

"You like it hard, maybe? Fast? You tell Ben what you like."

Her breath came in pants now. Apart from beads of sweat on his brow, he seemed in control. "You tell me what you like," she countered. "I want to make you happy."

"Oh, I'm gonna be very happy, Mrs. Lamar. I gonna plan so many surprises for you. So many new things."

Why had she picked him out? Because he'd been everywhere she looked yesterday, and because he was the kind of beautiful she couldn't resist. Even as his hands and body sucked at the last vestiges of reason, she struggled against panic. Rather than what she was accustomed to, an exciting, forbidden encounter quickly forgotten by both parties, she was threatened with a tough opportunist who knew how sexy he was, and who was sharp enough to also know he might have hit pay dirt with *Mrs. Lamar.*

"You tell that Opi he hire me to take care of the pool, yes? And Mr. Lamar's aquariums, of course?"

With no effort he spun her to face him and bent to suck at first one, then the other breast. He took his time, took long, heavy drags, and eased the gown up to her waist. His thumbs settled in the cleft of her bottom and he held the cheeks, forcing her against his jeans once more.

She looked at his thick black hair, his slanting black brows. He didn't close his eyes while he worked over her breasts. Sally had never seen a man who didn't close his eyes for that.

He was menacing.

But he was so damn good.

"What you say?" His blue eyes rose to hers. "We gonna have a whole lot of fun together, Mrs. Lamar?"

She stopped herself from asking, *What if I say no?* Instead, she passed her tongue over her lips and nodded. Her breasts felt bruised, but she wanted more of what he'd bruised them with. "We're going to have lots of fun, Ben," she said in the husky voice she could summon at will. "I'll speak to Opi."

"Good. You tell him I come recommended, me. And you not satisfied with the pool, huh?"

"You bet," she told him. "I'm going to tell him exactly that."

His intent expression became immobile. Concentration drew his mouth down at the corners again. "You never bored, Mrs. Lamar. I promise." With that he sank to kneel, parted her thighs, and used his tongue. A tongue that wasn't practicing a thing. A tongue that was a well-developed muscle like a small jackhammer whipping back and forth until she came. And she came so fast, there was no step between the start and the finish line.

"Hush, you," he said, clapping a hand over her mouth when she screamed. "You a lady who need a lot of attention, a lot of surprises."

On his feet again, he shrugged out of his shirt, unsnapped his jeans, and turned her to face the counter again. "Hold on, lady," he muttered, laughing very deep. He tipped her forward and she clung to a faucet while he pushed inside her.

"Oh" was the only word she could speak. She hadn't stopped throbbing from his tongue. "Oh, oh." Twenty-three, huh? Thank God she'd kept her body in the kind of shape that still made men drool.

Long, deep strokes became faster until he crossed his arms around her and held on to her breasts—and rested his face on the back of her neck.

His control wavered only with his own release, and even then he gave just a single keening moan before spilling into her.

Ben knew how to play a woman who was a connoisseur.

They breathed hard, and together. Slowly Sally became aware of how short a time had passed. He hadn't wasted a second. He'd made his demands—not that she intended to grant them—and then he was in, and out. But she would want him again once she could figure out how to do so and still call the shots.

"Nice," he said, stepping away from her. He stripped off his jeans—under which he wore nothing—and his shoes and efficiently removed the gown that was twisted around her waist. "When do I start here?"

Her stomach turned. "I'll have to talk to Opi."

"Opi make decisions like that? I don't think so. I think if Mrs. Lamar say she want Ben, Ben get the job, yes?"

She gave him a modest smile. "Probably."

His mouth covered hers so unexpectedly, she had no time to take a breath. Still kissing her, he lifted her, wrapped her legs around his waist, and carried her into the shower. Placing her head immediately beneath the pounding water, he ensured she kept her eyes squeezed shut.

"Probably, yes," he said. "I come tomorrow and Opi expect me. Your good friends recommend me."

He couldn't do anything to her, could he?

Ben showed just what he could do to her at that minute. He jerked into her again and held her around the waist to pump her up and down on him. When she squirmed, and whined, "I'm too sore," and meant it, he wrapped her against him and gave her his first complete surprise. A finger where she least expected it, massaging, horrified, then thrilled her. He sent her exploding over the edge while he laughed some more, or, more accurately, while his chest moved with silent laughter.

"Don't stop," she begged. "Oh, damn, oh, yes. Don't stop."

*   *   *

When Sally went back into the master suite, she avoided looking at Wilson and went directly to her dressing room.

"Get out here," he told her, his voice angry. "*Now.* Shit, this is a goddamn mess."

She looked at herself in the dressing room mirror. Even after toweling off and combing her hair, she still looked used. She'd left the gown hanging in the shower to dry and put on the robe. Now she grabbed a pair of orange cotton sweats and dragged them on over her still red and chafed skin. She trembled inside. Pulling her hair back, she secured it at her nape with a piece of ribbon, then pushed her feet into gold flats.

"Sally! Get here!"

"Sure, lover," she said, going as briskly as possible to his side and kicking the shoes off again to lie beside him on the bed. "What's eating you, Wilson?"

"That." He pointed at the television screen. "What the fuck do I pay all these people for?"

Sally looked at the set and saw the front of a familiar building in the Quarter. "Royal Street. Was there an accident?" There was always something going on in the Quarter, some drama.

"For God's sake, Sally, shut the fuck up." Wilson snatched up the phone and dialed. He waited, still naked but sitting up and leaning forward. "Yeah. Yeah, I know. And you know why I'm calling anyway. Yeah, so why not let me say my piece fast? The faster, the sooner we hang up and pretend you never heard from me today, right?"

Not just Royal Street, but that Errol Petrie's place. Sally strained to hear what was being said, but Wilson had turned down the sound while he made his phone call.

"Okay," Wilson said. "Maybe I need to speak to someone else. No. Shit, no, I'm not being funny. There's nothing funny about this. What's all the fuss about Petrie? Why the big TV splash? You're supposed to make sure this doesn't happen."

Sally got an unaccustomed tightening in her chest. Breath stuck in her throat. Even if she didn't know Wilson almost as well as she knew herself, she'd be able to see how angry he was, and how scared. He was more scared than angry, and that frightened her. He never let weakness show.

"Save it," he yelled into the receiver. "If you want to keep on getting the bennies, just do it." He hung up, snatched the remote, and turned up the volume again.

"Wilson," Sally said tentatively. "What's happened? Did something happen to that Petrie man?"

He slid her a pitying look. "That Petrie man is dead."

"Oh." Her heart thudded. "I didn't think you knew him well. Just from casual things."

"You don't know anything." He gripped her arm and jerked her face close to his. "And now you're going to forget what you just heard."

"Who were you talking to?"

"I haven't talked to anyone today."

"But—"

"Sally, I haven't—"

"No," she said quickly, trying to draw away from him. "You wanted to talk to me about something, Wilson? You called me."

He smiled, but his mouth quivered. "Good girl. You were always quick on your feet. Claude taught you that. Quite a guy, your old man."

The announcer's voice caught Sally's attention. She opened her mouth and shook her head. An aid car stood at the gates into the courtyard of Errol Petrie's house on Royal. Gradually she began to hear what the reporter said. And she watched medics carry out a loaded gurney and slide it into their vehicle.

"Dead?" she said, thinking fast. "That's sad. He did so much for children."

"Remind me to cry for him," Wilson said. "Maybe I'll play the friggin' harp at his funeral."

She hardly dared look at him. His reaction confused her.

". . . found early this morning by his old friend, Jack Charbonnet. Authorities haven't yet released details of exactly how he died, or when."

"Charbonnet," Sally said, recalling the several times she'd met the man who was getting so much publicity because he was a principal in the biggest, flashiest riverboat casino ever to open. She remembered him because no woman would ever forget him. "Is he invited tonight, Wilson?"

"Charbonnet wouldn't come near this house," he said. "He's made his affiliations more than clear. Not that we want or need him. He's no gentleman, and his money's dirty. Dirty money, we do not need, honey."

She noted the subtle change to the almost conspiratorial tone Wilson occasionally used to her—another cause for concern, since it inevitably meant Wilson was feeling insecure.

"Why is his money dirty?" she asked, aware that Wilson had never met as much as a dollar bill he considered "dirty."

"Never mind. I don't have time to give a local history lesson now. I've got to think. It could be okay. It could all blow over."

"Mr. LeChat," the reporter said. "Mr. LeChat could you give us a few words about what you saw in there."

A man Sally didn't recognize tried to push past the reporter but was stopped by the microphone that was pushed into his face. "I do not have a word to say to you nasty people," Mr. LeChat said. "Ask Mrs. Payne. Come along, Mrs. Payne, your cab will wait for you. This gentleman needs an informed view of what happened here today."

"Oh, my God!" Wilson fell flat on his back and put the back of a hand over his eyes.

No explanation for the reaction was necessary. "What's Bitsy doing there?" Sally said. "Wilson, this is awful. How could she get herself in a position like this? Call Neville at once."

Wilson shook his head from side to side.

"I guess Mrs. Bitsy Payne—would that be Mrs. Neville Payne?" the reporter asked Mr. LeChat, who appeared to be amused by the woman's ducking and turning away.

"That's right," LeChat said. "Mrs. Neville Payne, who doesn't feel like commenting. Any more than I do. We've both had a very distressing time of it. The unexpected death of a friend, and a truly good man, isn't likely to be a time for celebration. Now, excuse me, please."

Several policemen could be seen walking in the central courtyard at Errol Petrie's house. A man in plainclothes appeared and stretched yellow crime scene tape between the pillars of the tall metal gates.

The reporter duly noted the development and publicly dedicated himself to pursuing the truth of the situation for a public that "deserved to know what had happened at the heart of their own city, and to a philanthropist, an upstanding man respected by all."

"Crap," Wilson said behind his hand.

"It's sad," Sally said. "But you're just too softhearted, Wilson. You feel for everyone and you feel too deeply." The mixture of fear and fabulous sex must have gone to her head.

"I told you to shut your mouth," he muttered. "If the phone rings, answer it. Don't put anyone through to me unless I say I want to speak to them."

A flipping in her stomach joined the unpleasant thundering in her heart. "I don't understand."

"You don't have to. Just do as you're told. Remember that what affects me affects you—that should keep you from making any careless calls—or careless comments."

On the screen a man identified as a detective emerged from the courtyard and made for an unmarked car parked at the curb. The reporter cut him off and got a "No comment" for his pains.

Then the avid camera closed in on a woman with curly, dark red hair being escorted from Petrie's property by a tall man Sally instantly identified as Jack Charbonnet.

"Mr. Charbonnet, Mr. Charbonnet," the reporter shouted, closing in again. "We understand you found the body."

Jack Charbonnet aimed a glacial stare at the man.

"Ooh," Sally said, and shuddered, with deep excitement rather than any negative emotion. "I used to laugh when people said he looked like the devil when he was mad. But he looks like the devil. Look at him, Wilson."

"Get out of my way," Charbonnet was saying.

Undeterred, the reporter cleared his throat and said, "We saw the crime tape. People are speculating that we may be looking at a foul play situation."

"You'll have to get your information elsewhere," Charbonnet said, trying to walk on.

"Mr. Petrie's dead. Was he murdered?"

"Get out of my way," Charbonnet said, trying to shield his companion.

"So he was murdered."

The camera jerked and the picture swung wildly. "He pushed the cameraman," Sally said. "Wilson, Charbonnet pushed the cameraman. Won't he be arrested for that? Who was it who got arrested for that?"

"Stop this," a woman's voice said clearly. "Errol was a peaceful man. There's no call for this behavior. It's disrespectful."

"Yes," the reporter said. "Sorry, ma'am. Maybe you can shed a little light on what went on in there this morning."

"Errol Petrie died," she said. Charbonnet still stood between her and the camera. "We thought he had a heart attack. He had a weak heart."

"You thought he had a weak heart?"

"He did have a weak heart. But the police doubt if that's what killed him."

"That's it," Charbonnet said, steering his companion firmly along the sidewalk. "No further comment."

"Celina Payne, isn't it?" the reporter said, glowing with triumph. "Why, yes, I should have seen at once. We're talking with Celina Payne, folks, our former Miss Louisiana."

"Someone's going to pay for this," Wilson said.

Sally looked at him and got slowly to her feet. His face was pale, and sweat trickled down his temples. He scooted to sit on the end of the bed, where he was so close to the television screen, she was sure the picture would be too blurred for him to see.

"Bitch," he whispered through his teeth. "You are going to learn to do as you are told, *bitch*."

"I haven't—" Sally stopped, her lips parted. He wasn't talking to her. "Celina?" she said. "What do you mean?"

"You aren't taking me down," Wilson said. "Trust me, baby, it's time for a lesson."

"Wilson," Sally said quietly. "Please."

He turned on her, threw her down on the bed. His lips were drawn back from his teeth and veins stood out at his temples and in his neck. Too quietly he said, "You don't have to beg, Sally. Just spread your legs."

For the second time that morning a powerful male tore off her clothes and used her forcefully. For the first time in some months, Wilson entered his wife's body. He used her, and kept his eyes on the television while he did so. If she were stupid and blind, she might have enjoyed it. But Wilson Lamar had become aroused by an image on a screen, and his wife happened to be around as a substitute for Celina Payne.

Six

Jack heard Amelia's bare feet on the wooden floor in the corridor—again. He could also hear Tilly smacking pots and pans together in the kitchen.

He peeled off his reading glasses and lowered his feet from the leather ottoman in front of his chair. What a hell of a day. And now his daughter was mad at him, and his housekeeper was mad at him.

Women. He would never figure out what made any of them tick.

Amelia pushed the door to his study open and stood there, hanging on to the doorknob and clutching her oversized buddy, Frog Prince, beneath an arm.

He set aside the sheaf of papers he'd been studying. "What now, squirt?"

"There's an ugly ghost eating my toys. He's making loud chewing noises and he doesn't say he's sorry when he burps."

Jack struggled not to laugh. "Wow. You'd better not say that too loud. All the other kids will want one."

"There aren't any other kids, Daddy. Just me, and there's an ugly—"

"Amelia," Jack said, "I put you to bed. Tilly put you to bed. I put you to bed again. There isn't an ugly ghost."

She swung back and forth in her blue cotton nightie, and swung a small foot too. Her short black curls shone. There was no hint of either anxiety or remorse in her green eyes. "You didn't take me to school."

"No, and we already discussed that. I had something unexpected come up and I had to ask Tilly to take you."

"That's our time. You said that. It's our time when you take me to school. You didn't have breakfast with me either. That's our time too."

"It sure is, squirt. But sometimes we have to make allowances because of something important."

Amelia stopped swinging. "This is important."

Jack started to get up, but changed his mind. "Okay, shoot. What's important?"

"I'm upset because we missed our special times this morning, and you have to make allowances."

This was the price he paid for treating his little girl like a sidekick, and for talking to her as if she were an adult, and insisting her grandmother and Tilly talk to her in adult terms. "I'm sorry you're upset."

"I forgive you. A story would be a good allowance."

Jack shook his head and held out his arms to receive his daughter when she hurtled across the room and scrambled onto his lap. She went through her ritual of getting settled, and arranged her frog—with his shiny patches where the green fuzz had worn off—on top of them both. Jack wrinkled up his face as he got ready to continue the same story he'd been making up for years.

"Phillymeana and the Dragon Prince have rescued another elf baby from the Ice Wizard." Amelia inevitably provided a recap of the previous episode.

"Philomena," Jack automatically corrected her.

The sound of the doorbell surprised them both. They rarely got evening visitors.

"You want me to answer that, Mr. Charbonnet?" Tilly yelled as only Tilly could yell. "Or you want me to follow my instincts and ignore it?"

Jack set Amelia on the floor and called, "I'll go. Thanks, Tilly."

Tilly lived in. Jack's connections had allowed him to buy a coveted apartment above two antique stores on Chartres Street and Tilly lived in comfortably renovated third-floor quarters that had once housed servants.

Tilly was not a servant. She was Amelia's companion, Jack's household consultant.

The banging of pots resumed and Jack went down the stairs that led to the door from the street. An outside lamp glowed through the fanlight. Adhering to a rule he'd imposed on himself because of Amelia, he used the peephole before shooting back the old but effective bolt.

"Well, well," he murmured, and opened the door. "I hope you're going to tell me your bodyguard's somewhere around," he said to Celina Payne.

She frowned at him and glanced over her shoulder at the stream of people that trolled back and forth on the sidewalk, and spilled into the street. "You've got to be joking," she told him. "I know what I'm doing. I'm not a tourist."

"Does that mean you're immortal?"

Even in the gloom he saw her pale, and felt a morsel of guilt—a very small morsel. "What do you need?" Now he sounded rude—great.

"Please may I talk to you?"

"I didn't think you just wanted to look at my pretty face."

She ducked her head, but not before he saw a faint smile.

"Did I say something funny?"

"Not especially. You're so prickly. Looking at you is dangerous to the eyeballs."

He leaned on the doorjamb. "Okay. You do want to look at my pretty face."

Celina Payne gave him a cocky grin and said, "I don't want to prick my eyeballs." Their lunch together hadn't been exactly cozy, but it had broken a little ice. Tonight he saw a strong spark of the aplomb that had helped make her Miss Louisiana. She added, "But you do have a pretty face, Jack Charbonnet. Too bad you're such a nasty man."

Maybe more than a little ice. It was impossible not to smile back at her. "What d'you need, Celina?"

"Could I come in, please? I can't talk about this out here."

Jack had never brought a woman to Chartres Street. Not to his home. This was Amelia's territory, the territory she shared with Jack and Tilly—and Frog Prince—and where she didn't expect intruders. "Couldn't it wait until tomorrow? This has been a long day."

"Not for Errol," she said, all hint of humor gone. "It was really short for him."

"Grief counseling isn't my forté." *Sounding mean again.* He guessed it was just his nature.

"Errol was pretty good at it. Did you ever see him with the parents of a dying child? He was wonderful. Now he's the one who needs something. He needs champions who won't give up until whatever happened to him—and why—is brought into the open."

No wonder she was so good at her job. She knew how to drive the knife to the heart if that's what it took to get what she wanted.

Convincing people to make fabulous donations to Dreams must be child's play to Celina Payne. "Come in," he said, hoping Tilly—who frequently reminded him that Amelia needed a mother—would buy it that this was business and leave it at that.

He ushered Celina up the stairs in front of him and guided her to his study. When Celina entered the room, his daughter was seated in his leather chair with her arms crossed and her feet straight out in front of her.

"Would you run and tell Tilly a business associate has dropped by, Amelia? We have some things to discuss and we don't want to be interrupted. Then go to bed. Sorry about the story. If you're still awake when Miss Payne leaves, I'll tell you some when I tuck you in. Okay?"

"I'm Amelia Charbonnet and this is Frog Prince, F.P. for short," Amelia said to Celina. "Sometimes Daddy forgets his manners."

With a completely straight face, Celina said, "I'm Celina Payne. I'm pleased to meet you and F.P."

With evident reluctance his daughter climbed from the chair and went slowly from the room, not taking her eyes off Celina until she had to.

"I didn't know you had a child," Celina said. "Errol never mentioned her. Neither did you."

"You and I have hardly been in a situation where we swapped personal information. Errol knows—knew I prefer to keep my private life private."

"Is that because of what happened to your parents?"

She stopped him for an instant. He didn't answer her question. "As Amelia says, my manners are a little rusty. I don't suppose you want a drink, though."

"Charming offer," she said. "Thank you. I'll have a gin and tonic. Make it very light. Oh, actually just tonic."

"I don't have any tonic. Or gin."

She looked at him and said, "Oh."

"I've got some wine. At least, I think I do. A merlot."

"That would be nice."

He left the room and went deeper into the apartment, to the kitchen—and jumped at the sight of Tilly standing in the shadows with her arms crossed. This was where Amelia got many of her mannerisms. "Everything's under control," he told Tilly. "Thank you. I don't know what I'd do without you." That was very true.

"Who's the woman?"

He was accustomed to Tilly's blunt manner. "Celina Payne. She worked for Errol."

Tilly shook her head, an exercise that didn't move her tightly permed gray hair. "Mr. Petrie. What's this world coming to? A nicer man never walked the face of the earth. Picked off in the prime of his life. Plucked from the garden when his scent was still full. They say the Lord takes only the best blooms. It's hard, though. We need those blooms down here among the sinners."

"We do indeed," Jack said. "I need that bottle of merlot I got as a gift."

A pinched expression pulled Tilly's thin features together. "She's a drinking woman?"

At first Jack blanked, then he shook his head no. "Just being polite," he said. "Miss Payne was there this morning when we—when I found Errol. She suffered a terrible shock, just as I did. I'm concerned for her. She looks very pale."

Tilly didn't move, except to cross her arms even tighter. "You care about this Miss Payne? Are you planning something with her?"

"I'm planning to have a short business discussion with her."

"So why do you need to ply her with alcohol?"

Ply her with alcohol? "Where's the wine, please?"

Small and wiry, Tilly had large feet and wore "sensible" lace-up shoes with leather soles that slapped the floors. They slapped the floors now when Tilly marched to pull out a step stool, and climb up to remove the lone bottle of merlot from a cupboard above the refrigerator.

"Thank you," Jack said, searching for and finding a corkscrew, then taking down two wineglasses and dusting them.

"Looks like you're planning a seduction to me," Tilly said. "Don't forget there's an impressionable five-year-old child in this household."

"I won't," Jack said.

"Maybe I should take Amelia up with me. I could play music to drown out any sounds of passion from down here."

"We're going to talk," Jack said, dangling the glasses upside down between his fingers and picking up the bottle. "Amelia will be perfectly fine in her own room. It's time we worked on makin' sure she stays there when she's put to bed. The *first* time. I think we're spoiling her."

"I knew it. A woman comes into the picture and you lose your focus on what's important. Your first responsibility is to that motherless child."

"I thought you believed I should be looking for a new mother for Amelia." The devil made him say it, Jack thought, and grimaced. "Not that Miss Payne is in that sort of category. But how would I go about findin' someone if you don't even want another woman in the house."

"You're changing the subject. Certainly on a first visit it isn't suitable to be drinking and shutting yourselves away. You'll give everyone the wrong idea."

"Everyone?"

"You know what I mean." She pulled out a chair, produced a sewing basket, and sat down at the kitchen table. "I'll just stay here in case Amelia needs anything."

Jack rolled his eyes and left the room. When he returned to his study he found Celina exactly where he'd left her, standing in the middle of the carpet with the strap of her brown leather purse still over her shoulder. There were dark, purplish marks under her eyes, but that didn't stop them from being bright and beautiful—and very troubled.

He put the glasses down on his desk to one side of windows that opened onto the gallery, and poured wine into each. He gave one to Celina. "Sit there," he told her, pointing to his own chair, the only comfortable one in the room. "Put your feet up. You look as if you need some TLC."

Her raised eyebrows suggested that an offer of TLC from Jack Charbonnet had been the last thing she'd expected, but she said, "Thanks," and did as he suggested. "Errol trusted you, Jack. He used to relax when he heard your voice on the phone. I watched it happen time after time."

Jack swallowed hard. He'd never be able to forget Errol, but he wished he didn't have to think about the way he'd found him that morning.

"You were kind to me today. Thank you for that."

"I got you out of the Royal Street house, that's all," he told her. "Anyone would have done the same thing."

"Not if they hated my guts, and you do."

She silenced him with that.

"I appreciated the lunch and a chance to get myself together. I apologize for my mother. She didn't mean anything by what she said at the house. She's led a pretty sheltered life, and she doesn't think sometimes."

"I don't hate you, Celina." He wanted to let her down lightly where her mother was concerned, but the sight of a chink in his own armor scared him. "But you do have a way of believin' what you want to believe, don't you? Your mother is sheltered? It's too bad she didn't shelter you rather than push you through all those kiddie beauty pageants."

Celina looked away. "You know about that?"

"Everyone does. How could they not? You were Miss Louisiana and there was talk about how your mother pushed you from when you were a kid. They showed a lot of cute footage. As a parent, it scares the shit out of me to think that stuff still goes on."

"She did that for me."

"Bunk."

"I beg your pardon."

"I said *bunk*. Your mama had one chick and decided to live through that chick."

"My mother could have gone places herself. She chose to dedicate herself to me instead. I've got to respect her for that."

Maybe this was a nice woman after all. She had to know she was spouting what her ambitious mama would love to hear, which was absolute garbage. Jack detested people who didn't protect their children from the world as much as they could without stunting them and making them unable to cope. And the word he'd use for a parent who exploited a child was "criminal," and that would be on a day when he was feeling generous.

He sat in a straight-backed cane chair some distance from her and sipped his own wine.

"This is a nice room," she said.

"Thanks."

"I wouldn't have pegged you for a reading man."

"I've got a lot of books. That doesn't make me a reading man."

She looked sideways at him. "Aren't you?"

He ran his eyes over the cases of books that covered every available wall space. "I am, yes."

"Do you let anyone know you?"

"Errol knew me."

He saw her consider reminding him that Errol was dead. "How about Amelia's mother?"

Four and a half years and a stray mention of Elise still had the power to cast him into a black place he wanted to forget. "My wife died."

Celina turned very red. "I'm sorry. I had no right to ask something so personal."

"Why did you come here?"

Her eyes flickered away. "You own a big share in that new river-boat."

"I do." Whatever she wanted, she was finding it hard to get to.

"I thought all the offshore gambling was—well, you know."

"Do I?"

"They say you've got to have connections to that family—the criminal one—to be involved with anything like that."

Jack sipped his warm wine. "Is that what they say?"

She nodded.

"Well, what do *they* know? You can see what my life is. I'm a quiet man who looks after his daughter and his investments."

"You and Errol went into Dreams fifty-fifty." She stuck her nose into her glass but didn't actually drink any wine. "At the beginning it was almost a hundred percent your money because Errol didn't have it. He told me that. Then he paid you back but you wanted to be involved, so you've kept a half interest. I expect you do that for income tax purposes."

"I probably do." Watching her fascinated him. And listening to her. She thought her way along out loud, almost as if she didn't expect any answers. "What's your interest in Dreams, Celina?"

"I love it. I love working for children. It's everything I ever wanted to do. I've got a marketing background, which helps. And to be frank, the only good thing that came out of the pageant stuff was that it opens doors for me. People want to see me up close." She surprised him by giggling. "By the time they get over wondering what the big deal is, they've agreed to donate a round-the-world cruise, or a new Mercedes, or liposuction and a face-lift." Jack had never seen this lighter side of her. She electrified him—for an instant.

He deliberately studied his hands. "So you're good at asking for things. What else are you good at?"

Their eyes met. Celina looked away first, and color crept up her neck. "I'll be very good at running things—at least until everything settles down again. Errol would have wanted business as usual. We've got a lot in the works, including another auction."

"At your parents' house?"

"That was never my idea."

"Whose was it?"

She moved in the chair and crossed her legs. Tonight she wore a loose black linen dress that settled several inches above her knees, and her short curls were slicked severely against her head and back from her face. No makeup to speak of. Great bones.

Great legs.

He noted that she avoided clothes that drew attention to a figure he knew from photographs was spectacular. Maybe he was old-fashioned, but he approved of that.

"My parents have a lot of connections. To rich people—bored rich people who can afford to spend more than something's worth just for the kicks. Then, a lot of them like to see their name on contributor lists. I'm not saying they aren't nice people, only that they're the kind of people we need and my mother and father know them. Mama and Daddy also have the kind of home that lends itself to entertaining— entertaining the way Errol thought it should be done. Graciously."

He decided not to press her to say her parents had pushed for their house for the purpose, or that they kept their financial noses above water with the money they earned from foundation projects.

"You didn't come here tonight to give me a rundown on things I already know."

"No, I didn't." She popped up out of the chair and paced, rolling the glass between her palms. She wandered to the window and stood looking out into the darkness.

"Please don't stand in front of the windows," he said automatically.

She jumped, took several steps back, and stared at him, aghast. "Why?"

Because it's a good way to get shot. He stood too, and shrugged. "Just an old phobia. Don't mind me. I never liked the idea of being seen when I couldn't see."

"It's because of what happened when you were a kid, isn't it?"

"You haven't learned to figure out what subjects to avoid, have you?"

"Sorry. It's been quite a day. I guess my instincts aren't functioning too well."

She'd feel good to the touch.

Where had that come from? He bowed his head. He knew where it came from. His last, carefully chosen female companion had gotten too serious and he'd done what he always did, cut the cord. And that had been too long ago for a man with his kind of drive.

"How long have you lived here?" she asked.

"About four years. Why?"

"I didn't think anyone could get one of these unless . . . well, I know they're difficult to come by."

"Unless they've got connections? I have." She was wondering if what they said about Jack and the Giavanelli family was true. "You just have to know some of the right people."

"And have the right kind of money," she told him.

"You don't believe in subtlety, do you?"

"I didn't take you for a man who needed pussyfooted fawning, Jack. Was I wrong?"

"No." In fact, he almost liked her for her directness. "I really will need to get back to my daughter shortly. We ought to get to the point, Celina."

She tipped her glass, barely touched the wine to her lips, coughed, and held the glass out for more.

Jack raised his brows and added a few drops.

"I've never been good at guessing games," she said. "Or uncertainty. I can work as hard as I have to work, but until we find out what provisions Errol made for his death, I'm adrift. Sort of. I can run things just fine. I'll need some help. That won't be hard to find. What I need to know now is where I stand and, since you were Errol's best friend, and you helped him get started with Dreams, I thought you might have some thoughts on how he'd want me to continue."

Jack's courtly skills were rusty. Since Elise's death, his relationships with women had been selected to avoid the kinds of situations that would require champagne and roses. Sensing that Celina was a woman who might respond to the gentlemanly arts his mother had started to teach him—and Elise had made him want to practice naturally—he put a hand under her elbow and gave her a serious sideways glance. "Errol always said you were his right hand, and his left. I did suggest there ought to be a bigger staff, but he held out."

"He held out because he wanted to spend the minimum of funds on administration. And since we confined ourself to New Orleans rather than trying to go national, we managed very well. The operation is simple, Jack. I go after the kind of glamorous donations I know will pull people into an auction—and they do. Apart from Errol's running expenses . . ." She choked up so suddenly, Jack got the feeling she hadn't expected it.

Awkwardly patting her back, he let her cry. He produced a handkerchief and pressed it into her hands. She sobbed for only a couple of minutes, then sniffed and turned her back on him while she collected herself.

"Take a few days off," he said. "You can't expect to jump right back in after somethin' like this."

"We have things in the works," she said indistinctly. "Time to spare isn't something we ever have. The children we work with certainly don't have any."

"You never met Errol's boy, did you?" Jason Petrie had been a young, too-small version of his father. "Of course, you wouldn't have. Errol idolized that boy."

"Like you idolize your daughter."

The analogy made his skin cold. "Like that, yes. Jason had an autoimmune disorder. They put him in one of those tents, but somethin' went wrong and they lost him. Errol just about lived at the hospital. He hated it that there were kids who almost never had a visitor."

"I know."

He just bet she did. "You knew Errol very well, didn't you, Celina?"

"Yes, I did. He was the first man I ever met who didn't try to put the make on me."

So she said. "Errol had a hard time of it for some years, but he beat the bad stuff."

"You bet he did. He dedicated his life to helping other people—helping children. They became his, and their joy was his. He was a saint."

Jack didn't say what he thought, that he considered that a bit rash. "I would be more than happy to hire someone to help you with the day-to-day runnin' of things. Do you think you'd be comfortable takin' over as liaison with the hospital and parents?"

She was silent for a moment, and he knew he didn't imagine the chill that entered the room. "I'm comfortable taking over everything."

This was something else he'd been afraid of. "I wouldn't expect you to do that. It's too much for one person. Too much for two. You need someone to deal with your admin tasks. That'll free you up to concentrate on what you do best. Charm the people."

"I'm not just charming, Jack. I've got a mind. Errol made sure I could do his job if necessary."

"You and Errol were very close."

"So you keep reminding me, and we were. But not the way you think."

"What way do I think?"

She colored again. Blushing suited her. "You think there was some romantic attachment between Errol and me. There wasn't. You can choose to believe that or not—I can't make you. But it's true."

He shouldn't want to believe it quite as much as he did. "It isn't my business."

"But you keep alluding to it anyway. Look, I came here out of politeness. I know you have money in Dreams, but I also know you aren't the kind of man who's interested in a hands-on involvement. I'm ready to assume responsibility, but I do need some help, and I'll hire it."

"You do that," he said, thinking fast. "You'll be able to stay on in Royal Street, if that's what you want to do."

She faced him again. Up close she was translucent. Her mouth was the full-lipped, naturally slightly puckered type that made a man think thoughts he hadn't planned on.

"The Royal Street house was Errol's. He owned it."

Jack owned it—he'd bought it when Errol showed signs of losing it, and Errol had been making payments to Jack for years.

"There shouldn't be any hitch to keeping the headquarters where they are," he told her.

"I never knew anything about his extended family," Celina said. "He never mentioned them. But I expect they may want to sell the house."

"It belongs to me," he said without looking at her. "I have no plans to sell. Don't you think it would be a good idea to keep things as status quo as possible? People have an odd way of reacting negatively if they think there's anythin' shaky going on."

"The house belongs to you?"

He should have expected her to be shocked. "Errol had some problems—financial type—some years back. Jason's illness just about wiped him out. He sold to me and then started buying it back again. That house has been in his family since the late eighteen hundreds."

"Jack." She gave him her full, more than a little disconcerting attention. "I was no part of whatever happened to Errol. You believe that, don't you?"

He said, "Yes," more because it was what she needed to hear than because he absolutely believed it.

"When will we hear the results of the coroner's findings?"

"When they're ready to give them to us. You can be certain they're as busy as little bees right now, flitting back and forth seeing what they can dig up on each of us, and on Errol."

"I'm boring," she said. "There's nothing to dig up on me."

The timing was wrong for him to tell her he found her anything but boring, but wished he didn't. "Errol had a past," he said. "I'm not talking out of school when I say that. You know some of it yourself. My so-called past isn't my own, but it's plenty interestin', and if they decide to get into it all over again, we'll see stuff no one wants to see again—least of all me."

"When people are reminded of what made Errol want to start Dreams, they'll forget the other."

He wished he was as certain as she was. "Maybe."

"Oh, I just know they will. People are good at heart, especially when it comes to helping children."

There would never be an easy time to tell her what he'd decided—what he'd promised Errol several years back. "I'll be taking an active part in Dreams, Celina. That was Errol's wish."

"An active part?"

"A certain amount of time in Royal Street. And . . . Celina, I'm going to be taking over Errol's place. More or less. I'm hoping that if we get you more help you'll agree to take some of the routine things off my plate. I'm not a man who enjoys public appearances, although I will make them when you consider them necessary." And from the way she was looking at him, he doubted there would be many of those.

She sat down again, this time on the cane chair he'd vacated, and scrutinized the room from the old Aubusson carpet that had belonged to his grandmother on his mother's side to the green-painted wooden ceiling fan that wobbled on its rod. He supposed you'd call the decor ancient and modern and the color scheme mud, but he liked it. Celina's sleek presentation didn't fit here, but then, neither did Celina.

"Are you goin' to give me any thoughts on what I just told you?" he asked.

"When I can stop my brain from going in circles I'll give it a shot."

"Fair enough. Any estimates on how long that might take?"

"Look." She fastened him with a hard stare. "This isn't easy for either of us. You've just dropped a whole new concept on me. I'm used to being pretty much autonomous. I don't want to . . . no, that would sound like some sort of ultimatum. I hate ultimatums. Do you honestly think we could work together?"

"I think we're going to try."

"Why?"

"Why are we going to try to work together? You already said—"

"No. Why are you going to do this at all? You've got your fingers in a lot of pies. And this isn't exactly your kind of thing, is it?"

Jack began to wish he did keep some hard liquor around. "First of all, you don't have any idea how many pies I've got my fingers in—as you put it. Secondly, how the ... how do you know what is or isn't my kind of thing?"

She had the grace to color. "Tell me how it's going to work. You can't blame me for wondering."

"I don't blame you. You're going to do exactly what you're already doing. Solicitin' donations, layin' on functions. Plus, you're going to help me orchestrate the other end of things—with the recipients. By the way, I have no objection to continuing the arrangement you have with your parents."

"Errol had the arrangements." She looked at the floor again. "I'm not going to lie to you. He did it for me. But it does work very well, so, thank you."

"Do you think we can work along the lines I've set out?"

"This is going to sound wild, but I don't think it's the business I'm most worried about."

This ought to be good.

She played with the wineglass a little longer, then set it down. "I can't imagine working with you, Jack. I'd be lying if I said anything else, but I owe it to Errol to keep what he started afloat, and I think you want that too. So we'll work it out."

"Good. There isn't a security system in the house, is there?"

She blanched again. "No. Errol didn't believe in things like that."

"I'll deal with it tomorrow. You might want to go to your parents' place at night until it's installed."

"Going home to mama isn't something I do. I'll stay where I am."

"Suit yourself." But he didn't like the idea of her being alone over there. Antoine didn't live on the premises. "The police are goin' to be all over the place in the daytime."

"I know. I don't care."

He knew when to quit. "Okay, but if you find you aren't comfortable, don't stay just to be hardheaded."

That earned him a ladylike snort. "Doesn't gambling draw some unpleasant types?" she said.

He laughed and sat on the edge of his desk. "Where did that come from?"

She crossed her legs and jiggled the free toe. "I don't know. I'm so muddled up by what's happened. I wish the police would get back to us. What do you suppose they meant by 'what actually killed him'?"

"I think our trusty NOPD likes to dramatize itself. Beyond that, I don't know. It makes perfect sense to me that Errol died of a heart attack. He wasn't up to the kind of—"

"*Don't.* I can't imagine . . . I don't want to think about it."

"No." But she had known that Errol had supposedly beaten addiction problems. "What did Errol do with his spare time? Any idea?"

"Not a lot except go to church."

Jack almost dropped his wineglass. "What did you say?"

"Church. He was very devout. He went several evenings a week. And on weekends too. He didn't say a whole lot because he realized I'm private about that sort of thing, but he'd occasionally say he hoped I was taking care of my spiritual life, things like that."

If she'd told him Errol had taken up mud wrestling, Jack couldn't have been more bewildered.

"He must have mentioned it to you," she said.

Jack shook his head slowly. "Not a word. Where did he go? A church here in the Quarter?"

"I don't think so. I didn't ask and he never said. He was always gone a long time, though, I think. Or he was when I noticed."

"Well, different strokes, as they say. If it brought him some peace, I'm glad. There were a lot of years when he didn't have any."

Celina smoothed her dress over her thighs.

At first Jack watched with detached interest, then he dropped the detached bit. She really had gorgeous legs. and they went on and on. He wondered if she deliberately let her simple little pump fall free of her heel when she pointed her jiggling toe. Somehow he doubted it. She was just naturally sexy.

She fiddled with a seam in her dress, glanced at him, fiddled some more.

"Is there anything else on your mind?" he asked, and wished she'd say something she wasn't likely to say, such as how much she wished he could stay in Royal Street until the alarm system was in. What a dreamer he was.

Celina continued to pluck at the seam.

"You're going to make a hole in that," he said when he couldn't stand the wait any longer.

"Did Errol make his payments to you in cash? For the house?"

Jack felt blank. "Payments? Oh, no. They were an automatic bank payment."

"Probably from his personal account?"

"Of course."

"I see."

Jack crossed and recrossed his feet—and waited.

"I had to pay some bills today," she said. "I went through Errol's in basket and just picked out what was due."

"You can sign checks?"

She shook her head. "I was going to pay them myself, then get the money back."

"That won't be necessary. I'll pay them until I can get your name on an account. Okay?"

"Mmm. Yes, thank you." She picked up her big purse and produced a business-sized book of checks. "I thought I ought to take a look at this—just to see where we are. Here." She handed it to him. "It's the business account."

Jack stopped himself from saying that was obvious. He turned pages but didn't see anything that struck him as unusual.

"Oh," she said, delving into the bag again, "you need this. The last statement."

He took it from her and scanned the several sheets of check numbers and amounts, then looked at the balances and said, "Wow."

"Uh-huh. What do you think it means?"

"It means a great deal of money has been coming in, but in the last three weeks, even more money went out. This is overdrawn."

She got up and stood beside him, and leaned around him to look at the checkbook. "See this? And this? And this? Those wouldn't equal house payment amounts, would they?"

"No. I've already told you that money didn't come out of this account."

"They're for cash." She pointed to a deposit entered in the checkbook register. "I made all the deposits. This one never happened."

"Maybe Errol thought it did."

"I guess. But why? He never made deposits to this account himself, and I'm the one who balances the statement. I think he hoped to make it right before I saw it."

Jack felt queasy. "I see your point."

"I've tried everything I can think of, and there's nothing that would have called for that kind of expense. And if there had been, it wouldn't have been paid out in cash."

Jack looked into her face, at her eyes, then at her mouth, then he returned his attention to the checkbook. "Would you know if this had ever happened before?"

"I would now. I've checked back through several years of canceled checks. Nothing bigger than a few hundred for petty cash."

"In other words, Errol needed cash and didn't have enough in his personal account."

"I don't see how he could have," Celina said. "He took only bare living expenses out of the foundation. I had to beg him to buy socks or a new shirt. He didn't care about those things."

He used to care about those things—and a lot more. "Any ideas?" he asked her. "Hunches? Anything? We're desperate here, aren't we?"

"I can only think he hoped he could pay it back before he ever had to explain it to anyone. Although he didn't actually deal with incoming funds or deposits, he was in charge of the money. He was the only one who could write checks—except you, of course, and you didn't play an active part in this. Jack, you know Errol was an honest man."

"Yes, I do know."

The phone rang in the hall, and the slap of Tilly's shoes brought a startled expression to Celina's blue eyes.

"That's Tilly," Jack explained. "She looks after us—keeps us on the straight and narrow. There isn't a phone in here."

Tilly's tightly curled gray hair and florid face appeared around the edge of the door. "This is not good for an impressionable child, Mr. Charbonnet. All this upheaval when she should be quiet."

"Thank you, Tilly. I take it the call's for me?"

"Who else would it be for? Certainly no one would call me in the middle of the night."

"It isn't the middle of the night."

Jack excused himself to Celina and went to the phone, leaving his study door open. "This is Jack Charbonnet."

Detective O'Leary identified himself and kept his remarks short, so short that Jack found himself staring at the receiver after the other man had hung up.

He remembered Celina in his study and walked slowly back.

She said, "What is it?" and made an involuntary move toward him.

Jack took hold of her outstretched hands and held them tightly. He closed his eyes but couldn't shut out the picture of Errol on his bathroom floor.

Celina's hands trembled. He pulled her into his arms, rested his chin on top of her head, and held her tightly. She held him right back.

"Tell me what they said," she whispered.

"Somebody set it up," he told her quietly. "The whole scene. Dead men don't climb out of bathtubs. The autopsy showed Errol drowned."

Seven

The detective—Celina thought Jack had called him O'Leary—hadn't actually said they were calling Errol's death a murder. Couldn't he have slipped under the water, then struggled out and . . .

Errol had drowned. Someone had drowned him, then tried to make it look like something else killed him. He had, in fact, had a heart attack, but the coroner had been adamant—according to this O'Leary—that it hadn't been his heart that precipitated Errol's death.

Jack's embrace hadn't surprised her until she'd left him and had time to think about it. He wasn't the kind of man she associated with spontaneous kindness, but evidently she was wrong. She didn't know how long they had stood there, just holding each other, but the effect had been more disquieting than calming. He was a strong man in every way, a man with a heady ability to make a woman feel very much a woman—and like it.

The analysis was a waste of time. She doubted she'd spend more time wrapped in Jack Charbonnet's arms.

The cab she'd taken from Chartres Street dropped her in the driveway of the Lamar house. She paid the driver and he gave her a card with a number to call when she was ready to go home. She'd have liked to go then, but her mother would already be watching for her and worrying. How embarrassing it was when Celina, who had once been a part-time member of Wilson Lamar's campaign force, failed to show up on time, showed up many hours late, in fact. Mama and Daddy were turning their connections into cash again by smoothing Wilson Lamar's path to the old money New Orleans set. They needed and expected Celina's support.

She loathed the prospect of seeing Wilson.

Small white lights trembled in the oaks lining the drive. More lights outlined the two galleries along the front of the house. And from the volume of laughter and music issuing through the open front door, enough liquor had flowed to make it unlikely anyone would either notice her arrival, or care if she was or was not there. Except for Mama. And Wilson. Wilson noticed everything.

The first word Celina heard clearly when she entered the Lamars' elegant foyer was her own name. Someone screamed her name, and a sudden surge toward her made her consider retreat.

She stood her ground while drunken partygoers swarmed about her.

"Where have you *been*, Celina?" Mama's voice was always easily recognized. "We've been waiting for you for hours. There was no answer at your apartment."

"You aren't going to stay in that grizzly place, are you," Mrs. Sabina Lovelace asked, her thin-bridged nose very red. Mrs. Lovelace, of the timber Lovelaces, was a close friend of Mama and Daddy's. Many people here were their close friends.

"What grizzly place would that be?" Celina asked, deliberately widening her eyes.

"Why"—Sabina Lovelace's voice dropped—"the Royal Street place, of course. How could you even think of *sleeping* there. They say it takes the dead a while to vacate, if you know what I mean."

Celina let her eyes get even rounder. "Vacate? You mean Errol Petrie?"

"Well, I surely do. He's the only one who died there recently, isn't he? And they say violent deaths are the worst. The poor, dear departed has been violated and can't rest while he or she is watching and waiting for justice to be done."

Celina smiled suddenly, brilliantly, and said, "Why, Mrs. Lovelace, I thank you. I'll feel so comforted knowing Errol is still there with me."

The woman moaned and turned to Celina's mother. "Bitsy, you poor thing, I think your girl is unbalanced. Must be because of the shock. You need to get her to a good therapist, and soon. I'll call you with the name of mine in the morning. I need another drink."

Questions burst from all sides. Who had been the first to see Errol after he died? Who had been the last to see him before he died? What had he looked like when he was dead? Did the police think it was murder? Was it true that Errol had been involved in a sex orgy and that he passed out from . . . you know? Did he hit his head on the floor because he slipped? They always said most fatal accidents happened at home. And it *was* murder, wasn't it?

"Let the poor girl be." Wilson Lamar's voice boomed over the rest. "She's had a terrible day, I'm sure. Thank you for makin' yourself come, Celina. I take it as a personal compliment and a sign of your commitment to my senate bid. What will you have to drink?"

She didn't want anything, not if it came from Wilson, but she forced a smile and said, "I'll take a cranberry juice and tonic, please." Her breath always shortened around the man. Why couldn't her parents see that he was slime and wanted people only for what he could get out of them?

Wilson snapped his fingers and sent a waiter sliding through the throng to get the drink.

Sally Lamar appeared at her husband's side, her long, reddish hair caught up at each side with a diamond comb. More diamonds glittered at her ears. A soft face. Rounded cheekbones and jaw, a full mouth colored pale pink and moistly shiny, ingenuous brown eyes that managed to appear liquid and innocent at all times. Sally was a perfect compliment to her tall, fit husband. Wilson's blond good looks, his easy smile, usually drew attention away from a vaguely supercilious light in his intelligent eyes. The most stunning couple in the county, that was what was said about the Lamars. Sally's sequined shift was the color of Irish coffee and set little reflections dancing off her smooth white skin. Matching pumps with very high heels drew attention to beautiful legs shown to advantage all the way to mid-thigh.

Celina detested both of them.

"You do know how to draw attention to yourself, honey," Sally said to Celina. "All over the television screen all day."

"Oh, Sally, you couldn't even see her face," Mama said, not looking at the other woman. "And they just kept repeating the same footage. You know how those things go."

"No, I don't, thank goodness," Sally said sharply. "Unless I'm at my husband's side—which is my job and my pleasure—I manage to keep myself out of the limelight. We can only hope Celina's attachment to Wilson's campaign won't draw any negative attention."

For her mother's sake, Celina didn't remind the gathered company that she was no longer involved in helping with Wilson's senate bid. "Well," she said with forced cheer, "you all look as if you're having a time of it. Nice music, Sally, and the house looks gorgeous."

Sally simpered, and hung on Wilson's arm. "My daddy was famous for giving the best parties in the parish. Some said the best parties in Louisiana. I guess I inherited his talent."

"I guess you did, sugar," Wilson said, patting her hands while he took subtle advantage of the moment to release himself from her. "Here's your drink, Celina. It's hot in here. Let's find a couple of seats outside and you can catch me up on everythin' that's been happenin' to you. Old friends shouldn't lose touch."

Celina's skin crawled. Goose bumps shot out on her bare arms.

"There you are, little pet." Dear, ineffectual Daddy tottered up to Celina and dropped a liquor-laced kiss on her cheek. "You are lookin' lovely, as always, my child. You make your daddy proud. I worried about you today. All that unpleasantness. You ought to come home to your mother and me."

A big man who still showed remnants of how handsome he'd been when he'd married Celina's young, newly widowed mother—back before the liquor did its worst—silver strands glinted in his sandy hair. He still worked out—when he was sober enough. Neville's primary problem had been that although he was physically strong, he was one of the most emotionally ineffectual men she'd ever known.

Grateful that he hadn't yet drunk enough to turn nasty, she hugged him and felt the first rush of genuine warmth she'd felt all night . . . except for when Jack Charbonnet had embraced her, and that had been an entirely different kind of warmth. "Hi, Daddy," she whispered. "I love you, y'know."

He drew back and looked at her with eyes that didn't quite focus but which became instantly teary. He patted her arms, stroked her cheek, leaned close, and whispered back, "Forgive me, pet. I wish I could have done more for you. Never could quite . . . we'll, you know. Never mind, your mama's strong enough for all of us, hmm?"

Celina nodded and smiled, but sadness struck very deep. Neville Payne had married Bitsy and adopted her children. His deterioration had kept pace with the speed with which he'd spent his wife's fortune—which meant it had been relatively rapid.

"I'm borrowin' your daughter, Neville," Wilson announced. "This is one savvy girl you raised here." He affected the drawl of a southern gentleman—which he was not. When he looped a muscular arm around her shoulders, she was heavily pressed not to shrug away—or scream.

"You aren't leaving our guests, are you," Sally whined. "Marshall Compton wants to talk to you about something, darling."

Wilson ignored her and shepherded Celina outside and along the path that skirted the house until it reached the wide white marble ledge around an oval pool. The pool shone turquoise under soft lighting.

She didn't want to go with him, but neither did she want to make a scene.

He pulled up two Adirondack chairs and placed them so that the arms touched. "Now, you sit right here, Celina. You've had a terrible day. It would be terrible for anyone, but you're a sensitive little woman. You were never intended to deal with unpleasantness."

"Thank you for thinking of me," she said, gingerly taking a seat. "But I'm pretty tough, Wilson. I've got to be to do what I do."

"Did," he responded promptly, lowering himself into the chair beside her. "That's something I want to talk to you about. I need you, Celina. You made a memorable Dreams Girl, but obviously Dreams won't continue with Errol gone. He was the heart and soul of that little effort. Of course, I'm the first to say it's sad to see it disappear, and I intend to put forward a plan to provide special little services to these terminally ill children. And when I'm elected, I won't be one of those politicians who forgets the platform he ran on, so don't you worry about that. But in the meantime, I need you, my dear. I've missed you. Now, I know we haven't always seen eye to eye, but I do think that philosophically we're on the same side, and it's a thorn in my side to think of you doing anythin' but workin' for me, and for the good of your brother and sister Louisianans, and your countrymen. What do you say?"

She stared at the bright, lapping water and didn't trust herself to say anything.

Wilson covered her hand on the arm of her chair and Celina promptly pulled away.

If Wilson was offended, he hid it very well. He said, "Now, I know I've probably surprised you by moving so quickly, but you know that's how it has to be in my business. The man who misses a beat, misses the boat, so to speak. It's time to put any disagreements behind us for the good of the cause. You're too sophisticated a woman to dwell on little misunderstandings."

Her nerves felt sheared. He was incredible. Nothing stopped him, not the fact that he continued to laugh at her parents behind their backs while he used them and that he'd told Celina he would drop them the instant he'd got everything he could out of them, and not Celina's decision to leave his campaign staff because she'd discovered that he was skimming funds. She had told him what she knew, and he'd laughed at her, and threatened to make her "pathetic" parents look like fools in front of all they had left, their connections, if she made any move against him. But that hadn't been all Wilson Lamar had done to try to ensure her "loyalty."

"You think I can *forget* the past, Wilson?" Her voice sounded unused.

He guffawed and reached to pat her thigh. His hand lingered, and squeezed. "Might as well, sugar. It isn't as if deadbeat Mama and Daddy are going to take up your financial slack. You're going to need a job, and what better job than with someone who really appreciates your gifts? I'll make it well worth your while. Have you ever been to Washington?"

Glass splintering brought both of them to their feet. A boy in jeans and a striped T-shirt, with a hood pulled over his head, dashed from the house. He'd collided with a waiter carrying a tray of glasses and knocked both the man and his tray to the ground.

"He's a thief!" a slurred voice yelled. "God knows what he's taken. He's a thief, I tell you. A thief! Looking through the coats. Stop, thief!"

The boy dashed toward the pool, and the fence that skirted it on the side farthest from the house, then saw Wilson and Celina. Wilson was on his feet. The boy dithered, deciding which way to go.

Another figure, this one much bigger, emerged from the pool house. Dressed in jeans, but with his chest bare and shining slightly in the subdued garden lights, he launched himself. It would be some time before the intruder learned what hit him—and then only because someone would tell him.

Not even a cry escaped the boy. The newcomer tackled him at knee level from behind, sending him whipping down on the pool surround. Celina heard the crack of a skull hitting tile and winced.

Opi, the man who ran the Lamar household, walked rapidly from the terrace with Sally trotting behind him. Guests began to crowd forth from the house.

"Who is that?" Wilson asked Sally when she reached him. "The man who stopped him. He came from the pool house."

"Umm." Sally's uncertain tone made Celina look curiously at her. "Well, I do believe that's the person you hired to put in those beautiful aquariums of yours."

Having made certain their interloper wasn't going anywhere, first because he was semi-unconscious, and second because the bare-chested, dark-haired adonis had him pinned to the ground, Opi approached his employer. "Police on their way, Mr. Lamar."

Wilson didn't answer Opi but went to stand over the two men

beside the pool. "Fellow who put in the aquariums, aren't you?" he asked.

"Yes, sir. Ben Angel."

Wilson snorted. "It's a good thing you're big. No one would be stupid enough to make anything out of that name, Angel. What were you doing in the pool house?"

"I'm a perfectionist, me," Ben Angel said, and now Celina could see that he was young, probably not more than in his early twenties. "With the important party going on, I wanted to be close in case anythin' go wrong with my aquariums."

Wilson said, "I like that," and dropped to his haunches. He felt the prostrate boy's neck for his pulse, but drew back when the kid moaned and started to move. "He's going to have the mama and daddy of all headaches. Keep him where he is, Angel, there's a good man."

"Let the staff take care of it, Wilson, do," Sally said. "Come and be nice to our guests. You come too, Celina. Really, you've had more than enough to deal with for one day."

"I can handle things here if you need to go, Mr. Lamar," Ben Angel said.

"Not at all." Wilson eyed him speculatively. "I like a youngster who can act and think. You set on sticking with the aquarium business?"

"Oh, Wilson," Sally said, catching his sleeve and tugging. "What a question."

"I'm not plannin' to stay married to it, if that your meanin'," Ben replied.

"Come and talk to me in the mornin'," Wilson said. "Ten sharp. Opi, make sure he gets in to see me."

"Yes, sir," Opi said.

Celina couldn't take her eyes from Sally's face. The woman looked sick, and she looked sick while she stared from her husband to Ben Angel and back again.

Sirens sounded and rapidly grew closer. Flashing lights spun through the darkness outside the estate. Assuming his smooth, in-charge demeanor, Wilson was on his feet and standing over the culprit by the time the police—with several reporters in pursuit—made their way through the gibbering throng on the terrace.

Celina was amazed to see the gossip columnist Charmain Bienville in the lead, shouting orders at an accompanying cameraman as her high heels quickly covered the space to the drama area. Her close-cropped white-blond hair glinted. She was a tall woman but probably wore size four Armani suits. "Hello, Wilson," she said briskly, touching his arm lightly. "Fund-raiser turns into a drunken brawl, hmm? Anything you'd like to say about that? Fred, you know what to do."

"Fred" promptly dropped to make sure that his shots would include Wilson as well as the kid with blood running from his nose. The camera also captured Ben Angel and the bevy of inebriated guests who had finally gained enough courage to totter close.

A policeman ordered everyone to back off, but they were slow to react.

Charmain's sharp eyes singled out Celina. "Oh, my dear girl," she said, throwing her arms around Celina, who had no relationship whatsoever with the woman. "What a terrible day you have had. Listen, I've been trying to reach you. I want to do my best to help as much as I can. These will be difficult times. You'll have to deal with all the unpleasant rumors—"

"Good to see you here, Charmain," Wilson said. "How about some champagne?"

"Thanks," she said, and turned back to Celina. "People can be so nasty, dear. Are you staying on in Royal Street?"

Mesmerized, Celina nodded.

"Good. I shall come over and we'll have a girl-to-girl chat and I'll help you plan your counteroffense."

"Counteroffense?" Celina frowned. "To what?"

"The people who will want to undermine Dreams because of all the talk about Errol, of course. Aren't you . . . oh, you don't plan to keep things going. I should have thought of that. After all, you were just the Dreams Girl, not the foundation itself. Errol Petrie was the foundation, and he was well loved. It would be a pity if everything he did came to mean nothing because of what they'll say about him. But we should still talk."

More camera flashes popped, and reporters yelled questions. Celina noted that the police didn't seem at all annoyed at their presence, which lent credence to suggestions that the first item on the police dispatchers' list was to inform the media of anything interesting going down.

The boy sat up and hung his head forward while a policeman read him his rights.

Charmain slipped an arm beneath one of Celina's and said in a confidential tone, "Is it true that Jack Charbonnet helped fund Errol Petrie?"

"They were very close friends." Celina knew she was out of her depth with this, and the less she said the better.

"But Errol had money problems because of some, well, isn't it true that his wife left him because of certain differences of opinion about the kind of entertainment he preferred?"

Celina pressed her lips together and squelched her temper. "Errol Petrie's son died of an autoimmune disorder. That cost . . ." She was playing into this woman's hands. Smiling wasn't easy, but she managed. "I'm sorry. You're trying to help me with my job and I'm just too upset to know what to do or say at the moment. I must ask you to forgive me. Perhaps we can talk later." Much later. Like never.

"It's nice you've got Jack Charbonnet's shoulder to cry on now." Charmain raised dark eyebrows, and her oddly light eyes shone conspiratorially. "And what a shoulder, my dear. That's a coup no other woman has pulled off since his wife killed herself. Drove into a swamp. Drowned in there. Horrible story."

Suicide? Celina couldn't stop herself from registering distress, which she instantly realized would let Charmain know she'd delivered some news.

"Here's your champagne, Charmain darlin'," Wilson said, insinuating himself between Celina and the columnist. "We've had quite the fund-raiser here this evening. Anyone you may have been wanting to interview is undoubtedly here. Why not let me introduce you to a few people."

Charmain looked at him, and her eyes became old and knowing. "How's the campaign, Wilson?" Before he could respond, she said, "I'd better see what we have going on by your pool. Amazing how it's not safe to go to a party at the home of someone like Wilson Lamar."

"I hope you don't intend to print that," Wilson said with one of his most boyish smiles. "When I'm in the Senate I'm going to make crime in this country one of my priorities. And I'm not going to be one of those senators who goes to Washington and forgets the platform he ran on."

"We're taking this young man in," one of the policemen said. "Evidently he was interrupted before he actually got what he came for. We've searched him and he's clean. We'd appreciate it if you'd do the necessary."

"The necessary?" Sally said. "What do you mean, the necessary?"

"Nothing to get upset about, ma'am," the policeman said. "We need to have Mr. Lamar file charges."

"Of course, Officer," Wilson said.

Celina felt tired, so very tired. She'd done her part and come to the party because her parents had begged her to. And she realized she hadn't seen either of them among the group outside. Bitsy and Neville knew when to make themselves scarce.

"I'll be calling you," Charmain told her, and pressed a dry kiss on her cheek. "Take care of yourself, dear. You don't look well."

Wilson took Celina by the shoulders and studied her. "No, you don't, young lady. Not that you should after everything you've been through. But you will give serious thought to what I mentioned to you, won't you?"

"What was that?" Charmain asked so offhandedly, it was hardly a question at all.

"Why, I want Celina to join my staff again, of course," Wilson said heartily. "She used to work part-time for the campaign. Now she's going to have lots of free time. She's not just beautiful, she's brilliant, and I don't like to see that kind of talent going to waste."

Celina bowed her head and took a small step closer to Wilson, just close enough to murmur, "That was a mistake." Then she nodded in all directions and moved away from him. "I think I'm going to take the advice of my well-wishers and toddle off to get some rest, so I'll bid you all good night."

A chorus of good-byes followed her as she walked toward the house and made for the nearest telephone to call the cab back. A faint buzzing began in her head. Once before she'd felt the sensation, and she'd almost passed out. That had been when she'd had an encounter with Wilson, too, and it had terrified her.

She used the passage of the police through the house to make her getaway without having to speak to her parents again, and ran the length of the driveway until she could slip through the gates and wait outside.

Within moments the police cars pulled away, their lights flashing again.

Tired didn't come close to describing how she felt. Her limbs were heavy and her head ached so badly, she wanted to close her eyes.

"Are you out of your mind, Celina?"

She jumped, and clutched the neck of her dress.

Jack Charbonnet, his hands in his pockets, leaned menacingly over her. "You really have a thing for courting danger, don't you? What the hell are you doing out here on your own? Trying to see if you can pick up a murderer? Or maybe just a rapist?"

"Don't!"

His face moved, grew less distinct. She threw out her arms and was vaguely aware of hands gripping them as she began to fall.

She should ask him what he was doing there.

A cold place cleared at the center of her mind, and she saw another face—Wilson Lamar grinning at her.

She shook her head, willing the image away. Tears sprang in her eyes. She couldn't stop them.

"Celina?" *Jack Charbonnet.* "Hold on, kiddo, hold on. It's okay."

You never trusted men who told you things would be okay.

Wilson sweated and stood very close to her. "I need you, Celina. Trust me, it'll be okay." They were in the small sitting room on the second floor at her parents' home. "I swear if you won't talk to me, I'm going to kill myself. I've got a gun in the car and I'm going to drive out to the Atchafalaya Swamp and put the thing in my mouth. By the time they find me, there won't be anything left."

"Celina, can you hear me?" Jack asked. "I'm taking you home. I'm going to drive you home."

She hit him. Hit him again. And she cried.

Wilson had closed and locked the sitting room door and begged her to hold him, to let him tell her what was destroying him.

And she'd been afraid of him, but sorry for him too. Before she'd found out he was stealing, she'd believed in him and in what he said he wanted to do for Louisiana.

"It's okay, honey." Jack's voice again. "Hit me if you want to. I can take it. You're angry. Come on, hold on to me."

"Hold me, Celina, please hold me. I'm going to do great things for Louisiana, baby. You wouldn't want to get in the way of that by telling people things that don't matter. I needed that money. To help me get where I want to—where I need to go for everyone's sake."

How long ago had it been? Five months now? A little more? She couldn't make herself remember clearly anymore. She'd been afraid of him, and she'd asked him to go home and get some sleep, told him they'd talk things out when he was calmer.

Wilson Lamar had put his hands around her neck and smiled, and said that he would just have to make sure she saw things his way. He'd have to create some insurance for himself, and if she chose to keep on threatening him, her parents would be the ones to suffer. He'd just have to let their hypocritical little world know that their daughter was a tramp who had tried to trick him into leaving his wife. Celina had come on to him. That's what he'd tell the world.

She'd flaunted herself and he'd been weak. He'd throw himself on public mercy and get it. She'd never be believed. After all, there were precedents, and she was a beautiful, sexy woman. The former Miss Louisiana, a woman accustomed to using her body to get what she wanted.

Then Wilson Lamar took out his insurance.

He had raped her that night.

Eight

"This is an unexpected pleasure, Sonny." Win Giavanelli waved his underboss, Sonny Clete, into the private room at La Murèna, a small, expensive restaurant specializing in Italian fish dishes. The room was reserved for Win at all times. Win owned the restaurant.

Sonny Clete sweated, not a good omen. "Come and sit with me," Win said, spreading his hands. He'd just finished eating—he always ate around one in the morning. Helped him think more clearly.

Still hovering just inside the door, Sonny looked as if his expensive silk suit would soon be sodden under the arms. So far he hadn't said a word. Of average height, with thinning red hair and a plump face, Sonny had been little more than an ambitious, scrambling boy when he'd been inducted into the family. Now in his forties, he'd thickened around the belly and his beringed hands were soft.

Maybe Sonny had grown too soft, too complacent.

"Hey, what is this?" Win pulled the napkin from his neck and tossed it aside. He stood and reached his arms out to Sonny. "Is this the way family greet each other?"

Sonny walked into the embrace and patted Win's back. The piece Sonny wore in a shoulder holster pressed Win's chest.

"Good to see you, Win," Sonny said. "Thanks for lettin' me come on such short notice."

The formality was not lost on Win. "I always got time for you, you know that." He motioned Sonny into one of the heavy mahogany armchairs lined with plush red velvet pillows that circled the table. Glancing around, Sonny sat at Win's right elbow.

Win was left-handed. No one sat at his left—it was understood.

"I don't like to interrupt your dinner," Sonny said. "I've been worried. Otherwise anythin' I needed to discuss with you could have waited."

"My table is your table," Win told him. Those words gave a signal of which Sonny had no knowledge. A trigger man behind one of the intricately carved wall panels now had the sights of his submachine gun trained on Win's guest.

"I see you are deeply troubled, Sonny," Win said. "This pains me greatly. Pour yourself some wine."

Sonny poured the Chianti automatically. The offer was an order, and there was no choice but to follow instructions.

"You hungry, Sonny?"

"No, Win, I'm not hungry."

"You comfortable in that chair, Sonny?"

"Great, thanks. You're a considerate host."

Win poured himself more wine but didn't drink. "Am I like a father to you, Sonny?"

"More than a father, Win."

"Isn't a good father a man his son can turn to when he's troubled, and turn to with confidence?"

"That is true."

Win settled his considerable bulk more comfortably and said, "Then tell the father what is in your heart, son."

"Jack Charbonnet."

Win drank then, to give himself a moment to recover. He set down the glass and said, "Jack Charbonnet? What about him?"

"His parents had their unfortunate accident shortly after I had the good fortune to become a member of the family."

Win pushed out his lips and blotted them with his napkin. He frowned and made a show of casting his mind back, then nodded. "That would have been about right. You have an exceptional memory, Sonny. But that's history. Why does it worry you now?" And why, he wondered, had he ever hoped the issue was permanently buried along with the Charbonnets?

Sonny hunched his shoulders, propped his elbows, and laced his fingers together. "Jack Charbonnet was a ten-year-old kid at the time. I think perhaps there was some decision to look after that kid because he was an orphan and deservin' of pity. We all got a soft spot for an orphan kid, Win, and you're the most merciful man I know."

"Merciful?" Win said, meeting Sonny's eyes sharply. "Or soft? Would you be suggesting I'm soft, Sonny? I should be most hurt if I thought that was the case."

Sonny snickered and shook his head. "You, soft? Not you, Win. You're one hard son of a bitch." He snickered some more, but when Win didn't crack a smile, Sonny slowly sobered and added, "With all due respect, of course."

The memories of that day began to come back—all of them too brightly colored, too sharp. "If that's an apology, I accept. Now, back to what's on your mind."

"Charbonnet senior and his tart were taken out early in your administration, Win."

"Mrs. Charbonnet wasn't no tart. Remember that. Always give deserved respect to the dead. And it was my understandin' that she wasn't supposed to be part of the deal. Yeah, it was in my administration, but I never knew it was going down until it happened. Know what, Sonny, I don't think it was anythin' to do with the family—this one or any other one. We tried to find out, but came up empty every way we turned."

"Sure," Sonny said. "If you say so, Win. I guess it's all talk that Jack's father was tryin' to quit the family and that's why he and his lady got blown away."

"You callin' me a liar, Sonny?"

Sonny's eyes, the same reddish color as his hair, became as innocent as a babe's. "If there's one thing I wouldn't do, Win, it's call you—a man of integrity—a liar. I meant that if you think this was somethin' outside, somethin' Charbonnet had goin' on the side, then you're probably right."

"So," Win said expansively, gripping the edge of the food- and paper-strewn table and leaning back in his chair, "I hope that puts your mind at rest."

"That covers the parents. Why do you think Jack's gettin' the breaks?"

"Breaks?" Win managed to sound abjectly confused. "Why, Sonny, what breaks are you talkin' about? The guy's a free agent. Never was no part of anythin' we're into."

"That's not the way a lot of the boys see it. And maybe it's not the way I see it."

This was a time Win had expected to come, even while he'd hoped it never would. "Wanna tell me the way you and other members of my family do see it?"

Sonny sweated more profusely now. Rivulets ran down the sides of his face, and the top of his dark gray collar had a half-inch band around it that was even darker. "Charbonnet's a friggin millionaire."

"Millionaires are a dime a dozen, Sonny. You're a millionaire. I'm a millionaire. Why not Jack Charbonnet?"

"He's a millionaire on family money. Our family's money. Money his old man was trying to take out with him when he thought he could say *arrivederci* to the best friends he ever had and keep what they were responsible for helping him get. Even if you wasn't responsible for ordering his execution, you gotta admit you knew he wanted out."

Win considered lying, but there were too many of the older people still around who knew the truth. "He discussed something like that, yeah, but that was all. He discussed it. I had to point out to him that a made man can't do what he had in mind. I assume he understood. Then he met with his sad end before there could be anything more than that. What was the family supposed to do? Walk into the courtroom when all that was being settled and say, 'Hey, judge, the man's money belongs to us because Mr. Charbonnet made it carrying out certain assignments for us.' The judge might say, 'What assignments would those be, gentlemen?' 'Oh, a hit here, a little extortion there, prostitution, bid-rigging, and then there's—whatever . . .' I don't think so, Sonny. I think the best course was to let the kid inherit and forget it. What you got against Jack Charbonnet, anyway?"

"His goddamn gambling interests." Sonny's doughy face turned an interesting combination of red and purple mottling. "Wanna help me understand why he's the only owner—majority owner—in a riverboat casino who don't show his respect to the family by sharing his good fortune with us, and why he ain't even remotely scared about that?"

So it was all starting to get real sticky. The direct approach might be best here. "I own a part of that boat," Win said. "Plain and simple. I gotta provide for my children and I wanted it to be clean—just in case something changes with the family—so I bought into Charbonnet's venture."

"Nice for Charbonnet. Know what else I heard?"

"I'm sittin' on the edge of my seat."

"I heard you got a thing for Charbonnet. You got anythin' you wanna say about that?"

"A *thing*? Maybe I don't understand your generation's vocabulary so good. Sure as hell, I hope I don't."

Sonny's face became a solid, shiny red. "Like you feel responsible for him. You bein' the boss when his folks got whacked, and all."

Win decided he would be doing some investigation of his own.

Someone had talked out of school, and he didn't like that. No, he didn't like that one bit. "Jack Charbonnet's not my kid. I got my own kids to feel responsible for. And if I didn't make what went down with his parents, why would I feel I owed him something?" So far he'd managed to hide the reason Jack Charbonnet was important to him. Once he'd thought the truth would come out at any moment, but as the months and years passed, he'd become convinced his little secret was safe.

With a one-sided smile Sonny shrugged and turned up his palms. "I'm just tellin' you what I heard. You always said one of the reasons I was your underboss was because I got real good ears, Win."

Win brought his fists down on the table with enough force to make the used dishes jump. He enjoyed Sonny's flinching, and the way he threw himself backward in his chair. "I been good to you, Sonny. Real good."

"Real good," Sonny said, taking a dirty napkin from the table and wiping his eyes.

"I made you what you are—a real successful man."

"Yeah, Win."

"That means your ears belong to me. Got that?"

Sonny finished with the napkin, balled it up, and threw it down. "You got my respect, Win. Do I got your respect enough to ask you to hear me out?"

The change in the other man switched Win to full alert. "Sure," he said slowly. "Say your piece."

"You told me about your part in Charbonnet's action. I like that. Honesty. I like that. It makes me feel like things haven't changed between us."

Win kept silent, but he was making a decision about Sonny Clete. There were men you never questioned because they never put a foot wrong, never forgot who was boss. Then there were men who couldn't stop themselves from starting to think they knew more than you did. They began to believe they were bulletproof and had the right to tell you what decisions you should make. A man like that usually became too expensive to keep around. Things had been hard lately. The last thing Win needed was an impatient heir apparent.

"You got anythin' you want to say, Win? Or do I go on."

"Go on."

"If it wasn't out of some misplaced sense of responsibility for Charbonnet, why did you choose his operation for your investment? Did you think it wouldn't be noticed that he was never touched? I ran a check. That's all it took. And not one man could tell me it was his job to collect from Charbonnet's outfit."

"You checked on me?" Win said, but made sure he sounded real quiet, real reasonable. "Why would you do a thing like that?"

"I checked on Charbonnet because I was interested. I know a fat cat when I see one. Nothin'. He lives like Cinderella after the prince comes along. And you're the man who calls 'em, Win. If Jacko isn't in, it's because you never decided to have him invited."

Win knew when he was looking at a man who wanted his job. Things had been too quiet for too long. That should have made him suspicious. Sonny would have to become an example, but not there at La Murèna, and not that night. Win had indigestion tonight. "I told you why the guy isn't payin'. You don't choose to accept my explanation, that's your decision. Give my felicitations to your lovely wife. I hope you're bein' good to her—and those nice kids of yours. Family's everythin', Sonny, never forget that."

"I wouldn't," Sonny said, and Win saw his confidence waver— but not for long. Sonny lowered his face and breathed deep. "I don't want to say this. To me you been more than the boss in this family. You been more of a father than the man who married my mother."

"Oh, don't ever show disrespect to your father, Sonny."

"You hear what I said? I said, you became my father. Now I get the whisper that you're a man who gets tired of this son. I get word that I'd better be watchin' my back because you don't got room for two sons at your right hand and you're gettin' old and guilt is now a thing with you. You got guilt because Charbonnet lost both his parents and he saw it. And you feel real bad about that—you always did—but now you've been goin' to confession and thinkin' about what comes next and you want to make amends to the man who was that kid. So you're thinkin' you'd like him to take your place when you're gone. Only that means there's no place for me."

Win reached into his pocket. He grimaced and shook his head when Sonny went for his piece. "Forget it, Sonny," he said. "I ain't goin' for no gun. I don't do my own killing, or had you forgotten?"

Sonny relaxed a little.

The pain in Win's chest wasn't from indigestion. He found what he was looking for in his pocket, eased the top off the bottle, and hooked out a little pill. He coughed to hide what he was doing and slid the medication under his tongue. Weakness was something you never showed, especially to a man who wanted your chair while it was still warm.

"You finished?" he said, breathing a little deeper as the pain in his chest receded.

"Almost," Sonny said. "I got my own army, Win. Reserves, not regulars, so don't panic."

Win showed his teeth. He leaned toward Sonny and flipped his hand-painted silk tie out of his jacket. "Nice," he said. "You was always a nice dresser. You wouldn't be threatening me with some sort of mutiny, would you?" He patted Sonny's face, then patted it again, this time hard enough to bring a hiss through the other's teeth.

"I'm tellin' you that we got an understanding, you and me," Sonny said. "I've served you well—with absolute loyalty—for a lot of years. I'm tellin' you that if you've got a mind to do this thing and put Charbonnet in my place, there'll be war. Mutiny, if that's what you want to call it. There are others who don't feel real comfortable with the idea that you'd turn your back on faithful soldiers and take in strangers instead."

Win needed to lie down, but he'd sit right where he was for as long as he had to. "I'm wounded," he said, putting his brow on his fists. "After all I've done for you, you question the promises I've made to you." He used the opportunity—while his face was hidden—to order his thoughts. Someone had found out that Jack Charbonnet operated a riverboat casino without interference and decided to use the intelligence to stir up the New Orleans family. That was the Giavanelli family—no one else got any action in the parish. The big question was, who? Why? Well, "why" was easy. Divided, they fall—and there was plenty worth grabbing in this town.

"I'd like to go home now," Sonny said, and his steady voice didn't make Win more cheerful. "All I'm askin' is that you think about what I've said. You want to respect me, I'm your man, and things stay as they are."

"Or else?" Win raised his face and wiped all expression from his eyes. "You threatening me, boy?"

"I've told you what I want. I got a right to ask for that."

Win was grateful his next breath didn't hurt. "But? There's a 'but,' isn't there?"

"I'm not a man into threats. If I got somethin' I think needs to be done, I do it. But this is different. You and me—we're family. I owe you. So I'm gonna do what you taught me and take my time thinking and watching before I make any moves."

"You learned well." But Win was badly shaken by this bald confrontation.

"I had the best teacher. And I'm gonna hope everythin's fine. Meanwhile, I got a couple of trusted soldiers lookin' after my security for me."

A single three-word signal and Sonny Clete wouldn't need any security anymore.

"They know they don't make no moves as long as I'm healthy, but if they should get word that I was taken ill and it didn't look like I'd recover, they'd follow orders. I never said they were smart soldiers, see, just loyal."

"You about done now, Sonny? I got a real bad feeling about the way things are with you and me. I think we gotta call the consigliere and ask him how to proceed. If my underboss is threatening me, I got no choice but to get advice from our lawyer, then call a meeting of the family."

"We ain't gonna need no lawyer, nor no meeting. Just an agreement between you and me. You're a man who puts family first. All kinds of family. Even the family of a stranger like Jack Charbonnet."

Win's bad feeling grew worse. "Your point."

"Simple. You be good to me, look after my welfare, and nothing happens. But if I have an unpleasant accident, those loyal soldiers I mentioned, the ones lookin' out for me, are gonna know what happened. And they'll make sure what happens next gets traced right to your door."

"Your *point*, Sonny?" Win growled.

"They'll be in position. They're in position right now. Keepin' their fingers on the trigger and their eyes on the crosshairs. Watchin' Jack Charbonnet and that sweet little kid of his. Amelia, is it?"

Nine

Palms in the courtyard hustled in the wind. Lightning briefly soaked the darkness to the north, over Lake Pontchartrain, and bathed Celina Payne's Royal Street sitting room. Jack waited for the thunder, then wished he were at the old house his grandfather had left him at the edge of the lake. He didn't get to go there nearly often enough.

The thunder, when it came, was distant and disappointing. Tonight was worthy of cannon fire, an explosion to open the skies and bring the cleansing rain in torrents.

He'd left the lights off out of habit. Moving around in the darkness was comfortable. He smiled, but knew it was a bitter smile. A love of darkness probably came naturally, a legacy from his father—like the phobia about standing in front of windows.

His reaction to Celina wasn't welcome. It wasn't unpleasant, far from it, but it was inappropriate for too many reasons. What did he feel about her, or toward her? She made him angry.

Now there was a telling first reaction. Anger was a poor basis for a relationship, working or personal. Not that he intended to pursue anything personal. This time his smile felt vaguely embarrassed. If he thought the woman would welcome any advances from him, he was a masochist who enjoyed rejection. Her dislike of him had a whole lot more punch than the night's first pathetic roll of thunder.

Celina had gone to her bedroom—to change her shoes, she said. Jack had noted that a light showed on the phone in this room, meaning she was using the line and wanted privacy.

He wondered whom she was speaking to and considered, for a short, mad moment, carefully lifting the receiver. A very short, quickly quelled moment.

What the hell had all that been about at Wilson Lamar's place? He'd swear she'd passed out from some sort of incredible stress. He'd all but carried her into the taxi that mercifully arrived within seconds. But then she had rallied enough to pull into the farthest possible corner of the seat and sit, huddled, peering at houses they passed, and then at the buildings in the Quarter. She'd attempted to leave him in the cab when they got to Royal Street, but he'd ignored her protests and followed her into the house.

The illuminated button on the phone went out.

A gust of heavy rain on the windowpanes surprised him. No relief from the electric humidity had been forecast.

A muted snap sounded behind him and a floor lamp in one corner came on. "You're standing in the dark," Celina said.

"So I am."

"What were you doing at the Lamar house?"

It had been too much to hope for that she wouldn't ask the question. He was not going to tell her that he was curious about her as a woman outside the only arena where their lives had touched—Errol's arena. And he wasn't going to tell her that he'd done something completely contrary to his nature and followed her on a whim without knowing what, if anything, he intended to do when he arrived at his destination.

He took his time turning around to look at her. "The same thing you were doing there," he told her. The lie came easily enough. "Only I was even later than you were."

She entered the frankly threadbare room with her arms tightly pressed to her sides. Her hands were clenched into fists. An oversized gray sweatshirt and jeans had replaced the black linen dress. "You were on your way to the fund-raiser?" Celina looked out of place among mismatched predominantly brown furnishings.

He'd have to pray she never verified what he said. "Yeah."

"How come you didn't mention you were going too, when I left you? I told you where I was heading."

"I guess I was too tied up with thinkin' about Errol." He shrugged and forced himself to make eye contact with her. "I still can't believe he's gone."

At that she flexed her fingers and the abject sadness in her eyes loaded him with guilt. "I appreciate your kindness," she said. "For bringing me home. I'll be fine now."

In other words, get lost, Jack. "Good."

She looked directly into his face, then quickly away again. But she didn't look away quickly enough for him to miss either the naked misery, or the moist sheen in her eyes.

"It's raining," she said. "Maybe you should call a cab from here instead of—"

"Don't worry about me. I've lived in the Quarter a long time. I know my way around—even in the rain." What he hoped was an engaging smile didn't elicit a flicker of reaction. "Celina? Will you let me do something for you? Is there something you need?" Now he was getting soft.

"I"—she pulled her sleeves over her hands—"I don't need anything, but thank you for offering."

"You're very pale."

"I don't feel great." At last a smile appeared, but it wasn't convincing. "That doesn't mean I'm ill or something, just that I'm a bit wobbly. Shocked. You must be too, in your own way."

How right she was, Jack thought. He nodded, and it was his turn to look away. "I lost my best friend today." That was the kind of thing he never said aloud to anyone. Ms. Celina Payne had an unusual effect on a man. "We weren't very much alike, really. Not at all alike. But, y'know, I loved the guy. I always knew where I was with Errol. He told it like it was. Played it straight. Aw, hell, I sound like an athlete who's given one too many interviews."

"You sound like a sincere human being to me. You sound as if you aren't what you pretend to be."

He glanced at her sharply. "What does that mean? I'm really a creep? Or I'm not really a creep?"

She shook her head and caught her bottom lip between her teeth. And when her eyes crinkled, tears slipped free and he swallowed hard. After Elise died, he had cried, and he'd walked around for weeks with what felt like a block of wood in his throat. Since then he'd been able to become emotional only over Amelia. His daughter had become his link to her mother, the wife he'd loved and lost, and his link to a part of himself that would have frozen if he hadn't had a child. What he felt now, because very lovely Celina Payne shed tears prettily, was an autonomic reaction he might have to a well-produced, well-acted piece of cinematic pathos.

"I think you're more comfortable if you can make people think you're a tough guy, Jack," she said, clearly struggling for composure. "But I don't think you're so tough. Toughened, maybe, but not tough."

"When I was a kid, my mother told me I could make it on the stage." A laugh stuck in his throat. His mother? He'd mentioned his mother spontaneously after never saying her name or answering a question about her from the moment he knew she was dead.

"I think most mothers think that kind of thing about their children," Celina said. "My mother got completely carried away with . . . forget I said that."

He wouldn't forget, but he might never have a reason to raise the subject again. "Well, if you're sure you're okay, I'll go on down and find that cab." He felt inside his jacket for a card. "I know you've got my number in the office, but I'll leave this here. Don't hesitate to call, please. I can be here in a few minutes." He put the card near her phone.

"Thanks." Barefoot, with her hands hitched inside her sleeves and no makeup left, she looked very young and very alone. "I'll be at my desk in the morning."

He cleared his throat. "I meant to speak to you about that. Evidently we're going to have to put up with more visits from the NOPD. They were here all afternoon, so Antoine told me. Errol's rooms are taped off. They think they've done everything they need to do, but until they give the word, it's off limits over there."

Her expression turned haunted. She whispered, "Who would kill Errol?"

Jack said, "Not a living soul I can think of. No, I surely can't think of a soul. Celina, people grinned at the sight of him. It's corny, but he spread sunshine—you know that. He had a hard time of it for a few years there, but he faced up to his problems and beat them. And he didn't make enemies along the way." He looked at her. "Did he? Do you know of anyone with a grudge? Is there somethin' I don't know?" What he stopped himself from asking was if she was hiding somethin, an he believed she was.

She seemed to consider, then said, "No. No, nothing. Nobody."

"No." There wasn't anything else to be said, not now. "I'd better go."

"Yes. Amelia will be watching for you."

"Amelia had better be asleep."

"She's lovely."

"I know. I'm a lucky man."

"Children make you feel that way, I'm told. Your own children."

"Yes." For some reason, he could no longer visualize her on the runway in a beauty pageant. "You must be very tired."

"So must you."

He didn't like leaving her alone there. "Don't forget to lock up after me."

"I won't forget."

"Can you take business calls on this phone?"

"Yes." She tipped her face up to the ceiling. "I'd like to keep on working for Dreams, but if you have different plans, I'll understand. I know I can keep things afloat until you're ready to—"

"I'm ready now."

"I see." The next second seemed long, and the next. "You mean you'd like me to leave?"

Jack scrubbed at his face. "Of course I don't mean that. I don't have any idea what I'll decide about long-range plans for the foundation."

"It's self-sustaining," she said, so pathetically eager, he detested himself for all the doubts he still had about her.

"I'm not concerned about that," he told her. "But this was so important to Errol. The most important thing in his life since he lost his boy. Whatever I decide to do will be designed to make Dreams a tribute to a good man's life."

"And I might not be good enough to be a part of that?"

"I didn't say that." Nor did he mean it. "Could we take our time deciding what comes next?"

"You can take yours. The children we serve don't have time."

"I don't respond well to someone trying to make me feel guilty. Once it was easy to do, but not anymore."

If it was possible, Celina became even paler. Her blue eyes appeared black and too big for her face. She backed up, sat down suddenly on the lumpy brown tweed couch, and pushed her hands beneath her thighs.

"Do I make myself clear?" he asked. "I have no intention of putting things on hold around here. But I do have to take stock of where things stand. I should think you'd expect that after what you showed me earlier."

She breathed through her mouth and said nothing.

What the hell, this wasn't about money. He'd kept the books at his place. "I'll make things right with the foundation accounts. There won't be any problem with you writing necessary checks. I can sign them. Just keep on as you've been doing until we can talk again. Okay?"

Celina gave a single nod and pushed herself farther back on the couch.

His first instincts about her had been right. They would never be friends. "Good night, then. I'd appreciate it if you'd let me know about any developments."

Taking off his jacket as he went, he slung it over his shoulder and walked to the door. The rainfall hadn't done a thing to lessen the humidity, but then, it rarely did. He was too warm.

"Excuse me."

Jack stopped and looked over his shoulder. She'd spoken so softly, he barely heard her. "What is it?"

"Oh, nothing."

He turned and retraced his steps, and bent over her. "What did you want to say?" Why would a man who knew better keep walking toward trouble?

"You don't need this," she said.

"Now it's my turn to say, excuse me? What is it I don't need?" He looked closer. "Are you sick? Do you feel faint again?"

"No, of course not."

"You're shivering."

"Uh-uh. I'm highly strung. I—I'm okay. Good night, Jack. Thanks for helping me out when I needed it."

"You passed out, or just about passed out when you were leaving the Lamars'."

"I told you I got upset because of that boy being knocked down, then arrested."

Jack narrowed his eyes. Sweat stood out along her hairline. "I thought you said he'd been caught attempting to rob the place."

"He didn't have to be beaten like that." She slumped against the back of the couch. "I think I'm going to be sick."

"As in throw up?" Jack tossed his jacket aside and made to pick her up.

Celina pushed him away and struggled to her feet. "No. Thank you, but I like to be in control. You can get hurt if you give up control, if you trust someone."

A lot of sense the lady made? "Whatever you say. I'll just hang around while you decide if you're going to collapse, okay?"

She clapped a hand over her mouth and made a wavy path into the corridor. Jack followed her to her disordered bedroom and inside. He registered lots of white scattered with blue polka dots on the bed, and at the windows. He also noticed the scent of burning, or something that had burned.

By the time she reached the bathroom, her slim body was doubled over and she made retching sounds.

"Hey," Jack said, clicking into take-charge mode, "let's get you in there before we end up havin' to clean the carpet."

A hand waving him away was all the thanks he got. Jack ignored the embarrassed signal and all but lifted her into the bathroom. With one hand he whipped up the toilet seat and with the other he lowered her to her knees.

"Go away," she moaned, but without any force, before she gripped the edge of the toilet and no longer cared if he was witnessing her misery or not.

Jack gave thanks for her short hair, kept a hand under her arm, and reached for a washcloth. Celina's wasn't the first brow he'd sponged in the early hours of the morning. Single parents became experts at these things.

He didn't like the limp weakness he felt in her body. When she tried to get up, her legs showed little interest in supporting her, but he didn't lift her. Instead, he held the wet washcloth on the back of her neck and walked her to the bed. He sat her on the edge and lifted her legs.

Instantly her eyes shot wide open, and the terror he saw there made him angry. No woman had ever had a reason to be terrified of him. The instinctive urge to let her legs fall again passed quickly. She was ill, perhaps very ill. Rather than back off, he stretched her out carefully and pulled a sheet over her.

She closed her eyes.

An outer door slammed and footsteps came toward Celina's rooms. Jack looked around for something to arm himself with.

"Hey, Celina sugar, where are you? It's me, Dwayne. I'd have come earlier, but I had to close and you know how things get." Jack heard the other man go into the sitting room. "I called this afternoon, but you weren't back. Celina?"

"In here, Dwayne," Jack called. "In the bedroom."

There was silence before Dwayne called back, "Is that you, Jack Charbonnet?"

"It surely is."

"Why, you devil, you. I had no idea. I'm such an innocent. Celina? You okay, lamb? Just say yes and I'll be on my way. Big, strong Jack will keep you safe."

"Quit the crap and get your rear in here, Dwayne," Jack shouted. "Celina's ill. We need a doctor."

"No!" She sat up and gripped her stomach. "No doctor. I don't like doctors. I'll be fine."

Resplendent in a rain-spattered burgundy and gold caftan and wearing gold sandals, Dwayne rushed into the bedroom and directly to Celina's side. "What's happened to you?" he demanded, glaring at Jack before stroking her hair. "Did he hurt you?"

"Don't be silly," Celina said.

"Oh, thanks for that anyway," Jack muttered, and felt foolish. "Persuade her to let us call a doctor."

"Persuade?" Dwayne said, giving him a pitying look. "I'm calling one anyway."

Celina drew up her knees and rested her face on top.

"Excuse the camp getup," Dwayne said, flipping through a little book he produced from somewhere beneath the voluminous caftan. "One of those wretched girls didn't show up, and I had to go on. Happens all the time. Bitch. Wait till tomorrow." He found an entry in his book, picked up the phone, and punched in numbers. A few terse directions to someone who evidently didn't argue at two in the morning, and he hung up.

He stroked Celina's hair again and frowned meaningfully at Jack, silently indicating that her head was wet, and that he was worried. Jack had known and liked Dwayne LeChat for years, and he couldn't think of anyone he'd rather have around at that moment.

"How long will it take for the doctor to get here?"

Dwayne said, "Not long. Celina hon, would you like to put on a pretty nightie? Something cool. You aren't hot, but I've got to tell you, you're sweating like a bull, baby." He caught Jack's grin and made a small bow. "The English language has such infinite possibilities. I believe in using them just as colorfully as I can."

"Errol's dead," Celina said into her knees. "I can't believe it. I know it, but I can't make it stick in my head."

"Are you feeling any better?" Jack asked, heartened by the sound of her voice.

"Tell the doctor not to come," she said.

Jack's and Dwayne's eyes met, and they both shook their heads.

Dwayne went to a chest of drawers that had been painted white by someone who hadn't done much painting. He held his tongue between his teeth, frowned, and began searching the contents of the chest. "Turquoise? No, it'll clash with those horrible blue polka dots. I've got to give you some advice about the decor in here, Celina. You'll just have to wear white. Nothing else will do." He produced a short white cotton nightgown with a pair of abbreviated, matching shorts.

"We're going to turn our backs and you're going to slip these on. Okay?" He put his selections on the bed.

"If you stop the doctor from coming."

"This is not a time for striking bargains, my little flower," Dwayne said. "Put these on, please. I want you comfortable. And I want to straighten up this room, so be quick."

Following Dwayne's lead, Jack faced the wall farthest from the bed and crossed his arms. In a full and beautiful bass, Dwayne broke into a familiar number from *Porgy and Bess*.

"I had no idea," Jack said when his companion paused for breath. "The last time I heard you sing that, you were Bess, not Porgy."

"I'm very versatile," Dwayne told him, putting a finger to his lips. "And sometimes I just can't help myself, I have to show off."

They were silent, listening to movements on the bed.

"Do you know that fabulous piece from *Phantom?*" Dwayne said. "Christine and the Phantom. You must know the one. He tells her, 'Sing for me, Sing for me.' "

"Sure I know it," Jack said.

"Oh, good. Shall we?"

Jack screwed up his face. "Shall we what? Sing it? You've got to be kidding."

· "Oh, be a sport. I'll sing Christine."

This time it was Jack who put a finger to his mouth. Celina had grown silent. "Is it okay if we turn around?" he asked.

She didn't say anything.

Jack raised his brows to Dwayne, and they both looked at the bed. With the sheet pulled up to her chin—and her sweatshirt and jeans in a heap on the floor—Celina lay on her back with one hand thrown over her head, the other curled into a fist against her throat.

"I think she's got food poisoning," Jack said. "Where the hell is the doctor?"

"He'll be here. He was just finishing with his last client."

"Client?" Jack said. "He calls his patients clients?"

Dwayne hovered over Celina. "Don't be ridiculous. He's a medium. In his spare time, naturally. He's very popular, so I'm told. Personally, I have enough trouble talking to the living."

"Is—" Jack motioned for Dwayne to join him at the bottom of the bed, then whispered, "Are you telling me this is some sort of witch doctor?"

"What do you think I am?" Dwayne hissed back. "The man has one of the most prestigious practices in New Orleans."

"But in his spare time he conducts séances on Conti?"

"Yes, Jack. Loosen up. Some people accept the possibility that there may be more to the world than whatever they can see or touch. And they do say that séances can reduce the blood pressure. Al's an internist. And he's a very nice man. He's good with people and he'll put our little friend at ease. He'll also tell it like it is. I don't like the way she looks."

Jack glanced at the bed. The only noticeable difference between Celina's skin and the sheets was that she didn't have blue polka dots. She opened her eyes and looked at him. "I think this is some sort of delayed reaction to what's happened," she said, and wetted her lips. "I'd be a liar if I said I didn't feel awful."

"What have you eaten today, sugar?" Dwayne asked.

"We're wondering if you've got food poisoning," Jack said. "They say most of us get varying doses of it."

"That's what it is," Celina said. "Call the doctor back."

"What did you eat?" Dwayne repeated.

"I've forgotten."

The street bell sounded, tinny and echoing, through the thick-walled building.

"That'll be Al," Dwayne said, and hurried away.

"You picked at lunch," Jack said to Celina. "Jeez, why didn't I think of that? You didn't eat anything. Or nothing to speak of. Did you drink at the Lamars'?"

"Oh, yes, I did."

Her enthusiastic response made him suspicious. "What, exactly?"

"Um, spritzers."

A strong booze lush. "How many?"

"One—a sip of one."

Dwayne breezed back in with a dapper, damp, and prematurely gray man striding behind him. "Al Vauban. That's Dr. Alain Vauban for our purposes."

Bag in hand, Dr. Vauban went directly to Celina and smiled down at her. "Hello, Celina. We met at an auction at your parents' house. Not that you'll remember. I liked Errol very much, and respected him. His death is a great loss. There aren't enough people like him." He was, Jack decided, a small but handsome devil. The thought didn't please him. A picture of him presiding over bumping tabletops wouldn't quite take shape.

Dwayne slid a hand firmly around Jack's arm and tugged. "Come along, Jacko. We'll let the professional do his job."

They went back to Celina's sitting room, where Dwayne trailed around, clucking and threatening to do foul and deadly things to the furniture. He picked up a metal wastebasket, held it to his nose, and sniffed with distaste. "Something burned in here. I swear that baby girl will kill herself if we don't look after her."

Yesterday Jack would have protested that her welfare was no concern of his. Tonight he realized he couldn't say that with conviction. "Waste paper?" he asked.

"Oooh, no. Somethin' nylon—or maybe silk with some nylon. Looks melted. Rubber too. That's the worst. Disgustin'."

Jack's interest was instantly piqued. He took the stainless basket and peered inside. He said, "Promise me you'll forget this," without intending to say any such thing. "Unless I change my mind. Okay?"

"Okay," Dwayne said.

"It's just that—"

"'Nuff said. A friend I respect asks somethin' of me, he gets it."

"Thanks." Celina had done a bad job of trying to burn the black underwear and silk bonds that had been in Errol's room. Jack had already started to regret holding the evidence back—unless it did, indeed, belong to Celina.

Damn, he couldn't get emotionally involved with her.

"Hush," Dwayne said abruptly, holding up a hand. "I do believe we've got more company."

They looked at each other and listened. There was no doubt that someone was climbing the outside steps from the courtyard to the second story.

"Let us not forget that our dear friend was murdered in this house less than forty-eight hours ago," Dwayne whispered. "Could be whoever did that to him decided to come back for somethin'."

Jack slanted a glance at the wastebasket and said, "Could be."

The outside door to the corridor opened, then closed, and the footsteps advanced.

"We don't want Celina upset anymore," Dwayne said, going for the corridor himself. "I'll deal with this."

"Not on your own, you won't," Jack told him, and they went to greet the latest visitor side by side.

And stopped—side by side.

Jack didn't tend to spend a lot of time analyzing men's looks, but the man he confronted now was probably the most handsome specimen he'd ever encountered.

Dwayne murmured, "Oh, my," under his breath, then, "good

evenin', could we ask you to come into the sittin' room before you explain yourself. There's someone sick here." When Dwayne said, "here," it was so pronouncedly "heeyah" as to sound affected—which it wasn't.

The very tall newcomer nodded and approached. Jack and Dwayne stood back to allow him access to the sitting room.

"Where is Celina?" the man asked, facing them. "How sick is she?"

The navy-blue slicker he wore dripped on the worn carpet. Jack noted that water beaded on well-polished shoes that were nevertheless old and deeply creased. His dark, curly hair was cut short and currently soaked.

"How *did* you get that wet?" Dwayne asked. "Where did the cabdriver let you out, for goodness' sake?"

"I walked," the man said shortly. "I asked about Celina." If he was surprised by Dwayne's caftan, he gave no sign.

"The doctor's with her now," Dwayne said. "She's had a terrible day. We all have. A shock, you know."

"Yes, I know. I'm deeply sorry about Errol. Such a loss." His eyes were an extraordinary color, not blue or green, but a mixture of the two. Every line of his face was sharply defined and ruggedly perfect. He had the straight-backed, leanly solid physique of an athlete, per- haps a rower. "Celina told me about it on the phone. That's why I came at once. Fortunately I had to come into New Orleans for a meeting and I'd given her a number where she could reach me when I got in tonight. I'm glad I was here."

The phone call, Jack thought. He was sure he'd never met the man, yet he seemed familiar. "I'm Jack Charbonnet," he said, extending a hand.

"Cyrus Payne." A long-fingered hand enveloped Jack's in a firm shake. "I'm sorry, I don't think I said I was Celina's brother."

Jack smiled, and immediately hoped he didn't look as relieved as he felt. And then didn't want to think too hard about why he felt relieved. "I didn't know Celina had a brother."

"The *priest*," Dwayne said, taking his turn at shaking Cyrus's hand. "Of course. I should have known the moment I saw you. You look like Celina. Oh, priests are so fascinating to some of us, you know. So mysterious."

Cyrus raised one very well-defined eyebrow and said, "Really?"

"Yes," Dwayne continued, apparently unaware that he'd amused his audience. He gestured expansively and got closer to Cyrus. "I'm Dwayne LeChat, by the way. A friend of Celina's. There's a forbidden quality about priests—maybe a keep-away quality would explain it better. *Do not touch.* There, that's it. It's the whole thing—the collar, those lovely robes. You don't even have to *say* anything to cast a spell."

"I wish I could just stand in front of the congregation at mass and cast a spell without saying anything. How long has the doctor been with my sister?"

"Not very long," Jack said. "She hasn't felt well all evening. We think she may have food poisoning."

Cyrus took off his slicker and looked around for somewhere to hang it. Dwayne took it from him and tossed it on a chair. "A little rain can't make that monstrosity any worse."

"Celina doesn't care about material possessions herself," Cyrus said. Despite already knowing he was a priest, the clerical collar was almost a shock. "She was born with her priorities straight."

"Is that why she competed all the way to the Miss USA Pageant?" Jack began to feel his tongue was a liability tonight.

"If Celina wants to talk to you about that, she will." The lady's brother had a hard edge to his deep voice, and the eyes might just be able to see their way to a man's world-worn soul. Not at all a comforting idea.

Dr. Vauban joined them. He nodded when Cyrus introduced himself, and took a seat on the couch, where he started writing prescriptions. These finished, he dropped the pad into his bag and took out a notebook. "I'm going to leave some instructions," he said. "She's tired. Emotionally as well as physically. She needs sleep and care. She needs to eat properly. And she needs understanding, support."

"She doesn't have food poisoning?" Dwayne asked.

"No, and she doesn't wish she did," Vauban said. "She's resting now. She told me I could talk to you, Father Payne. I was going to leave a number where you could reach me. But we'll chat right here, if it's all right with you."

"It's fine, but I prefer to be called Father Cyrus."

Dr. Vauban cast a significant glance at Dwayne and Jack. Naturally he wanted them to leave.

"Lordy," Dwayne said, grinning. "I know what this is all about. We're going to have a baby, Al, aren't we?"

Dr. Vauban wasn't quite successful in smothering his own smile. "Not unless you've only been passing all these years."

Dwayne laughed aloud. "You know what I mean. *Celina.* She's pregnant, isn't she? Why didn't I think of that?"

Jack's mind refused to deal with what he was hearing, or what he was thinking.

"I'm not at liberty to discuss that with you," the doctor said. "If Celina and her brother choose to share information with you, that will be their decision."

Father Cyrus went, very deliberately, to the door and closed it. He looked from man to man, and said, "Obviously, there's no secret here. But as far as what you've learned tonight goes, you've got short memories. This is my sister we're talking about, and I won't see her hurt any more than she's already been hurt. Do we understand each other?"

Dwayne nodded.

Jack barely stopped himself from swearing. He needed to be alone, to think.

"Celina is pregnant," Cyrus Payne said. "That's why she asked me to come this evening."

Ten

Several nights of storms, and the temperature only seemed to rise. Buffeted by the warm wind, Celina rested her umbrella on top of her head and angled it to allow her to see. Lamps illuminated the approach to Jack Charbonnet's riverboat, but the surface was slippery underfoot.

She'd taken advantage of Cyrus going to an evening mass to sneak out of the house. He would be disappointed when he got back and discovered she had failed to keep her promise and stay put. And he would be there waiting, and worrying, until she got back, but he wouldn't be angry, only glad to see her safe again.

Cyrus, the son of a demanding mother and a weak father, had somehow managed to grow into a strong man who was most happy when he was serving others. She had never told him how much she had missed him when he left to go into a seminary. He would be deeply troubled only if she explained that the loss of him had doubled their parents' demands upon her.

Boats slipped along the river, their running lights blurred by a steamy mist that hung in the air. The legs of Celina's cotton slacks clung moistly to her shins. She ought to be uncomfortable, but she liked the mystery of the water at night.

Avoiding Jack Charbonnet in recent days would have been simple even if he had tried to see her—which he hadn't. The doctor's instructions that she sleep had as much as possible allowed her to evade everyone else but Cyrus—and Dwayne. Dear, dear Dwayne who loved with such abandon and such utter loyalty. He'd wheedled his way past Cyrus to bubble about the wonders of new life. Celina smiled at the memory. Dwayne had promised that no mention of Celina's pregnancy would pass his lips without her permission and she knew she could trust him.

Jack Charbonnet was a different matter. She had no idea what he might do with the information she'd hoped to keep from him. A fresh gust of wind carried fine rain into her face and she wiped her eyes. The instant Cyrus had left for St. Louis Cathedral in Jackson Square, she'd called Jack's home number and been told tersely by Tilly that Mr. Charbonnet was not at home. On a hunch she'd caught a cab to the river. His floating casino soared above her, the lights outlining its decks and hull shimmering in the darkness. He might not be aboard, but on the other hand, he might, and if he was, she'd be the last person he expected to see. Celina was a neophyte at intrigue—a neophyte rapidly gathering experience—but she thought surprise might be a useful advantage.

Somehow she had to convince him to keep her secret. For how long? She didn't know the answer yet. Even the doctor had been surprised to confirm that she was approximately five and a half months pregnant. He'd remarked that some women, particularly women in good physical condition, did show little sign of their condition until quite late. He'd reassured her that despite her smallness, the baby did seem to be developing at an acceptable rate—and he'd commented that she could probably plan on being unable to conceal the pregnancy for much longer, if at all.

She had to make plans for the future. Wilson Lamar must never be able to assume this was his child, and to pull that off she needed time, as much time as she could snatch.

Steam rose from the wooden railings and boardwalk beside the boat. Celina leaned on the railing and stared down at the black water sucking and blowing between the *Lucky Lady*'s side, and the wharf. Heavy lines sawed at their moorings, and the air carried the scents of oil and tar.

Raucous people plied to and fro on the ramps that led to a booth where Celina could see two women in short, fringed skirts, and a very large man with a bald head. This world didn't feel as if it could belong to the cool, aloof man with the sweet little daughter.

Memories of the night when Jack took her back to Royal Street from the Lamars' swept back, and Celina gritted her teeth, mortified to think that someone who was almost a stranger, someone who had never let her doubt that he didn't like her, had held her head while she vomited.

Jack had been kind. She would cling to that and hope her misery had allowed her to see a side of him that might be her best hope for making him her ally rather than her enemy.

Slowly she climbed the ramps to the booth, lowering the umbrella as she went. The brunette who took her money—the price of admission—smiled but didn't make eye contact.

She trod between rows of slot machines. The lights were bright, conversation loud, laughter and shouts of disgust or triumph louder. More women in short skirts delivered drinks to preoccupied customers.

Ahead a wide flight of steps rose to another deck, and Celina walked halfway up so that she could study the scene she was leaving carefully, searching for any sign of Jack Charbonnet. She could ask if he was aboard, but that would snuff out the minor advantage she might get from her surprise theory.

Celina didn't see Jack, but she did see Charmain Bienville.

Horrified at the possibility of the woman cornering her again, Celina fled to the next deck where she was confronted by a bar backed with mirrors. On one side of the bar was a small lounge where elevated video screens allowed patrons to play keno while they drank. A larger area at the opposite end of the bar was devoted to a restaurant called Velvet's. Celina wondered if Jack had selected the name, and if so, why?

Charmain's voice reached her from the stairway.

Above lay only an open air deck. It had to be coincidence that she was there on the same evening as one of the women who ranked as her least favorite. If there was a way to let Charmain pass, then escape downward, Celina decided she would give up this obviously ill-fated quest.

Hooking her umbrella over a forearm, she approached the bar and slid onto a single vacant stool between two men deeply engrossed in their companions. One of the men turned to look her over thoroughly enough to be annoying, but Celina was no stranger to men taking more than casual inventories.

Apparently unconcerned by the way his female friend fidgeted on her stool, he smiled at her and snapped his fingers at the bartender. "What'll you have, pretty lady?"

If she couldn't see Charmain Bienville, her cameraman sidekick in tow, arriving at the top of the stairs, she would leave. Trapped, she said, "Thank you, but I'm waiting for someone," and felt lame.

"So, *chère*." Dark eyes could show so little, or so much. These dark eyes were too interested. "Just because you wait for someone who isn't here means you can't have a drink with me?"

She faced him squarely, then looked past him to the woman at his side. "You're both so very kind," she said to the obvious surprise of the other. "I'll have an orange juice, please."

The dark-eyed man tipped his head back and laughed. The lady with him ordered the orange juice and Celina found herself, for the present, a member of a party of three. She'd make her getaway as soon as Charmain passed. At the moment the woman remained too close to the head of the stairway.

The orange juice arrived and Celina thanked her newfound "friends."

"I'm Mavis," the woman said. "This is Hector, him."

Musicians wandered onto a stage that separated the lounge from the gambling floor and began testing mikes before soothing their way into a gentle Dixieland number Celina didn't recognize.

"You like Dixieland, you?" Mavis asked.

"A lot," Celina told her, and laughed. "Probably because my parents don't."

This brought laughter. Celina decided that Mavis had enjoyed the rebuff Hector had received, pleasant as it had been.

"Oh, my *God!* It's Miss Louisiana herself! *Celina.*"

Celina slowly raised her eyes—and met Charmain's in the mirror. All conversation faded.

"Well, look at you, Celina Payne." Charmain, resplendent in a short red-sequined dress, her white cap of hair spiked, rushed toward Celina with outstretched arms. "You are such an enigma, darling. You can't resist doing the unexpected, can you?"

Celina braced herself and swung the seat of her stool around. Both Hector and Mavis did likewise, as did the couple on the other side. Mavis leaned over and said, "You're Miss Louisiana?"

"I told you I had good taste, *chère,*" Hector said.

The photographer's camera flashed, flashed again, and again. Celina felt angry and helpless.

Charmain embraced her at arm's length and came in a little closer to land a peck on her cheek.

Celina said, "I haven't been Miss Louisiana for some years, Charmain."

"Oh, you'll always be Miss Louisiana to me, darlin'. This is perfect.

I called your place today and spoke to some man with a dark-honey-and-gravel voice. Oooh!'' She winked at Mavis. "He said you were *otherwise* occupied. And I thought, I'll just bet she is. Who was that man?"

"My brother," Celina said shortly, bringing another gust of laughter from a rapt audience.

A sly light entered Charmain's fascinating eyes. "Is *that* who that was? Now, there's an interesting story, I'm sure. The beauty queen whose brother became a priest. The priest from the society family. Why, one wonders?"

If Charmain's design was to pry Celina from the stool, she got her way. Celina stood up and made purposefully for the stairs. She paused to call back a thank-you to Hector and Mavis, and gave the reporter the instant she needed to slip a hand beneath Celina's arm and make it impossible for her to escape without making a scene.

"I just know there are people who come here who wouldn't want the world to know it," Charmain said, leaning close to Celina and whispering as if they were friends sharing confidences. "These places are only supposed to be the playgrounds of the wanna-be movers. I've meant to come and take a look for ages. I think a lot of money changes hands here, and wanna-be movers don't have that kind of money."

Celina made a polite noise. She didn't ask which category she'd been judged to belong to, the wanna-be's, or the real movers.

"Let's sit over there." Without waiting for a response, Charmain half dragged her captive to a table in the lounge. "Why don't we have a bottle of champagne? Just to celebrate? Get lost for now," she told the photographer, who obliged.

"What would we be celebrating?"

A momentary blank look smoothed Charmain's face, then she said, "Why, you and me getting together at last, of course." She signaled for a server.

"No champagne for me, thanks," Celina said.

Charmain ordered a bottle of Dom Pérignon anyway and whipped out a small notebook and a gold pen from an enameled evening purse molded like a scarlet apple with bright green leaves. Charmain lifted the purse, said, "Judith Lieber, isn't she the *end?*" and stroked the hard, shiny surface.

"I need to get home," Celina said. "I've already been gone longer than I should have been."

"Oh, nonsense. You're a big girl. Don't tell me that lovely brother of yours imposes a curfew when he's in town—even if he is a priest. I want to talk to you about poor Errol."

"I thought you were here looking for celebrity sinners."

Charmain batted her arm playfully. "I *am,* darling. But then I saw you and you are much more interesting. Why did you say you were here?"

"I didn't."

"Oh, dear, you think I'm being pushy. I'm not, Celina, I just find you engrossing, and I always have. You're such a dichotomy. The kind of woman every man drools over—that's on the outside—but so quiet and thoughtful. Still waters run deep? Isn't that what they say?"

"Whoever 'they' are," Celina agreed. Coming here had been one of her poorer inspirations.

"So talk to me about yourself. What turns you on? *Who* turns you on? Did Errol Petrie turn you on?"

Celina made a move to get up, but Charmain caught her hand. "Forgive me. I'm a reporter and I've been a reporter for too long, I suppose. Too long for a gentle thing like you. Sit down again, please."

She did sit, but only because people were looking their way again.

"You don't even know what an enigma you are, do you?" Charmain asked. "You move about as if you weren't anyone at all."

"I'm who I am, and that's not very interesting. I don't believe I can help you with a story, and that should mean you'll be perfectly happy for me to go home."

"*Au contraire,* darling." Charmain didn't release Celina's hand. "I *know* you're interesting. And it's only a matter of time before I find out where all the little pieces of you come together for me. The woman who looks like a movie star. Who worked for a charity. Who has parents who are a joke. A whining barracuda mother, a lush for a father."

Celina's mouth felt like a desert. Her heart thumped. She pulled against the woman's strong, thin fingers.

"Settle down. I'm going to have my say. Whatever you think of me, I'm fair. You play ball with me and I'll play ball with you. Make sure I get first shot at this story—and there *is* a story—and I'll make sure you don't come out covered with shit."

"Don't," Celina said.

"Oh, no, of course I mustn't shock your delicate sensibilities. Why did your brother run away to a seminary?"

"My brother had a calling. He didn't run away."

"Were you sleeping with Errol Petrie?"

"No. *No.*"

"Intelligence says you were. After all, he was a handsome man with a reputation for having quite an appetite." She held up her free hand. "Don't argue. I've got a long memory, and I remember everything I read anyway. Maybe I won't have to use some things. That could depend on you. What about the night he died? What happened? All the sex stuff."

How could that kind of information have been leaked? Or known at all. Celina composed her features into a semblance of empty confusion. Only she and Jack knew exactly how Errol had been found.

"Did he always like to be tied down?" Charmain chuckled. "How prosaic that's starting to sound. Do you like to be tied down? They say it's the quiet ones who gravitate to the kinky stuff."

"I don't have any idea where all this is coming from," Celina said while her heart pumped even faster. She must be cautious not to get overstressed or she'd become ill again. The prospect of not being in control here panicked her. "Errol was found on his bathroom floor. I don't mind telling you that, because it's public record."

"But there were skin burns on his wrists and ankles. From some sort of fabric, they think."

"Who are these—*they?* Who are the people you say are telling you things?"

"The marks on his penis were different."

Celina fell back in her chair and jerked her hand free. "Go away."

"Oh, I do believe I hit a nerve at last." Fishing a gold case from her purse, Charmain lit a cigarette and took a deep drag. "You do see why you should talk to me, don't you? There's no power like the power of the press, sweets. And I didn't get on top because I've got tender skin. You can either give me what I want and I'll be kind to you, or I won't be kind to you."

"Go away."

"You're repeating yourself. Why did you come here tonight? To see Jack Charbonnet?"

What could she say? Celina got a faceful of cigarette smoke, and her stomach turned.

"That's right, Charmain. Celina's here to see me. To meet me, actually. Errol and I were partners in Dreams. Now he's gone and we intend to make sure his work keeps right on going. I need Celina's help with that. If there's anything else you want to know, give me a call sometime."

Celina stared up at Jack and decided that she had never been more pleased to see anyone. Relief made her tingle.

"Hello, Jack," Charmain sang out, unfazed. "Both of you at once. I must be living right. Sit yourself down."

"It's late," Jack said. "Celina doesn't need any beauty sleep, but she might prefer to get home before dawn, and we've got a lot to talk about."

"Where is that Dom Pérignon I ordered?" Stretching her neck, Charmain peered toward the bar with a crease between her brows. "You need better help here, Jack love."

Jack looked around, smiled, and said, "You seem to be the only one who thinks so. You wouldn't believe what a good time people have here. They throw money at me to prove just how much, and all but bury me in the lovely stuff. How are you doing, Celina? Sorry I got held up."

"It's okay. Some nice people bought me some orange juice." She could tell he saw the humor in her eyes. "I've been very entertained. I'm a sheltered girl, and a look at the sinful side of life fascinates me."

"Good, good," he told her. "I'm glad you find my orange juice sinful. I have those figures you need for tomorrow. Why don't we go to my office."

"What figures?" Charmain asked baldly. "Jack, do you have any idea what caused the marks on Errol's penis?"

For once Jack Charbonnet wasn't quite collected enough not to show surprise.

"They know the ones on his wrists and ankles were probably from fabric bonds. But evidently they're still working on his genitalia."

Jack winced a little and said, "Thanks for sharing that with me."

"You're welcome. Is that man waiting for you?"

Celina looked at the man Charmain pointed out but didn't recognize him.

"What man?" Jack said.

"If I remember rightly, his name is Sonny Clete and he's Win Giavanelli's underboss."

"Sonny?" Jack said, sounding amazed, and looking closer at the paunchy red-haired man who leaned on the bar smoking, and staring their way. "Of course it's Sonny. What would he be doing visitin' here? He doesn't even like me. Sonny, over here."

"You aren't even going to pretend you're not on first-name terms with members of the mob?"

"Mob?" Jack snorted. "I don't think Sonny would appreciate you makin' that kind of connection. Hey, Sonny, welcome to my humble boat."

Sonny Clete dragged his feet on the way to the table. He didn't look particularly pleased to be hailed in a crowded area. He glanced around, his hand spread over his tie. "Thanks," he said. "Just stoppin' by to drop some bucks at the tables."

"That's great," Jack said, standing up. He motioned to Celina to join him. "Meet Charmain Bienville. She surely wants to meet you."

Sonny regarded Charmain with frank interest, and she looked back with her reporter's alert eyes.

"Sit down, Sonny, sit down. Hey"—Jack snapped his fingers— "get that champagne over here for my friends, Lem."

The bartender gave him a high sign and picked up the bucket and glasses he'd already placed on the counter for their server.

Sonny sat beside Charmain, who no longer appeared as fascinated. *Edgy* would be a more accurate description of her body language.

"Where you goin', Jack," Sonny said when Jack took Celina's hand. "I come for that chat we been goin' to have."

Jack sighed. "What can I tell you, Sonny? There's nothing I'd like to do more than speak with you. It's been too long. Far too long. But I've got to get my friend here home. She works for me, and I like my people bright-eyed in the mornin'."

"But you—"

"Soon. We'll talk soon. Talk to Charmain. She's one of the most entertainin' women I know. Ask her anything—she'll tell you what you want to know."

"I talked to Win. He complained about one or two things. That's what we need to discuss."

"Win?" Jack laughed loudly. "Oh, Win doesn't change. He'd complain if they used a new rope to hang him."

"He wouldn't consider that humorous," Sonny said, his doughy face a study in serious disapproval.

"It's not," Jack said. "It certainly is not. Charmain, tell Sonny some of the interesting things you know about bondage. Don't miss out on the penis stuff."

Celina managed to keep her mouth closed at Jack's diversionary tactics. She barely managed to keep her feet on the ground when he took off across the deck, gripping her hand so tightly her fingers were pinched together.

He led her from the enclosed area to the deck outside, and hurried her aft. A door with a single curtained porthole led to a small unfurnished room that became utterly silent once the door was closed again. Jack didn't pause there, but carried on through another door to large quarters that were evidently office and living areas in one combined space. Again he closed the door.

The next instant he dropped her hand and pushed back his dark dinner jacket. With his fists on his slim hips, he regarded her with an expression she couldn't read.

"I called your home," she told him. "You gave me your card the other night."

He waited.

"Tilly said you were out. I had a hunch you might be here, so I came."

"Sounds plausible."

"I don't tell lies. At least, I don't tell lies that don't have to be told."

"I didn't think any lies *had* to be told."

A vestige of the unpleasant exhausted feeling began to seep into Celina's body. "My brother would agree with you. You'd make him very proud."

"Sarcasm doesn't suit you."

"It doesn't suit anyone." She considered sitting on his comfortable-looking burgundy-colored couch, but instinctively knew he wouldn't welcome any move toward relaxing the atmosphere. "You were very kind to me when I got sick. Thank you for that. I know you don't like me, but you're a good person—a generous person. I'm still smarting from thinking about embarrassing myself in front of you."

"Don't. It was nothing. I'd have done the same for anyone."

"Thanks." She had no right to be hurt, nor should she be hurt. "Thanks anyway. You nurse with flair."

He bowed slightly without taking his eyes from her.

"I understand you were with Cyrus and Dwayne when the doctor left me."

"Uh-huh."

"Cyrus told me you're aware that I'm pregnant."

"Yes."

"That isn't something I'm ready to have discussed at this point."

"Why?"

"I have my reasons. And I've got a right to those reasons. My private business is my own."

"If that's the case, I suggest you avoid talking to Charmain Bienville."

"I didn't talk to her, I—" He was baiting her. "That would be good advice if I had any intention of saying one important word to the woman."

"When are you having the abortion?"

Celina heard her own small cry of shock. She turned and ran—but didn't get far. Jack stopped her—carefully but quite effectively, by wrapping an arm around her middle.

She made no attempt to struggle against him. "Let me go."

"No way. I want you to sit down."

"You can't always have what you want. I'm not yours to command."

"Sit down, please."

"I came to ask—"

Very neatly he caught hold of her waist, lifted, and deposited her on the couch she'd admired. "I know you like to be in control," he told her. "You made that clear the other night, but evidently you aren't always in control. Rather like my not always being able to have what I want. Annoying, but a fact of life. Is it Errol's child?"

The nightmare went on and on. "What did you say?"

"You heard me. Are you carrying Errol's baby?"

She should have expected him to think of that, but still the idea caught her by surprise. "What if it is Errol's baby? What does it matter to you?" She'd just told him how much she disliked lies, but suddenly she knew she was going to tell one, to live one.

"I intend to make sure a good man who happens to be dead doesn't get maligned any more than I can help. That means I don't want him accused of fathering a child by a woman he wasn't prepared to marry."

"How do you know what he was and wasn't prepared to do?"

"Don't play around with me," he snapped. "Errol would never have married again. He swore to that after the mess at the end of his first marriage."

Celina said nothing.

"There's already enough potential for any competent reporter to make him sound like a pervert. Take a small leap from there to his involvement with young children, and there'll be a bunch of people ready to accuse his memory of some sort of pedophilic tendencies. The foundation would wallow and sink over something like that. I don't think you want that."

"I don't." She ought to get up and leave. "I want Dreams to go on every bit as much as you do. Probably much more. I'm not just the pretty face that begs for donations. I've been involved with the children, Jack. I *am* involved with them. Not the way Errol was—he was wonderful. But I'm going to take over for him."

"Are you? Let's get back to what's happening here tonight. You heard that woman in there. I don't know who she's getting her information from, but I'm going to do my best to find out. Maybe someone in the NOPD will want to help me with that."

"They don't know we took those things," she said in a small voice. "It scares me. All of it scares me. It's as if all that matters is the sensationalism of the sex stuff. He was murdered. Why isn't that what everyone's interested in?"

"It's what I'm interested in. They will probably find out we got rid of evidence. Since there must be marks on him that I didn't notice, they'll be lookin' for whatever was used."

"I burned it."

His smile didn't comfort her. "Yeah. In your wastebasket. Dwayne picked it up and said silk and nylon smelled bad when they burned, but rubber is the worst. Unless you plan to ask him to perjure himself, we'll just have to hope the police don't question him and lead him back to that wastebasket. Then it's a little hop to you—and then to me."

"I wouldn't tell them you had anything to do with it."

"How chivalrous of you. You'd tell them anything once they started working on you."

She looked around. "I left my umbrella in the bar."

"If it's gone, I'll buy you another one."

"The police don't torture people," Celina said. "They won't drive toothpicks under my fingernails. I'm a decent citizen. I've never hurt anyone."

"Is that right? Good. We'll make sure you don't start now. Most of all, we'll make sure you don't do anything to hang scandal on Errol's memory. Any more scandal than some people already intend to hang. Damn, I'd like to muzzle that female."

"I only came here to ask you to keep my secret. At least until I'm ready to reveal it—or until I can't hide it anymore, whichever comes first."

"The way I've got it figured, you're about out of time anyway. I can't believe you're more than five months pregnant—I wouldn't believe it if the doctor hadn't insisted he was right. You haven't answered my question. Are you going to say this is Errol's child?"

Was she going to "say" this was Errol's child? "Why does the thought bother you so much?"

"What bothers me is the thought of someone he trusted taking advantage of him now that he's dead."

He still wasn't making enough sense. "How would I do that?"

"By saying he . . . by saying he took advantage of you."

Celina couldn't form a coherent thought.

"If you were in a relationship that was healthy, you'd either be happy about this child, or you'd be planning an abortion. Are you? Planning an abortion?"

Tears filled her eyes. "No," she said quietly. "Even if I could have considered such a thing, it wouldn't be this late in the pregnancy."

"Are you in a healthy relationship?"

"No . . . I mean I'm not in a relationship at all."

"You didn't get pregnant all on your own."

"Stop it."

He pulled an ottoman in front of her knees and sat down facing her. "That's what I'm asking you to do. Stop it. Don't use Errol."

"I never said I would use Errol." The idea sickened her, the idea that this man thought she would do such a thing.

"You never said you wouldn't. What did you tell your brother, the priest?"

"You already know. That I was pregnant."

"You people don't believe in abortion, do you?"

"We people?"

"Practicing Catholics."

She averted her face. "Aren't you a Catholic?"

"My beliefs aren't the issue here. Yours are."

"You think that, in the name of faith, I'd keep a baby I supposedly don't want, but that I'd lie about the paternity of that baby? Why wouldn't I just not identify the father?"

"Because you're part of a social set that would make your beloved parents' lives miserable if you turn up pregnant but without a well-connected father for the kid. And you know Errol's history. What a perfect cover. A dead man who used to have a problem controlling his sex drive. The very least you'll get is sympathy to your face."

"You're a bitter man, Jack Charbonnet. You're so bitter you can't think good of anyone you can't immediately stick in a box and categorize—or anyone you haven't known forever."

"If you're not ashamed of this pregnancy, why are you hiding it?"

He would never know if she could help it. "That's my business, Jack."

"I'm going to make it mine."

"I'm not ready to deal with this in a public way yet."

"Because you've got to make sure you've got your story straight. And the stage set before you start tearfully giving out the so-called truth."

Wilson intended to try to draw her back into his clutches; she'd seen it in his face the other night. She could elude him on that, but if he found out she was pregnant, he'd hound her to get rid of the baby regardless of how advanced the pregnancy was. And he'd use the same old threats against her family to try to force her hand. "I'm going home," she said abruptly, and stood up. "Please honor my wishes. My private life is none of your affair."

"I think you've answered my question. I really hoped I was wrong, but the more I thought my way through the possibilities, the more the hunch grew to conviction that you had a plan I'd have to do something about."

She couldn't do this anymore. Sidestepping him, she looked down into his face. "What can you do, Jack? Apart from hope I can keep this as quiet as possible—with your help, of course."

Jack stood up, a formidably attractive man in evening clothes who would make any woman weak at the knees. He made her weak at the knees, but not because he was attractive, not tonight. Tonight Jack Charbonnet scared Celina to the bone. She really believed he detested her.

"How am I supposed to help you exactly?" he asked in the deceptively quiet voice she now recognized as the one he used when he was truly angry.

"You know what I want from you. Job security. I want to know you won't get rid of me because I'm pregnant. It's not going to stop me from doing my work just as well as I ever have."

"I've already told you that I have no intention of firing you."

"You didn't make me feel you wouldn't change your mind later."

Jack shrugged and said, "You'll have to hope I don't. Will that keep you more or less happy?"

"No." She shook her head. "I need an absolute promise that you'll be silent about what doesn't concern you. I'll be the one to decide when it's time to name Errol as my baby's father."

Eleven

Jack had made up his mind what he had to do. The way he'd got through the difficult years after his parents' death had been to make up a code of ethics known only to himself, and live by that code. The first tenet had been that he was never to completely rely upon anyone. He'd kept that one. Even with his grandfather—his mother's father, who had largely brought him up—he'd held a part of himself back, although Granddaddy never knew, at least, Jack didn't think he did. Another rule was that once he made up his mind to do something, it got done, and unless they killed him, nobody would stop him.

So today Jack would do what he'd spent most of two nights and a day thinking about. He'd dropped Amelia at school and returned the car to the garage before setting off again on foot. He hoped to catch Dwayne at his club before doubling back to Royal Street.

The city was heating up, but there was still a breeze to make the walk pleasant enough. Plastic cups from margarita bars littered Bourbon Street. An early-bird street artist had set up her easel, and displayed her sketches of Tom Cruise, of Billy Crystal, of Whoopi Goldberg, and other famous faces who hadn't sat on her rickety metal chair, on this celebrated and stained sidewalk, to win a place in the pictured company. Even Wilson Lamar was there, showing his perfect teeth, teeth the common folk could trust. Jack smiled a little. The smells were old; old buildings, old memories, older sins. Sin. Now there was a stench Lamar could generate all on his own. Jack knew that Wilson and trust were strangers. Unfortunately Wilson had once stumbled into a situation Jack intended to keep private—for Amelia's sake, and that piece of knowledge kept the other man safe from Jack.

"Mornin', gorgeous. Hey, Jack Charbonnet, I am talking to you."

Dwayne hailed Jack from the open front doors of Les Chats. "Are you looking for something special? Something different? You surprise me, so early in the day. Why, Jack, I do believe you are insatiable."

"Save it," Jack called back, laughing. "I don't embarrass that easily."

When Jack drew close to Dwayne, he took quick note of the other man's tired eyes and the tense expression he wasn't quite managing to hide. "Could we hope for some decent coffee in this high-class establishment of yours? I need to wake up, and you look as if you need to go to sleep. Probably means we both need that coffee."

Dwayne gave up on the grin. He lowered his voice and said, "I tell you, Jack, I am dead where I stand. I mean, I am aware that the whole world isn't necessarily as uncomplicated as I am, but there are things going down around here that shake me."

"Me, too," Jack agreed.

"There are some who think it isn't safe here anymore."

"It never was."

"You know what I mean."

"No," Jack said, "I don't think I do."

"Forget the coffee. We probably shouldn't even be seen together."

Jack looked behind him. "Now you've got me jumping. Did something else happen?"

"Other than the murder of our mutual best friend?" Dwayne asked, drawing Jack into his glittering, mirrored club. The debris of the previous night had already been cleared, and the flashing neon lights inside groups of velvet-covered "scratching posts" were being checked out for the next performance of *Catting Around*. Dwayne said, "You had better be ready to jump, my dear friend. Perhaps very quickly and with no warning."

Dwayne's dramatics were legendary. "I agree that Errol's death has shaken me," Jack told him. "I wouldn't be normal if it hadn't. But I'm still not convinced it was murder." He had already created a new scenario, one involving the lady visitor to Errol. Why couldn't he have drowned accidentally and been removed from the bath? Terrified people could find unnatural strength.

Dwayne watched him as if expecting him to say more. When he didn't, Dwayne said, "I do not know what you may be thinking, Jack, but you are probably wrong."

"Why so sure?"

Dwayne shook stiffened fingers in the air. "I do not know anymore. Perhaps I am trying to say that not one of us knows what's going on.

I keep waiting for an announcement on Errol. *Why* aren't the police saying anything?"

"Perhaps because they don't know anythin'," Jack suggested.

A great, frustrated sigh raised Dwayne's chest. "None of this feels right. They *should* know something by now."

A lithe man with a glass in one hand and a cigarette between pursed lips seated himself at a piano and tinkered, one-handed, through the melody of "Careless Love."

"He is so talented," Dwayne said of his partner, Jean-Claude. "I'm a lucky man. At least I find a little peace with him."

Jean-Claude set his glass on top of the piano, squinted through his cigarette smoke, and showed just how talented he was. He grinned at Jack and Dwayne.

"You are lucky," Jack said.

"I know. But I don't enjoy being scared."

"Okay." Jack faced Dwayne. "Concentrate. I came by to touch bases and find out if you know something I don't know about Celina Payne. Do you?"

"Oh, I am sure I do."

Jack looked at the toes of his boat shoes. "Don't keep me in suspense."

"Celina Payne is special. She's kind, generous, and honest. And she is not an empty-headed bimbo. The whole pageant routine was her mama's thing. That woman and her big, useless husband drove her son away and came close to ruining her daughter's life before she had any chance to live it at all. Bitsy Payne thinks that if her family had not been *so* refined, she would have been winning those paste crowns herself. From when she was a little child, Celina kept quiet and did what her mama told her to do. You don't know a whole lot about family, Jack, any more than I do. Yours wasn't around long enough—God rest their souls. Mine, we will not discuss. But Celina is still working herself free of her parents' sticky fingers."

Jack pretended to gasp. "That was some speech. Is the lady running for office? If she is, she'd better make sure your friend Dr. Al doesn't have a big mouth."

"The only potentially big mouth we have to worry about is yours, Jack." The deadly serious caste of Dwayne's face surprised Jack. "People in Al's job don't discuss cases. Evidently Cyrus is another walking miracle, a Bitsy offspring who outran the odds and became a really decent human being. He'll always protect his sister. I wouldn't discuss Celina's business with the Angel Gabriel if she didn't want me to—

even though I do celebrate this baby. A baby is a blessing, friend, an innocent creature meant to be loved and nothing else."

"Yeah." How could he point out that this particular innocent, lovable creature wasn't exactly coming along at a perfect time, not as far as he could see? "Who's the father?"

Jean-Claude quit the piano and hopped onto a stage, where he leaped into a tap routine. To Jack's uneducated but appreciative eye, the performance looked like competition for Gregory Hines.

"I'm not going to talk to anyone about Celina's pregnancy," Dwayne said, an unexpectedly steel edge in his voice. "That's what you came to ask about, and I've told you all I'm going to tell you."

"Does that mean you do know who the father is?"

"It means, dear Jack, that you can fuck off and die before I'll play a game of whodunit with you on this one."

"You don't know? Or you do?"

"I don't fuck—"

"All right, all right. But do you think it might have been Errol?"

Dwayne's mouth opened and closed. He shook his head and walked away, then turned around and came back. "You're unbelievable. Or you would be if I hadn't known you long enough to almost expect you to be outrageous."

"*Me* outrageous?" With an expansive gesture Jack took in the entire club. "What does that make this—and you?"

"I'm just a working fool trying to keep bread in my mouth," Dwayne informed him primly.

"So you say it wasn't Errol?"

"I did not say any such thing. I said you are outrageous to ask personal questions about Celina."

"You thrive on gossip."

Dwayne rounded on him so abruptly that Jack stepped backward. "Listen up, Jack baby. I thought you were listening, but I was wrong. Celina is my friend. I respect her. I told you I can be trusted with my friends' most intimate secrets, and I meant it. Those are the things I don't gossip about."

"You do think it was Errol."

Dwayne yelled, "Jean-Claude, *save* me," threw up his hands, and fell into a chair. "I have to keep different company. You are all driving me mad. Jean-Claude! Go away, Jack. Go ask Celina if you dare. That little lady might eat you up, but ask her anyway, because she'd be doing us all a favor."

"Well, thanks," Jack said, but he grinned, and snapped his fingers to a Dr. John disc Jean-Claude snapped in behind the bar. "Maybe I'd like it if she did too."

Dwayne pretended not to hear. He batted at imaginary dust on his bleach-splattered but carefully creased jeans. "Listen to me, Jack. But don't look as if I'm saying anything important."

"What . . ." Closing his mouth, Jack studied Jean-Claude's long, loose-limbed walk—his dancer's walk—when he slowly approached, chatting to employees on the way.

"I had a visitor a while ago. He came through the kitchens. Wore a cowboy hat with his usual getup. As if the hat was some sort of disguise. Pretty scary, I can tell you. He made my stomach loop-de-loop. Felt like it was getting ready for a Blue Angels' audition."

Dwayne became silent. He glanced in every direction.

"Okay," Jack said. "Put me out of my misery here. Who are we talking about?"

"Antoine."

"Antoine?"

"Keep your voice *down*. Yes, Antoine."

"He came here in a cowboy hat? I don't believe you. *Here?* He wouldn't be caught dead—"

"*Don't* say that," Dwayne ordered. "I am well aware of Antoine's religious beliefs. He is a good man. He came here because"—he dragged Jack so close, their noses all but touched—"he came because he saw something."

Jack watched the other man's pupils dilate. "Antoine saw something?" he whispered. "You don't mean . . . you do mean the night Errol died, don't you?"

"Very early in the morning. Antoine likes to start early, but on that morning he got there *really* early because he had some things left over from the previous day that needed to be finished. Antoine is a very industrious man."

"But the coroner said Errol died around midnight."

"This *person* came into the courtyard with the dawn—Antoine's terms, not mine—he came with the dawn, carrying a bag, and left soon after, still carrying a bag, and still moving with the shadows."

Dwayne must once have had acne. The pores around his nose were enlarged. Jack realized he was refusing to concentrate because he wasn't ready to deal with potentially tangible facts about Errol's death—and his killer.

"Well?" Dwayne said.

"Antoine went up then?" Jack asked. "When I arrived, he already knew Errol was dead? Why didn't he do something? And why didn't he say something when he saw me?"

"I don't know. And I don't know if he did go into the house. He may not have thought it was for him to interfere."

"Of course you know. Antoine came to tell you all this."

"I do not know the rest of his story. He said he knew too much. Then he told me he must be careful not to hurt good people who were his friends, then he stopped talking. Not another word, I tell you. He said he was afraid. He said he thought he'd been followed here, and he was leaving."

Jack threw up his hands. Jean-Claude was still making slow progress toward Dwayne, but he was on his way. "Tell me quickly, please. What was he afraid of?"

"It's obvious, dear. He thinks he saw the murderer—who evidently went back into the house because he'd forgotten something, and then sneaked out again, never expecting to be seen. All that would be good news, or it could be, if Antoine didn't think this guy—although he's not certain it was a guy—it could have been really useful information for the police if Antoine hadn't told me he'd clam up if we told them because he's afraid he'll be the next one to turn up dead."

Celina stood at the single window in her small sitting room and looked down into the street. A silver Mercedes was parked at the curb with a tall, broad-shouldered young man leaning against the driver's door. "Is that yours?" she asked without looking at either Sally or Wilson Lamar. "The new Mercedes?"

"Isn't it lovely?" Sally said. "Actually it's all mine. Wilson insisted."

The man by the car was familiar, but Celina couldn't place him. "And the chauffeur? Is that man leaning on the car yours too, or should you go down and tell him to go away." *Then get in your "lovely" car and leave.*

Sally giggled. "That's Ben. He's supposed to be Wilson's chauffeur, but that's not really what he is." She sent Celina a knowing glance.

"What is he, then?"

"Oh, don't be naive. He's Wilson's bodyguard. There are dangers attached to running for public office, you know. Aren't there, Wilson darlin'?"

"We aren't here to discuss our household staff," Wilson said brusquely. "We came to talk about you, Celina, and our concern for you."

She hated him. One of her hands went to her stomach. She hated the father of the child she carried, and loved. That shook her deeply.

"I heard your brother is with you," Sally said, peering around as if Cyrus might be hiding behind a piece of furniture. "Your parents would have come with us this morning, but they are very upset that their only son—and he a priest—has returned to their very doorstep, so to speak. And he's been here for *ages*, but he hasn't bothered to go and see them."

"Cyrus is here on personal business." Could she really lie about something like this? Celina glanced involuntarily upward. "Visiting the diocese. He had to come on short notice and he needed a place to stay. I'm closer to the chancery than our parents." Cyrus had come to New Orleans to visit the diocese, but he'd had no plans to stay until he'd discovered Celina's plight.

Sally had lost interest in why Cyrus was there. "Where is he?" She pressed her palms together. "At mass? Such an unusual man."

"That's right, he's at mass. Why did you say you were here?"

"To make sure you're all right, of course," Sally said, trotting on her inevitable high heels to put an unwelcome arm around Celina's shoulders. "We are all so worried about you. Your mother and father begged us to come and persuade you to do what you should do."

"Which is?"

"Now, just a minute, ladies." Wilson had yet to meet Celina's eyes. Dressed in a light gray silk suit and luminously white shirt with a black tie, he exuded health and vitality from every tanned inch of skin. "There are a few things I'd like to say at this juncture. I owe it to Bitsy and Neville—without whom I'm not sure I should be in quite so enviable a position—I owe it to them to follow their instructions to the letter. So I must ask you both to let me talk for them. And I must ask you to listen without interrupting me."

Sally rolled her eyes, wrinkled her nose, and flopped down on Celina's couch.

"Your parents are very worried about you," Wilson said solemnly. "And so are Sally and myself. There is a murderer on the loose."

How could she ever have thought he was a good man who cared for people? She wanted him anywhere but near her. She said, "In New Orleans, one murderer on the loose would be good news."

"That's not the point, Celina. This man struck in this very house."

"Oh, *don't!*" Sally said, rubbing her bare arms. "You make me prickly all over."

"Good. I hope I make Celina prickly all over too. Perhaps that will persuade her that she's foolish to remain here."

Celina shifted her weight from one foot to the other. "I am safe here. Probably more safe than if poor Errol hadn't been killed. Whoever did that awful thing isn't likely to come back."

"How can you be so sure?"

"It's logical, isn't it? He'll assume the house is being watched. And he'll also notice that Cyrus is staying here at the moment."

"Aha!" Sally pointed a pink nail at Celina. "Now we have it. That darling Cyrus came because he was worried about you too. But she does have a point, Wilson. I hardly think whoever did it will come back to the same place, especially since there's a man staying here. A man who would make anyone think twice about trying anything."

Sally's smile and faraway look disquieted Celina. She knew how much Cyrus disliked any attention that had sexual overtones.

"You are both kind to come and check on me," Celina said, every word a stone in her throat. "But this is my home at present. And my work is here. So it's natural for me to remain."

"Bitsy and Neville want you back at home. Now." Wilson was never convincing in the masterful but reasonable mode—not to Celina. Violent suppression of someone weaker was his style. "We want to take you with us when we leave this morning. You get packed while we wait for your brother. When he gets back, you can tell him you're moving home."

"And we're going to help you through these difficult times," Sally said. "Wilson and I know how much Errol and Dreams meant to you. It's going to be a difficult transition, and we don't want to make light of that. So Wilson has something wonderful to tell you."

Celina didn't trust herself to speak at all.

"I have a job for you, Celina," Wilson said, rocking from his heels to his toes and lacing his hands behind his back. "I want to put you in charge of publicity for the campaign. I haven't been pleased with the current arrangement. I need your expertise. You can be *our* Dreams Girl." His smug smile nauseated her.

"Isn't that wonderful?" Sally said.

Wilson continued. "We all know it isn't realistic to think Dreams can carry on now. Not with everything that's coming out about Errol. But I won't forget those children and their needs. I'll make sure their needs—"

"What are you talking about? What's coming out about Errol?"

Sally opened the large straw bag she carried and took out a newspaper. "I should be angry with Charmain, but she's only doing her job and she's so interesting." She held the front page up for Celina to see. "I never knew Errol was a sex addict."

"He wasn't anymore," Celina said, scanning a headline that blared: *Saint or Sinner. Local Philanthropist Had History of Sexual Addiction.*

"This is only one paper," Sally said. "And it happens to be Charmain's byline. But there are similar pieces—not as informed—but similar pieces in other papers."

Celina returned to the window and pulled a curtain aside. She didn't trust herself to speak.

"We should be ready to leave when—"

"I'm not going anywhere. And that stuff about Errol is so unfair. It was a long time ago and he's made up for it in so many ways. These people are despicable."

"It says he used to pick up women and bring them back here," Sally said, reading.

"Please leave." Celina went to the door and held it open. "Please go now. I want to be alone. And I will be carrying on with my work for Dreams. In fact, I have a very full schedule of appointments today. Jack Charbonnet. You know him, of course. Although Jack didn't take an active part in the foundation, he was Errol's partner. Now he intends to take over from Errol, and he wants me to do exactly what I've been doing."

"Charbonnet?" Sneers didn't suit Wilson. "You really think you are goin' to have any luck gettin' support in this town with a man like that at the helm? He's a gangster's son and he owns a casino. A riverboat. Somethin' else I intend to work to eradicate. Law-abidin' people don't want the element that comes in with gamblin'."

"Organized crime is what comes in," Sally said, elevating her chin. "For your dear mother's and father's sakes, you won't have a thing to do with that man. He's bad, Celina. Everyone knows it."

Pointing out that he wasn't so bad that they hadn't invited him to their last fund-raiser would be pointless. She already knew they would take anybody's money. She made herself breathe deeply. "I know you mean well, but I can't leave my work here, especially not now, with so much left undone."

"It's not going to happen now," Sally told her, her mouth in a thin line. "None of it. You've just got to accept reality, Celina. Donations aren't going to be made. There'll be no auctions, and no big bucks to play Lady Bountiful with. People all over the country have read about

Errol today. Some of them will be worrying about whether or not he was dangerous to have around their children."

"Errol's dead," Celina said quietly.

"Well, I *know* he is. But I mean that when he wasn't he could have been doing goodness knows what when he was alone with one of those children."

Wilson had the sense to cough and shake a hand at his wife. "That's not important, Sally. All that rumor stuff. From what the papers say, Errol wasn't likely to be into pedophilia."

"Shut up," Celina said loudly. "Shut *up* and get out. How dare you come here making such disgusting suggestions. Here's the door. Use it."

"We're not going without you," Sally said, all huff. "I hear Cyrus coming. He'll talk sense into you."

Not Cyrus, but Antoine appeared in the doorway. "I been lookin' for you, Miss Celina. I need to talk to you about somethin', me. Somethin' I saw. I should have said before, much before."

"Of course, Antoine. My company's leaving."

Antoine looked past her and backed away. "You got comp'ny. I'm sorry, Miss Celina, I didn't notice. I come back later, me."

"No. Stay." She didn't even know for sure that Antoine heard her last words, because he'd already reached the door to the outside and in seconds she heard his feet thudding down the steps.

"Celina—"

"Please, Wilson, go away. You have no tact. Neither of you has any tact. My parents think a great deal of you, or I would never speak to you again." Whatever she did or said she must keep some semblance of detachment with this man—a distance that would help establish that she had no connection to him and never had. How she wished that were true.

Sally got up and smoothed her tight white dress over her very nice body. "She'll change her mind," she told Wilson. "She's not thinking properly. We'll give her time."

Wilson looked dubious.

"How insightful of you, Sally," Celina said. She'd do anything to get rid of them. "I'm on overload. Be careful going down the steps in those heels. I wouldn't want you to break your neck." She smiled.

Sally didn't smile. She went to Wilson and took a firm hold of his hand. "We'll be going directly to Bitsy and Neville. Those poor dears are beside themselves. If you were a dutiful daughter, you'd want to save them that."

Celina wanted to say that Sally would make a great mother in the Bitsy Payne school of mothering. Ladle on the guilt whenever possible was Mama's theory.

"We'll be back," Wilson said, giving Celina a long look. Reason had left his eyes, and she saw again the man who had violated her. If she were alone with him now, he'd be likely to try force again.

She held her tongue until they left, then marched back and forth with gritted teeth and clenched fists. There was a new focus in her life, and she mustn't forget it no matter how hard that focus was going to make the immediate future. The Lamars had to be kept at bay.

She'd bought several new dresses that skimmed her breasts and flared just enough to look stylish and soft. In bright shades and made of georgette or challis, they flipped about her knees. The look was good and drew attention away from her stomach, but someone with a practiced eye could look at her now and guess she was pregnant.

Celina spread a hand over her belly. A flare of tenderness brought tightness to her throat. She'd begun to visualize the child within her, and to wait. Mothers throughout time must have known that sense of waiting.

On the heels of warmth and possessiveness came a fear so deep and strange, she caught her breath. What if she should lose her baby? She couldn't. Oh, please let her baby be safe and healthy.

There was too much to do for her to wallow in anxiety.

The first order of business must be to locate Antoine and find out what was disturbing him. Celina looked down at her tummy. She couldn't help remembering Dwayne's enthusiasm, and it made her smile. He'd been right. A new life was reason for celebration. When she held her child in her arms, he or she would be all that mattered. This little one was innocent, and she would not give her up.

She left her sitting room but didn't get much farther. Jack let himself into the house. He didn't immediately realize she was there, and his bowed head showed off the dramatic angles of his face. It also accented a deeply troubled expression.

Her heart lifted at the sight of him. That had to be because she felt alone and vulnerable and he was a strong man who seemed afraid of nothing.

"Hi, Jack," she said, not wanting him to think she was watching him covertly—even though that's exactly what she'd like to do. "I swear I shall never get any work done today. I'm so popular. The visitors keep on coming."

"I'm not a visitor."

He had a talent for cutting through any attempt at lightening the mood. "No, of course not."

"What did Lamar and his wife want?"

"They wanted me to move home with my parents and go to work for Wilson." Not that Jack had a right to know what her visitors had said.

"Sounds like a nightmare."

"And you sound rude. I avoid insulting people's parents."

"Don't be coy. You know what I mean."

"Perhaps I do. Errol's room is still taped. The police have said I can use the rest of his suite now. I should go there and get on the phone. I need to start picking up some pieces."

The denim shirt Jack wore was open at the throat and the sleeves were rolled up over his tanned and strongly made forearms. He studied her more carefully than made for comfort.

"I really should get on, Jack. Are there things you need to look over? I'd be happy to organize whatever you need."

He shook his head once. "Have you seen the papers?"

"Yes."

"What we have to do is work on damage control."

She liked him for his matter-of-fact response to trouble. "I think so too. Do you think it would be useful to contact Charmain Bienville? I was trying to think of something we could offer her to call off the dogs."

Again she got the short, sharp shake of the head. He ran his eyes over old black and white Petrie family photographs that covered the walls in every corridor. "Errol was the last Petrie," he said absently. Then he looked at her. "I think we meet the gossip head-on and play to public sympathy. Yes, Errol had problems, big problems. But he faced up to them and sought treatment. He was an example to be followed. And this was years ago."

"I agree." Just having some sort of plan brought a rush of relief. "I'll get right on it and write a press release."

"I'll help you. First there's something you and I have to talk about."

Apprehension turned her palms moist. "It's probably not a good idea to waste time. I also want to reach the local TV stations."

"That too. But you and I need to talk about our last two meetings."

The corridor began to feel too small for the two of them. "There's nothing to say, Jack. You know what you know. But you won't talk about it because you don't want more mud on Errol's name—any more than I do. Can we let it drop, please?"

"Pregnancies don't stand still, Celina."

"Thanks for the information."

"I'm not in the mood for sarcasm. I'm deadly serious about this." He studied her body so frankly, her cheeks began to burn. "You choose your clothes well, but you must be starting to thicken at the waist."

She pressed her hands to her cheeks. "Please, don't."

"I think pregnancy looks great, but then, I've always thought pregnant women look great. I'm just stating facts."

"I'm taking care of things. I'm making slow changes in my clothes, but I've got to be careful to avoid anything too flamboyant, or I'll do the opposite of what I want to do."

"Which is?"

"Buy time, of course. Disguise my pregnancy for as long as possible."

Jack put his hands in his jeans pockets. He turned sideways, but looked at her. "This means you've decided to keep the baby."

"I think I already told you that. Jack, I'm five and a half months. Think about it."

"I'm just making sure you haven't changed your mind."

"I want this baby. And I'm never going to change my mind about that. End of discussion."

He sucked in a breath, then blew it out through pursed lips. "Have you examined your reasons? Babies aren't toys. And they don't replace love you think you've missed elsewhere. They need. They need everything you have to give, and they deserve that."

"Finally we agree on something."

He was too involved in his own thoughts to react to comments that she would expect to irritate him. "I was thinking that you've obviously been avoiding alcohol. That's very important."

"I know." Now she was going to get a well-baby lecture.

"What did you have for breakfast this morning?"

The change of topic disoriented her. "Um—I haven't yet."

"Pregnant women need to pay attention to those things. Come on, I'll buy you a good meal."

She opened her mouth to refuse, but voices in the courtyard stopped her. "This place has never been so busy," she said. "People keep showing up."

"Have you had a lot of calls from the press?"

"Early this morning. I refused to say anything, then I turned off the phones."

"We've definitely got more company on the way. Maybe we should go to the office."

He headed in that direction and Celina followed. They'd barely entered the office Celina had shared with Errol, when the voices became louder.

Celina opened floor-to-ceiling drapes of dark brown tapestry and hurriedly straightened items on top of her own small desk. Dust flew.

A timid knock on the open door preceded the entrance of a man and woman who looked to be in their sixties.

"Good morning," Celina said.

Jack muttered something unintelligible.

"We're Joan and Walt Reed," the man said, holding out a big, workworn hand which Celina promptly shook. "We had to come as soon as we could. It would have been sooner, but we had to make arrangements."

The accent was southern, heavily southern, but Celina couldn't place it.

Joan's blue eyes watered, and she sniffed. "Did he—did Errol talk to you about us? You are Celina, aren't you?"

"Yes."

"I just knew you were. He talked so sweetly about you always. Oh, Walt and I are beside ourselves."

Jack came forward. "I'm Jack Charbonnet, Mr. and Mrs. Reed. Errol's partner. You were friends of his?"

Walt Reed sighed. He held a broad-brimmed hat in both hands and his scalp shone through a helmet of carefully styled silver hair. "That boy was like a son to Joan and me. We felt the good Lord sent him to us, because although Joan had a boy from her first husband— God rest his soul—the two of us was never blessed with children of our own, and the Lord knew Errol and us needed each other."

Joan Reed bleached her hair, and wore it "big" with bangs that obscured her eyebrows. "I can't believe what those horrible people are sayin' about him in the papers. Why, he fought so hard against his demons."

Celina's spine tingled and she looked at Jack. He raised his eyebrows and went to Errol's desk, where he sat down and opened the top drawer.

"We are humble people," Walt said. "We came from humble beginnings, but thanks to the Lord, we've made a good life, isn't that so, Joan?"

Joan swayed, and nodded sadly. Her dowdy gray and white

checked dress didn't go with the hair. She wore flat lace-up shoes and no hose but plenty of makeup.

"We want to help shut those devils up," Walt said, putting his hat on the arm of a chair and unbuttoning the jacket of his black suit. "If you have the Lord on your side, you can overcome. Never forget that. Errol didn't."

"Didn't keep him alive," Jack said, taking papers from the drawer and heaping them on top of the desk.

"You're grieving, son," Walt said. He went to Jack's side and settled a big hand on his shoulder. "Errol must have been your friend as well as your partner."

"He was. I couldn't have asked for a better friend."

"Neither could we," Joan said, and burst into tears. She located a handful of tissues and blotted her eyes, looking upward to avoid smudging her mascara. "When the tent needed repairin', Errol paid for it all. And he replaced our trailer. Bought us a brand-new one out of his own pocket. He would not take no for an answer. We've got to do something for him now."

"The people who saved Errol's soul," Jack said slowly. "Yes, you were mentioned. Or the event was mentioned."

"God saved his soul, boy," Walt said severely. "Never underestimate the power of the Lord."

"What exactly are you here for?" Jack asked.

"To help," Joan said, her voice shifting higher. "It's the very least we can do. We have suffered a great loss, but it's not for us to question the Lord's ways."

"You think the Lord lines up killers?"

"I think the Lord cries when we cry," the woman said, twining her hands together in front of her. "But we must put these awful stories straight. Errol had repented and started a new life in the Lord."

Celina felt out of her depth. She'd been aware of Errol's religious convictions but knew nothing of his practices.

"Well," Jack said, ceasing his fiddling, "I do thank you for feeling you want to help. I'm sorry if I sound less than grateful, but we're trying to rescue the foundation that was Errol's life, as well as his reputation, and we're under a lot of pressure."

"Why, of course you are, son," Walt said. "But don't forget that Errol had turned his face to higher things, the way a man does when he realizes his soul is in danger. Why don't we all say a prayer together?"

Celina curled her hands into fists, not daring to meet Jack's eyes.

"You're kind," he said. "But I'm not ready for that yet. I'm still too angry. Why don't you leave us your address and we'll arrange a more suitable time to talk about your old times with Errol."

"He was so kind to us," Joan said.

"You told us." An aura of impatience vibrated about Jack. "Perhaps Errol had promised you some ongoing financial help?"

Celina cringed and held her breath. She couldn't bear to see people embarrassed.

"Oh, we didn't come because we want anything," Walt said with no hint of anger at Jack's suggestion. "All we aim to do is be around to offer our assistance as we can. Joan and I use our lives in the service of the Lord, and we know He would want us to be here for both of you."

"Thank you," Celina said quickly, drawing a doleful smile from Joan.

"We took us a room at the Pontchartrain. Nothing fancy, but it's quieter there and still close enough so as to be easy for us to get here."

"Nice hotel," Jack said offhandedly. "When will you be leaving town again?"

"Oh, not too soon," Joan said, looking sideways at her husband. "We know our duty, and our duty is to the memory of a man who became like a son to us."

Jack's frustration was palpable. "It's always nice to have a change of pace. I imagine living in a confined space can become tedious, even if you like life on the road."

"We don't spend much time on the road," Walt said. "We've got a nice little spot just south of Baton Rouge. Permanent place for the tent. Fill it up every night, we do. That's how we met Errol. But the money isn't for us. We use it for the greater glory of the Lord. We serve Him."

Celina smiled and got up. "I'll touch bases with you at the Pontchartrain," she said. "Thank you for coming by."

"We wouldn't have done anything else." Joan wore what Celina recognized as Cartier's So Pretty. The soft perfume wafted through the room where the air had grown stale from being closed in.

"We'll wish you good-bye, then." The upward turn at the corners of Jack's mouth hardly qualified as a smile. "Thank you for being good to Errol."

The Reeds stood side by side. Walt cleared his throat and glanced at his wife, who said, "I suppose you're in charge of his affairs?"

Jack frowned but said, "Yes."

"He told us you would be."

"Why would he tell you that?"

The woman shrugged. "So we'd know where to come if we ever had to."

"Do you want to spit out what that means?"

Reed picked up his hat and waved it. "Nothin', really. Just that Errol pledged ongoing support and we were wonderin' about his will."

Anger blossomed in Celina. The tears that pricked her eyes were tears of frustration.

"We should be there when it's read. Errol would surely want it that way."

Twelve

How would it feel to be loved by Jack Charbonnet?

Celina averted her face and pretended to look into the windows of the closed shops they passed. The fragmented thoughts and feelings caught her off guard, and they were becoming more frequent.

"Exercise is good for pregnant women," Jack said. "So I understand anyway. Nothing violent—at least, I wouldn't think that would be a great idea. And not when it's too hot. But a walk like this in the evenin' is something you should make part of your routine. Not alone, of course. In fact . . . well, not alone."

His dissertation rendered Celina at a loss for a response. He'd left that morning, shortly after the abominable Reeds, excusing himself on some pretext of having forgotten something. But before he'd gone he asked her very seriously if she would come to his place this evening. He'd decided they needed an opportunity to discuss what they might face in the coming weeks, and he'd also decided that interruptions would be less likely in Chartres Street. Celina had been too captivated by his slow, quiet voice and his intensity to consider that she might have refused, and she'd nodded when he'd said he would come for her.

"Diet is also very important," he said, holding her elbow as they crossed at the next corner and turned right onto Conti. "I remember . . . there are definitely fads in the whole pregnancy thing. The medical profession seems to change its mind about how much weight you're supposed to gain, and so on. Did you see a doctor? Apart from Dwayne's friend?"

Celina couldn't believe she was having this conversation with Jack Charbonnet. "Not yet."

"I don't have to tell you how irresponsible that is at such a late stage. I'll make some inquiries in the mornin'. It shouldn't be too tough to find out which obstetricians are highly regarded in the area. Are you takin' vitamins?"

"No." She chose not to tell him she didn't need a lecture. Maybe she did. Maybe she needed someone to at least be interested in the baby's welfare—and her own.

"You've got to get this under control."

She sidestepped a boy in oversized jeans who danced beneath a streetlight to music from a boom box. Jack settled a hand at the back of her waist. Celina looked away from him again. A strong, fascinating man showed her a little attention, a little of the courtliness that must come naturally and that he'd undoubtedly show any woman in her position, and she began to have feelings she couldn't afford to have.

He was instinctively protective.

Celina liked it.

The man wouldn't be anywhere near her if she hadn't worked for his friend.

"Did you hear what I was saying, Celina?"

"About getting something under control? You mean vitamins?"

"I mean a well-designed regimen to make certain you do everything possible to assure that you have a healthy baby. And to come through healthy yourself. How many weeks is five and a half months?"

He was so blunt. "I'm about twenty-two weeks."

"You should be bigger, I'd think. Did Dr. Al say he thought everything was okay?"

"Yes."

"But you've been doing too much. Why would you vomit this late?"

"Sickness isn't unusual. Some women have it throughout pregnancy. Everyone knows that. But I got sick the way I did that night because I was upset. I'm still upset, and I expect to be for a very long time. But don't worry, I intend to make sure I don't collapse on you or anyone else again."

They made another turn, onto Chartres this time, and Jack had either run out of wisdom for pregnant women or his mind had moved on to other things. He produced keys from the pocket of his jeans and let them into a small vestibule at the bottom of the steps leading to his apartment. She went ahead of him up the stairs, and almost bumped into a wiry little woman at the top.

"There you are, Tilly," Jack said. "Meet my associate, Celina Payne."

She visited me the other evening. Celina, Tilly is Amelia's companion and my right hand around here."

Celina said, "I'm happy to meet you, ma'am."

Tilly said, "Hmm."

Jack said, "Is Amelia okay?"

"Amelia is as well as you can expect a neglected, confused child to be."

Startled, Celina looked at Jack. He said, "If Amelia Elise Charbonnet is a neglected, confused child, she hides it well. I'm here now, Tilly. Thanks for covering for me, but I won't take up any more of your evening."

Tilly produced glasses from one of the pockets in her floral shirt-waist dress and a pocket New Testament from the other. "I'll be in the kitchen if you want me," she said. *"Reading."*

"I wouldn't hear of it," Jack said, and Celina marveled at how calm he sounded in the face of a woman he employed but who upbraided him as she might a naughty child. He grinned at Tilly and told her, "Off with you. It's long past time for you to start your beauty regimen."

Several loaded seconds passed before Tilly flounced away without another word. Her rather large feet slapped along in lace-up shoes. When she was gone Jack said, "I couldn't manage without Tilly. She's wonderful. I never have to worry about Amelia getting the care she needs when I can't be with her."

"That's nice. But your Tilly isn't thrilled about you bringing me here."

He laughed and went past her to open his study door. "She considers Amelia and me her family. She's motherin' me too. Come on in."

Celina did as he asked and jumped when she sighted Amelia in the same leather chair she'd occupied the other evening. The child cradled her big stuffed frog as if it were an infant.

"What are you doing up, young lady?" Jack asked from behind Celina. "You're supposed to be asleep."

"I need to talk to you, Daddy. Serious."

Jack plucked his daughter from his chair and she promptly wrapped her arms around his neck and kissed him soundly. He ruffled her black curls and said, "Thank you, missy. That was very nice. Now you're going back to bed."

"It was hard to get in here without Tilly catching me."

"I'll just bet it was. Do you remember Ms. Payne?"

Amelia studied Celina. "Of course. I'm not a baby. Are you dating her?"

Get out of this one, Jack. Celina put her hands behind her back.

"It isn't appropriate for five-year-old girls to ask pointed questions of much older people. Celina is a colleague."

"What's that?"

"We work together."

Amelia wrinkled her nose and regarded Celina with green eyes of a similar shade to her father's. "You never worked with a lady before."

"Bedtime," Jack said firmly. "Say good night to Celina, please."

"When you work with a lady, do you always bring her home?"

"*Amelia.*"

"That rude ghost came back."

"No, it didn't. Please excuse us, Celina."

"Of course," she said. "Sweet dreams, Amelia. And F.P."

"Do you have any children?" Amelia asked her.

"Not—no." She'd like to touch the child, to feel her skin and her soft, curly hair. And she'd like to be kissed the way Amelia had kissed Jack. She touched her stomach, then let her hand fall.

"Say good night, Amelia," Jack said. "I mean it."

"Good night. Do you have a daddy?"

"Yes."

"Then why don't you have any children?"

"She meant husband," Jack explained quite unnecessarily. "Celina isn't married, Amelia. I'll be right back."

As he made to leave the room, Amelia clutched the edge of the door. "There's a ghost in my room, Celina. It comes all the time when it knows Daddy's not thinking about me. And it eats my toys, and burps, and doesn't say sorry. Has Daddy told you about Phillymeana?"

"Philomena," Jack said, prying small fingers loose. "And I haven't."

"She has trouble with ghosts sometimes," Amelia said. "And the ice wizard who tries to steal elf babies. Some of the elves are bad too. Right now Phillymeana's on her way to the North Pole to help Santa Claus get ready. There's another ghost that lives across the street." She pointed toward the windows. "I've seen it looking at me from behind the curtains."

Jack got his child into the corridor and closed the door behind them.

Celina took it that Jack made up stories for his little girl. Darn it, but all these rushes of emotion were a pain.

Was her baby going to be a boy or a girl? A girl. A girl who would need a strong father as much as Amelia Charbonnet did. And as much as Amelia needed a mother. Celina massaged her temples. Single parents had to do the best they could, and there were legions of them out there doing a wonderful job. She'd work at being wonderful too.

Within minutes Jack returned. "Sorry about all that. She's really a very good little girl."

"I can tell she is. And I can tell you love her a lot."

"A lot. She's got quite an imagination."

Celina looked at him quizzically. "I wonder if she gets that from a daddy who makes up some pretty wild stories."

He smiled at that and nodded. "Would you like some milk?"

This health stuff could get very old, very fast. "I don't drink milk."

"But—"

"Yes, I know. I'm going to get my diet straightened out. And I'm going to work on a health regimen." Anything, she would say anything to make him change the subject. "Not that I eat badly anyway, but I do need to make some changes."

"Sit there." He pointed to his comfortable old chair, and kept pointing until Celina sat down. "We've got a lot of ground to cover this evenin'. How about some juice?"

"Nothing now, thank you. But don't let me stop you."

If he heard her, he didn't react. Instead, he fell into one of his favorite pastimes—pacing. "I've been doing a lot of thinking since you came to see me on the *Lucky Lady*."

"I believe you. I'm sure we've both been doing a lot of thinking."

"You're going to say Errol was your baby's father. That is what you meant, isn't it?"

There wasn't any room for remorse, not now, not when all that mattered was the future of her baby. "I don't know what I'm going to do without him," she said, not intending to. "I could tell him anything. If he thought I was foolish sometimes, he never said so." But she'd never seen him as angry as he had been when she told him she was pregnant, and what Wilson had done to her. That had been only days before Errol died. Before she'd thought—crazy as it seemed now—that she could somehow manage not to tell anyone ever. But then she'd started getting messages from Wilson again. Not a lot, but even one would have been too many. And he'd showed up in Royal Street when she was alone, with some phony pretense of wanting to make a donation to Dreams. Then he had tried to put his arms around her and the fixed look had entered his eyes, the same look he'd had that other night. Celina managed to contain a shudder. Wilson had tried to put his arms around her and she'd heard the buzzing in her head—and felt herself begin to faint. Antoine had appeared and the moment passed, but she'd realized how vulnerable she was and how much she needed a good friend. Errol had been the only one she trusted enough to approach with her story.

"I know you thought a lot of him," Jack said.

Errol had threatened to tear Wilson apart. Only Celina's pleading and her insistence that she didn't want anyone to know Wilson was her baby's father had stopped Errol from going after the man.

She brought her attention back to Jack. "I'm going to try to get by without naming anyone in this. If I don't have to, I won't."

"Either you will or you won't."

"This isn't cut-and-dried, Jack. Please don't ask me to explain."

"There could be a situation that would make you decide to say Errol fathered your child?"

"I thought we were going to discuss business," Celina said. "We didn't get anything done this morning. I want to approach the administrator at St. Peter's Hospital and see if he'll endorse a statement in Errol's defense. And I've got to act as quickly as possible to keep our work moving along. There are projects in every phase. The need for them isn't going away."

"Going directly to Garth Fletcher at St. Peter's is a good idea. I'll talk to him."

His take-charge instincts annoyed Celina. "I know Garth too. I was often with Errol when he went to see him."

Jack paced on in silence.

"I need to feel as if I'm doing something," she told him. "You can understand that, can't you?"

"Yes. Were you ever engaged?"

Celina drummed her fingers on the arms of the chair. "I've never been engaged. Would it work for you if we both went to talk to Garth?"

"Possibly. I take family very seriously."

"Because you lost yours?" She waved a hand in front of her face. "I'm sorry, I shouldn't have said that."

"Why not? You said it because you thought it. I did lose my parents. And I lost my wife. But I always thought family was important. You don't like me, do you?"

She laughed, then coughed.

"Do you need some water?"

"No. And I like you as much as you will allow me to like you. You are not a soft and cuddly person, Jack."

A faint smile brought some humanity to his austere face. "How would you know?"

He managed to make her blush yet again. "You're cold, that's what I should have said."

"No, I'm not. I'm just out of practice in some areas, so I seem cold. People who know me really well do like me. Some people."

This man was the king of bizarre conversation. "I'm sure lots of people like you."

"You could come to like me too. People grow on you if you let them."

She absolutely would not tell him that she couldn't understand why he cared what she thought of him, or that she wished far too frequently that . . . She was in an "interesting" condition. Any yearning for male attention could be blamed on that.

No, it couldn't. And she didn't yearn for attention from any man but Jack Charbonnet, darn it.

He watched her with absolute concentration. The denim shirt he'd had on in the morning had been replaced by a white shirt that drew attention to his tan, and to the darkness of his hair. "You've never been engaged," he said. "Is that because you don't like the idea of marriage?"

"No." If his probing questions drew only monosyllabic answers, he might give up the interrogation.

"I take marriage very seriously too."

"Good. You take family and marriage seriously." Drat, sometimes she couldn't hold her tongue.

"You think that's a bad thing?" His eyes were so green tonight that they were hard to look at, then hard to look away from. "Celina, what do you think?"

Why did he care what she thought? "I agree with you on both points."

"I loved my wife very much. We met in high school. There was never anyone else for either of us."

It was no good, she had to try to understand him. "Why are you telling me these things?"

"Because I want you to know me."

"I suppose you'd be insulted if I told you I'm completely bemused by this entire conversation."

That stopped him. He dropped to sit on the floor beside her chair.

With his long legs crossed and his face turned up to hers, he appeared younger, less sure of himself.

"Elise's death was the kind of shock you think you'll never get over," he said. "And maybe you never do—not completely. She . . . Elise struggled with depression. I never realized how serious it was until it was too late. Postnatal depression added to what she'd already been fighting was too much. She killed herself. My parents were murdered."

Celina touched his face impulsively. She couldn't answer. There was nothing to say, especially not *I'm sorry*. I'm sorry would be so inadequate. Certainly she couldn't brush him off with a reminder that everyone knew his parents had been murdered. Instead, she looked into his eyes and smiled a little, and let her hand come to rest on his shoulder.

He smiled back and put her hand on the arm of the chair again, and kept one of his own on top. "Thanks. I'm okay about it now."

"You can't be."

"If you're going to be close to someone—for whatever reason—there has to be honesty between you."

All sensation centered where his skin met hers. "I believe in honesty. And I don't believe in posturing. I've had to spend too much time with people who posture. You don't do that."

His smile broadened. "Does that mean you find somethin' honorable in me? Somethin' you might even like?"

Celina made herself look away. "You could get that lucky. Who knows?"

"I'd like Amelia to have a woman in her life. Tilly's a godsend, but she isn't a mother figure."

"If you want to marry again, Jack, you know you can. I'm sure women would line up to be your wife." Now he would think she was telling him how attractive he was.

"How about you? Would you line up?"

"I don't like lines. I'm too impatient."

"You just want to be at the head of the line?"

Word games, word games. "I'm getting tired." And she was exhausted by this verbal sparring. "We haven't done a whole lot that's useful, but I do think going to St. Peter's is a good idea, and I'm glad you agree."

"Good. We'll do what you suggest, and go together."

He sounded different, not relaxed or more gentle, just different.

"Right after Elise died, I didn't want to consider marrying again.

Not ever. Once I did think about it, I decided the most important thing would be to make sure Amelia wasn't going to be exposed to something unpleasant. Like a divorce."

Okay, she would play along. "Divorce can happen. It's too bad when a marriage fails, but I can understand how it happens."

"If you're careful from the outset, it doesn't have to. Errol would have married you if the baby was his."

"Errol asked me to marry him," she told Jack with total honesty. "He died before I had a chance to give him an answer." Errol had wanted to marry her the moment she told him there was a baby. She'd just about decided to take him up on the offer, when he'd died.

"Why would you need time to think about a thing like that?"

"No one should marry out of a sense of responsibility."

"Errol wanted to marry you only because of the baby?"

Celina let her eyelids lower. Her hand was still beneath Jack's on the chair. "I think Errol might have wanted to marry me anyway." She knew he had. "The baby made him reach a decision." Errol had even tried to take her to buy an engagement ring.

"You didn't love him?"

"Not in that way."

"So let me get this straight." His fingers closed around her wrist. "You only wanted Errol for sex. And you say the baby you're carrying is the result of some of that mindless sex. You couldn't make up your mind to marry Errol because you didn't think of him in *that* way."

"I was going to marry him." She wasn't in a position to make any protests.

She heard him suck in a sharp breath. He touched her cheek and she jumped. He turned her face toward him, but she kept her eyes almost shut.

"Look at me, please. I want to see your eyes."

Slowly she did as he asked.

"I'm sorry for Errol's sake that you couldn't love him."

Celina smiled and felt sadness deep inside. "I'm sorry about that too, but we can't force love."

His thumb stroked back and forth on her cheek. "Could I try something and hope you won't scream, or slap me." Rising to his knees, he regarded her face minutely as if he could somehow find a way to see inside her. "I'll take my chances."

Jack Charbonnet's mouth should be outlawed. He settled it over hers. Firm, but gentle, gentle but insistent, insistent but carefully so.

He kissed her with insistent pressure, but without attempting to open her mouth. With a hand behind her head, he kept on kissing her.

And Celina started to kiss him back. She ached all over, a wonderful ache, a sensation more intense than she'd ever felt. The most natural thing imaginable was to slip her own hands around his neck and tangle her fingers in his hair. He smelled clean, clean skin, clean shirt. The start of his beard growth rubbed her chin, and she shuddered with pleasure. For this one suspended fraction of time she wouldn't question what was happening. His mouth tasted like coffee and mint.

She tightened her arms around his neck, and he wrapped her tightly to him. They kissed and kissed, and Celina didn't care that kissing Jack Charbonnet should be the most unlikely thing ever to happen to her.

His fingertips brushing up and down her spine left a sensitive trail that spread. Her breasts were crushed to his chest. Their increased fullness was something she had tried to hide, but his hard chest against them brought potently erotic pleasure.

With a reluctance she felt, he took his mouth from hers. With the backs of his fingers he stroked the sides of her neck. "A successful experiment," he said, his voice even quieter than usual. "What do you think?"

"I think I'm amazed. The kiss was great—lovely. Thank you. But why would you kiss me?"

"Just to find out what it was like. And because I wanted to. I liked it very much too. I'm going to want to do it again. But maybe we shouldn't push it too soon."

"Are you trying to suggest you think we're going to be doing a lot of kissing?" She was Celina Payne and she wasn't in the habit of talking to men about whether or not they intended to kiss her.

"You are a very lovely woman. I'm not surprised you won beauty pageants."

She cleared her throat. "I'm trying to forget I was ever in those pageants. It embarrasses me."

"You glow, Celina. Did you know that? It's not an old wives' tale. Pregnancy makes even plain women pretty, and you are not plain, my dear."

My dear. Was that actually a term of endearment, or just a figure of speech?

"I'd better go home."

"I'm going to take you soon. Will Cyrus be there?"

"Yes. He was only stepping out for a little while."

"Did Antoine come back and talk to you this afternoon?"

"No. He really looked upset again this morning. He and his wife are very close, so I'm sure he wanted to be with her."

Jack's hands, settling on her stomach, stunned Celina. "You don't mind, do you?" he asked.

"Well . . . I don't suppose I do."

"People want to touch babies in the womb. I guess it's a hangover from when a baby belonged to a whole tribe and everyone felt proprietary toward it."

"Could be," she agreed.

He fanned his fingers and stroked, then shocked her again by settling his ear on her navel. "Who's in there? Speak up. What's your name?"

She giggled and said, "You're silly," then couldn't believe she'd said such a thing to him.

His expression, when he raised his head, was softly smug. "Wait till you feel that little tyke move. We'll see who gets silly then."

"Maybe. Why are you being so nice to me?"

"Somebody should be. You're pregnant and pretty much alone. You're going to keep the baby against difficult odds. I admire you for that."

"I never had any choice. I wouldn't want one."

"Okay, on your feet." He pulled her up, but instead of moving away he held her hands. "I'd like to get to know Cyrus better. He seems like a really nice guy."

"He is. Cyrus is my champion. He always had been."

"That's great to hear." The strangest expression entered his eyes. "My mother was pregnant when she died. I was going to have a brother."

She clung to him, horrified. "That's awful. How do you know it was a boy?"

He looked her straight in the eyes. "It was a boy."

In other words, back off.

"It's obvious what has to happen here, you know that, don't you?"

Celina went blank. "No. Right now I'm a very fragmented woman."

"You're a Catholic, I presume."

"I am, but I'd be keeping my baby anyway. It's different for different people, but I couldn't live with myself if I did anything else."

"I like that. What do you think of prenuptial agreements?"

She frowned. "I suppose I can see where they're sometimes necessary."

"Would you be offended if you were asked to sign one?"

"I don't know." She thought about it. "It could be that I'd think the man didn't trust me not to take him for a ride or something."

"I used to think like you. And at that point I was right. Things have changed, especially with this situation."

She made a polite noise.

"Errol would never have asked for one," he said.

"Do you mind if we don't talk about Errol for a while. I don't want to cry, but I'm starting to feel a little shaky."

"Sorry. I do believe I was thinking out loud. But that's not what we're dealing with here."

"Isn't it?" She wasn't sure what they were dealing with anymore.

"By now you know exactly what I've got on my mind. It's the only thing that makes sense. If we get right on it, we can be married within a week or so. I know you aren't in love with me, but you need me and I'm prepared to do what needs to be done. Would you like your brother to marry us? If that's important to you, it's okay with me."

"Marry us?"

"Perhaps he wouldn't be able to. I'm not sure what that would entail with the Church, are you?"

Not a single coherent thought would settle long enough for Celina to respond.

Jack inclined his head and watched her face. He pressed her palms together and kept his hands over hers. "I'd decided this was the thing to do by this morning. There won't even be a question about who the baby's father is. It'll be accepted that it's mine. Later on we'll have to decide what—"

"We?" She gathered enough wit to pull away from him. *"We?"*

"Celina—"

"Please *stop*. Not another word—please. You decided? This isn't something you can decide."

"But it makes sense."

"You, Jack Charbonnet, are an arrogant . . . *ass!"*

Thirteen

A tiny staircase led from a narrow doorway in the corridor, behind Tilly's rooms, and up to the attic, The stairs creaked, and the dust made Amelia want to cough. She had closed the door carefully behind her so no one could see the shine of her flashlight as she climbed.

She wasn't supposed to go to the attic, but when she was lucky, she got to play up there almost every day. Tilly liked her to come home from school, eat her snack, and lie down to rest for a while. Amelia often waited until she heard Tilly go upstairs to her apartment again, then slipped from her own room and up the stairs.

This was the first time she'd come at night. Daddy would be angry if he found out, but he'd left with that lady Celina and probably wouldn't be back too soon. Amelia was certain Daddy was dating Celina and didn't know how she felt about that yet. Tilly often talked about how Daddy should get married again because he was too young not to have a wife for the rest of his life, and because it would be a good thing for Amelia to have a mother. Amelia didn't want a mother. She liked looking at the pictures of her real mother, and being with her daddy. But if Daddy needed a wife, then Amelia supposed she wouldn't be a brat about it. She'd try anyway—unless Celina called her precocious like that lady Amelia and Daddy had met in the street once. The lady had kissed Daddy, and Amelia had told her she didn't think that was appropriate. Then the lady said she was precocious.

She'd just wait and see about Celina. She was pretty. Tilly was waiting to see too, but said she thought Celina might be okay. Nanny Summers wouldn't like it though. Mama had been Nanny's only child and she said they should never forget Mama.

At the top of the stairs another door opened into the attic. A pointed ceiling rose high over Amelia's head, and boxes were stacked against every wall. There was also an old sewing machine with ivy leaves painted on it, and a dummy thing for pinning clothes on. The dummy didn't have a head, so Amelia had put a hat on it and draped a piece of lace over the top so you couldn't tell about the head unless you looked really close.

In one corner was a trunk. On the front, fancy letters on a dirty metal label spelled out ELISE SUMMERS. That was Amelia's mama. She lifted the lid carefully so it wouldn't bang when she leaned it against the wall. Inside was a big box with a window of plastic in the top. The box was taped and Amelia had left it that way. She knew this was Mama's wedding dress. She's seen it in photographs of Mama and Daddy on their wedding day anyway, but one day she'd get to take it out of the box because she was going to wear it when she got married. That reminded her that she needed to get going on that. Daddy said you should take your time finding someone to marry, just to be certain you'd keep on loving them no matter what. Amelia wasn't sure what he meant by "no matter what."

Under the box were other pretty things wrapped in tissue paper. Pieces of lace. A white nightie and robe, and slippers with little pearls sewn on them. And there were books from when Mama and Daddy were in school. Amelia had found their pictures. They looked funny.

And there were baby clothes. She was sure they had been hers, and it was hard to wait to ask Daddy. Meanwhile she had brought her big baby doll, Fanny, up to live in the attic and she wore Amelia's baby clothes all the time.

Would Celina come to live in their house, Amelia wondered. And if she did, would everything change?

Daddy had taken Celina home, but would probably be back soon.

Roland's mama had got married again just before he came to kindergarten. Amelia knew because she and Roland were friends and he'd told her. She'd tried not to be rude when she asked questions, but she'd asked them anyway. Roland said it was okay to have a new dad, that his new dad played ball with him. But now his mama was having another baby. Amelia said, "Yuck" aloud. She wouldn't like it if Daddy got married and there was a new baby. It would probably want to touch all her things.

She cuddled Fanny and closed the trunk again. From the little window set low in the sloping roof, Amelia could peek all the way down to the street. She went to climb on the suitcase she kept there.

She could watch for Daddy to come home. Then she'd run down to bed.

Outside it was very dark. There wasn't any moon, but she'd see him come under the streetlights.

She wasn't going to look at the house across the street anymore. There was a lady who lived there who didn't go out. She had another lady who looked after her. Tilly had told Amelia that.

Amelia thought the lady who lived there might not be nice. Of course she wasn't a ghost, Amelia had made that up, but she might be a witch, and she might be the kind of witch who wanted to kidnap little girls and make them work for her. That nearly happened to Phillymeana once when she'd been mean to the dragon prince and he'd gone away to mend his heart. She didn't have him to help her then. If she hadn't sent a message to the North Pole so Santa's friend, Polar Bear, could tie up the witch with a rope made from her own broom bristles, the witch would have got Phillymeana.

A little light flashed on and off—a red light, but really small. It was in the window in the lady's house.

Amelia had turned off her flashlight before she climbed onto the suitcase. She pressed her nose to the glass and peered down at the red light. It went out and didn't come back on again.

The lady had lace curtains in her windows.

One of them moved, one in the same window where the red light had come on and off.

Amelia shivered. She wasn't cold, just scared of that mean old lady over there who stayed up in the night to spy on people. At least, Amelia was almost certain that's what she did. And she'd seen the curtain move in the daytime too.

The curtain moved again.

A face. Amelia covered her own face, then separated her fingers and looked through them.

A white face was looking through the window, and after a moment or two it put something over its eyes. Amelia made herself look as closely as she could.

Why that wicked lady had binoculars, didn't she? And she was looking straight into Amelia's own apartment—right into Amelia's bedroom.

Fourteen

Antoine needed to relieve himself. He moved on the hard metal chair and made noises. Noises were the best he could do with a dirty rag crammed into his mouth and tied behind his head.

"Hey, I do believe the boy's got some'tin he wants t'say. That's very smart of you, boy. Our patience is gettin' short, and you ain't even met the guy with the really short fuse." A man whose face he couldn't see, a man who stayed beyond the blinding glare of a white light that swung from the ceiling, delivered a kick to Antoine's shin, and then kicked him again. "You got some'tin to say, boy? Nod your fuckin' head if the answer's yes."

Pain blasted in his legs, but Antoine nodded. He knew who these people must be and why they'd grabbed him and stuffed him into a car while he was walking to catch the cable car. He'd got scared after he tried to talk to Miss Celina the second time. The other people left and he went back, but Mr. Charbonnet was still there and Antoine wasn't sure he should talk in front of him, so he decided to leave Royal Street. Now he wished he'd stayed.

"The boy's got some'tin t'say," the man behind the light shouted. "What say we find out what it is?"

"You do that," another voice said, a deeper, slower voice. "It better be what we want to hear, old man, or you'll be goin' to heaven sooner than you planned."

The light swung in an arc, casting crazy shadows on brick walls. He'd been blindfolded in the car, and although he'd tried to note what turns they'd made, he'd soon lost all sense of where he was. Smells made him suspect they were near the river. And he'd heard what sounded like a ship's horn in the distance.

The cloth was taken from his mouth and he coughed, and thought he might get sick.

Another kick, this one to his knee, made him lean forward and choke back vomit. His arms were tied behind the chair, and his ankles were lashed together.

"You puke, you eat it, boy," the man with the hard shoes said. "I don't like smellin' what someone else ate. You got that?"

"Go easy," the other voice said.

"I'm doin' this for you, boss. And you know how stupid his kind are. You gotta keep remindin' 'em who's in charge and what they're supposed to do. They ain't got no natural respect for their betters. That's because they been around dumb fuckers who make 'em think they're equal or some'tin stupid like that."

"Antoine," the quieter man said. "What is it you want to tell us? We're all ears, and we want to be your friends."

"I . . . I got to use the facilities, me."

In the silence that followed Antoine could hear the beat of his own heart.

"You gotta use the *facilities?*" He saw the dark shadows of the face that bent over him. "You gotta take a shit, you mean? Or a piss? Both, maybe?"

Antoine swallowed his disgust. These were not good men, not men with any of the grace his own quiet parents, poor, hardworking parents, had instilled in him. He and Rose had taught their boys the same things, although it was harder now.

"Answer me, boy!" A blow to the side of his head with a closed fist caught the corner of his eye, and he felt blood there. "What you gotta do in the *facilities?* You gonna try to escape, ain't that it? You gonna try to make us look like fools in front of the nice people we work for."

"I need to relieve myself," Antoine said quietly. "You got my word I don't try to get away. I'm an honest man, me."

"You a stupid man who minds other people's business. You got pants on, use 'em. You ain't goin' to no *facilities.*"

"Maybe you should take him."

"You goin' soft or somethin'?" The man who struck another with such pleasure sounded angry with his companion. "You're the one who asked for insurance. I'm givin' it to you."

"Make this faster," the other man said. "I'm tired of it already. You don't gotta prove nothin' to me. You're doin' a good job for me. And I need you back on the other thing. I don't trust your buddy not to do somethin' I wouldn't like. You hurry up here and get back there. Then you tell him he does nothin' without I say so. Got that?"

"Got it. Okay, *Antoine*, I'm gonna ask you again. What do you think you saw the mornin' after your owner bought it?"

"Mr. Petrie he don't own me. Nobody own nobody no more."

"Well, *excuse* me, sir. Maybe I'll help you get more comfortable."

Cold water drenched Antoine from head to foot. Then, while he shook his head to clear his eyes, a punch landed on his full bladder, and another, and another. He cried out, and couldn't stop himself from crying out again. And his bladder let go. He felt the warm urine soil his trousers, and he burned with shame.

"Better now?"

He didn't answer.

"What did you see that morning?"

"Nothing."

"What time was it?"

"I did not see nothing."

"Didn't you tell someone you saw a person early in the mornin'. This person came to Petrie's place before it was light and went into the house."

"No. I did not see nothing." He had to lie, because if he didn't he could put Dwayne in danger. Antoine didn't want to think what these men might do to someone like Dwayne.

"So why'd you say so, dummy? You know why? Because I think you did see someone and I think you could do a very nice job of describin' that person. Why don't you prove me right? I get real happy when I'm right. I might just let you go home to that wife you're so fond of—and those boys."

Despite his soaked clothes and his misery, Antoine sat straighter. They knew about his family. "I saw nothin', me."

"THE TRUTH WILL SET YOU FREE. That's what your fuckin' T-shirt says, Antoine. Maybe you can't read so good. Can you fuckin' read?"

"We don't have time for this," the man behind Antoine said. "If Win finds out someone made a careless move, he's goin' to be even harder to deal with."

"You never did tell me why Win's on your case, boss."

"I don't pay you to ask questions."

Antoine wondered who Win was but knew better than to ask. "It was a difficult day," he said, trying to figure a way to make them think he wasn't worth their time. "They found Mr. Petrie dead in his bathroom. You can read it in the papers, you. Old papers, but you get them at the paper office, they say."

"Shut the fuck up."

Antoine decided to press on. "You can ask for the old ones. I see him with my own eyes. He on the bathroom floor. They say his heart kill him, but now it the word of the man from the police. He say Mr. Petrie drown. No one know how. Perhaps he hit his head."

"He was on the floor," the quiet man said. "Isn't that what you just told us?"

"That's what I say, me."

"So," his tormentor said, "how the fuck does a drowned man get out of the tub and onto the floor?"

Another knuckle blow landed on Antoine's temple and pain blossomed inside his head. Two more punches, in quick succession, made certain he couldn't see out of his left eye at all. The swelling instantly grew tight.

"What did you see, fucker?"

Antoine shook his head slowly from side to side. Blood ran into the corner of his mouth.

"You didn't get around to telling the LeChat queen everythin'. You saw someone was watchin' you at the fairy palace and quit talkin', didn't you?"

Dwayne LeChat was a kind man. Antoine didn't want to say anything that might hurt him. "I didn't tell Dwayne nothin'."

"Stupid," he was told before a flurry of punches battered his face and neck, then his belly. The man sounded breathless when he said, "All you gotta do is tell me who else you talked to about this and we'll take you home to Rose. How's that?"

Antoine's brain was on fire. How did they know Rose's name? *They weren't going to let him go.*

"All you gotta do is let us know you respect us. Let us know you got honest feelin's of admiration for us. You revere us. When you revere someone, you don't try to keep things from them. Who else did you tell about what you thought you saw that mornin'?"

"No one."

He braced himself for whatever punishment might come. When it didn't, he relaxed a little.

Something cracked his front teeth, but Antoine didn't know what it was. He let his head hang forward, not that he could have held it up. A piece of a tooth went down his throat. He spat another piece out. His mouth was filled with blood now.

"We saw the queen talk to Jack Charbonnet. You like Jack Charbonnet?"

Antoine nodded, every move bringing a fresh agony.

"Wrong answer. We don't. We think the queen told Charbonnet about your little visit."

He didn't want to die. But more than that, he didn't want his family to suffer because of him.

"He—" Antoine spat blood into his lap. It didn't seem to matter anymore that he'd relieved himself in his pants, or that he could smell his own urine and excrement. "Dwayne, he can't tell Mr. Charbonnet. I don't finish tellin' Dwayne, so he can't tell anyone."

"Oh, the boy's decided to believe his shirt and be honest with the best friends he's ever goin' to have. Ain't that nice? But you went to LeChat to tell tales, ain't that right?"

"I went to ask him advice. Him wise, Mr. LeChat. Not many know him wise."

"His kind make real men sick," his brave questioner said. "We gotta stamp out dirt like that. Unnatural, that's what they are. But you asked him advice. And what advice does he give you?"

"No advice. I don't finish askin', me. I get nervous because I not sure I see anythin'. Maybe I just get a visit from a spirit come to wish me peace in the mornin', only I don' recognize him."

"I think our friend here is tryin' to divert us," the second man said. "And I think his time is runnin' out. What do you think?"

The man behind Antoine was obviously the boss. The one who was giving Antoine the hands-on attention wanted to impress his boss. He said, "You got it. His time's runnin' out. I'm gonna ask one more time. Who else did you tell about what you thought you saw?"

"No one."

"Rose is a lot younger than you, old man. Ain't that true?"

He saw the shadowed bricks through a haze of blood and spittle, and tears he didn't remember shedding.

"Ain't it the case that your woman's a lot younger than you? They say that black meat is sweet. At least, that's what I heard. Maybe if your lady's lonely, I could go over and keep her company."

The agony of helplessness and fear closed Antoine's throat as tightly as any pair of hands could. He moaned and rocked his head from side to side.

"Trust us, Antoine," the boss man said. "We don't intend to hurt anyone. It is very regretful that we've had to cause you a little discomfort, but we have to know who else you spoke to about whatever it was you thought you saw in the Royal Street courtyard the morning after Errol Petrie died."

"I no see nothin'. Believe me. I tell you if I see somethin'."

"Then why did you go to Dwayne LeChat?"

If only his mind would stay clear long enough. "I go because Mr. LeChat, him, believe in the old ways, and him respectful of the old arts. I know he listen when I talk about the spirit."

"You're a goddamn liar, boy. And you ain't good at it."

The next swat knocked him backward, and he crashed to the concrete floor. He screamed. His weight landed on his arms, and his arms were strapped behind the chair. The cracking he heard had to be bones, and the pain that exploded afterward all but made him faint.

"Okay, boss, I say we leave him here and go visit his old lady."

"Oh, why disrupt the whole home like that. We could always bring one of his boys here. Simon, is it? Pretentious name, but kinda cute for a cute little ass like that. How old is Simon, Antoine?"

No one would come to his aid, but Antoine didn't care anymore. He wouldn't answer these people again. Sound gurgled. It came from his own throat.

"He's fifteen," the boss man said. "I remember now. I asked a few questions and learned he was fifteen and very good in school. You and Rose are proud of him. He wants to be a doctor and you save money all the time to help him. I'd say you people got ideas above your station, but why shouldn't people make up dreams. You saw someone come into the courtyard at Royal Street and go up into the house. Is that right?"

Simon was gentle and clever and wise. He saw good where there was no good.

A solid toe connected with Antoine's right kidney. "Is that right?"

He nodded. What could they make of that anyway?

The boss said, "Push him on his side. He's chokin'."

The chair rolled. Antoine saw the floor rise toward him, then his face met concrete. Blood flowed back into his arms, but it only brought more pain.

"You didn't say anything to the police because your kind is naturally afraid of those people. But later you wanted to feel important, so you started shootin' your mouth off."

"I left without tellin' Dwayne everythin'."

"You didn't tell me what the person look like."

He took in a choking, wet breath. "I didn't see what the person looked like, me."

"You know what this is, boy?"

Antoine squinted up. His left eye saw nothing. With his right eye he made out a wire. He nodded and said, "Wire."

Sudden pealing laughter made him lose control of his bowels again.

"Whooeee, would you smell that?" the funny one said. "You'll thank me later for giving you a good clean-out. This is wire. You're right about that. But what else? No, you don't gotta figure it out. It's a live wire"—more laughter—"get it, a live wire. Fuck, I don't want to think about what you'd smell like if you burned right now."

"Let me go," Antoine said, coughing between each word. "Just let me go and no one ever knows about this. No one. And no one knows about what I see in the courtyard."

"So what did you see?" the man shouted. He ground a foot into Antoine's arms, ground them against the back of the metal chair. "And who else did you tell? You went up to the house in the middle of this morning, didn't you?"

He murmured yes, and felt his mind slip away. He wanted silence and dark. He tried to pray to himself, to tell himself he was a child of God and full of joy. They couldn't find the part of him that was God's. They couldn't kick that and make it bleed.

"That was because you wanted to tell someone about your secret, right, *Antoine*? You wanted to be important, right?"

"I never be important, me. Not important. Just an honest man."

"Honest. Will you listen to that? The man is honest, so we got nothin' to worry about. You went up to the house to tell your story, but someone else was there. So you waited until later and then you finish, huh? This time you tell what you saw. The description and everythin'."

He couldn't clear his thoughts. "Nice dresser," he said. "Black leather bag. Cost plenty."

"Oh, plenty. What else?"

"Nothin'. Red hair, maybe. Him wear a hat, but the light shine on his hair. But I do not know him, me. No, I do not know him."

"Oh, yeah. I think we got our answer, boss. Okay, boy. One last thing before we let you go. You told someone else what you saw and we want you to let us know who that was."

How would Rose and the boys manage without him? Mr. Petrie had paid him well. Miss Celina would keep on paying him well—or Mr. Charbonnet. They'd want the place kept up.

"Who?" He heard the voice, but it was distant.

"He's passing out on us."

"We gotta have a name. I gotta have somethin' to prove we done our job—and we got a problem to fix. I gotta be able to tell Win I used my initiative, and I got good instincts."

"Because it's goin' to help you prove somethin', boss? You afraid you ain't so popular with him no more?"

"When you get to ask me questions, I'll let you know. Stick to what I pay you to do. Get him to give us a name and not Charbonnet, please God. I can't use Charbonnet or Win will think I'm making the whole goddamn thing up."

The voices wafted over Antoine. He liked the cold concrete beneath his cheek. He'd like to melt into the floor and be gone.

"Okay, you're watchin, boss, right." A mouth came close to his ear. "All you got to do is nod, Antoine. Did you tell Celina Payne what you saw?"

He began to sink. The concrete opened to take him.

Antoine nodded.

Fifteen

"The job must pay well," Jack said, sizing up Garth Fletcher's plush office suite at St. Peter's Hospital for Children. He was making conversation, but Celina didn't show any sign of having heard him.

"If he's tryin' to make a point, he's made it." They'd been in the green and gray waiting room almost an hour. "We're convinced he's important and busy. He can show up now."

Not a word from Celina.

"I've never had a professional reason to see him before. Does he make a habit of running behind schedule? Way behind schedule?"

"No."

It was a start. She'd refused to let him pick her up in Royal Street. No explanation, just "No, thanks, I'll meet you there," and a hangup while his mouth was still open. He'd phoned St. Peter's first thing that morning and made an appointment with Garth. After last night's disaster he had needed an excuse to call Celina. He had a feeling that if her brother hadn't been the one to answer the phone and say she was there, she would have screened his call out.

Perhaps she'd told her brother about his "arrogance," and Cyrus had been pragmatic enough to think marriage to Jack would be a good opportunity for his sister, or at least one she should consider. "How long is Cyrus staying with you?"

"Indefinitely." She was adept at conversation stoppers.

"About last night, Celina. I—"

"Don't."

"It's a perfect solution for you. You and the baby would never want for anything. And you won't have to think about whether or not you want to name Errol. And—"

"Don't. I'm not here to discuss anything personal with you."

"Marriage. Yours and mine. It would be a useful arrangement for both of us. And you wouldn't have to worry about your child having a father. If I say it's mine, nobody's going to say otherwise—not where they're likely to be heard." Oh, yes, Jack Charbonnet was known for his suave approach. Too bad the magic had deserted him today.

He sank lower in his soft green leather chair. Celina sat in a similar chair, as far from him as possible. He said, "I'm glad these are comfortable," then indicated the receptionist's vacant rosewood desk. "Do you suppose wherever they are, they're together?"

Taking her briefcase with her, Celina got up and walked, stiff-backed, to the open door into Garth's acres of office. From where Jack sat the decor in the other room looked like a re-creation of an oversized study in an English manor house. Studded brown leather abounded.

"Red suits you, Celina." The understated lines of her linen suit drew attention to the woman, not the clothes. She was vivid, and if you knew what to look for . . . "You are startin' to show no matter what you wear."

She stared at him and he decided he'd earned the contempt he saw in her eyes. "You shouldn't have to hide it," he told her quietly. "But I don't have the right to be so personal. I apologize."

Celina nodded, and faced Garth's office again.

"You are lovely," he said, surprising himself. "I think you only get lovelier. Pregnancy does that. At least, I believe it does."

"Thank you."

He ran the back of a thumbnail over his bottom lip and kept on studying her. "I'm not going to forget kissing you."

"It wasn't important."

Jack almost laughed. He deserved the put-down. "I hope we can find a common ground. Perhaps I should say I'd *like* to find a common ground."

Heavy steps sounded outside. "There you are!" Garth Fletcher bounded into the waiting room with his large head thrust forward on broad shoulders, and exuding energy. The atmosphere changed. It almost crackled.

"Were you lookin' for us, Garth?" Jack asked mildly. "I thought I clearly heard your receptionist tell me the meetin' was here."

"Just a figure of speech," their host said with a honking laugh. His mane of gray hair rippled back from his wide forehead like a retreating tide. "You're lookin' mighty fine, as usual, Celina. Come on into my parlor, both of you." He put a hand on the back of Celina's neck and guided her ahead of him.

Jack followed and closed the door. "Busy day?" he said, beginning to simmer at the other man's condescension.

"They're all busy."

But the bastard wasn't going to apologize for wasting an hour of another busy man's time. "I was starting to think you were tryin' to avoid us, Garth. I called yesterday, and the day before, and was told you didn't have an open appointment. I'm glad we finally got to the head of the line." There had been little doubt that Garth would have preferred to put them off indefinitely.

"You always make this room look clumsy, Celina," Garth said, not looking at Jack, or acknowledging he'd heard what he said. "Such a lovely, feminine little bit of a thing."

More than lovely in Jack's opinion, even if she was more peaked than he would have preferred. Wasn't there something they said about redheads not wearing red? Her hair was a red-brown with flashes of coppery color among the short curls. Celina should wear lots of red because it was terrific on her. She needed him. What would it take to make her see that? Did she have something to hide from him, something that made her want to keep her distance from him?

She sat down and put her briefcase on the floor. She smiled at Garth, but it looked as if the effort cost her something. She didn't thank him for the paternalistic compliment. He patted her shoulder and his hand lingered.

Jack resented that Garth thought he had a right to touch Celina with that familiar, jovial informality. It gave the man—or so he thought—a way to disguise a gesture with sexual undertones. "We did have the time right today, didn't we?" Jack asked. "Two?"

"You did. Now, what can I do for you? Oh, I'm sure you don't want anythin' to drink so soon after lunch, do you?"

This time Celina's blue eyes sought out Jack's. She said, "No, I'm sure we don't. How is Derek Columbier?"

"Doin' well, quite well."

"He's not rejecting the implant?"

Garth's jovial facade fell away. He sniffed and rocked onto his heels. "Not yet. His mother is euphoric, o'course. It's never easy to strike the balance between supportin' hope and avoidin' false hope."

"Garth," Jack said. "Celina and I have somethin' we want to ask you. A favor. We know we could have sent a note, or called, and you'd have done it, but we wanted to come and see you face-to-face. These are difficult times. I'm sure you understand."

"Times are inevitably difficult." Garth walked around his oak desk and sat down. "I'm faced with a special meeting of the board of trustees this evenin'. That's enough to make a man quake in his shoes, I can tell you. You can't imagine what a group that is."

"Oh, I think I can, I—"

"Not that they aren't all well meanin', of course. They give their all to this hospital. But they do expect a great deal from me and the entire staff of St. Peter's. They scrutinize everythin', I can tell you, and if somethin' looks like it might cast a shadow on this fine institution, well then, they expect me to fix it."

"Very demanding," Jack said. He sat down. "But you do a fine job of it. That's why this hospital is held up as an example across the country."

"We've come to talk to you about Errol," Celina said. She took a file from her briefcase. "I'm hoping there will be time to talk about progress, time schedule, and so on for a few projects, but Errol is the first order of business for us."

Garth pushed his chair back, propped his heels on the desk, and tented his fingers. "Errol is dead."

An uncomfortable silence followed before Jack's temper finally overloaded. "No shit! I'm glad we came to see you today, Garth, or we might have missed that important piece of information. How about you, Celina? Aren't you relieved to know the truth about Errol? And did you notice the fine balance Garth struck. He knew this was not the time to give false hope, so he went straight for complete disclosure. Now we can stop hoping Errol will open that drawer at the morgue and walk into our open arms. He's still there because the police won't release his body yet."

"There's no call for that," Garth said.

"Don't," Celina said, her voice barely audible. "Please, don't argue at a time like this."

"You're upsettin' the little lady," Garth said, leaning forward, adjusting his tie. "The shock has been too much for you, Jack. You're overwrought."

"Overwrought? *Overwrought?* What are you . . . Work on your vocabulary, Garth, you're not talkin' to a girl about to swoon." He stood up and paced. "You deal with this, Celina. I don't trust myself right now."

"We're all shocked," Celina said. "We need your help, Garth. If we're going to save Dreams, we need your confidence."

He was quiet for a while and tapped his touching forefingers against his lips. "Errol was the heart and soul of the foundation," he said at last. "When something like this happens, it's often best to step back and give it time. Now, I wouldn't want you to think I don't think it's a great idea. It is. And you and Errol brought a lot of joy to a bundle of children, but there's a time for grievin'. An appropriate time. And that's now for you and Dreams."

"Why would you refer to Dreams as a *good idea?*" Celina said, and Jack glanced at her sharply. The anger he heard in her voice was new, different. "You didn't call it a good idea when we were able to raise the money for a patient library you wanted but the trustees didn't think was necessary. Then we were angels. Your term, not ours. Ideas are notions that haven't yet taken shape."

"Semantics, Celina, semantics."

"Don't talk down to her," Jack said. "I don't like it."

"Is that a fact?" Garth tapped his fingertips together and regarded Jack with knowing eyes. "Steppin' right into Errol's shoes, are we?"

The implication was impossible to miss. "What do you mean by that?" Let the man put it into words.

"Obvious, isn't it," Garth said smoothly. "You're steppin' right up to make sure the things Errol cared for continue. I like that."

"You just said you thought this was a time for grieving," Celina said. "For us, and for Dreams. That sounded as if you meant you didn't think we should be continuing with our work."

Garth smiled at her and his glance took her in from head to toe. "I meant it might be a good idea not to draw too much attention to the foundation right now."

"Why would that be?" Jack asked.

"All I'm tryin' to do," Garth said, looking aggrieved, "is what's best for everyone. Now, if you want to work here with the children, Celina, I know I can find somethin' for you. I'm about to institute a fund-raiser for an additional rehab wing and there's nothin' that would please me more than to have you on board."

"I bet," Jack said, not so much to himself that Garth Fletcher wouldn't hear. "Did you know that Errol and I were partners in Dreams? His idea. His sweat and tears. But I have a financial stake and Errol and I had an understanding that I'd step in and take an active role if it was ever necessary." He and Errol had never discussed what would happen if Errol couldn't act, but Garth didn't have to know that detail.

"Is that so?"

"It is. But we're here for another reason. We know you're going to want to help us out."

An impassive mask spread over Garth's wide face, but his eyes remained alert and wary.

"We want you to do something for Errol," Celina said, sitting forward in her chair. "He loved this hospital. You weren't the administrator when it happened, but his son was kept alive here. And then he died here. Errol never stopped feeling he owed this place a great deal."

Garth studied his fingernails. "Took him a while to remember though. So I understand. I suppose you can forgive a man for turnin' to liquor—and other things—at a time like that."

They ought to leave—now.

Celina sprang to her feet. "That wasn't when Errol had his difficulties."

"But he did have them," Garth said, sizing her up yet again.

"Yes, he did," Celina agreed. "And that's why we're here. There are people who are capitalizing on history. Rather than mourn the death of a good man, they're having a great time dragging up things he had the courage to overcome a long time ago."

"From what I've heard," Garth said, "he was found in, shall we say, unfortunate circumstances."

"He was found dead," Jack said, barely restraining himself from pulling Garth across his desk.

He sounded as if he knew what only Celina and Jack were supposed to know about Errol's death—unless Garth had the same sources as Charmain Bienville. Then there was the question of what had been on Antoine's mind the last time Jack was in Royal Street. He had intended to speak with him, but there hadn't been an appropriate time.

Celina said, "Errol was murdered. And now we're in a bind because some people are getting in the way of us continuing his work because they enjoy pulling out things that are long past. History. Instead of mourning for a truly good and honorable man, they want to find a way to blame him for what was done to him. You and I know that for some years Errol's life revolved around helping children. Primarily children in this hospital. What we're asking you to do is issue a statement of support for Errol. A statement about your gratitude for all he did. We'd be very thankful if you'd tell anyone who wants to listen, and plenty do, that you had great admiration for Errol, that he was beyond reproach, and that any effort to tarnish his memory is a miscarriage of justice."

Garth actually looked amused. "You were very close to him, weren't you?" he asked.

"Very. I loved and admired him."

Wrong word, darlin'. "So did I," Jack said, seeking to defang any negative comeback of Garth's. "You could find hundreds in this town who feel very close to Errol."

"Really? I didn't know him that well myself."

"You"—Celina gripped the arms of her chair—"you did know Errol well. You came to him often, Garth, very often. No week went by when you didn't call. And the two of us spent hours in this office with you."

Garth picked up a pen and doodled on a pad. Apart from a telephone, only the pad marred the perfect, shining surface of the desk.

"Isn't that true?" Celina persisted.

Jack shoved his hands in his pockets where they'd have difficulty doing what he'd like to do with them. Either Garth Fletcher was slime, or he was doing his darnedest to make them think he was.

"The last thing I want to do is add to your grief, but I do have to think you've exaggerated a few things in your mind. Probably because you have a natural need to look for good things to think about Errol." He held up a hand to interrupt the start of an outburst from Celina. "Hear me out, my dear. I understand the grievin' process. I work with it every day."

Slime, Jack decided. "Garth, Celina and I hope you'll do something to help us—in memory of Errol. I'll cut right to it. As you've plainly heard, there are a lot of rumors flying around about him."

"*Rumors.* I fully accept the tendency to canonize the dead, but we can't change the fact that those aren't rumors."

"Will you put out an announcement about Errol?" Jack pushed ahead as if Garth hadn't already damned a good man. "A public statement. This was a man who dedicated the last five years of his life to the support of dying children. He had no concern for himself, for personal gain. His reason to live was bound up in those children and you're the one in the best position to let the world know it. They will believe you when the same statement coming from me would be just the words of an old friend, and from Celina they'd be his employee speaking."

Garth smiled with one side of his mouth. "Quite. His employee and close companion. That wouldn't be at all the thing. And you remember that, Celina. You've got a bright future ahead of you. But if you say too much about Errol, you'll be jumpin' into his grave with him—at least professionally. There are people who can use the talents you've got. Don't forget that. A good-lookin' woman like you is always an asset. But not if she's seen as potential trouble."

The crawling sensation that attacked Jack's nerves wasn't completely unfamiliar. He knew he'd felt it before, but he didn't want to identify the occasion. For now he still needed something from this asshole. "We're glad you see our point of view, Garth. I'd like to take out a full page in the *Times* to publish endorsements from various people. Your statement would be the highlighted piece we lean on for most impact."

"I've brought tear sheets of pieces written about him," Celina said, and Jack noted that her hand shook slightly when she placed a folder on Garth's desk. "I thought you might appreciate them as references."

Garth didn't touch the folder. He laced his fingers behind his neck and rocked his chair backward. "Do you intend to try carryin' on with Dreams?"

"Try, nothing," Jack said. He looked at the ceiling. This guy was unbelievable. "We will carry on. What I don't get is why you're taking this line. Who got to you, Garth? Who are you afraid of?"

Garth's hands slowly fell to the arms of his chair and he rocked forward. He narrowed his eyes. "What makes you feel safe enough to make suggestions like that? If I were you, I'd be very careful who I insulted. You may think this town has forgotten who you are and what you came from. It hasn't."

"I repeat," Jack said, although his heart beat harder, "who are you afraid of? Who is tellin' you what to say and what to do?"

Garth stood up and leaned on his desk. He pointed an imperious finger. "There's the door, boy. Use it."

"What's happening here?" Celina said, her face chalk white. "You asked if we're continuing with our work and Jack told you we are. Now you two are insulting each other—you're insulting Jack and telling him to leave. Why? Why don't you explain yourself, Garth?"

With visible effort, Garth pulled his overgenerous lips back in a smile. "Don't you worry your pretty head. This is nothin' for you to concern yourself with. And you know we'll be more than happy to accept any help you can give us here at St. Peter's."

"And you'll have it," she told him. "But we're asking you for some sign of gratitude for all Errol did. We can count on you for that statement, I assume."

Garth spread his meaty hands and said, "We all answer to a higher power, my dear. I told you about that meetin' with the board of trustees. They call my shots."

"As in they are your God?" Jack said quietly.

Fletcher gave up on the smile. "Better a group of well-meanin', solid citizens, than your daddy's old boss and his soldiers. No, I'm afraid we can't speak out on Errol Petrie's behalf, not when the hospital has already agreed to an investigation aimed at reassuring the public that this isn't a hospital where their children could be coerced into submittin' to performin' sexual acts in exchange for a new tractor for the farm back home."

"*What* are you talking about?" Celina said. She turned to Jack, an appeal in her eyes. "Why would he say things like that about Errol?"

"Could be I smell Charmain Bienville," Jack said, unnerved by the pulsing throb behind his temples. "And big bucks for offerin' a load of bull to an unscrupulous reporter. And maybe, just maybe, I also smell that fear I already mentioned. Are you afraid of someone, Garth? Come on, you can tell me. With my questionable background I probably have the right connections to call off whatever nasty dogs are on your tail."

The man's face turned a dull red before he said, "You're goin' to pay for that suggestion, Charbonnet," and went to throw open the door. "*Out.*"

Sixteen

The courtyard was shady, but sunlight polished the highest tips of palm fronds that waved, silk-smooth, against a blue sky so clear it seared the eyes.

"This property is yours now," Celina said. She'd been too involved with Errol's murder to concentrate on some obvious changes that must occur.

In the filtered brilliance Jack Charbonnet's eyes were an intense green-gold. He stood still, but managed to give the impression that nothing about him was still at all; restless energy tightly controlled.

"I'm living here. My brother's staying with me. I can't imagine why I didn't ask if that was all right with you before now. I'm behaving as if I have a right to be here. I don't."

"Yes, you do. I already told you so."

Not for the first time, she found that looking back into his eyes was an uncomfortable experience, yet she couldn't look away. "You did say I could stay. I remember that now. But you didn't necessarily mean indefinitely. Or that I could have guests."

"I meant you can stay as long as you want to. And I'm glad Cyrus is here with you. I also meant that . . . Celina, you were right to call me an ass last night."

"We should forget last night," she told him.

Water sparkled over the three tiers of a stone fountain in the center of the courtyard. Celina let herself focus on the softly calming sound. Contradiction surrounded her. This place she'd come to love harbored the echoes of violence amid its charm, and yet she could not find it ugly. With Jack beside her, Jack, who could almost make her believe he cared about her, there was magic here.

Their eyes met.

He didn't care about her and she must not pretend otherwise. He had an agenda. A true friend who mourned Errol's loss deeply, he was dedicated to preserving that friend's reputation. In truth she was nothing more than a potential hindrance to him.

"We've got to talk seriously." His low, slow voice with its faint Cajun emphasis could lull even the most wary. "The people who should be outraged by Errol's murder are lining up to bad-mouth him. I don't think he's got anyone but you and me and Dwayne to fight the good fight for him, but I'm game."

"So am I." Watching Jack Charbonnet's mouth was a pleasure. Feeling his mouth had been a pleasure. She was not herself. They said pregnant women were slaves to their emotions. This must fall into that area of the condition. "Dwayne would walk a mile on hot coals for Errol. We can do it. We can see justice done."

"Not at the expense of your health, and not if it's going to jeopardize the baby."

Celina felt her lips part but didn't care. He was an enigma. Berating her one minute, heaping apparent concern on her the next. Her throat ached. She had to be on guard against overreacting to kindness—especially from this man. He was capable of using her fragile sentiments against her.

"No wonder they made you Miss Louisiana," he said, smiling slightly. "I'm no poet, but if I were, I'd say something about sun and shadows on your face. And that glow they talk about in a pregnant woman's eyes. I'd better not touch you, but I surely want to."

When she caught her breath, she said, "I don't understand you at all. Most of the time I'd swear you hate me, then you say something like that."

"I don't hate you. I almost wish I could, but I haven't been able to manage it. Don't you like it when a man tells you you're irresistible?"

"I don't like it when I'm not sure a man isn't playing with me."

"Oh, I'm not playin', *chère*. But I'd like to play with you—the best kind of play. All alone, just the two of us, and all the time in the world. I'd like to stretch you out on a cool bed, or anywhere else for that matter, and see if I could find every delicate, touchy, responsive spot on your body."

She couldn't speak, could scarcely breathe. Her skin burned, and her flesh. Places ached that had never ached in quite that way.

He raised a hand and let it hover over her shoulder, as if considering whether or not to rest it there. Slowly he did so, and his touch was hot through her linen jacket. With his other hand he stroked her neck with his fingertips, then ran them so lightly downward, over her left breast, that she might have thought she'd imagined the outlandish intimacy if her nipple hadn't hardened and tingled.

"Sorry," he said. "No, I'm not. That wasn't enough, not nearly enough. I want to undo those buttons. What are you wearing underneath?"

"You can't talk like that."

"Surely I can. Somethin's pulling us together, and it's stronger than I am. I'm known as a reticent man, but not with you, ma'am, oh, no, not with you. Come on. What's underneath the jacket? One of those lacy bras that don't quite cover your nipples? You're demure on the outside, did you know that. In a way. Does that cover up the other Celina Payne? A red bra?" He glanced down. "I think you're feelin' somethin' too, darlin'. In fact, I can see you are. Red?"

"White," she said, never intending to answer him at all. "I need to get into the house and see what's been going on since I left."

"I can see you in my mind, Celina. Without the red suit. You've got beautiful legs. Is all the hair on your body the same color?"

She absolutely could not catch her breath. "A nice woman would slap you and walk away."

"Should I prepare to be slapped?"

"I didn't say I was nice."

"You excite me."

"You shouldn't excite me. It isn't right."

"Why? We're both adults."

"I'm pregnant. I'm not supposed to have these feelings."

"That's garbage, ma'am. What old books have you been reading? Pregnant women don't stop feeling sexy. And men don't stop finding them sexy—this man certainly finds you sexy. I want to be with you. Ain't that the darnedest thing? We both know we're dancin' around each other, watchin' and sizin' up. You don't trust me, and I can't trust you. But I would like to. And I'd like you to trust me. Maybe those old fates will shine, huh?"

"Why are we having this conversation?"

Outside the courtyard, in the street, a musician broke into "Such a Night" on a horn, and Jack whispered, "If I don't do it, somebody else will," and he might have sung the words to the music. Celina felt as if she were made entirely of light, and the open ends of nerves.

"Such a night." Jack sang this time, and breathed in, narrowing his nostrils. "Or should that be such a day?" With his fingers surrounding her neck, and his thumbs on the point of her chin, he swayed until she swayed with him. She rested her hands on his chest and he said, "You make me tremble, lady. Keep on makin' me tremble."

"Someone's going to come, Jack. What will they think?"

"If it's a man, he'll wish he was me. Especially if he takes a look at my pants."

"Oh!" She made to move away, but he laughed and kept right on holding her neck and moving with her. "It's broad daylight, Jack Charbonnet, and you are saying things a man ought to be jailed for saying."

"Since when?" He tipped his face up to the sky and laughed louder. "Free expression ain't against the law, my lovely. I would mention to you that my condition isn't real comfortable, but I'm enjoyin' it. I'll enjoy it more under other circumstances."

"This is what's called talking dirty isn't it?"

Evidently her every word was cause for fresh mirth. "Are you tryin' to tell me no man ever talked to you this way before?"

Celina assumed her haughtiest expression. "The men of my acquaintance have been gentlemen." With one very notable exception.

"Then you have missed a great deal and I intend to make up for that. Do you like music when you make love? Did you ever come to the rhythm of a horn like that one? Did anyone ever stretch you out on a table and lick you from your toes to your nose without missing any point in between? Especially that one special spot between? It would feel good if I did that for you. Then I'd concentrate on a couple of other spots. I'd lick them until you begged me to get inside you. I'll bet we could go upstairs right now and find a table in the sun where we could do just that. Oh, *chère,* I'm not sure I could wait very long if I had you naked in the sun, on a table, like a feast. I would eat you up."

He spoke in quiet, even, conversational tones, offered her sex with his voice, undressed her with his eyes, stroked her with fingers that hypnotized.

"This isn't you," she said, regaining a fragment of reason. "You're teasing me. Trying to embarrass me. Why?"

"I am not tryin' to embarrass you, Celina." His features fell into such somber, intensely watchful lines, one would have sworn he didn't know how to smile. "You and I just went through a battle together at that hospital—or at least a skirmish. After a thing like that, people need to celebrate what's good. Makin' love is good."

"I'm going upstairs."

"I'm comin' with you."

"I don't think that's a good idea."

"I think it's the best idea I've had in a long time. I'm not a womanizer, Celina. I'm very selective, and I select you. D'you think you could enjoy me?"

Overcome, she closed her eyes and he reeled her in until her face pressed his chest.

"Well," he prompted. "Could you enjoy gettin' naked with me and spendin' a few hours findin' out just how many things we could teach each other about makin' love?"

She rolled her head from side to side.

"No? Well, how about if I teach you things this time and you can teach me next time?"

"I think you're mad, but you have made a pregnant lady feel desirable. Thank you for that."

"How about you make me feel desirable?"

"You are desirable." She made a fist on either side of her face and grimaced into his shirt, and felt the rumble of laughter in his chest.

"Thank you, ma'am. I think I'd better get you upstairs before I really do somethin' against the law down here."

She moved away, but he promptly caught her hand and spun her into a swing. Aware of the outrageousness of it all, she danced with him, twirled on the uneven stones beneath her feet, giggled when he tugged her close, gasped when he slid a hand beneath her jacket and around her waist. The tips of his fingers were slightly roughened and he played them up and down her spine until she fell against him and held on.

"Everywhere in every way," he murmured into her ear. He ran the end of his tongue into each fold, then nipped the lobe. She gasped. He said, "Upstairs, I think. We've got things to do."

Celina placed a hand flat on his chest and removed his hand from the skin of her back. "You're not yourself. You've probably got a fever. Go home and get some rest. I'll bet if you tell Amelia you don't feel good, she'll tell *you* the next installment of Phillymeana and the Dragon Prince."

"Philomena."

"Yes. Well, she'll tell you. Ask her how things are going with Santa's wicked bear. Isn't there a wicked bear?"

"A mischievous polar bear."

She looked up at him. "Fine. And make sure you check for rude ghosts under your bed."

"I do believe you're laughing at me," he said, grabbing her hand when she would have made a run for the outside staircase. He fell in beside her. "I'm coming up to check for pushy ghosts under your bed."

"I think I'd better check for pushy men *in* my bed. Go home, Jack. We'll talk everything through later."

"Uh, uh, uh, we're goin' to talk now—among other things."

"You can't force . . ." She turned instantly cold and stopped running.

Jack immediately swung her to face him. "Look at me. *Now*."

She did so before she had the wit to do otherwise.

"Do you want to talk to me about that? About force? Did someone force you, Celina?"

"I—no." She would not allow anyone to know her secret. To share that horror would be to court exactly what she must avoid—opening a trail that could lead to Wilson Lamar. "The heat's gotten to you, Jack. Come on up and I'll find us some iced tea."

"Iced tea?" The question was loaded with something other than interest in tea.

"Perfect for moments like this."

"Moments when a lady wants to cool a man's ardor. May I kiss you?"

"No."

"We kiss so well."

"You're right, but the answer is still no."

"Can I tell you what I've been dreamin' about?"

She slanted him a sideways glance. "I'm not sure you wouldn't be breaking a law if you said something like that out here in the fresh air."

"I'll say it anyway. I've been dreaming about kissing you again, and kissing your breasts, and your pretty belly, and your clitoris. I want to kiss you there until you beg me not to stop."

Celina looked around. And she flinched when a burst of raw heat shot from her breasts to bury itself between her legs. He was deliberately taking her apart. She lowered her voice to a hiss and said, "Don't, Jack. You know anything between us would be a mistake. What has gotten into you?"

"You don't like the idea?"

"Iced tea. And you're not to talk like that anymore."

"When you were ready, I'd let you take over the licking. That mouth of yours looks as if I'd like it on—"

"*Don't.* That's not a warning or a request, it's an order. Either drink iced tea and talk like a civilized man, or go away."

His chest rose with the great breath he took. A deep frown drew his dark brows together, and with his inevitable dark beard shadow he resembled an angry pirate. "Iced tea," he said finally, and took her elbow in an excellent imitation of a gentleman.

They reached the foot of the staircase and looked up. And Celina sucked in a sharp breath.

Seventeen

Shaving a thin strip of peel from an apple with a pocket knife, Cyrus sat on the top step. He waved a greeting with the hand that held the knife. "This is an art. Take the whole peel off in one strip. Remember Granddaddy Payne doin' that, Celina?"

She saw amusement in her brother's eyes, and some of the old deviltry that had so often put him on the wrong side of their parents when he'd been a boy.

Ignoring his question, she said, "How long have you been sitting there?"

"Long enough."

Jack chuckled.

"Spying, Cyrus. You were spying on me."

"No such thing, little sister. I was sittin' here—just as large as life, and that's pretty large—when you walked into that courtyard. Is it my fault if you were too preoccupied to look my way?"

"You should have gone inside."

"Why?" His eyes, with their oddly hypnotic mixture of blue and green, crinkled at the corners. Celina was certain the ladies Cyrus ministered to in his little parish west of New Orleans spent more than the occasional moment thinking about those eyes. Cyrus continued. "I've seen people dance before. You look very good together."

"Thank you," Jack said in perfect command of himself. "Your peel broke."

"Oh—fossilized fishooks, so it did."

Celina snorted and Jack tried, unsuccessfully, to hide a grin.

"Cyrus, *fossilized fishooks?*" Celina said.

He had the grace to look abashed. "An altar boy said that when he dropped a salver. I thought it was mighty inventive."

"Don't use it," Celina suggested. "Why are you sitting out here anyway?"

"It's nice. And our esteemed parents are within. They peeled my skin in many pieces, and I think they're preparing to peel yours, sister dear."

"I can't face them now," Celina murmured. She shouldn't have wasted time indulging her fantasies with Jack. He'd think she was the kind of woman who liked sexual advances—which was probably exactly what he wanted to believe. The step to believing she had enticed Errol would be a simple one for him to take. "Jack, we do need a plan. Is it okay if I tell Cyrus what happened with Garth at St. Peter's?"

"Surely."

"Thank you. I need to go and deal with my parents first. I don't seem to do anything that pleases them these days. Would it be all right if I called you later? We could talk on the phone."

"I'd rather talk in person. I'll come on in and get on with some paperwork while you visit. Then we'll get together."

She didn't miss the emphasis he placed on the last sentence, but she wasn't about to argue in front of Cyrus. "Okay. If you're sure that's what you want. Amelia isn't waiting for you?"

"Amelia's my daughter," Jack told Cyrus. "She's five and keeps me in line. Tilly's taking her on the bus to visit her grandmother in Baton Rouge for the weekend, so I'm a bachelor till Sunday night."

Cyrus regarded Jack silently.

"I lost my wife," Jack said. "She died shortly after Amelia Elise was born. Elise was my wife's name. Tilly looks after us."

"God rest your wife's soul," Cyrus said. "And may He bless you. It isn't easy to be a parent alone." He looked from Jack to Celina, stood up, and went to the door. He held it open until the two of them went inside the house.

"Anything else from the police this afternoon?" Jack said when he was in the gloomy hall.

"Nothing since this mornin'," Cyrus said. "I keep expectin' them to be crawlin' all over this place all the time, but it's not happenin', is it? They seem to be takin' their time."

"They told me they were finished with everything but Errol's bedroom and bathroom," Celina said. "They said the integrity of every other area was too compromised, whatever that means. I guess I know what they mean, but I'd still think they could spend more time checking."

"Is that you, Celina?" Bitsy's voice trilled from the direction of Errol's parlor.

"What are they doing there?" Celina asked. "It makes me sad to go into the parlor. Errol loved it once I'd helped him redo everything. He said it made him feel warm, as if the sunshine came inside."

"Oh, that old devil, sunshine," Jack murmured, and Celina heated up yet again. "It uses its magic fingers to do all kinds of things. Have you noticed how a little sun can paint already beautiful things until they're so lovely they almost make your eyes hurt, Cyrus?"

Bringing up the rear, Cyrus said, "The world is beautiful. I'm glad you're a man who appreciates that. My sister is sensuous too. She reminds me of a cat. She almost stretches with pleasure when she's excited by something."

"Does she? I guess I'd expect that." He left them and headed for the study.

Celina looked straight ahead and walked into the parlor she'd decorated in shades of yellow and gold with soft white walls that drew light to them. "Hello, Mama, Daddy. It's great to see you. But what a surprise."

"If you stayed in touch as you should, you'd never be surprised to see us—you'd expect it," Bitsy said. "You'd visit all the time, the way a child ought to. You behaved badly at Wilson and Sally's party. Withdrawn. Difficult. And leaving like that, almost without a word? That Charmain person hinted that there were secrets you weren't sharing. And she hinted at other things that are just too embarrassin', Celina. She's got to be put in her place."

"Mama," Cyrus said, moving from behind Celina and going to his mother. He led her to the couch where his father sat, a large whiskey in hand, and sat her down. "You are overreacting. And you can't expect Celina to spend her life catering to the whims of the Lamars. She owes them nothing as far as I know."

"We're very involved in their campaign, son," Neville said, the faintest slur in his voice. "Your mother's right. We're a family. And families support each other. Celina can be a great help to us in difficult times, and she should want to do that."

Celina couldn't separate herself from the knowledge that although Jack had slipped past her in the dark hallway, he'd almost undoubtedly heard every word. "I do support you and Mama, Daddy," she told him. "But I see no reason why I have to feel a responsibility toward the Lamars. They're more than capable of making sure they get everything they want."

"That's exactly the kind of comment that shows how selfish you are, young lady," Bitsy said. "After all I've done for you, all I've sacrificed for you, you won't do the little things that would make our lives—your father's and mine—easier. We aren't gettin' any younger. We need to feel more sure of our future. For that to happen, we're forced to do things that are abhorrent to people of our social status. We need the money from the auctions, Celina. Surely you're going to make certain we're paid for the last ones we arranged. And what about more auctions? Whether you're the one arranging them or not. Don't tell me children stop wanting their little dreams to come true just because one man gets himself murdered."

Celina covered her eyes and shook her head. "Please think before you speak, Mama. And try to consider someone other than yourself."

"*Celina.*" Bitsy loaded the word with horror. "How can you talk to your poor mother like that? We're in danger of getting into trouble. I loathe mentionin' the word, but I'm talkin' about *money* troubles. That won't help you, my girl. But you can put everything right. You hold the key. Make sure we continue to hold the auctions."

"I'm not sure when or if there'll be more auctions." Celina detested voicing the truth, but covering up was pointless. "We have some people to convince first."

"Talk to her about Wilson," Neville said, upending his glass, and getting up to wend a wavery trail to the decanter for a refill. "He's a good man, Celina, and he thinks the world of you—just as he does of your mother and me. He wants to hire you. And he wants to pay you more money than I thought anyone got paid for these aide jobs."

"Wilson Lamar wants me as an *aide?*" Her stomach turned. "What exactly does that mean?" The last time she'd seen Wilson he'd spoken of her taking over publicity. He wanted her under his control and he didn't care what excuse he dreamed up.

Neville retraced his steps, placing his feet carefully, and gestured with his overfull glass so that it dripped. "As in being his right hand. He's got respect for your mind, girl, real respect. He wants you to travel with him as his aide during the real gearing-up of the campaign. And he wants you there at the house."

"Oh, Celina, it's perfect," Bitsy said. "What were you trained to be but a beautiful, accomplished *impression?* That's what Wilson wants, a beautiful impression to confront everyone who comes his way. You're going to be the gateway to him. You'll decide who comes in and who stays out. We will never want for another penny, I tell you. Oh, I am so excited. Think of all the parties. And then . . . Celina, then there's Washington and . . . oh, it steals my breath away. It could be the White House eventually, couldn't it? And with you at the President's side."

"I'd think it would be the first lady who would be at the President's side," Cyrus remarked mildly. "Or do you have plans about that too."

"I don't like what you seem to be suggestin'," Bitsy said. "I'd have thought a priest would be more careful what he said to his mother. But you've never been careful, and the Church hasn't made you any kinder."

Celina felt tired. She'd noticed that by the afternoon of each day she began to wilt. Her parents were simply intensifying the process. "I know you'd like this to happen, but it won't. I'm going to continue right here and try to help Jack keep Dreams going. Even though it will not be easy."

Whiskey disappeared steadily down Neville's throat. He paused for breath and blinked slowly, pointing a finger at Celina. "You're going to do as you're told this time. From what we're hearin', the sooner you put distance between yourself and anythin' to do with Errol Petrie, the better. The auctions are somethin' different. We can keep on doin' them as long as you make the right arrangements before you leave. Draw somethin' up. A contract. Wilson will look it over and make sure it's legal."

Cyrus came to her side and put an arm around her shoulders. "Celina's tired. This conversation will have to wait."

"We have the most ungrateful children, Neville," Bitsy whined. "Ungrateful and disrespectful. Celina, are there going to be more auctions?"

"I told you I don't know."

"We have to know."

"Well, you can't know for sure until I do."

"It's because of what they're saying about Errol, isn't it?" Bitsy said, chewing a fingernail. "What were you doing living in a house with a man like that? Alone with him?"

"Errol was a fine man. He's been murdered, Mama. How can you malign the dead like this."

Bitsy gestured airily. "Don't give me that righteous act. The man was a sex addict. It's all over town. And to think I was right there in the very bedroom where all that perversion had gone on. Oh, I shudder at the thought." She gave a demonstration.

"An alcoholic," Neville said, closing an eye in an effort to focus his vision. "Living alone with an alcoholic sex-addict. My God, if you've any reputation left, you'd better be grateful. It shows Wilson's high regard for us that he's prepared to overlook all that and take you on."

Cyrus's grip tightened. "Let it go," he murmured to Celina.

"What are you whisperin' about, Cyrus?" Bitsy said. "You don't understand what we've been through because you chose to abandon us and save yourself. By the way, Sally Lamar wants to see you. She's a very kind woman and she's interested in the Church. She'd like you to help her explore her desire to become a Catholic. She's been afraid to go to a church where she doesn't know anyone. But she feels that with just the two of you alone, she'd wouldn't feel embarrassed."

Celina didn't dare look at her brother. His grip tightened even more and he said, "I doubt I'll be here long enough to be of much help to her."

"Oh," Bitsy exclaimed. "Our salvation is within our grasp if only you two would cooperate, but you're too selfish."

Cyrus cleared his throat. "If you need money, all you have to do is ask. I have some savings."

Neville guffawed. "Thanks, son, but payin' the paper boy isn't going to help a whole lot."

"I see," Cyrus said quietly. "You need a great deal of money. How exactly would it help you if Celina and I agreed to whatever the Lamars want?"

The blustering noises Neville made didn't make sense.

"He said he'd take care of us," Bitsy said loudly. "There. Now you have it. The onus is on you. If you and Celina do what Wilson and Sally want you to do, we won't have any money worries and we won't be shamed in front of our friends. And before you ask again why they want you, it's because you're from a fine old family, and having you around impresses people."

Celina put her arm around Cyrus's waist. She felt sick. He must be remembering how Sally had chased him when they'd been in high school. He'd been too kind to turn her down when she invited him to the senior prom, but he'd come home early and would never discuss why.

"You mean Mrs. Lamar wants to *retain* me for some spiritual reason?" Cyrus asked. "And Wilson wants to employ Celina? And if you deliver us both to them, they'll pay you a finder's fee."

"Oh, would you listen to him, Neville? He makes it sound so

tawdry. Some of us have to be pragmatic, my boy. When Neville married me, he adopted you children. How many men would do that? We spent a fortune on you children when you were growing up. Your education. Your sister's education and all the money it cost to support her pageant ambitions."

"Scholarships are wonderful things," Cyrus said. "And—"

"Mama, Daddy," Celina interrupted Cyrus. Another moment and he'd be reminding Bitsy that it had never been Celina's idea that she compete in beauty contests. "I'm going to ask you to try to relax and give me time to deal with what's absolutely pressing now."

"What's absolutely pressin' now is your obligation to your family and our needs," Bitsy said. "Isn't that right, Neville?"

"S'right."

"There, you see? Your father and I are in agreement."

"My first responsibility is to help Jack Charbonnet keep Dreams going while the dust settles. For that to happen, we've got to hope and pray they find out who killed Errol. When those things are straightened out, I'll be able to try to think of a way to help you."

"The house is a terrific expense," Cyrus said. "You don't need anything that large anymore, why not—"

Bitsy sent up a wail. "My house. My beautiful house. My daddy left that house to me, and it's not goin' out of the family as long as I have breath in my body. You have to do as you're told, Celina. And so do you, Cyrus. You ask for a sabbatical and look after your parents. They'll give it to you. You call yourself a Christian, prove it. I told Wilson you'd be speakin' to him tonight, Celina. He's such a good man. He said he'd come over here to see you himself. Now, think of that. A man destined for the White House comin' to see you when he could insist you go to him, but no, he's too considerate."

Wilson wanted to come back alone to try to force her hand. The weakness Celina had hoped never to feel again started to creep into her limbs. "That won't be convenient this evening. I already have plans."

"Cancel them." Her mother's powder-blue designer dress and jacket were too pale and made her features appear harsh. "What could possibly be more important? Haven't I told you how much we're relyin' on you?"

"Yes," Celina said softly. "And haven't I told you what my priorities have to be at the moment? You are standing in a house where an unsolved murder has taken place."

"Don't remind me, please." Bitsy pressed her hands together.

Celina continued. "And Jack and I have to continue the work of the victim. For the sake of his memory, and for the sake of the children he served."

"That's the other thing we have to make clear to you," Bitsy said. "Neville, tell her."

Neville squinted at his wife. "What's that?"

"*Tell* her. About that man."

Neville looked into his glass, found it empty, and started another wobbly journey toward the decanter.

"See how you've upset your father?" Bitsy said. "He's beside himself. Jack Charbonnet. I've told you he's dangerous, and *low* class. He comes from the dregs, Celina. The fact that he's got a lot of money that doesn't belong to him only makes it worse. Dirty money. It's money his father took for illegal activities. And he runs a gamblin' boat, for goodness' sake. I shouldn't think Errol Petrie's death would be much of a puzzle with connections to a man like that."

"Hush, Celina," Cyrus warned as he must have sensed her rising fury. "A lack of understanding is a sad thing."

"Don't you sermonize around me, son," Bitsy informed him. "I know what I'm talkin' about. That man's father was found dead at a big house he and his wife had no right to own. I went to the library and read it all up. He offended the hand that fed him. You ought to understand that, Cyrus. They nailed him to the wall and mutilated him, but they didn't let him die until they'd finished with his wife. They found her in the pool. *Naked.* Can you imagine that. Naked and on one of those air pillows. She was no better than she ought to be. She was related to those awful people somehow. And she was pregnant at the time when they killed her."

Celina felt her legs sag.

"Those people don't do things like that to their own unless they're *really* awful. And that Jack is their son. There, now do you see why you are not to have another thing to do with him?"

"Poor Jack," Celina murmured. "Oh, poor, poor Jack."

"Speak up," Bitsy ordered.

"Afternoon all," Jack said, entering the room and planting himself at Celina's other side. He looked at Cyrus over her head. "Thanks for being here for Celina."

Bitsy stared, open-mouthed, as if she were afraid Jack would produce a submachine gun from some invisible violin case.

"How are you, Mrs. Payne?" Jack said. "At least we meet again under slightly less tense circumstances. Did I hear you expressing regret over my having lost both of my parents when I was ten years old? My parents and my unborn brother."

Something seemed to break inside Celina. A sob rose in her throat. She turned to Jack and he studied her upturned face. "I'm sorry," he said. "I shouldn't have said that, not now. Self-indulgent." He put his arms around her and held her against him.

"You unhand her," Neville said, rising unsteadily to his feet and pointing with a finger that couldn't locate its target. He closed one eye again, then the other, and sat back down. "Take your hands off my daughter."

"I know how you feel, Mr. Payne," Jack said in an unbelievably reasonable voice. "I've got a daughter myself, and I'm very protective of her. But you don't have to worry. I'm going to take very good care of Celina."

She held her breath, knowing what he intended to say, and why. Marshaling her courage and strength, she rose to tiptoe, put her mouth to his ear, and whispered, "God help both of us," before turning to her parents and saying, "Jack and I are getting married."

Eighteen

An irreverent thought brought a grin to Jack's face. He doubted either Celina or Cyrus would appreciate his sharing the notion that they couldn't be related to Bitsy and Neville, that they must both have been mixed up in the hospital nursery after birth, and that somewhere there were two families with an impossibly shallow offspring they frequently wished they could drown.

Bitsy and Neville Payne had left minutes earlier, but still no one had said a word. Bitsy Payne had expressed horror at the prospect of having a "gangster's" son as a relative. Neville Payne had issued bombastic orders that Celina not dare to proceed with such an outrageous idea, and that she return to the bosom of her loving family at once.

"I apologize for my parents," Cyrus said, and Jack saw Celina jump. Seated on the couch, she had been deep in thought. Cyrus continued. "They are ill equipped to deal with life. They both came from wealthy families, and they still think like spoiled people whom the world will always accommodate. Not having the money to keep up the lifestyle they expect has made them childish in their efforts to make others—primarily Celina and myself—responsible for supplying their needs. I should mention that Neville married our mother when she was a young widow with two children. He was good to us. He isn't all bad."

The formal apology made Jack uncomfortable. He gave a short laugh. "Show me a so-called functional family, fully functional, and I'll show you people who are afraid to confront the truth. We're all just trying to survive and find some peace."

"You sound like a cynical man," Cyrus said.

"Not at all. I'm a realistic man."

Cyrus raised one dark brow and nodded. He spoke to Celina. "They didn't get to it today, although I think you headed them off with your news, but accordin' to our parents, word has it that you and Errol were more than workin' acquaintances. That was one of the *terrible* suggestions the lady reporter made at the Lamars'."

Jack gave Celina enough time to answer. When she didn't, he said, "They were. They were friends. A man and a woman can be friends, can't they, Father?"

Cyrus's stare wasn't as open as usual. "Just Cyrus, Jack. I believe some men and some women can be friends. Others can't. I didn't know Errol well."

"And since you've heard about the problems he used to have, you doubt he'd make a great platonic buddy?" He kept returning his attention to Celina. Even though more than an hour had passed since she made it, her announcement to her family—and to him—continued to amaze him. "Celina was goin' to talk to you about what happened at St. Peter's when we went to ask Garth Fletcher to endorse Errol. I might as well do the honors. He refused. Said people were already starting to wonder if their children had been molested by Errol."

"Sick." Cyrus looked tired. In an open-necked white shirt and jeans, he also looked very unpriestlike. "It's as if we're suspended in the middle of something horrifying. Like bein' in the eye of a storm. D'you feel that?"

"I do," Celina said. In her scarlet suit she was an exotic creature on the yellow couch. "And nothing is real. Since the original pieces in the paper right after the murder, there's been almost no mention, except for the horrible thing Charmain wrote. I don't understand her. You'd think that in a city like this there would be enough stories to make her move on from this one by now."

One small woman—one small, pregnant woman—would change his life, Jack thought. Nothing would ever be the same, and that would primarily be because of Celina Payne.

And the idea held some appeal.

The idea held a lot of appeal.

"I think that's what I'm sensing," Cyrus said. "It's all unreal. Murder is unreal anyway, of course, but this happened—right here—and apart from a gossip columnist who seems interested in anything but who killed Errol, nothing's being done about it. That's surely the way it seems to me."

"And to me," Jack said. "There's plenty of talk. That was obvious when Celina and I spoke with Fletcher at the hospital. But officially? Nothing. I called O'Leary this morning. I call him every morning, and I drop by. He gives me the blank-wall treatment. They're looking for leads and don't have any. But Dwayne says he'd know if questions were being asked in the Quarter. He hasn't heard a thing."

Celina had curled herself up at one end of the couch. With a burst of motion she swung her feet to the floor and stood up. "It's all wrong and it's all frightening," she said. "The silence is as if there are people waiting everywhere. Watching us. But we can't see them." She looked at the windows and took a step backward. "Some of the time we're even behaving as if nothing happened. It isn't as if the motive could have been theft. Something really sick went on in this house."

"I'm sure the police are at work on the problem," Cyrus said. "We have only the TV interpretation of the way they go about these things. They've got a lot of cases they're working on at the same time."

"Errol was loved by so many people," Celina told him. "Could someone with a lot of influence *stop* a real investigation?"

Jack met her eyes and said, "They could."

The possibility had already occurred to her, but she'd tried not to believe it possible. "It's all wrong that the city isn't demanding more action."

"I know." Cyrus appeared oblivious to the depth of his sister's tension. "We'll have to be patient though. Our parents aren't going to make life any easier either. I think they truly expected us to jump instantly and do what the Lamars want. Not that I have any idea why those people are so anxious—well, I can see why Wilson would see you as an asset, Celina, but for Sally to decide I'm the only candidate to become her spiritual adviser doesn't make sense."

Celina chafed her upper arms. "You were always an innocent," she said. "Sally Lamar hasn't stopped wanting you. End of story."

Cyrus appeared more amused than shocked. "She's a married woman. I think you're seeing plots everywhere. Why didn't you tell me you were carryin' Jack's child?"

The man might be naive about what would or would not stop a woman like Sally Lamar from going after a man she wanted, but he didn't pull any punches. Jack studied Celina's face, and she lowered her eyes.

"And why hadn't you told him about the baby by the time I got here?" Cyrus continued. "You were beside yourself when you called me. You said you were pregnant, and when I asked who the father was, you said you couldn't tell me and the most important thing was that he never find out. What happened between then and now? What changed your mind?"

What changed your mind, Celina? Jack knew he would give a great deal to know why she'd suddenly made her declaration. And he could hardly wait to hear what excuse she intended to give Cyrus.

She had kicked off her shoes. Barefoot, she appeared even smaller, and if you knew what you were looking for, there was evidence that she was going to have a child. He swallowed. Even though he feared it, he wanted to know the truth about the father's identity. He also wanted Celina. That probably made him a reckless fool, especially at a time when it was too late to step back from what he'd already set in motion elsewhere. Those responsible for his parents' death were going to be punished. They were going to suffer almost as much as his innocent mother had. Would he step back from that now if he could? He didn't think so.

"If I'm causing you too much pain, say so," Cyrus told his sister. "But it isn't good to live with lies, and I think you are. Jack isn't the baby's father, is he?"

Celina looked at Jack, question in her eyes.

"This is your card to play," he told her.

"Okay. I didn't say my baby was Jack's. I said we were going to be married."

"To give the baby a father? If there's no love between you, the child will suffer more than ever."

So said the priest. There were times when finesse was essential. "Celina and I are both real fond of children, Cyrus."

"Jack's right," Celina said. Her blue eyes were too bright, the patches of color in her cheeks too bright.

"Oh, Celina," Cyrus murmured. "You don't have to tell me who really is the father, but I shall pray for all of you. And I'll pray that whatever makes you want to deny your child's real father will heal."

"It will *never* heal!"

In the shocked stillness that followed, Jack dropped his hands to his sides and flexed his fingers. The desire to go to Celina and hold her was overwhelming, but she wouldn't be grateful.

"You're angry," Cyrus said gently. "Not the kind of anger that comes from sadness. I know that anger too well. Were you violated?"

Jack stared at the other man.

Cyrus pressed his palms together and tapped his fingertips against his mouth. He watched his sister with deeply troubled eyes.

And Celina bowed her head. She didn't speak, didn't move, except to slowly bow her head.

"I see." Cyrus closed his eyes, and Jack saw his lips move as he appeared to pray silently.

When Celina raised her face, tears glinted on her cheeks. She cried with wide-open eyes and without making a sound.

And Jack felt yet again the urge to take another man—this one faceless—by the throat. His rage made its presence known too often, and could not be allowed to surface. Even if he choked on his fury, he must not show its depth. "Celina and her baby will be safe with me," he said, hardly recognizing his own voice. "I know I don't need to say it, but I have to. Please don't disclose anything we've discussed among us."

"No," Cyrus said simply. "Perhaps I should leave."

"You don't mean leave New Orleans?" Something near panic surfaced in Celina's expression. "I need you. We need you."

"To perform a marriage, if nothing else," Jack said, trying to grasp for something light.

"I didn't mean I intend to leave New Orleans," Cyrus said as if Jack hadn't said anything. "I meant leave this house. Just to go and visit our parents. And to give the two of you a chance to talk through the decisions you're making. I've never been a husband or a father— I never will be—but I've listened to so many who are and I've learned from them. That's what I'm charged to do. To learn from those I am to counsel. Then we help each other. I hope that's what happens. When you're ready to talk to me about what you decide to do—if you decide—I'll be there for you. I wouldn't, of course, ask you to lie for me, but I'd prefer it if only the three of us knew that I have, in fact, already taken an indefinite leave of absence from my parish."

"Cyrus—"

"Hush," he told Celina. "You are my sister and you mean a very great deal to me." He dropped a kiss on her brow, nodded at Jack, and walked out.

Jack waited only long enough for the outer door to click before scrubbing his face and asking, "Who, Celina? Why didn't you turn the bastard in?"

She shook her head.

A chill raised the hair at the back of his neck. "Not Errol?"

"How could you say that? How could you?" She flew at him, stopping with her fists raised. She let them fall impotently against his chest. "You have defended him every bit as strongly as I have. Now you ask me if he raped me?"

"You told me he was your baby's father."

"I—" Narrowing her eyes, she gripped his forearms. "You and I are going to be locked together in whatever comes, Jack. And I'm not talking about marriage. You don't have to marry me. I would never hold you to a thing like that, and I'm sorry I blurted it out in front of my parents, but I thought you were going to ask me again. Right then, while they were here."

"I was."

"Cyrus is very wise. Maybe we shouldn't—"

"Cyrus is a good man. He's doing what he has to do—trying to make us change our minds if they can be changed. I'm not changing mine."

"Because my pregnancy shows? And you know the questions will begin soon, and even if I don't say anything, there are those who will decide Errol and I were lovers?"

"That used to be the reason."

Her gaze flickered away and back again. "Errol was gentle. You know that. He would never have forced himself on me." She frowned. "Is that what you're worrying about, that I'll accuse Errol of rape?"

"No. Even asking if he did it was reflex on my part. He never forced himself on women—he wouldn't know how to be physically violent. There was never anything like that."

"I think he came close to rushing out and getting violent when I told him," she said, sounding distracted. "He was so angry."

His mind grew still. "You told Errol who assaulted you?"

Celina hesitated an instant too long before saying, "No. I only meant he was really angry."

Jack decided he wouldn't delve any deeper now.

"I don't know if you understand this, but I have never felt more safe than I did with Errol," Celina told him.

She was right, he didn't understand. "I'm glad. If you felt so safe, why did you refuse to marry him as soon as he asked you?"

"I wasn't—" She turned her back on him.

Jack waited, then said, "You weren't what?"

"Errol was a father figure to me."

In other words . . . "Are you payin' me a compliment, ma'am? Accidentally, of course?" He should know better than to press the issue of what she did or didn't feel for him, especially now. "Forget I asked that. It isn't important."

"It is. Very. But we've got too much to work our way through. Once Cyrus has spent some time with my parents, I'll talk to him and decide how to deal with them."

"You'll tell them you will have nothing to do with Wilson Lamar. *Nothing*."

The slow way she blinked suggested his comment surprised her.

"I'd like to take you back to my place. We can be on our own there and no one will interrupt. I don't want to wait, Celina. There's no reason to wait. We can be married in a couple of days."

The slow blinking continued.

"I didn't put that well. We should make some plans and we don't have a lot of time. The sooner we get the marriage out of the way, the better."

She smiled.

"You know what I mean," Jack told her. "We won't pretend the baby was still a twinkle in your eye on our wedding day, but if we move quickly, some people will forget that it wasn't."

"An old-fashioned man," Celina said wryly. "I'm surprised, but I think I like it. Why so adamant about Wilson? I didn't even realize you knew him."

He had to be careful. "I don't know him well."

"But you were going to the fund-raiser. I'd forgotten that."

"I decided to go only because you'd told me you'd be there." It was partly true. He had gone because of Celina, but he hadn't been invited.

"Should I take *that* as a compliment?"

"It was a compliment. I don't like it that Lamar thinks he can issue orders to you. I don't like it, and I don't understand it. But I don't necessarily have to on either count. I'm going to make it impossible for him to ask anything of you without running head-on into me."

Celina regarded him speculatively. "You have some sort of history with Wilson, don't you?"

He wasn't ready to share every facet of his life's history with her. "It's nothing that need concern you. Just some philosophical differences of opinion." Like whether a man was or was not responsible for his gambling debts, and whether that man should be extended special privileges because he regarded himself as a public figure rather than an overambitious lawyer.

After slightly too long a pause, Celina said, "Okay. I don't think it's a great idea for me to come to your place right now, Jack."

He gauged how best to handle her without coming on too strong. "I'm not comfortable leaving you here alone."

"Cyrus will be back."

"Either you come with me or I stay until he does come back."

"That's ridiculous. Nothing's going to happen to me. And I've got to see if I can find out why Antoine didn't show up for work today. He tried to talk to me. It was when those awful Reeds came. Earlier. But he left without saying anything, and I haven't seen him since."

"*Damn*," Jack said. "*Damn, damn, damn.* I've been so preoccupied. Dwayne told me Antoine went to him in disguise and—"

"Antoine in *disguise*? What are you talking about? And he wouldn't go to Les Chats."

"His disguise consisted of a Stetson pulled over his eyes. And he did go to Les Chats. Dwayne said the same thing as you, that Antoine's the kind of man who thinks his soul's in jeopardy if he goes near what he regards as sin, but he did go there."

"Why? What did he say?"

The hair on the back of Jack's neck prickled. "I shouldn't have set this aside. Antoine told Dwayne he saw something early in the morning after Errol was killed. I don't know what because Antoine got spooked and left."

"He went to Dwayne." Celina was speaking to herself. "He likes Dwayne. He seems comfortable with him. He's nervous about places like Les Chats, but that goes for a lot of people, and it wouldn't necessarily stop him from going to ask Dwayne's advice about something, I guess."

"You're right. It didn't. Not until he behaved like he thought someone was watchin' him and scooted outta there."

"But what could he have seen here? If he saw something, he'd have told the police, wouldn't he?"

Jack shrugged. "I have no way of knowin', Celina. But he surely has taken off. Can we contact his home?"

"They don't have a telephone."

"Go there, then?"

"I'd have to find an address. Errol always dealt with Antoine. He paid him and told him what his duties were. Everything like that was between the two of them. I think Antoine had been with him a long time."

"Well, we can't just pretend he was never here—or wait and hope he shows up someday."

The bell outside the door from the courtyard rang. A heavy, green-coated brass piece you rang with a chain, its clanger bonged inside an elongated casing.

"I'll go," Jack said when Celina started for the hallway. "Please see if you can find Antoine's records among Errol's files."

He hurried to open the door at the top of the courtyard steps. A tall woman stood there. Tall, with a strongly boned face and large eyes that were so dark as to seem black, and with no pupils. Her hair was a tightly curly black cap and her skin was the color of chocolate without milk. Perhaps forty, her inexpensive blue floral dress, although shapeless, didn't hide a voluptuously statuesque body that she carried with grace. She held a large brown purse.

"Good afternoon," Jack said, although evening was almost upon them. "How can I help you?"

"Good afternoon." Her voice was a surprise. Light, and Jack thought he heard something of New York. "I'm Antoine's wife. I've come to see Celina Payne. Is she in, please?" The woman was also agitated but trying not to let it show.

Jack smiled at her and put out a hand. "Jack Charbonnet. I like your husband a great deal, Mrs.—"

"Thank you." She made no attempt to fill in the name Jack now realized he'd never known. "I'm Rose." She glanced around, and Jack knew without her saying another word that she wanted to get inside where she couldn't be seen by anyone who came into the courtyard.

He obliged, ushering her into the hallway and waving her ahead of him. "Celina's in. We were just tryin' to figure out how to contact Antoine. Apparently you don't have a phone."

"No phone," she said. "Why'd you want to contact him?"

They went into the study where Celina was going through a file cabinet. She turned and smiled, and Jack said, "This is Rose, Antoine's wife."

"Oh," Celina said. "Coincidence. I was looking for his records. Is he okay, Rose? He wanted to talk to me the other day and I had visitors so I wanted him to wait until we could speak alone. Then he must have had to leave, and I haven't seen him since."

The woman fidgeted with her purse. She stood very straight and was almost as tall as Jack.

"Is Antoine sick, Rose?"

"I come to talk with you, Miss Payne. Antoine says you're okay."

"Thank you." Celina glanced to Jack and back at Rose. "Please sit down."

"I like standing."

Celina closed the file drawer. "You aren't from Louisiana?"

"New York. Brooklyn."

An awkward pause settled in.

"You didn't say if Antoine's sick," Jack said.

"I come to speak with Miss Payne." There was more anxiety than stubbornness in Rose's attitude. "Alone."

Rose—who said she preferred to be called just that—didn't relax when she was left alone with Celina. Rather she became more tense, looking over her shoulder frequently, her eyes sliding away and narrowing as she obviously listened for something.

"We're alone, Rose," Celina said, feeling edgy herself. "Jack has gone to his apartment. He won't be back for an hour or so." The thought of her being alone here didn't have any more appeal to Celina than it had evidently had to Jack.

Rose put herself where she could see both Celina and the door. "You got to say you don't tell nobody about me talkin' to you. Nobody. You understand?"

"Yes."

"That man. That Jack. Who is he? Antoine don't talk about him."

"Jack Charbonnet was a friend of Errol Petrie's for many years." She considered for a moment before saying, "Jack is a good man," and feeling strange afterward. Only weeks ago she would not have imagined paying Jack's character a compliment.

"No one but you. That's the way it's got to be," Rose said. When she closed her mouth, she pressed her lips tightly together, but not before they trembled.

Celina felt an increasing premonition that bad times were going to get worse and that Rose was the herald of very bad times.

"You got to tell me you won't tell that man what I come to say." Still alternating her attention between the door and Celina, Rose fiddled with a button at the neck of her dress. Her hands were long-fingered, the knuckles large. A worker's hands.

"Won't you sit down, Rose?" Celina asked. "Let me get you some iced tea?"

"I need to get home. Tell me you won't tell no one what I come to say?"

"What is it?" The premonition began to point toward danger. "Just talk to me, Rose. Antoine sent you, didn't he? I wish I'd stopped everything and talked to him when he wanted me to. What's wrong?"

"You got to tell me you don't say nothing to anyone. Not to *anyone.*"

"Jack is my friend. He's my boss now, and Antoine's boss. Surely—"

"No! Not him. Not anyone. Otherwise . . . You tell me you don't say nothin' to him? Please?"

What could it hurt? And it meant so much to this woman. "I will, as long as you tell me why it's so important."

Rose held the purse higher and went to the window. She peered down into the street. "I was told only you. He said if I couldn't get you to understand, it wouldn't matter anymore." To Celina's horror, Rose began to shake steadily. "You understand? You don't give me your word, they punish us."

"Rose, it'll be all right." The other woman's reserve was something Celina felt. Touching her, even in an attempt to comfort, was out of the question. "I promise I won't mention a word of what you say to anyone. Tell him he's got my word." If it was this important to Antoine for her to keep his confidence, she'd do it.

"Thank you." Rose extended an arm and hitched up a short sleeve. "They bad people who got him. The man who come to me did this. Just so I remember he's not making fun, that's what he said."

High on the inside of Rose's arm two circular red wounds sent a shudder racing up Celina's spine. "What man? I thought— A burn? This man burned you with a cigarette?"

Rose nodded. "He said next time he do other stuff. He said next time maybe he decide he rather have some fun with our boys." She swallowed loudly. "He ain't no good, that man. He's a sick man, a bully. But I tell you, I'm scared. Antoine always told me he liked you and he trusted you. I got no other person to trust."

"It's goin' to be all right, Rose. Trust me, please. First we need to put something on your arm."

Pulling down the sleeve, Rose shook her head. "I can tend myself. If you be a friend to Antoine and me, that's all I ask. Silence. That's what the man said you gotta give. A promise you don't never say nothing."

Celina said, "I promise I won't," but felt confused. "Someone's got Antoine? They're keeping him?"

"They doing that."

"What am I supposed to keep secret, Rose?"

"Whatever Antoine told you."

With an even stronger sensation of unreality, Celina said, "Antoine didn't tell me anything. He didn't have time." She remembered what Jack had said. "And he didn't tell Dwayne either. He went to Dwayne to talk about seeing someone here the morning after Errol died, but he didn't finish. So he didn't tell anyone."

Rose opened her mouth and pressed her flattened fingers over it. A strangled sound came in bursts. "They think he could have though," she said indistinctly. "And they want to be sure no one tells no one else. I got to be able to say you won't."

"I won't. But we need to go to the police and—"

"No!" Rose fell to her knees and bent over, her back heaving. "No. Please, Miss Payne, don't you go doing that, or Antoine won't ever come home to me."

Celina's heart beat so hard she backed to sit with a thud on the nearest chair. "I can't believe any of this. You're sure someone has Antoine?"

Rose rolled her head from side to side. "He gone. Since he left for work yesterday, I don't see him. Then this man come and push into the place. Praise be he come when the boys at school, but I'm so scared."

"The police—"

"You tell the police, Antoine dies. Maybe our boys be molested. And me." Rose extended a hand, pleading. "Please, please, believe me. He said all I gotta do is make sure you understand that if they hear anyone's comin' their way, they'll make sure there's no one left who can point the finger at them."

"I don't even know who *they* are."

"But Antoine do," Rose moaned. "And they don't believe he ain't told no one."

"It's okay." It wasn't and probably never would be again. "I won't say anything. Tell them you got my word and you believe me."

"Thank you."

"He's coming back, this man?" A fresh wave of horror engulfed Celina. "He said he was coming back anyway?"

"He's coming."

"But— You've seen him. Rose, think about it. You've seen this man, so he must be watching and waiting right this very minute. He isn't going to let you go to the authorities to report what happened and give a description of him, and he can't be sure you won't."

"He got a thing over his head, a stocking. He inside my place, waiting for me to come home. He don't look like nothin' human. I been looking for Antoine." Hopelessness drew its lines on Rose's face.

"I walk everywhere. Looking. I stood outside this place this mornin', waiting. For hours. I don't see him. Then I go home and when I shut the door, the man's there with a stocking over his face, and a hat on. I don't mind telling you, I screamed and screamed. He hit me, and I stopped. Then he tell me what I got to do. Make sure you understand you ain't to say nothing. He burned me so I show you. He say if he gotta do other stuff to me and my boys, he might have to do stuff to you, too."

Desperation all but overwhelmed Celina. How could she help Rose if she couldn't tell anyone what was going on? "So you're going home to wait for this sadistic pervert to come and *do other stuff* to you and your boys if he feels like it? And you absolutely believe that if you can tell him I've given my word not to mention Antoine to anyone, he won't hurt you? How can you believe that?"

"It's all I got," Rose said, her voice falling low. "He say I gotta tell you if you don't do like he says, he can get to you, just like he got to Antoine."

Celina wanted Jack. And she didn't care if it was bizarre to want him so desperately when she'd thought of him as the enemy such a short time ago.

The light was waning outside. She wanted to close the drapes but dreaded going near the windows. At that thought she almost smiled. Already she was catching Jack's hang-ups.

"I'm sorry, Miss Payne," Rose said. She climbed laboriously to her feet, a strikingly handsome woman with the most tired face Celina recalled seeing—ever. "I don't want to bring no trouble on you. I say to the man that I gotta have proof or I ain't coming to you. So he give me proof."

Rose fumbled to open her shabby bag.

"I don't need any proof," Celina said. "I believe you. We've got to have some sort of plan. We've got to get Antoine back."

"The man said Antoine will come home when they decide the time's right. If I make sure no one says nothing they don't want them to say. Oh, Miss Payne, if I lose my Antoine, I'm not sure I can live no more."

"Don't talk like that. You aren't going to lose him."

Rose took out a crumpled brown sack and dropped her bag on the floor. She opened the sack and pulled out a wad of cloth that had once been white but was now filthy and bloodstained.

Celina couldn't stop herself from exclaiming and drawing back.

While she straightened the ruined fabric, Rose cried openly. What emerged was a ruined T-shirt, mostly soaked in blood, but with the words THE TRUTH WILL SET YOU FREE still visible on the front.

"Antoine's," Celina whispered. "He was wearing it the last time I saw him."

Rose hiccuped and nodded her head. "Me, too. That man give me this, too, just in case I don't believe him." She unwound a scrap of tissue and held it toward Celina.

Resting there was part of a front tooth with a gold rim.

Nineteen

Ben had moved into a room next to the one Sally shared with Wilson. It made her nervous, his proximity. His arrogant treatment of her only grew more overt. He behaved as if she were absolutely no threat to him. He ought to be cautious around her and the fact that he wasn't had to mean there was something she didn't know.

Tonight Sally intended to find out exactly what she didn't know about Ben.

Every morning he came strolling into Sally and Wilson's bedroom and Wilson actually asked her to go into the bathroom and "start makin' herself pretty" while he talked to his new bodyguard about the plans for the day. And Ben never as much as looked in her direction, even when she climbed half-naked from the bed.

She would find out what that was all about too. So much for the wonderful surprises he'd promised her back on that first delicious morning when all he'd been angling for was a permanent job on the household staff. He hadn't touched her since.

On the night of that same day, at the last fund-raiser, Wilson had singled Ben out and appointed him his almost constant sidekick. Sally had begun to wonder if Wilson's tastes ran in directions she'd never guessed at. There was no doubt that Ben had a cute ass.

Sally was looking at that ass now. Once more the house was filled with Wilson's adoring followers, including Neville Payne, who had surprised them by arriving without Bitsy and with some excuse that she wasn't feeling well. Wilson had barely hidden his anger when Neville told him that Celina would not be coming. Cyrus has been invited too but hadn't arrived. So far this evening wasn't going at all as Sally had planned.

But it was time to do something about Ben.

She waited until Wilson was deep in conversation with the president of one of the most prestigious banks in the South, then walked nonchalantly close to Ben, who looked so irresistible in evening dress.

She put a hand on his shoulder and said, "Evenin', sugar," in a voice meant only for him. "I'm really wounded that you haven't found the time to thank me for your wonderful new job yet."

He glanced sideways at her with those marvelous smoldering eyes of his and said, "Thank you for helping me be in the right place at the right time."

"Think nothing of it, lover. Don't I remember you talkin' about some *surprises* you had in mind for me. Didn't you tell me I was goin' to have to be on my toes because I was never goin' to know when you'd decide to give me one of those surprises?"

His blank stare angered her.

"Well, Ben, you may think you don't need me anymore, but you're wrong. I'm goin' for a walk in the gardens. I anticipate bein' in the old pergola in about five minutes. In case you don't know where that is—it's out back of the house. On the other side of the greenhouses. No one goes there anymore. If you want to keep your wonderful new job, you'll meet me there."

Sally walked quickly away, smiling and nodding to the guests she passed. Holding her head high and swinging her hips in the short, stretchy, black-sequin-covered halter dress she wore, she left the house by an open door at the end of the passageway that bordered the kitchens.

Excitement mounted with every step, and confidence. She would teach him to respect her. Her backless high-heeled sandals slowed her down, so she took them off and carried them in one hand. And she hurried, because she wanted to have time to collect herself before Ben got to the pergola.

This wasn't the first time Sally had received gentlemen callers in the pergola that dated back to her grandmother's time. The thought made her smile and remember some pleasurable interludes.

She arrived at the birdcage-shaped iron structure, opened the door that squealed on its ancient hinges, and went inside. Clematis vines completely covered the wrought iron bars that curved to a point overhead. A circular stone bench with a hole in the middle was the only inner adornment. Huge white blooms on the vines loaded the air with a heavy night fragrance.

Sally went to the far side of the pergola. She put on her sandals again, faced the door, and reached to grip bars behind her head. Even from this distance she could hear the strains of the Dixieland band playing in the house, and she swayed from side to side with her eyes partly closed. Anticipation was half the fun, so they said. Well, she wouldn't put it quite that high, but she did enjoy feeling her body get ready for a man.

The door whined open.

She leaned her head against the bars and watched Ben come in. In the almost complete darkness his eyes glittered, and his teeth shone very white. His high cheekbones gleamed paler than the rest of his face. He looked frightening. Almost satanic.

Sally wriggled a little with delicious apprehension. "Hello, Ben."

"What is it?" he said. "What do you need to say that couldn't be said in the house."

She was older, wiser, and a whole lot tougher than he was. "Sit down, Ben. We need to talk."

Rather than do as she told him, he pushed his hands in his pockets and sauntered around the pergola.

"You don't get it, do you?" she said. "You're here because of me, because I showed an interest in you that first day. You think that gave you the upper hand. But all I have to do is talk to Wilson, and you're out."

Ben picked a clematis blossom and held it to his nose.

Sally's skin prickled. He was too sure of himself. "What is it about you?" She was surprised she'd asked the question aloud.

He crossed his arms, held the flower against his mouth, and regarded her with inscrutable calm.

"You arrogant little bastard," she said through her teeth. "If you think you're bulletproof, you are so wrong. My husband is a jealous man, Ben. What's his is most definitely his. If I tell him you took advantage of me, you are in big trouble, honey."

The flower's petals took a twirl on Ben's chin.

She gathered her composure and sauntered toward him, snapping her fingers as she went. "I've got it. You used me. Hah! Who would have thought it? You planned the whole thing. You intended to get close to me so you could figure out a way into a fat job with my husband. Oh, you couldn't have expected that kid to try to rob us. That was an unexpected bonus. It speeded up the process. But that's it, isn't it?"

"Is that all you wanted to tell me?" he asked when she paused to take a breath. "If it is, I'd better get back. Mr. Lamar might need me."

Tears of rage smarted in Sally's eyes. Her jaw trembled with fury. "You have met your match, *Angel*. I see it all now. You're afraid to touch me again because you don't want to jeopardize your wonderful, cozy position with Wilson. Guess what, lover? You need to get a lot smarter before you try playing in the big leagues. If you don't do what I tell you to do, when I tell you to do it, *I'll* make sure you go back where you came from, and I don't mean you'll get the consolation prize. No one in this town would touch you once I finished with you—they wouldn't touch you or your aquariums. I will destroy you—not that you're anything but a pretty face and an efficient body anyway."

"Thank you for sharin' that with me, Mrs. Lamar. Would you like me to escort you back to the house?"

"I'd like to take you apart piece by piece. You want me. I can feel how much you want me. I can smell it. But you're too scared to take me. You must have been terrified you wouldn't pull it off that morning when I took you upstairs. But you held yourself together until you could do what you wanted to do and get out safely. You decided you'd try to frighten me, to make me think you could call the shots. And you wanted sex with me so you could have something on me, but you sure as hell didn't want to get caught."

"Oh, dear lady," he said softly. "Your mind is certainly goin' in little circles. Could it be you drank too much? Mr. Lamar will never forgive me if I don't make sure you get home safely."

She seethed. Sweat broke out on her back. "If there's one thing I don't have to put up with, it's a fuck-and-run artist." Half expecting him to push her away, Sally reached for his bow tie. "You can run, honey, but I'm getting one for the road. And if you expect to last around here, I'll get it again and again."

Ben didn't stop her from wrenching his tie undone and pulling the studs on his shirt free. He did push the bruised blossom nonchalantly inside her dress. He kept his hand inside and kneaded a breast until she fought to tear his shirt aside, panting in her hurry, angling her pelvis toward him.

"Mrs. Lamar," he said, the tone of his voice unbelievably even, "you really should try to control yourself, you."

He plucked at her nipple, rolled it, freed her breast from the dress she'd imagined him taking off her.

"Oh, Ben, Ben," she said, "you have a kinky sense of humor, but I could come to love it. Don't stop. Oh, don't you stop."

"You're not yourself."

"I am very much myself. And myself is getting better every second. Help me get your clothes off. I want to see your body shine in the dark."

She didn't have to guess if he wanted what she wanted. He was hard enough to make holes in concrete. Sally pressed her thighs together and dipped, reveled in what she felt while she got his pants undone.

He removed his hand from her breast.

"I told you not to stop," she said, gasping and looking up at him. He pushed out the tip of his tongue, pulled it in again, and grinned. "You are teasin' me, you beast."

Laughing, she released him and struggled out of the halter top of her dress until she was nude to the waist. Hands on hips, she backed away, turned sideways, always looking at him while she posed, knowing the moonlight shone on her breasts.

It also shone on Ben's strongly muscled chest, and on a beautiful promise that rose from a thick mat of pubic hair. His pants clung at the level of his massive thighs. He stared, and that thrilled her, but he didn't make a move toward her.

"I do believe we're going to hold a little lady's-choice." Giggling breathlessly, Sally inched her abbreviated skirt upward until it joined her bodice and revealed the tiny black G-string she wore.

Ben beckoned with a single finger. He held his tongue between his teeth now and ate her with his eyes.

"Yes," she told him. "Oh, yes."

He wasn't passive anymore. With one arm he swept her up and planted her on the bench. With the other he held her to him while he buried his face in her breasts. He took as much of her as he could suck into his mouth. It hurt, but she liked it that way.

She ripped the G-string away herself, and gasped when he turned his face up to hers. He was every bit as beautiful as she'd ever thought he was. Another powerful move and he had her legs wrapped around his waist while he took her to the only paradise she cared to visit. How could one man have so much? Every part of her ached and clenched. He stretched her, and she loved it.

With a great burst of motion, he made her come. He did it, and did it carrying her while he rammed her up and down. And he didn't come out of her when he was finally still. Waves kept right on blasting all those good places.

"Careful," he said. "Hold on to something, please." And he backed against the bars.

Sally giggled and bumped up and down until she felt him growing hard again. Ben let her go and she squealed, clinging to her handholds on the bars. When he raised his hands again, he held two fresh blossoms. He licked each one slowly, smiling at her all the while. Then he crowned each of her nipples with his damp tributes that stuck to her skin, and she closed her eyes.

A snick sounded, and something sent light across her closed eyelids.

"What was that?" she said, opening her eyes and twisting around.

"Oh, no," Ben said. "Stop it. You, get away, you."

A camera strobe flashed again, and Sally screamed.

Twenty

Celina had never felt more aware of being alone with a man than she did now, here in Jack's home, and with the knowledge that he knew she was there because she'd wanted to be with him.

He'd shown surprise when he'd opened the door to her, but then she'd been almost certain he was pleased she'd come. But people often saw what they wanted to see.

As on her two previous visits, he settled her in his study, but the phone in the hall had rung before anything could be said, and he was talking to someone. She felt more gratified than she should that he'd made no attempt to find privacy for his conversation, but she soon realized he was talking to Tilly about Amelia. Why would he want privacy for that?

"Put her on," he told Tilly after a series of exchanges, then he said, "hi, squirt. You havin' a good time with your grandmother?"

Celina eased out of the chair and went to study photos on Jack's desk. They were all of Amelia—at various ages—apart from one of a very young woman who was so like Amelia that she was obviously the child's mother.

"I have told you not to go up there, young lady," Jack said. "No. And I am not amused that you're makin' a scene like this in front of your grandmother. She looks forward to seeing you, and it isn't kind to make up stories to try to get home the minute you get there."

He'd raised a little girl who, understandably, adored her daddy and didn't want to be with anyone else. He was also responsible for her storytelling penchant.

Looking into the older version of Amelia's face made Celina deeply sad. How could someone with so much decide to leave it all behind?

"Amelia Elise Charbonnet, there are no witches in this house—no, no, right, no witches across the street, then. And no ghosts with binoculars either. Sweetheart, I have told you to stay out of the attic. You could fall and hurt yourself up there."

Celina glanced at the windows. It was dark outside, but the moon iced grillwork on galleries overhanging sidewalks across the street. She moved closer.

"You haven't seen the people who live there because they're very old." Jack sounded less patient. "Two old ladies who never go out. No they aren't witches, Amelia. And that's enough. What? No, you don't turn into a ghost when you get real old, and their food must be delivered. Now— You imagined little red lights, squirt. That's *it*, Amelia. Now be kind to Tilly and your grandmother. I love you. Good night."

It took Jack several more firm instructions before he could finally hang up.

Celina parted the curtains and stared at the windows opposite. They were all dark. "I couldn't help overhearing," she said when he returned to the room. She nodded at the buildings they faced. "They do look closed up, don't they? I expect Amelia's been practicing the skills she's inherited from you."

"Why don't you come and—"

"Sit down?" she finished for him. "And stay away from the windows, maybe?"

"I didn't say that, you did." He sounded aggrieved.

"So I did. I have absolutely no right to intrude upon you, and I'm not going to dream up an excuse. You get the truth. Cyrus has decided to try to please our parents by going to the Lamars' party, and I didn't want to stay in Royal Street on my own. I left a note to say I'd be here with you and asked him to call when he gets back."

"I wanted you here with me."

She smiled nervously. "Thank you." Since Rose left, there hadn't been a moment's respite from the struggle to decide what to do about the information she'd been given, the evidence of bestiality she'd been shown.

"Antoine's wife was a surprise."

Celina was startled. She said, "She wasn't what I'd expected."

"What's the excuse for Antoine's absence? Is he ill? Did she say anything about his visit to Dwayne—or about what he thinks he saw?"

She could tell him, ask him what she ought to do. "I'm still not sure about why he wasn't at work today." Her mouth was dry. Rose had been so adamant that Celina not tell anyone anything.

"The woman was edgy. I thought maybe she was afraid of something."

"I don't think she liked coming to me. She . . . she didn't say anything much."

Celina saw the instant when Jack lost interest in Rose. He said, "Are you hungry?"

"I've eaten. And I've had juice and milk. And I took some vitamins."

"You need prenatal vitamins."

He made her smile again. "You aren't my daddy, Jack."

"Thank God, *chère*. I am your future husband, your soon-to-be husband. And I'm going to be that child's father." He indicated her stomach. "That's part of the deal. I'm not takin' it on lightly. But I am in a hurry. I have to think of Amelia. She needs to be made part of the whole baby sibling thing, and I don't want it sprung on her a couple of weeks before you give birth."

"You are so matter-of-fact."

"What . . . sorry. I've been organizing my own life for a long time."

Celina shivered a little without knowing why. She crossed her arms. "You were going to ask me what I expect other than a no-nonsense approach to this. And you're right. I'm going to keep on being direct, Jack. If you're sure about this marriage, then I'm sure. Part of me keeps whispering that I want you because you'll give me and the baby safety. And that's true. But I can be good for you too."

His sudden wicked grin confused her. "I know you can be good for me, *chère*," he told her. "I know we can be good for each other— and with each other."

Men were unbelievable. "You aren't talking about sex again. You can't be."

He shrugged and appeared the slightest bit abashed. "I might be. Indirectly, of course. But it was accidental, honestly."

"Of course it was." To hide her smile, she turned back to the window. She shouldn't be having a moment's rest or cheerfulness when she knew Antoine was being held prisoner by some depraved creatures and Rose was beside herself with worry over her husband. The bloody shirt had been terrible, but the tooth had reduced Celina to trembling horror.

"Would you like to see the rest of the place?" Jack asked.

Rose had made her promise not to tell anyone what she now knew. Talking to Jack about it would be such a relief. Surely she should ask someone for help.

"Celina? Can I show you around? I think it'll work out just fine. There's plenty of room, and with Tilly's quarters upstairs, I don't see any problems."

If she broke her word to Rose and something happened to her, and Antoine . . . and their boys . . . She couldn't say anything, not yet. Maybe Cyrus was the one to talk to. He was accustomed to keeping confidences.

She didn't know Jack had come up behind her until he touched her back and turned her to face him.

"Do you want to share what's on your mind?" he asked.

This was the time to tell him. "No. Except that everything is so strange. If we go ahead with this, it'll be a modern-day marriage of convenience, won't it?"

"Not entirely. Not anymore. And we are going ahead with it. I asked you. You've accepted. By sometime next week you'll be my wife. I expect you'll want to keep your own name."

"Moving right along?" Somehow she didn't feel like laughing. "Would you prefer that I keep my own name?"

He raised his brows. "Isn't that back to front? Aren't you supposed to ask me if I'd prefer you to take my name, then politely suggest you're a thoroughly modern woman who would never consider such a thing?"

No more games. "I think Charbonnet is a lovely name. If you feel comfortable, I'd like to take it. And I'll expect to sign a prenuptial agreement. It shouldn't be hard to get it drawn up. I have no right to anything of yours. You're already giving me a great deal."

"I'm getting a great deal," he said, silencing her entirely. "But I appreciate your being sensitive to sensitive issues."

She would speak to Cyrus. Perhaps she should return there now, just in case he'd got home and hadn't seen the note.

"Celina?"

"Yes," she said sharply. "Yes, Jack. Thank you. Whatever you say."

He became quiet and the lamp on his desk picked up the gold flecks in his eyes. No man she'd ever known could look quite as serious as Jack when he was serious.

"Well, if we've covered everything, I should get home."

"This is going to be your home. And you're waiting for Cyrus to call, remember?"

"I was. I've already intruded long enough."

"Not nearly long enough. Tilly and Amelia are gone until tomorrow."

"And you must be looking forward to a little peace. We all need that from time to time."

"I hated that discussion we just had."

For an instant she wasn't sure what he meant. She watched his face and suddenly knew exactly what he'd been talking about. "It's necessary for us to cover these things sensibly. I understand that."

Jack bowed and tapped the end of her nose with a forefinger. "It's not necessary to be cold about something that should be warm. I'm attracted to you. If I weren't, I would be worried about what we're going to do. I'm not worried."

She considered only a moment before saying, "I'm not worried either." This should all feel outrageous. Perhaps it did, but she wasn't backing away.

"Would you stay here with me tonight, Celina? Please?"

He asked her a question, a particularly personal question—just like that?

"I want us to be very comfortable together. This weekend will be the only opportunity we have to get a little used to each other before you move in permanently."

Dithery. A simple question from a mature man to a mature woman, and that woman's response was to feel like a dithery kid. "Perhaps we should put it off until Amelia's had more time to get used to the idea."

"If things were different, I'd agree."

"If things were different, we wouldn't be doing this."

He put his hands in his pockets. "I'm not so sure we wouldn't eventually have been doing something together, Celina."

She had known her share of uncomfortable reactions, but Jack's ability to make her throb beneath the skin ranked at the top of the intensity scale.

"Surely, adversity threw us together," he persisted. "Now. But I couldn't have remained blind to what you really are forever."

"You don't know what I really am. That kind of thing takes time."

"I'm terminatin' this discussion. We are movin' on. The front door is locked. There's just you and me, *chère*. What do you say? Shall we see how we are together?"

Celina cast about. She needed to sit down, to think, to regroup.

"I am too cold," he told her. "I am an ass. Tell me I'm an ass and you wouldn't stay with me if I were the last man on earth. *Shall we see how we are together? I'm sorry.*"

His frown revealed the vulnerability he usually hid completely. His frown and the worried set of his features, the way he ducked his head to study her face.

"I'm not sorry, Jack. I'll leave a message for Cyrus so he'll know I'm not coming back tonight."

Once Jack Charbonnet hadn't known a moment's uncertainty with a woman. He didn't feel uncertain now, did he? Strange, because the situation was strange, maybe, but not uncertain.

He felt uncertain.

In a quaint, old-world way, the two-floor apartment delighted Celina. She'd dutifully allowed Jack to show her around—more quickly than she would have preferred tonight—before ushering her into his bedroom. Two small rooms separated the master bedroom from Amelia's little-girl-feminine domain. Celina had acknowledged to herself that she'd calculated the layout of the rooms because she worried about sleeping with Jack and having his small daughter very near. The rooms between relieved her.

Sleeping with Jack.

They'd kissed. Danced in a courtyard in the sun. Held each other a couple of times. He'd "talked dirty," to shock her—she smiled at that, while she observed how he drew heavy bronze-colored draperies over the windows. Their shared experience was almost nothing, yet he'd coolly asked her to spend the night, and she'd coolly accepted. Not coolly, but she had accepted.

Jack faced her across the bed and thought that the colors in his room might have been chosen for her. Against the browns, beiges, and dull golds her skin took on a bloom, and the red in her hair became more obvious.

"I haven't been sleeping too well, Celina."

"It's hard," she told him. "We've been through so much."

"I wasn't talking about what happened to Errol. I've spent plenty of time thinking about him, but you've been the one on my mind at night."

Her eyes were the kind that held a person's soul. And if they were hiding a whole lot, he'd be surprised. She was full of hope, hope that they'd pull off a miracle and form a great relationship from the bones of a disaster. She wanted him to care about her, not just for her. And she wanted to care for him. He was sure those were the hopes he saw in her eyes. She'd give this thing her best shot.

And he was turning into a romantic fool at the age of thirty-seven, when any man ought to know better.

Romantic? Or had he deprived himself of a woman for long enough to make him mistake hormones for emotions. Dangerous stuff.

He looked away.

"I'm afraid to hope for anything," she told him quietly. "I'm afraid we're making a horrible mistake. I— From the first time I met you I've felt something. That thing you feel when— You took my breath away." She laughed, and he returned his eyes to hers. "This should be taped and given to women in danger of making fools of themselves over men. It would save them."

"If it was taped and given to men who thought they didn't need or want someone in their lives, it would change their minds." He was stepping in too deep to climb out, but, hell, he was a big boy. If this was a giant error, he'd survive.

Celina felt light-headed. Not the kind of light-headed she'd come to dread, but the kind she'd only read about. He didn't have to say these things. "We won't be the first couple to decide to make a marriage work, Jack. We've both got good reasons, the best reasons." She refused to examine all her own too deeply. A pregnant woman was known to be susceptible to her emotions, and hers were trying to lead her around.

"I don't have anything to wear to bed." An instant flush suffused her entire body. She blushed entirely too easily these days. "Perhaps I could borrow something?"

The brilliant twinkle in his eyes only intensified the heat she felt. He spread his arms and said, "What's mine is yours. Anythin' that appeals, just appropriate it, *chère*. I don't expect anythin', you know. Just your company, to hold you, and feel you. I've become a very lonely man and I didn't know it until I suddenly knew I was going to have you."

Either he was the most talented seducer in the world, or he was saying the only things she needed to hear to feel she could be in love with him and like it. "You're being very kind to me," she said, plucking at braided piping on the quilt. "We both know you don't have to be lonely for one second unless you want to be."

"A warm and willing body doesn't guarantee you aren't lonely," he said, and he blessed the words that came to his aid so easily tonight. The right words, or so he thought from the gently accepting expression on Celina's face. He would have to be very careful with her. She was so damn fragile. "Would you feel more comfortable if I slept on the couch?"

She glanced at the couch in question. Books and magazines covered one end. Dull marks on the table in front of it were evidence that he'd spent hours reading there with his feet propped on the wood.

"A reading man," she commented. "You already told me that. I wouldn't hear of you disturbin' your books. I can tell you know exactly where every one of them is."

He chuckled. "I surely do."

They had fenced long enough. She went to the open bathroom door and looked inside. The brown marble was probably original. It was rich. Towels the color of chocolate were heaped on a low rattan cabinet.

"There's a new toothbrush in the top drawer on the left," he said behind her. "Do you want a T-shirt, or one of my regular shirts?"

"I don't like being restricted when . . . anything."

"I'll pull out some things for you to choose from."

He could have made a crack about what would offer the least restriction in bed. She admired his sense of the appropriate.

Appropriate? Her life was the most inappropriate life imaginable, yet she was dissecting this man's behavior?

"Would you like to take a warm shower? It might relax you."

"I showered before I left Royal Street."

"Well, I'll put out the shirts. I should check some things out before I come to bed."

Come to bed.

The simplest comments took on intense significance when you were about to . . . She wasn't an innocent kid anymore. "You mean you think you should go away and give me a discreet amount of time to get ready for bed. It's not necessary."

Deliberately avoiding eye contact, she turned back to the bedroom, where he was tossing shirts on the bed. "That's enough, thank you. Anything will do. Just throw me one."

He shouldn't feel so triumphant that she didn't intend to procrastinate. He shouldn't feel so damnably turned on either, should he? She'd

been right when she said this was a convenience thing. "Will a long
T-shirt work? It's huge, which should mean it'll be comfortable."

"Great. The bigger the better under the circumstances."

She laughed.

Jack didn't.

As she'd suggested, he threw the shirt to her and she caught it
one-handed.

Celina Payne put that T-shirt on the end of the couch and com-
menced to strip. She kicked off her brown sandals, stripped off her
baggy white gauze pants, took her loose white top off over her head.

She obviously had no intention of looking at him while she executed
her brave performance, and he identified it as brave. This woman
might have been Miss Louisiana—and that was no surprise right
now—but he was increasingly certain she was shy in some ways.

And some bastard raped her.

He took a deep breath and forced away the images he'd started
having, images that made him sweat with rage.

Her belly was more than gently rounded, her legs very long and
perfectly shaped. She folded her pants and put them on the couch
cushion that wasn't covered with books. Then she folded the matching
top and added it. The sandals she placed precisely beside each other.

Jack came close to commenting that he hadn't noted her being
particularly tidy in her own bedroom.

Standing before him in only her white bra and panties, she caused
the kind of erection that wasn't going away without some satisfaction.
His question about red hair was answered. He could see the triangle
clearly through thin nylon. "You are the stuff of wet dreams," he said,
and looked at the ceiling. "I'm losing it. That was unforgivable."

Her laugh made him smile. She said, "I don't think either of us
has rehearsed this particular scene too many times. Some of the lines
are coming too smoothly."

"Thank you," he told her. "For bailing me out."

Her smile disappeared. "I thought I might—I thought this might
be hard after what happened to me. So far, so good." She reached
behind her to undo her bra and take it off.

"I would never force you, Celina—do anything—or hurt you."

She nodded.

Jack couldn't look away from her breasts. Large, undoubtedly
larger than usual, they were round, the big, honey-colored nipples
just a little uptilted. A faint tracing of blue veins traversed very pale
skin.

He unbuttoned and took off his own shirt. And he didn't decide to approach her, he just did. Approached and framed her face, turned it up to his. "Are you still okay?" he asked her quietly. "I don't ever want to do something to frighten you—or put you off."

"I'm okay, Jack. Very okay."

Restraining the fierceness that would have made him wild, he kissed Celina. With his tongue he eased her mouth open, then tasted the moist flesh inside.

She kissed him back, stood on tiptoe, slipped her arms around his neck, and kissed him as if she needed the kind of meal he had in mind.

Still he held himself back. The time to let go would come, but not tonight.

Her breasts pressed his chest. He felt each nipple, hard and more erotic than anything he ever remembered. His breath started to come in shorter bursts. He moved his hands from her waist, upward between their bodies until he could spread his first fingers and thumbs on the undersides of her breasts. Not enough. He pushed them upward.

Celina gasped, and he remembered. "Tender, still? I'm sorry."

"No," she murmured. "It's so great. I didn't think . . ."

He pulled his head back and looked down into her face. "You didn't think pregnant women were supposed to be interested in sex. Yeah, you already said somethin' like that. And I told you this was the way it would be. At least, I think you may not mind."

She looked down at his hands on her breasts. Tanned skin on white flesh that never saw the sun. He would have to control himself if he was going to last. Very carefully he plucked at her aroused nipples, and she moaned.

"Did you want to clean your teeth?" he asked, fighting for a shred of composure. "I don't want you to think I'm a complete animal."

Her eyes were glazed. Slowly they cleared. "Come with me," she whispered. "I want you with me." She surprised him by taking his hand and tugging him into the bathroom with every sign of not caring that she was all but naked in front of him.

Jack found her a toothbrush and took it from its package.

And all the time she touched him, his shoulder, his chest, a nipple, his jaw, his mouth. He was dying a great death, but dying nevertheless. And loving it.

He let her go on touching him and put toothpaste on her brush before handing it to her. She turned to the sink and turned on the water, and looked at him in the mirror when she bent over.

Her panties were cut high and showed off a firm bottom that punched the wind out of him yet again. Jack's attention went back to her breasts. They were incredible.

"Hold them," she said.

A liquid sensation hardened the muscles in his thighs. He was hard everywhere that mattered, everywhere that had nerves he particularly valued.

"Jack?"

Praying for self-control, he traced her spine vertebra by vertebra, stroked her sides, tucked his fingers under her bottom, and ran his thumbs down the cleft while her muscles tensed and she jerked upright.

"Sorry," he said, not sorry at all. When she bent to brush her teeth some more, he put his arms under hers and obeyed her command to hold her breasts. "Such a sacrifice," he managed to mutter. "Oh, *chère,* I must have been waitin' for you."

With her mouth full of toothpaste, she couldn't answer him, but she grazed her bottom back and forth over his distended penis. He squeezed her breasts in automatic reaction, and she strained to rub him harder.

"Finish the teeth," he said through his own. "They're as clean as they need to be."

She rinsed her mouth, still bumping and enticing him with her sweet derriere.

Jack took a hand from her breasts, rested it on her belly for a second, then slipped inside her panties to find the wet, distended spot buried in springy little red curls. He stroked her clitoris softly, insistently, and smiled—with his teeth still gritted—when she let out a keening sound and locked her elbows to gain some stability.

He kissed her back and kept on stimulating her. Her breasts swayed against his hand, and her pelvis moved rhythmically, making sure his fingers didn't err. He dipped into the slick essence inside her, and continued his task—his pleasure, and hers.

"I'm . . . Jack, I can't say what I am. Or what I want. Ah! Don't stop. Please don't stop."

"Oh, I'm not stoppin', darlin'. Give yourself to me. Just let me take you where you want to go."

"I'm going. Yes, yes, I'm going!"

"Coming." He smiled against her smooth back. "Come, sweet thing. Come to me."

The intensity of what he made her feel ripped through Celina. He slid his fingers inside her repeatedly, making the entry a prelude to stoking the fire that hovered ready to explode.

His penis pressed against her bottom. She wanted her panties off. Holding on to the counter with one hand, she worked them down but couldn't get them off entirely.

She climaxed. She squeezed her eyes shut and pressed her head back against his shoulder. And she shuddered, and abandoned herself to voluptuous wanting.

They had only just begun this night.

Celina turned in his arms and brushed her breasts slowly from side to side on his chest. The grazing of his hair on her nipples was an exquisite torture. Her tentativeness when she went to touch his crotch surprised her, but she quelled any remaining fragment of hesitation and slipped both her hands under him. His scrotum was drawn up, tight and hard and heavy. Squeezing, she watched his face. He nodded, and Celina squeezed him again. She was overwhelmed with the need to give him as much pleasure as he'd given her.

Her fingers dealt with his pants as if she undid men's clothes every day. She didn't even fumble. Sliding around to test the hardness of his buttocks was irresistible. She found the intensity of his stare, the repeated flexing of muscles in his jaw, a total turn-on.

There was danger in that stare, the most irresistible danger. "Okay," she told him. "You're impatient. I can take a hint. Your turn, Jack." She pushed him away enough to allow her to kneel, and she tugged his pants down far enough to let him spring free. He made a sound she thought was a protest, but she shut it out and took him deep into her mouth.

Lust. She lusted for him. It sang in her ears and pulsed in her veins, this lust for a man, something she'd never guessed herself capable of experiencing.

"Celina, I'm goin' nuts, chère. Oh, God, you're drivin' me mad. Oh . . . oh, yes."

She clung to him when he would have bucked her off with his pelvis, and swallowed, and couldn't believe she was this kind of woman—without inhibitions—with this man.

He could have fallen to the floor so easily. She'd sucked him dry while she revved him up at the same time. There had never been anything like this for him. He couldn't even summon another experience of any kind at this moment.

"Now, lovely lady," he said when he could speak. "Now we have played enough. You will allow me to decide on the rest of our entertainment, yes?" He heard his own tendency to summon up more of his French roots when he was close to losing all control. And he was close in the best possible way.

"Jack," she said, her face turned up to him.

He bent to kiss her, and used the advantage of her upraised hands to capture and sweep her into his arms.

"I'm heavy," she protested.

"You weigh nothing." Not that he'd notice if she did. "I'm going to settle for lamplight."

"Lamplight?"

"You probably didn't notice there's no sun at the moment."

He kicked aside his trousers and shoes and carried her, pushing against him and making sounds of protest, into the corridor outside his bedroom.

"Jack! We're naked. What if someone comes?"

"They'd have to break down the door. I'd hear them. Or they could fly up to the gallery. I don't believe in flying people."

"Where are we going?"

"To find a table."

"Oh, Jack. Oh, no."

"Oh, yes," he said, pushing open the kitchen door with a shoulder. "Tell me, oh, yes, Jack."

"I'm not myself."

"I surely hope you are very much yourself. I like yourself exactly as it is."

"I'm a pregnant woman."

"Uh-huh. I think we should keep you that way permanently. It's sooo sexy. You're so sexy."

"Isn't it bad for the baby?"

"No, it's not bad for the baby. Forget the tales, and concentrate on what I say to you. Sex does not harm an unborn baby. And this baby needs to get the picture that he's going to have a mama and daddy who love each other, and love him."

"Her."

"Him or her. It will probably be one or the other. Do you like the tablecloth, chère?"

She peered around. "Very nice if you like a lot of flowers."

"I'm going to pretend I'm taking you in a green field among lots of little white daisies. First I have to spread you out for an examination."

Celina squealed. He was amazing. There was nothing about him in this mood that remotely resembled the austere man she'd known. "I don't want to be spread out, thank you."

He deposited her on top of the table. "Need a pillow?"

She waggled her head, no. "I guess I'm just a wanton and I never knew it. Isn't that the word, wanton?"

"Lovely word." He bent over her and proceeded to kiss her to silence. He kissed her silly and she loved losing her mind. Holding her head, he gave those kisses his all, and his all was really something. No man had ever chewed her lips with a gentle persistence that pulled on her insides until her breasts ached and the place between her legs started to throb without any help at all. He nibbled and sucked, and lifted his head enough to look into her eyes, then kissed the place between her eyes before standing up.

She made to get off the table, but he stopped her, and how he stopped her. Taking her nipples into his fingers again and pulling repeatedly, made sure she wasn't going anywhere. He pulled, and when she flopped back on the hard surface he bowed over her to suck in first one, then the other nipple. And he pulled her bottom to the edge of the table. She felt him between her thighs, felt him touching her with parts of himself that undid her completely.

Torn apart by his every touch, she drew up her knees. They fell helplessly apart. "I want you inside me," she managed to tell him. "It's too much, Jack."

"Really?" he murmured, his mouth full. "Don't quite believe you yet."

Soft brushing over her sensitive genitals brought her back off the table. "Jack! Oh, you can't do that. Oh, Jack, no."

"No?" What he did with the tip of his penis was designed to make sure she begged for a whole lot more.

Her head dropped back and she thrust out her breasts. "You are drivin' me to distraction, Jack Charbonnet. I can't believe I'm lettin' you do this to me. You are an evil tease."

His laughter was deep and rumbly. "I thought you'd love it. Say the word and I'll stop."

"Don't stop." Not that she thought he would anyway. His mouth fastened on one of her breasts again. The gentle stimulation, over and over again, drove her wild, made her thrash. She brought her knees together, but missed what he was doing at once and parted them again.

Jack said, "I hope this old table is as solid as it's supposed to be."

He moved her fully onto the table again and vaulted to straddle her hips. Parts of him rested on her belly, and she took hold of them without particular finesse.

He winced, and closed his eyes, and promptly went to work with his little brushing strokes on other parts of her body.

Celina grabbed his wrist and held on. "Okay, okay. You have phenomenal control. Guess what? Tonight I've discovered I don't."

His control was pretty fantastic, Jack decided. That was the last really clear thought he did have. She pushed his bursting penis to the entrance into her body, swung her very limber legs up until she could lock her ankles behind his back, and pushed him all the way home. Almost before he could start to move, she worked her hips back and forth, and a sob came from her throat. The sob jarred with each impact of their bodies, with each thrust.

She managed to grasp his balls, and he yelled.

Her response was to squeeze.

His response was to go for it like a mini-jackhammer out of control. So much for control.

"Jack," she panted, and squeezed again.

"*Chère*," was the only word he could form, and it was a hoarse whisper. "Do that. Do it."

She milked him, and he drove into her until his open eyes saw nothing but shifting shapes, her swollen, moist lips, her sweat-wet hair, her sweat-slicked skin, her jiggling breasts.

Celina had to release her hold on him. She clung to the sides of the table and raised her hips to receive each stroke. She was sore, but it was the kind of sore she'd like to suffer regularly.

"Jack! I'm coming. Jack, you've got to—"

"I am, *chère*, I am." His voice broke. He spilled his warm flood of the stuff of life into her, flooded her, and still he moved and kept on moving until she cried out and threw her hands above her head, gave herself up to Jack and what she was with him.

Gradually in the moments that followed, their breathing slowed a fraction, and sweat cooled on their bodies. Gently, Jack pushed her until he could lie with her. Wrapping her in his arms, he rotated until she rested on top of him, her face in the crook of his neck, her chest on his, her sticky stomach on his, her legs on his.

"We should go to bed," she told him, although she nestled as close as she could.

He mumbled nothing coherent.

"You'll wish you hadn't spent time on this table soon," she warned him.

Jack chuckled and found her breasts once more.

Celina struggled to push him away. "Don't, you beast. I'm sensitive all over."

"Good. Because I'm never going to wish I wasn't on this table with you. I'm just resting between courses."

Twenty-one

"Promise me, Cyrus," his mother said, clutching his arm as he helped her out of the cab. "Promise me you won't mention a thing about Celina and that man."

He paid off the cabdriver. "I will not bring the issue up."

"What will you say when they ask where she is?"

"The truth. I don't know where she is."

"Say she's at that place. At Errol Petrie's place. Say she's upset and not feelin' well. She wants to be alone. Promise me you will."

Cyrus smiled at her, longing to be far away, and detesting whatever weakness made him want to flee the constant upheaval that surrounded his parents.

"*Cyrus*. Say it."

"Look at me," he told her. She glared up at him and he said, "I am at the Lamar house because you begged me to come, to bring you. I have promised you I won't say a word when people start asking why you were too ill to come earlier, but you're fine to be here now. I—"

"I *was* too ill. My children have made me ill. You refuse to understand the sacrifices your daddy and I have made for you. But I know my duty, and my duty is to be at my husband's side while he tries to make the best of what few resources we have left to us."

"Yes." The brief flurry of fight left Cyrus. "Let's go in. You probably shouldn't stay too long when you've been so upset." He said a silent prayer that he'd be forgiven for his hypocrisy.

His mother held his arm tightly and clipped up the Lamars' tree-lined driveway in her high-heeled Ferragamo pumps. Bitsy Payne had always worn Ferragamo pumps because her feet were "so small and narrow, nothin' else would possibly fit."

"It's late," he said when they reached the open front doors and he saw and heard people who had already partied too long. "I'm not sure this is a good idea." He knew it wasn't a good idea, but he was a man of peace and intended to get some. Since he'd arrived at his parents' home to discover his mother alone, Cyrus had listened to her wailing against the evils of ungrateful children. Her tearful suggestion that he should take her to the Lamars' had sickened him, but he'd given in—in the name of peace.

"Smile," his mother said. "Go on, *smile*. Why do you have to wear the collar when you aren't working?"

At that, the smile she'd wanted came readily. "God's work is never done, especially in this kind of place."

She stopped on the black and white tiles in the Lamars' elaborately decorated, crowded foyer. "This kind of place?" she echoed in a hissing whisper. "What can you mean?"

"I don't mean anything. How does a lawyer keep up his practice while he runs for political office? These campaigns are so long. And how does he afford all this? The house was Sally's mother's."

Mama sighed hugely, smiled at a woman who passed with a glass in her hand, then sighed again. "Money came with the house, Cyrus. And Wilson is a very successful lawyer. That's all we need to know. I'm sure there are ways of doing these things. After all, most politicians are lawyers, and they do very well from both things, don't they?"

"Bitsy!" Sally Lamar forced her way through the throng. "You're here! Oh, how lovely. Oh, Bitsy, I am so glad to see you." All the time she spoke to his mother, she looked at Cyrus.

Drunk, he thought. So drunk she hardly knew what she said, and he hoped she didn't know how disheveled she appeared.

"And Cyrus," she whooped, winking at him. "The dark horse."

Wilson appeared at his wife's side and put an arm around her waist. "We heard you weren't well, Bitsy," he said. He nodded at Cyrus, said, "Where's Celina?"

Cyrus resented the man's curt, demanding attitude.

"Celina's upset," Bitsy said. "She's at that awful place in Royal Street and won't come out for anything. I just had a little headache, but dear Cyrus looked after me and it went away."

Sally pointed at him and wriggled inside a black dress that gaped to give a display of her breasts that made Cyrus uncomfortable. "Did you put a bad spirit out of Bitsy, Father?" she asked, and assumed an almost innocent expression. "My, perhaps you aren't in that little parish Bitsy talks about after all. Perhaps you're really hiding out somewhere right here. In the Quarter? Practicin' voodoo?" She hiccuped and leaned heavily on Wilson.

Wilson snapped his fingers at a good-looking, dark-haired man who came smoothly forward and put a hand beneath Sally's elbow.

"Let me go!" She jerked away and launched herself at Cyrus. "Thank you for coming. I knew you would help me."

He had to catch her, and steady her.

She gazed up into his face with eyes that weren't quite focused. "Thank you, Cyrus," she said, her mouth trembling. "I need you."

"We all need spiritual help sometimes," his mother said, loudly enough to make sure the curious who were still sober enough to care would hear. "When Cyrus heard you were troubled—"

"Sally is so concerned about the inequities we live with," Wilson said rapidly, also in a raised voice. "I'm afraid society's ills weigh very heavily on her. That's why I suggested she might like to talk to you." He propelled his wife toward a closed door, indicating that he wanted Cyrus to follow.

"Do it," Bitsy said. "Go and help them, Cyrus."

The dark-haired man was already a few steps behind Wilson. "Who is that?" Cyrus asked.

"Who?" Bitsy frowned. "Oh, him. The bodyguard, of course. It's very dangerous being a public figure. Wilson needs protection."

Wilson was, and always had been a man who looked after his own wants and needs, and he was a man of vast appetites. Cyrus remembered him from school, and not with fondness.

"Are you coming?" Wilson called from the door that now stood open to a sitting room.

Cyrus saw his stepfather shambling toward them, his heavy face florid and sullen. He bumped into another male guest, scowled, and pushed the man hard enough to all but knock him down. Neville Payne was usually a pleasant enough drunk, but there were times when the wrong brand of scotch, or just a combination of the right scotch and a bad humor, made him vicious. In his childhood years Cyrus had worn more than a few bruises that had to be hidden.

"Cyrus?" Wilson's tone had turned irritable.

"Coming," Cyrus said, and hurried after Wilson and Sally into a room furnished with comfortable but shabby antiques. Wilson's bodyguard was also there. He stood behind a green brocade couch with his arms crossed. Too young to have such old eyes, Cyrus decided.

Wilson closed the door. "Sit down, Sally," he said brusquely, and hustled her to a chair. "And keep your mouth shut if you can. Glad you came, Cyrus. How's Celina? What did your mama mean when she said Celina's upset?"

"Celina," Sally said, sniffling and wiping the back of a hand vaguely over her nose. "He thinks she can do him *so* much good. He thinks she's perfect."

"Shut *up*," Wilson told her. "Ben, get Mrs. Lamar another drink."

"Don't you come near me," she told the other man. "I only want Cyrus." She began to cry brokenly.

"Oh, my God," Wilson moaned, rolling up his eyes. The man looked tired, but otherwise he was his old, smoothly tanned, blond and handsome self. And he oozed self-assurance. "Get her a drink, I said."

Trying not to look at her chest, Cyrus studied Sally's hunched figure. The dress appeared to have stretched—or he assumed it must have. "Leave Sally to me," he said, suddenly certain that he ought to help her. "With all due respect, Wilson, she doesn't need anything else to drink. I understand you're interested in pursuing a return to the Church, Sally? My parents told me that was the case."

She fell back in the chair and nodded. "That's what I want. And I couldn't talk to a stranger." She glowered at Wilson. "I've got so much I need to get out of my heart, Father."

"This is fucking unbelievable," Wilson said, his finely chiseled nostrils flared. "I need a strong woman at my side, a strong partner, and my fucking wife falls apart."

"Wilson," Cyrus said automatically. "I don't think—"

"Yeah, yeah. Sorry about that. I'll say a thousand Hail Mary's when I've got a minute to spare. I'd appreciate it if you could calm her down and talk some sense into her. I've got to get back to my guests. There are important people here tonight, people I need."

"People with a lot of money?" Cyrus said, deliberately making his voice and face expressionless.

"Holy . . ." Wilson closed his mouth. Then he smiled. "We're both pimps in our own way, huh, Cyrus. I pimp for the good of the country. You pimp for the Church. Not so different, really."

The bodyguard laughed.

Cyrus didn't, but neither did he argue.

Wilson opened the door to leave and said, "Make sure she doesn't give the priest too much trouble, Ben."

Sally moaned, and Cyrus said, "I don't need any help here, thank you. These things are between the penitent and God. I'm his physical body. We don't have audiences on such occasions."

"Ben stays," Wilson said.

"Ben goes," Cyrus told him. "Sally is troubled and needs someone to listen to what's on her mind. I'm good at those things."

"From what she told me after the famous prom, that's about all you are good at," Wilson commented. He jerked his head, indicating that Ben should leave the room, then went out and slammed the door.

"Do you remember the prom?" Sally said. She tried to kick off her sandals but couldn't coordinate the effort. "I took off all my clothes and you wouldn't look. I thought you were a nancy boy, but you were just a man of God. Who'd have thought that?" Her eyes almost closed, but she forced them open again. "I should have known you were the best thing I'd ever be that close to, then maybe I'd have done the right things to make you want me."

"Are you comfortable, Sally? Would you like to lie down on the couch? You might fall asleep, and I think that would be good."

"And you'd go away." She cried afresh.

"I wouldn't go away. I'd sit right in this room until you woke up." She had been a sweet kid when she was real young. It wasn't until she got in with Wilson and his clique in high school that she changed.

She got unsteadily to her feet and managed to step out of the sandals. "I shouldn't have done that to you," she said, wandering to the couch and sitting with a thud. She slid sideways to lie with her head on a large cushion. When she wrapped her arm beneath the cushion, her right breast was naked. The abbreviated skirt of her dress had risen to the tops of her thighs, where ruined black stockings ended in lace tops.

Cyrus felt stirrings he tried to feel as infrequently as possible. He'd fought against his own sexual urges for a long time and could pass a number of weeks, and sometimes months, without discomfort now. But tonight he was confronted with a lovely woman's body and his erection was both an embarrassment and a potential disaster.

"Will you be my thingie?" Sally mumbled. "You know, who I tell everythin' to?"

"Your spiritual director," he told her, fixing his gaze on the middle distance. "Are you sure you shouldn't go to a church nearby and attend classes first?"

"No. I won't go. I won't do anything if you don't help me. I don't trust anyone else."

When had he got so lucky? "Why me, Sally? You and I haven't been anything to each other—not ever, really. You never did understand me because you thought I was different."

"You *are* different. You're lovely. Holy. Untouched. You're what I need. I can talk to you. I'm askin' you to save me, Cyrus. If you don't, I'm afraid I'm going to hell. I'm a sinner, Cyrus, a terrible sinner. I've cheated—committed adultery. Lots of times. And I've wanted things that belong to other people. And sometimes I've got them, too. And I've hurt people."

This wasn't the way these things usually went. Even murderers and rapists made excuses for themselves. Sally wasn't even trying to soften her story.

He went to her and sat beside her on the couch. With his head bowed he asked, "Do you want to ask for absolution?"

"I do. Oh, yes, I do. I feel safe with you because you're not like other men. You don't want me for my body. You don't think about sex. You don't even see me, really, do you? You never did."

Cyrus closed his eyes and moved his lips in prayer. Please God let him be granted the strength to resist temptation. It was a prayer that had kept him company through many difficult nights.

"Will you give me classes? Just me? I know it's a lot to ask, but I'll make it worth your while."

He looked at her sharply and shook his head. "This isn't about money, Sally. Get that out of your head. I'll counsel you, but not for money. If you choose to give to the Church out of a need to give, that will be wonderful. What is between you and me and your conscience is another matter."

Sniffing, she pulled herself to sit up and hugged her knees. "Thank you. We can meet as often as you have time. I'm goin' to give this my whole attention. You can come here, or I can come to you and we'll be completely alone together."

"I'm not sure how long I'll be in New Orleans."

She burst into tears again and thrust her fingers into her hair. "I'm dying, Cyrus. My spirit is dying. Please, please—"

"I'll do what I can," he said hurriedly. "I'm sure I can spend some time with you twice a week while I'm in New Orleans anyway. Relax. You've done the right thing in reaching out."

"Oh, thank you." Letting her rich hair slip down again, she captured one of his hands and took it to her mouth. "Thank you, Cyrus." She turned up his palm and pressed her parted lips there.

The door opened abruptly, and a silver-haired man peered into the room. He looked at Cyrus and Sally and shook his head. "I suppose

I'm sorry to intrude. But beware of the sins of the flesh. The flesh is weak, and—"

"Thank you," Cyrus said. "I'm a priest and this lady is in my counsel. Can I help you?"

The man entered the room and a woman came in with him. Her blond hair was combed into a smooth style that turned up sharply on the ends and stood out a long way from her head. She wore simple clothes but a lot of makeup. They came toward Cyrus and Sally with avid attention in their eyes.

"A Catholic priest?" the man asked.

Cyrus nodded.

"It's not too late for you to become a Christian, son," the woman said. "This is Mrs. Wilson Lamar, isn't it. I know you from your picture in the papers."

"I'm Sally Lamar."

"I just knew it." The woman smiled delightedly. "I'm Joan Reed. This is my husband, Walt. We came lookin' for someone and walked right into your lovely party."

Cyrus looked sideways at Sally and noted she appeared bemused. He decided to step in for her. "Pleased to meet you. Who are you lookin' for?"

The couple looked significantly at each other. "Oh, you wouldn't know him, I don't suppose. We came because we were told everyone had been invited tonight, and since he's important in these parts, we decided to take a chance."

"And crash a private party," Sally said, sounding less drunk. "I'm going to have to ask you to leave. If you don't, our bodyguard will help you."

"Well, I never," Joan Reed said. "Walt, will you listen to her? She sits there showin' things meant only for her husband to a pagan priest, and she gets high and mighty with two humble servants of the Lord."

"Hush, Joan," Walt said. "The lady isn't quite herself, I don't think."

"I'll deal with this," Cyrus said, standing up. "I'm sure if you tell me who you're looking for, I may be able to help you."

"We're preachers. Simple teachers of the word. No airs or graces and no wants or desires to speak of except a bare livin' to get by. We came to New Orleans to collect something that's ours. Something we need. We told the people concerned, and they know where we're stayin', but they haven't contacted us and things are gettin' a mite thin, if you take my meanin'."

"I'm sorry to hear that," Cyrus said, still recovering from being called pagan. "I'm sure Mr. Lamar would be sympathetic to your needs."

Sally made a disgusted sound.

"We'll find Mr. Lamar," Joan Reed said primly. She stared at Sally and shook her head. "That poor man must be beside himself. An important man like him needs a wife who can be his right hand, not a harlot."

Cyrus caught Sally by the hand and squeezed. "It's okay," he told her.

Walt Reed came farther into the room until Cyrus had to turn his head to see the man. "I think it's a fine idea for you to find Wilson," he told him. "The last I saw of him he . . . well, he was here, but I think he was joining my parents. Mr. and Mrs. Payne."

"Walt!" Joan pointed at Cyrus. "Payne. Are you related to Celina Payne?"

"My sister."

"Is she here?"

Cyrus didn't feel good about any of this. "Celina isn't here tonight."

"Where is she?"

"I don't know."

"Well, she isn't in Royal Street. We already went there."

"My sister is a very busy woman."

"We know all about her," Joan said. "We've been asking questions. But she's not the one who's got what belongs to us."

Cyrus felt Sally move. She rested back on the pillow, flung her hands over her head, and raised her legs to prop them on the back of the couch.

Joan tutted and averted her eyes. Walt moved in closer, and his eyes threatened to leave his head.

Joan went to her husband and hooked an arm around one of his. "Come along, Mr. Reed. We've got to get to that man before he spends everything that should be ours."

"What man?" Sally asked very clearly. "What should be yours?"

"Jack Charbonnet." Joan raised her chin. "We won't be put off again. Errol would have been the first to say we saved his soul for him. He was grateful. He promised us he'd always take care of us. It's time his will was read. We don't like thinking that Charbonnet is probably findin' ways to take Errol's money before it can go to its rightful owners."

Cyrus knew people like this existed, but he'd never actually been confronted by any. "Mr. Charbonnet isn't here either," he said. "But I know he'll want to make sure everything's exactly as it should be. And by the way, he is a very wealthy man in his own right."

"From gambling money," Joan said, her lip curled. "And other unsavory things, from what I've learned. His sort never has enough to make them happy."

He wouldn't argue, there was no point. "On Jack's behalf, I suggest you contact him at his office in the Royal Street property. On Monday. He likes his weekends free." Cyrus had no idea what Jack liked to do with his weekends, but on a hunch, he thought he'd try to head off distractions on this particular weekend. Jack and Celina needed uninterrupted opportunities to decide if they'd made a wise choice.

"Come on, Walt," Joan said. "We don't stay where we're not wanted. The Lord said that we should brush the dust off our feet when we came up against people like you. Sinners who won't see the light."

"That's right," Sally said, and to Cyrus's deep humiliation, she rocked from side to side, setting her voluptuous breasts swinging, swinging and showing the nipples and full contours. "We're sinners who won't see the light. Go look for some good people."

Walt Reed watched her with hot eyes. He backed slowly away, staring at Sally until the instant his wife yanked him from the room.

"Well," Sally said. "Now, I just wonder what that's all about. Errol paying money to some holy rollers. Who'd have thought it? I'll just bet there's another story there. It's too late to make you listen to me anymore tonight. But please talk to me tomorrow, Cyrus."

"Well—"

"Don't refuse me. I couldn't bear it. I'll get an address to you where we can meet and not be interrupted."

"Well—"

"I need you." Tears welled in her lovely eyes. "I didn't know until tonight just how much I was going to need you. I don't want to say too much, but I may be in a lot of trouble and getting out of it may mean ... Well, enough of that for now. I'll get in touch with you tomorrow."

"Sally, I can't be sure I'll be able to make it."

"Didn't the shepherd go after the one sheep that was lost? I'm that one sheep."

He wasn't in the mood to discuss the parable of the missing sheep. "All right, Sally. All right. Let me know what time and I'll be over. I do want you to include Wilson in this though. Not in our sessions, of course, but in your decisions regarding the Church. He's your husband."

She pouted, finally smiled, and said, "Oh, very well. If that's the way it has to be. Now, run along and look after Bitsy. She's been having a bad time. Neville's been out of hand for some time. He drinks everything they make, you know."

Cyrus stared at her. "I'd appreciate it if you didn't say things like that in company. All my mother has are her illusions. Public talk along those lines would destroy her."

"What would destroy her more would be for it to get out that Neville's turned violent."

"My stepfather?" His laugh sounded as forced as it felt. "He's a passive man. Always has been." For his mother's sake, he must try to make sure that fiction was kept intact.

"He might have been once, but he's forever getting belligerent with people now. Maybe he needs to see a doctor. Wilson's been talking about not inviting him to functions for a while. He doesn't want to go that far, because your folks have been so useful . . . so good to us."

Cyrus stood up. "I'm sure they have been useful. I'll gather some reading materials to give to you tomorrow."

She stacked her hands under her head and smiled up at him. "That would be dandy. I'll read every word." The smile faded. "I'd do anythin' to satisfy you, Cyrus."

He stepped away, and felt a bolt in his belly and privates that would have sent him to his knees if he hadn't locked them.

Little wonder Walt Reed had moved to find a different angle on Sally. Her skirt had risen high enough to show that she wore no panties.

Twenty-two

A sense of urgency drove Jack. He wanted Celina to be his wife—yesterday if that could be accomplished—and he wanted Amelia to love her stepmother and be crazy about the coming baby, when she was told about the coming baby, and he wanted everything that threatened their mad grab for happiness to be solved and then to go away.

"What are you thinking?" Celina asked him. Freshly showered, and dressed in the white shirt and gauze pants she'd arrived in the previous evening, she looked fabulous. Lovely, glowing, and wholesome.

"A penny for them."

He jumped and looked into her navy blue eyes, now so close to his that he blinked. Seated on a kitchen chair, he'd been watching her prepare the breakfast she'd said she wanted to "cook." He hadn't commented that bowls of dry cereal, apples cut in quarters, and glasses of orange juice didn't constitute cooking. Neither had he mentioned that as the first meal of the day, but served at two in the afternoon, this might be adequate for her, but he might be tempted to take a bite or two out of the "cook" afterward if he were to stave off starvation.

She pressed her nose to his.

"Okay." He laughed and pulled her onto his lap. "I was thinking that I'm a bit nervous about Amelia's reaction. And Tilly's reaction. And I hope your parents come around. And I hope Cyrus decides to abandon the dire warnings of impending doom when we go ahead with our marriage. And I want to know exactly what happened to Errol and put it behind us as best we can." And he also wanted to deal with the oldest, biggest outstanding debt owed him, and move on.

Celina eased from his lap and pulled a chair to face his. She'd removed the daisy-scattered tablecloth of the night before—blushing profusely as expected—and replaced it with two of Amelia's frog-strewn plastic place mats.

"We've got a lot to overcome, Jack. If you've got doubts that we can do it, speak now. I'll manage, I promise I will. And I will never, ever suggest that Errol had anything to do with my condition."

"You changed your mind?"

"Of course I changed my mind. I'd have changed it anyway in time. You just speeded the process. I wouldn't do anything to hurt you, and you treasure his memory, just as I do."

"Tell me who raped you."

She flinched, and kept her eyes closed. "Please don't ask me."

"Tell me."

"I'm never going to tell you. He's never going to know what he really did to me. And he's never going to know that while he thought . . . He's never going to know that he brought me far more joy than pain. I want my baby. I've wanted her almost since I knew I was expecting her. At first I was too shocked to know what I thought or wanted, but that passed quickly enough."

He leaned forward to hold her hands. "Will you let the baby be mine, too?"

Her soft smile undid him. Her full lips curved upward, and her eyes sparkled. "I want the baby to be yours too." She sobered and looked at the floor, and said quietly, "I wish she really were yours."

"I wish he were, too."

In the silence that followed, they held hands and stared at each other.

"Celina, I know you're easily embarrassed, but I'm never going to forget last night—or this morning."

"I'd better check the cereal."

"Check the cereal?" he said, keeping a straight face.

"You don't like it soggy, do you?"

"Nope." Something told him his future wife was unlikely to spend a lot of time in the kitchen. "Can you put into words why you're so determined that . . . You seem even more determined to have nothing to do with the baby's father than one might expect. You seem fearful that he might find out. Will you tell me why?"

She got up and carried the bowls to the table, then fetched the apples that had begun to turn brown, and the orange juice. "It's

probably not an issue at all, but I'm afraid he'd either hold the pregnancy over me and try to use it. Or decide he wanted the baby."

Jack turned cold. "So this wasn't a random thing with a stranger."

"I never said it was."

"You never said one way or the other. He's someone you know
well?"

"I've answered your question about my fears. Can we drop the
subject now?"

"Of course." He took up a spoonful of flakes turned to the mush
Celina dreaded, and ate valiantly. The apples were fine if you didn't
look at them.

"The apples look funny," Celina said. "I think you're supposed
to put vinegar on them to stop that. I remember Ms. Simmons saying
that when we were in school. Or was it salt?"

Jack made an interested sound. He didn't want to drop the question
of the baby's father, but it could wait. "When did Cyrus say he could
get over?"

She pushed the brown glop around her bowl. "He's agreed to
counsel Sally Lamar."

Jack put down his spoon. "You're kiddin'."

"Uh uh. She was in a terrible state last night. That's what Cyrus
was talking about for so long on the phone. I've got a hunch there
may have been a lot he didn't say, too. Cyrus is very discreet, but he
sounded worried. Evidently he's going to meet with her today, and
she wants them to get together a couple of times a week."

"A pretty serious sinner, hmm?" He didn't like Sally Lamar any
more than he liked her husband.

"In pretty serious trouble emotionally, so Cyrus said," Celina told
him. "I don't trust her. She had a thing for him from when we were
children. And he's an innocent when it comes to women and the way
they react to him."

"He's a big boy."

"He'll be mortified if she really comes on to him. You know what
she's capable of. He said they're going to be meeting in private. Not
at her home and not in Royal Street."

Jack couldn't help grinning. "Maybe you're right to be worried.
And you'd better hope Sally really is trying to save her soul, rather
than capture Cyrus's for the devil."

"That's not funny."

"No. Sorry." He promptly laughed, tried to stop, but gave up.

Celina punched his shoulder.

Jack coughed and managed to control himself. "The main thing I'm thinking about is Amelia. When Tilly gets back with her, I want to tell her about us."

With her spoon halfway to her mouth, Celina stopped. She looked at the food and set the spoon down again. "I think it's too soon."

"Tomorrow we're taking care of the formalities. I intend to do the deed on Friday or Saturday, whichever suits you. And Amelia must be there. Tilly too. I'm sure Cyrus will come, and I'd like to see your parents attend, but I won't expect them."

"Friday or Saturday?" Her voice squeaked.

He chomped a piece of apple and swallowed. "I thought we could have the marriage blessed later, if that's what you want."

She looked blank.

"We don't have time to waste, Celina. You're already quite obviously pregnant. Which reminds me. You probably should do something about a whole new wardrobe. I'd like to take you away afterwards, but we'll have to wait, I suppose."

"You're going too fast for me again, Jack."

He got up and bent over her until she raised her face. He stroked a forefinger back and forth over her lips, then kissed her. At first the kiss was soft and sweet, but quickly it became passionate. How was he going to manage what she did to him? He only had to look at her to want to get her naked and feel her body pressed to his.

He took his lips a fraction away from hers. "All I have to do is think your name and I'm hard. When you were asleep this morning, before it got light, I watched you and you wouldn't believe the urges I had. A lesser man would have given in to them."

"I love humility in a man, Mr. Charbonnet."

"Mmm." He shut his eyes. "I see dark places, and dark things that move in those dark places. There's hot music playing, and your body is hot, and so is mine. *Chère,* I want to throw you down, get rid of all that virginal white, and leap aboard for the kind of ride I doubt any man even dreams of—even in his best wet dreams. Argh, I said it again!"

"Jack, you make me . . ."

He opened his eyes and regarded her expectantly. "Don't stop. I make you?" He turned up a hand and urged her to finish the thought.

"You make me wet where I shouldn't be wet, and you make my breasts feel swollen, and my nipples sting, and all my veins pulse. I can hardly sit still because of what I feel . . . You know, what I *feel.*"

Jack felt short of breath. "Let's do it."

"I want to. I do."

"Come on, then." He kissed her again, and while he kissed her he fondled her breasts. "We didn't do it in the bath yet. Or in the shower. Or outside. I've got a house by Lake Pontchartrain with a gallery high off the ground, only the stars at night and the sun in the day as an audience. My mother's father left it to me. I spent a lot of time there when I was growing up. Oh, Celina, tonight's supposed to be clear. Lots of stars, sweet thing. It wouldn't take long to drive up there."

"I'm feeling very overheated, Jack."

"Good. In a rowboat. Rocking gently."

"Until we turn the thing over," she told him, struggling not to smile. "If performances to date are any measure, we'd be on the bottom of the lake feeding the alligators in no time."

"I'll settle for bed, then."

"No."

He wasn't joking anymore. His penis threatened to break his zipper. A simple solution presented itself. He unzipped his pants, opened them, and something else presented itself.

"Jack!"

"That sounds like approval. Why, thank you, ma'am. Come here."

"It's daylight and we have things to do."

"I couldn't agree with you more." He pulled his shirt over his head.

"Oh, Jack," she moaned. "Oh, you're doing it to me again."

"I intend to." He beckoned to her. "Come here. I've got something for you."

She hesitated, turned her back, turned to him again, and approached very slowly. But she ate him up with her eyes. Her pink cheeks made her look very young. Her lips were moist and slightly parted. Her breasts rose and fell with each short breath.

When she stood beside him, he pulled her face down and kissed her again, and slipped a hand beneath her top to maneuver her bra undone. She gasped when her breasts were freed, and he lifted the top to allow him to apply the tip of his tongue to the very tip of each nipple. She wriggled, and grasped for something to hold on to. What she found suited both of them.

Celina took her own slacks and panties off, but Jack lifted her astride his thighs. She came with his thumb on her clitoris, and his penis stroking deep—and with his face buried in her beautiful breasts, and he was right with her.

They collapsed together in the chair.

Minutes passed. Jack cooled a little, but not so much that he wasn't already thinking of the next time.

"Maybe I shouldn't marry you," she murmured.

"Huh?" He pushed her upright. He didn't remember taking off her top, but it was on the floor. "You can't what?"

"Oh, I was going to make some cute joke about if we get married we'll both be dead in a couple of weeks. Exhausted. Probably we'll have heart attacks. Forget it." She arched forward to rub her breasts slowly from side to side over his chest. "That is heavenly. I've been fooling myself. I didn't know this side of me at all."

"It's my influence," he said smugly. "You find me irresistible."

"When do Amelia and Tilly get back?"

"Not for at least an hour."

Her eyes cleared instantly. "An hour? Jack, why didn't you tell me? Oh, look at us."

"I'm looking."

"We've got to hurry. And you've got to be careful in front of your daughter. She's very impressionable, even more impressionable than most children her age."

"We'll be careful. Her grandmother—Elise's mother—loves having her for the weekends though, and she's been complaining that I don't let Amelia visit often enough."

"You won't be sending your daughter away to accommodate our sex lives," she told him.

"You are so right. I will not be doin' that. I just wish you wouldn't be in such a hurry to run away from me every time I try to touch you. And refuse to enter into anythin' I suggest. And I'm hurt you felt you had to make love and rush away like you just did."

She frowned, and glanced down to where her white thighs splayed over his darker skinned, black-hair-sprinkled skin, and where his black pubic hair tangled with her red curls. She said, "You can be quite sarcastic, Mr. Charbonnet."

He caught her by the waist and slowly lifted her up while they both watched their bodies part.

This time it was Celina who initiated the kiss. "You and I have some things to talk about," she told him when they paused for breath. "We've proved we do this sex thing really well. But beyond that our lives are a mess, Jack. We're still plumb in the middle of a drama."

She had no idea just how many dramas. One, singular, didn't come close. "We haven't begun to address how we'll get around Garth

Fletcher's little bombshell. I can't stand having everything at Dreams on hold like this."

He stood up and pulled on his pants while she picked up her own clothes and began to dress.

The phone rang, but he ignored it.

He felt Celina looking at him and raised his brows in question.

"Aren't you going to answer that?"

"They'll give up soon enough."

"What if it's Amelia?"

Jack paused in the act of putting on his shirt. "Jeez," he said. "What am I thinking of? That's the problem. I've quit thinking entirely." He dashed for the phone and yanked the receiver off the wall in mid-ring. "Charbonnet."

"Yeah. Get here, Jack, or I won't be responsible for what happens."

He pressed the phone hard against his ear. "Is that any way to speak to an old friend."

"This isn't a friendly how-are-ya," Win Giavanelli said. "This is one of those times when I wouldn't be making a call at all if I didn't want to save your hide—or the hide of someone you care about."

Twenty-three

"You got anything you want to tell me, Jack?"

When Win Giavanelli was an unhappy man, he avoided eye contact. Win wasn't looking at Jack today.

"You losin' your hearin' or somethin'?" he asked, shredding a napkin and piling the pieces into a small hill in the center of his sauce-smeared place. La Murèna might boast a fantastic fish menu, but Win was a meatball man.

Jack pulled out a chair he hadn't been invited to use and sat down. "My hearing's very good, thank you, Win. You called with some warnings I didn't like getting. You wanted to see me. I came."

"And I asked you a question. How come you're a stranger to La Murèna these days? What the fuck ain't you botherin' to tell me about your life? Ain't we good friends? The best of friends? Didn't I make it my business to be sure you were okay, even when you were— especially when you were a snot-nosed kid?"

"Always, Win. And especially when I was a kid. I am grateful for that." Grateful because Win's unexpected conscience had kept Jack safe from the goons who would almost certainly have wanted to close his eyes for good. Jack knew Win had told his trigger boys that Jack had been too young to be a threat to them; he also knew they couldn't be sure of that. These were men who only put their money on a sure thing.

"So how come things happen and you don't come to Win? You don't care about family connections no more? You think you don't need me no more, maybe? Dangerous thoughts, Jack. This is a dangerous town for a man with dangerous thoughts. You gotta remember the rules. You know that. I always been good to you. Looked after you. For old time's sake—and because I like you. I want to keep you safe. Didn't I always keep you safe?"

"I'm a man, Win," Jack said, capturing a fragment of napkin that floated away, and placing it carefully on Win's pile. "A man has to do for himself."

Win brought a beefy fist down on the table. "You think you can take care of yourself? Your papa thought he could take care of himself. Look what happened to him and your poor, dear little mama." He crossed himself and shook his head. With his eyes closed he murmured a prayer. "I shall always blame myself for what happened. Even though I never had any part of it—never would have had any part of a thing like that. But I shoulda known there was some rival activity. We got too fat and happy. They moved while we were havin' a siesta and . . . well, no point goin' into that. You suffered enough. We all suffered enough. But don't you forget who it was took you outta there in one piece. They'd have come back for you, Jacko. They thought you seen too much."

"I'm grateful, Win. I'll always be grateful."

Win grunted, and drank from a tumbler of heavy red wine.

Jack sucked in his gut and forced his heart to slow down. Win had never given any indication that he thought Jack might actually have seen what happened to his parents—or, more important from the survival point of view—that he knew who made what happened, happen. When they'd come for his parents, Jack was supposed to be with his grandfather at the house by Lake Pontchartrain. Only later had the truth come out that Jack hadn't gone to the lake that weekend. Win had found out from Granddaddy that Jack was at home. Then the young don had gone in search of the boy, and when he'd found him hiding, had believed the story that Jack had heard gunshots and run for cover in the pool house. Afterward Win had persuaded the triggers who did the job that Jack hadn't seen anything. Only things had been said, things that let Jack know there were some uneasy thugs who didn't believe he hadn't looked through the windows of the pool house and seen what they did to his mother in the turquoise water where she'd been swimming.

"I was sorry to hear about Errol Petrie," Win said.

"You already told me that, but thanks."

"You gonna be runnin' things for the little dyin' kids now."

Jack was accustomed to Win's less-than-subtle verbal skills, but still he winced. "I intend to make sure Errol's work is carried on."

Win nodded slowly, sagely. "A man oughta have a hobby. I gotta get me one sometime. Jack, I been hearin' things about you, things that don't make me happy."

"Who's been doing the talking, Win?"

"It don't matter. We'll just say it's a source I gotta take notice of. You been puttin' it around I'm lookin' favorable on you, Jack?"

For once the older man's meaning wasn't clear. "It's not something I'd have a reason to discuss, but I thought you did look on me favorably."

Win, vast and pasty, his thin, still-black hair slicked in strings over his skull, sucked a cherry off its stalk, chewed, spat out the pit, and wiped his fingers on the tablecloth before bending to use it on his mouth.

"Drink," he said, indicating a second tumbler of red wine. "I shoulda taken some time explainin' the facts of life to you, but I wanted to keep you out of it—in your mama's memory, and because a man's gotta do what he thinks is right. When I say someone thinks I look favorable on you, I mean they was suggestin' I might be considerin' you to take my place one day."

Jack came close to grinning with triumph. "What would give anyone an idea like that?" It was working.

"I'm askin' you if you might have suggested somethin' like that."

"Who would I suggest it to? And why would I do somethin' like that? I'm not a member of the family. I know Sonny Clete is your boy. Always has been. It's understood. Sonny and I get along just fine. He drops by the boat from time to time and shoots the breeze. Why would I say somethin' stupid like that?"

Win's tiny black eyes glittered out from holes in his pudgy white face. He grunted. "You tell me." Another cherry gave up its flesh, stem, and pit.

"Talk to Sonny," Jack told him. "He'll tell you how well we get along."

"You get along so well, you told him you don't pay no contributions to the family funds?"

"You mean *protection*? Win, what would I need to pay protection for? You and I are partners in the *Lucky Lady*. Fifty-fifty. You get half of the take—on everything. One partner doesn't ask another partner for *protection*."

Win chewed steadily on a mouthful of bread. He waved the rest of a thick slice into the air. "Maybe there's been a misunderstandin'. I'll look into it. Different subject. Listen up, Jack boy. You know Dwayne LeChat?"

"Yeah. Everyone who lives in the Quarter knows Dwayne."

"Is he some sort of buddy to a guy called Antoine?"

Jack turned cold. "Not that I know. Oh, they know each other because Antoine worked for Errol, and Errol and Dwayne were friends for years. Why?"

"Nothin', just explorin' a notion. How about Celina Payne?"

Careful. "What about Celina?"

"You know her at all?"

"I'm engaged to her."

Win threw what was left of the slice of bread on the tablecloth. "Since when?" He shoved his dirty plate aside. "See that? I never eat in the middle of the day, but you got me eatin' because I'm upset. I'm hurt, Jack. How come you don't come to me with good news? Ain't I like a father to you? Don't a son make sure he honors his father by givin' him that kind of news before anyone else?"

"I've been busy," Jack said. His heart wasn't slowing down. "Errol's murder was a terrible thing, and it left me with a lot to clean up."

Win ran his left hand down his face until it rested over his mouth. His face shone, and beads of sweat stood out on his scalp.

"Win," Jack said, "you don't look so good. You should get out more. Get more fresh air."

"Did this Antoine talk to you? About something he thought he saw?"

Jack's palms were moist. "What kind of thing?" He drank some of the wine and made sure he looked steadily into Win's eyes.

"You tell me."

Jack put down the glass. "You made a threat to me on the phone. You intimated a threat to someone I care about. That's why I broke away from something important to get here."

Win pointed a short forefinger at Jack. "You gotta work on the respect, Jack. I don't gotta give a shit about what you're doing. If I say come, you come."

"I did." He kept right on looking into the other man's eyes.

"I been hearing stories, and you better be grateful I'm lookin' after you, Jack. So walk this walk with me, okay?"

"Okay." Jack nodded. He'd never considered Errol's death might have been connected to organized crime in the parish.

"This Antoine. He never talked to you about seein' somethin'?"

"No."

"And this Dwayne—the queer—did he talk to you about Antoine seein' somethin'?''

Win's private dining room was too warm. The man himself rarely left the place anymore, and the air smelled used. Jack said, "I see Dwayne regularly. If Antoine had said anything of note to him, he'd have told me. He hasn't."

"How's Amelia?" Win raised his sparse eyebrows and examined his fingernails.

Instant tightness closed on Jack's chest. "She's wonderful, thanks."

"Happy she's gonna have a new mama?"

"Delighted," Jack lied.

"That's nice. And Celina Payne's a real looker, huh?"

Turquoise water and blood. And dead eyes open to the sky.

"Jack? I asked you a question."

"Celina's very attractive. But she's a great woman. She'll be good for Amelia and me."

"That's nice. Look, Jack. Sometimes things happen. Things I may not have anything to do with directly, but they are my concern. You understand?"

"Maybe."

"You're a smart man. If someone close to me gets some action going I don't know nothin' about, I don't like that. But if he says he's sorry and he's been a faithful soldier, then I'm gonna forgive—and I'm gonna help him out if he's in a tight spot. I'm gonna support him. Are you still followin' me, Jack?"

"Are we talking about Antoine? And something he could have seen? Something to do with one of your people?"

"It don't matter. The details don't matter. I'm lookin' out for you. That's all you gotta think about. For you and Amelia—and attractive Celina Payne, who's gonna be Amelia's new mama."

Jack rarely felt sick, but he felt sick now. He was going to have to be very, very careful. "Thanks for looking out for us, Win."

"Yeah. Now, you do what I tell you. You think about every word that comes from your mouth to Sonny Clete's ears. Got that?"

"Sure." Jack shrugged.

"This ain't no joke."

"No."

"And you talk to your very attractive Celina, and ask her if Antoine managed to talk to her about anything before he took a vacation from work."

Ice wouldn't melt in Jack's veins. He frowned, worked on looking puzzled. "Antoine hasn't been to work for days. How do you know that? He didn't tell Celina or me he intended to take time off." Without showing too much interest, he needed to see just how much Win knew about Antoine. "Did you hear where Antoine went? And for how long? We're short of help in Royal Street."

"I regret your problems with your help, but I can't help you further with that." Win was fascinated by his fingernails this afternoon. "Talk to Celina. And watch your mouth. I love you like a son, but I gotta lot of people dependin' on me. I gotta put their welfare first."

"I understand that."

"Do you?" Win's little black eyes skewered Jack. "I hope you do. I'll do my best for you because I always have. But if you should make a mistake and step outta line—make me have to look out for my own and forget I ever knew you—you do that, and you better never let Amelia and attractive Celina Payne outta your sight."

Twenty-four

Celina heard a key turn in Jack's front door and walked to the top of the stairs. The door started to open, and she was tempted to retreat. This could be Tilly and Amelia. Jack had told her that if they arrived before he got back, Celina should say he'd been called away and had asked her to wait. She wanted to get back to Cyrus, whom she'd talked to on the phone. He was going out to meet Sally Lamar and Celina wanted to talk to him before he left.

First up the stairs came Amelia, her balding frog beneath an arm. She climbed so fast, she stumbled halfway up.

Jack bounded behind his daughter and caught her up. He carried Amelia much the same as Amelia carried her frog, and both father and daughter laughed.

Last, after closing and locking the door, Tilly clomped upward.

"Look what I found outside," Jack said to Celina, and swung Amelia onto his shoulders.

"You are going to hit that child's head one of these days," Tilly said crossly. "She's growing fast, Mr. Charbonnet. Growing taller. If your attention was where it should be, I wouldn't have to point such things out to you."

"Taller?" Jack said, arriving beside Celina and reaching up to find the top of Amelia's head. "Why, I do believe Tilly's right. My little girl is taller than her daddy. Will you look at that, Celina?"

"Daddy, you are silly!"

Celina folded her arms and smiled, watching them. This man's love for his child beamed from him. And his child's happiness was his reward for loving her without reserve.

"You'll make Amelia sick, Mr. Charbonnet. Throwing her around like that."

Tilly dropped a canvas shopping bag on the floor at the top of the stairs. She avoided looking at Celina.

"I want to tell you and Amelia something important," Jack said to Tilly. "You'll want to unpack your bag first. Take your time. I'll send Amelia up to get you later."

The woman didn't have to say a word to convey her disapproval. She swept up her bag and left for her rooms.

"Is it okay if we talk in your bedroom, Amelia?" Jack said. He gave Celina a slight smile that didn't lessen her apprehension.

They went into the very pink room and Jack plopped Amelia on the bed. She still kept her armlock on the frog, but her grin wavered and faded.

"Jack, maybe this isn't—"

"Of course it is," he said, cutting Celina off. "Is that a new dress, squirt? Nice. That granny of yours spoils you."

Celina cleared her throat and said, "Yellow suits you. I love yellow."

"Granny bought it. I don't like it, but Daddy says it's not nice to make someone else sad, so I said I did."

"We'll talk about that later," Jack said. He pulled a chair toward the bed and indicated for Celina to sit. He perched beside Amelia. "What do you think I'm going to tell you?"

She pulled her shoulders up to her ears and let them drop. The corners of her mouth turned down.

Celina took a deep breath to calm her jiggling nerves.

Jack put a finger under his daughter's pointed chin and raised her face. "If you don't think you know what I am goin' to say, then why the soggy face?"

Amelia squeezed her eyes shut. "I'm not crying, so my face isn't soggy. I don't mind if you want a new mommy for me. Tilly told me you were probably going to get one soon."

"Thank you," Jack said. He kissed her nose and Amelia opened her green eyes to look into his. "You are so much like your mama," he added.

Thickness closed Celina's throat. In a rush she felt such longing to be part of this forever, and for them to want her just as much.

"We could have planned this better, sweetheart. Taken longer for you to get to know Celina. But we don't want to wait, so we decided to go ahead now. You're a grown-up little girl, but you're still a little girl, and we don't want you to worry about things you don't have to think about. Celina and I are getting married. But that doesn't mean you and I are going to do things differently. We'll have our special time together, the same as we always have. But you'll have a stepmama who will share a lot of things with us."

Surely no other five-year-old could manage the magnificent frown Amelia produced. Her fine, dark brows came down in a straight line. She wrinkled her nose and regarded Celina with the kind of intensity few adults could achieve.

"Amelia?"

"Yes, Daddy. I might like a new mama, but how do I know she's the right one?"

"That's not an agreeable thing to say, young lady. Celina—"

"Hush," Celina told him. "I'm a stranger to her." *And still a stranger to you in too many important ways.*

Father and daughter looked at Celina. Their likeness was startling, yet in his child Jack saw the wife he'd lost. He always would.

"I asked Celina to marry me and she's said she will," Jack said. His gentle finality overwhelmed her. "By the end of this week we'll be a family and she will live here with us."

Amelia lowered her eyes. She pressed her lips together and leaned against Jack. He stroked her soft black curls.

There seemed nothing to say. Celina held very still. She heard her own breathing, and theirs. Was that the way their life would be? Her, and them, at least when they were together.

He wanted to marry her, and she'd told him she wanted it, too.

Their hours alone no longer seemed real. For an instant Celina saw the kitchen, Jack's intent face above hers, the ceiling behind his head. She closed the visions out. They embarrassed her, now in the company of the child. That woman, the one naked in the kitchen, seemed a stranger, her actions inappropriate.

Jack kissed the top of Amelia's head and hugged her. He winked at Celina. "I thought you could move in here today. There's a spare bedroom next to Amelia's."

Celina felt something near panic. "I'm just fine in Royal Street at present."

"I would prefer you here." His pleasant expression slipped away. "You and Amelia need time together as soon as possible. I'd attend to the formalities while you two discuss how you'll keep me under your combined thumbs."

Celina wasn't amused. This was a new side of Jack, a manipulative angle that intended to get its own way.

"Have you heard anything from Antoine?"

She stared at him. "No. You'd know if I had. We—" Her mouth remained open and she clicked her jaw. "I haven't heard from Antoine."

"You're sure? Not a quick phone call, nothing?"

Why would he ask her these questions when he'd been with her all weekend? "No, Jack. How about you?"

He held his breath. She saw him. And his grip on Amelia tightened. "What is it? What's wrong?" she asked, forgetting the child.

"Not a thing," he told her, but the slight shake of his head was a warning to be careful what she said.

Celina sat quite still. She watched for some hint of what was really on his mind, but his expression had closed again.

"I need to go out," he said. "Stay with Amelia and Tilly, okay?"

"I want to go and talk to Cyrus."

"Have him come here. I'll call him."

She gripped the arms of the chair. Something was very, very wrong. And it related to the telephone call that summoned him away earlier. He'd looked grim afterward, grimly angry. When he'd come back he'd managed to cover his true feelings with the playful greeting of Amelia. Then he'd used his announcement about his marriage to Celina as a temporary diversion—for himself as well as for Celina and Amelia. Now he couldn't hide his agitation any longer.

"Don't call Cyrus," she told him. Jack could not be master of all he saw. "I'll speak to him myself."

"Good enough. Tell Celina all about us, squirt. Tell her about your school and your grandmother. And what you do each day—your tap lessons."

He kissed Amelia's hair again and got up. At first Celina thought he would walk out without as much as saying a word to her, but at the door he turned back and held out a hand to her. When she got up, he met her in the middle of the room and touched his lips lightly to hers. She wondered if he knew that the sweetness of that touch was a powerful weapon. It stunned her.

"Talk about being a family," he told her, and glanced down at her stomach. "Families are good things if you trust enough to be honest."

She should tell him about Rose, and what she had shown her.

"Daddy," Amelia said. "Can I come with you?"

"You and Celina have a lot of talking to do. See you later, squirt."

Even when his footsteps had faded and he'd left the house, Celina continued to face the door. She wasn't going to "obey" him. That he'd assumed she would astounded her. If they were to go ahead with the marriage, the time to establish rules was now. The first rule would be that neither party issued orders to the other, or expected their desires would come first.

"Amelia, will you forgive me if we don't talk now, darlin'?" She turned around. "I have a brother, Cyrus. He's a priest and he's staying with me at the moment. I need to go and see him."

Amelia had left the bed. She stood at the window.

Celina smiled and walked to join the child. "Watching your daddy?"

"He's gone now." Such a controlled voice for one so young. "But that ghost was looking at my room again. It went away when it saw me."

It might be a good idea for Jack to dream up some stories that didn't stir visions of ghosts and goblins.

Twenty-five

Artistic Fool. Cyrus glanced from the name of the shop to its windows. Exotic clothing, just as advertised. And spangled and feathered masks in Rumors. He hadn't window-shopped along Royal Street for years, and he wouldn't be doing so today if he weren't walking slowly, reluctant to keep his appointment with Sally Lamar.

At Toulouse Street he made a turn toward Bourbon and his steps slowed even more.

He'd agreed to meet Sally in the courtyard at the Hôtel Maison de Ville at three. The prospect of being alone with her concerned him, but he must not allow his personal reticence to stand in the way of helping the woman if he could.

A small hotel, the Maison de Ville was one of the city's best. Bypassing reception, Cyrus made his way to the brick courtyard, where a tiered fountain cascaded and flowers bloomed among banana trees.

At first he didn't see Sally. Then he realized with surprise that she was dressed in a long, shapeless black dress with a black scarf over her coppery hair, and dark glasses. She sat on a bench looking directly at him.

When Cyrus waved, she didn't wave back. And when he walked toward her, she got up and hurried toward an entrance into the hotel.

He wanted to call out for her to stop, but the stiff set of her body, her hurried, almost scrambling walk, made him look around instead and start to follow her. There were no obvious onlookers, no signs of an ominous presence that might have frightened her.

Sally didn't slow, except to look back and make sure Cyrus was behind her. He followed her all the way to a guest room, where she opened the door and beckoned frantically for him to come in.

Cyrus hesitated, but only for a moment. If he couldn't deal with one woman, he was less than a man. The thought brought a grimace. He wasn't less than a man in any respect, though he sometimes wished he were.

Once he was inside, Sally closed and locked the door and put her ear to a panel. She held up a hand for him to be silent, and listened.

A brief glance showed a room where the bed was untouched and there was no sign of luggage. Antique furniture, a glimpse into a bathroom at a marble basin with brass and ceramic fittings, the place was rich and quiet.

"I've got to be careful," Sally said, backing away from the door. She turned to him and took off the glasses. "Please sit down."

Being there with her couldn't be considered a good idea. He looked at her pale face and got another surprise. She wore little makeup and seemed younger. He was forcibly reminded of the Sally he took to the high school prom. "I thought we were going to talk in the courtyard."

"We might be seen."

"Why would that be a problem?"

Her eyes slid away from his. "Someone might make something of it. They might wonder what I was doing meeting a man who isn't my husband."

"We're old friends, and I'm a priest."

She laughed self-consciously. "I'm going to sit down anyway." Two Empire fauteuils with elegant gilt arms and legs flanked a Queen Anne–style demilune table. Sally sat in one of the chairs.

Taking a thin book from the inside pocket of his black jacket, Cyrus sat in the other chair. "I brought this for you. C. S. Lewis. There are plenty more when you've finished this one. If you like it."

"Thank you." She didn't pick up the book, didn't look at it. Rather, she fiddled with her shapeless dress. It was made of some material that was slightly shiny and pleated all over, although the pleats looked as if they'd been wrung out when wet and left to dry but not ironed.

"Sally, a lot of time has passed since you and I were in high school. Yet you said you felt you wanted me to help you spiritually. I'm a stranger."

"You don't feel like a stranger to me. I couldn't try to talk to a stranger. You were always different, kind. It never bothered you that you were on your own so much. It never bothered you that other kids picked on you."

He smiled. "They tried to pick on me. It isn't easy to pick on someone who doesn't react."

"That was your defense, wasn't it?" she said, looking sideways at him with her lovely golden-brown eyes. "Passive aggression, that's what they call it."

"Lack of interest is what I would have called it. I'm not proud of it now, but they didn't bother me. I didn't care about them one way or the other. And there wasn't much they could do to me physically unless . . . well, I wasn't afraid of that either."

She kept on looking at him. "Because you were always the tallest and the fittest."

"I was the tallest, and I could run," he told her, grinning. "Good combination for a man of peace in hostile situations."

Pulling slowly at one end, she removed the scarf and shook her hair. "You were always different from the others. That's why I couldn't stop thinking about you."

This wasn't totally unfamiliar ground. From time to time a lonely or a bored woman decided she was attracted to him. "How long ago did you leave the Church?"

"I was never really there. I went because my parents made me, then because the other Catholic kids I knew went. I was confirmed only because Guy Wilder went through the instruction at the same time and I had a thing for him. I need something to hang on to, Cyrus. Something strong. I need faith."

"You're very honest."

"You'd see straight through me if I wasn't. Will you help me?"

He took note of his shoes. They were too old. He'd have to break down and get a new pair. "I already said I'd help you for as long as I'm in New Orleans."

"There are other things. Other things than the Church. I'm in big trouble, Cyrus, and there's nobody but you I'd dare to ask for advice."

"Why me?" he asked. "You don't really know me that well."

She rolled in her lips and shook her head. "Why would you understand? You wouldn't understand a woman loving you the way a woman loves a man, but I love you that way."

She told him calmly, so calmly he might have missed the impact of her words entirely if he'd been distracted. He wasn't distracted.

"Don't look like that," she told him. "So shocked. I don't expect you to reciprocate, but I wanted to be honest with you. I haven't been honest with many people in my life, but I'd like you to think well of me. Loving someone isn't something you can choose—not usually. I didn't choose. And when I had a chance to be with you, I blew it by behaving like a tramp."

"The prom? That was a very long time ago."

"I've never forgotten the shame."

He rested an elbow on the table and braced a finger and thumb against his temple. "Forget it now. It's over and it was very unimportant."

"I'll read the book." She picked it up and flipped through the pages. "At least it's short. It surely looks dull."

"It isn't. It's humorous. A sly pointing of the finger at the frailty of mankind. A way to recognize ourselves and laugh. We shouldn't be here long, Sally."

"Wilson wants Celina."

He blinked and frowned, and didn't answer at once.

"Did you hear what I said, Cyrus?"

"I heard. Our parents mentioned that he'd like her to be an aide. To have her travel with him—and oversee the PR stuff."

The book slapped back down on the table. "And she wants that too, doesn't she?"

Was this what it was all about? Sally felt threatened by Celina and wanted Cyrus to help make sure his sister never got too close to Wilson. "You are wrong, Sally," he told her, twisting in his chair to face her. "Celina has no interest in politics anymore. When she worked part-time for Wilson, it was because she was in a phase when she wanted to do her bit to help. She believed she could and should help. Then she seemed to get to a point when she lost her optimism. She doesn't want any part of it anymore. All she wants now is to make sure Errol Petrie's work continues." And that she could bring her baby safely into the world and care for it.

"I think there's more than that," Sally said stubbornly. She stood up and trailed about the room. Even the shapeless dress couldn't disguise her lush curves. Cyrus had the disturbing thought that Sally covered from neck to toe was more seductive than Sally hardly covered at all.

Cyrus checked his watch.

"You want to get away from me," Sally said. "You think I'm bad.

Well, I am. But I wanted to be a good wife and I would have been if
Wilson had let me. He doesn't touch me. I know you probably aren't
comfortable discussing these things, but he doesn't have sex with me
anymore. I'm a sensual woman and I need love—I need to be *touched*,
Cyrus, to be held. When we were first married, he couldn't get enough
of me. Now he hardly notices I'm there. He's too busy loving himself
and his ambitions. He'd use anyone to get where he wants to be. I
can't help him, so I'm dispensable."

"He needs you," Cyrus said. He'd once thought he didn't like
Wilson Lamar. Today he was sure he didn't. "An intelligent, supportive wife is essential to a politician."

"And if she happens to look good, that helps too."

"You look good."

She stopped moving and turned needy eyes on him. "You think
so? Still?"

"I certainly do."

"Thank you. I think Wilson wishes I were dead."

Cyrus became quite cold. Again she didn't speak as if seeking pity.
"Men and women communicate on different levels," he told her.
"Women always need intimacy. Men don't. Men become completely
caught up in their other drives, the drives that make them perfect for
entrepreneurial pursuits that take a fighter's instincts. When they've
got fighting on their mind, they don't necessarily have loving on their
minds at the same time. For women it seems love has to be there all
the time or they wilt."

"Women give sex to get love. Men give love to get sex."

Her comment discomforted Cyrus. "In a way, yes. Some men,
some of the time. And some women, some of the time."

"You admitted women need love all the time."

"Some women. I should have qualified that."

"I need it all the time," Sally said. She crossed her arms beneath
her breasts and Cyrus looked away. "Wilson's using business as an
excuse, you know."

"An excuse?" When they'd been kids, he'd thought Sally Dufour
the prettiest girl around. Night after night he'd rehearsed what he'd
say to her when he saw her, then, when he did see her, he forgot
every word.

She stood before the windows with their sheer draperies. Little
sunlight reached into the courtyard outside, but it still sent a wash
through the windows and curtains, and polished Sally's hair.

"He wants her. Not as an aide, or whatever. That's an excuse. He wants Celina in his bed."

"Sally!" He stood up. "You torture yourself with these thoughts, and they aren't real."

"They most certainly are. Things have been happening. He and Neville, your dear sot of a father, have been holding private meetings. Afterward Wilson looks mad and Neville looks scared. I know I shouldn't, but I've listened when I could. I can't hear much, just the occasional word. I hear Celina's name. And I hear Wilson talking in a threatening way. He's good at that. I believe he's telling Neville he'd better help him get Celina."

"Wilson is married to you," Cyrus said, but his lungs felt squeezed. Their daddy had shown himself capable of betrayal in the past. "And a married politician doesn't want the kind of talk that would come his way if he started some sort of relationship with another woman."

She laughed, actually let her head fall back, and laughed aloud at him. When she brought herself under control, she said, "I cannot believe your innocence, *Father*. You can look at the political arena in this country and say that talk of sexual misconduct gets in the way of a man's political ambitions? No siree, it does not. And if Wilson manages to get rid of me because of some perceived sin of mine, then he'll be free to pursue Celina anyway. I believe that's what he intends to do. He's wanted her for years."

Disclosing that Celina and Jack had plans to marry wasn't his place. In addition, and although his sister had spent a night alone with Jack at his home, there had been no formal announcement.

"You're not talking because you know something." No sign of her laughter remained, and a deep line formed between her brows. "That's it, isn't it. You know Celina wants Wilson, too. They're in it together with Neville. Bitsy doesn't know the full extent of it because she's too stupid to be trusted. But—"

"No!" He went to her and lowered his head to look into her face. "You're not even making sense anymore. You're a very unhappy woman and you're searching for some way—someone to blame so that you don't have to look too closely at yourself."

She crossed her wrists over her breasts. "I'm a very . . . How do you tell a priest you love sex? I'm sexual, Cyrus."

"Most human beings are sexual."

"Except you."

He took a deep, calming breath. "I didn't say that. And neither do I have to discuss my sexuality with you. I have a calling. That calling demands celibacy of me. It isn't easy, Sally. Sometimes there are days or weeks when I'm virtually an asexual creature because I'm too busy to think about it. But that doesn't happen very often, not nearly often enough."

"Look at this dress," she said, her head bowed while she spread the skirt. "I put it on partly so I was less likely to be recognized, and partly because I'm still embarrassed—about the night of the stupid prom, a hundred years ago, and because I was all but naked in front of you again at the fund-raiser. People think I'm outrageous. They think I'm hard and manipulative. I'm not. I scare myself. Cyrus, I don't want to lose Wilson."

"I don't think you will."

"You are a trusting man. I know what I know. He never touches me anymore." Pain crossed her features. "Sometimes I think he might prefer men."

"Don't talk wildly. Not if you're going to hurt someone to make yourself feel better."

"It's just that— Oh, nothing. But I'm right about Celina. Wilson wants to get rid of me and be with her. He's trying to get damning evidence that I've been unfaithful so people will feel sorry for him and forgive him for getting involved with another woman."

Cyrus regarded her without blinking, and waited.

She lifted her chin defiantly. "I have been unfaithful. Lots of times."

"Do you want to ask for reconciliation?"

"Not yet. Not until I think I can intend to change the way I am. I don't intend to yet."

This was a pointless exchange—except for giving him a warning he should pass on to Celina. "If you aren't interested in changing, then why would you want help from me?"

"I need it. I need a champion. I'm alone, Cyrus. Since my daddy died, there's been no one I can trust."

"Surely, Wilson—"

"I don't trust Wilson!"

"Hush," he told her. "We don't want to draw attention to ourselves."

Sally raised her chin again. She went to him and rested her fingertips and palms on his chest. "Not a soul, Cyrus. I am surrounded by people, but alone. And I try to fill myself up by taking men to bed, or anywhere else I can get them. Are you shocked?"

He glanced down at her lowered eyelids. "It would be hard for you to say something I haven't heard before."

She slipped her arms around his waist and pressed her face into the hollow beneath his shoulder, and he felt her tense as she expected him to push her away.

Cyrus didn't push Sally away, neither did he put a hand on her.

"You loathe me, don't you," she murmured. "I'm everything you and your kind fight against in this world. I'm the other side."

"You are a woman in need. It's my job to try to help you."

"Because it's your *job*. Gee, thanks."

Her breasts were a softly obvious pressure on his ribs. Her body layered his, and he called all his carefully honed control into action.

"I think I walked into a trap Wilson set," she told him. "He put a man in my way knowing this man is just the type I'm likely to notice—and want. I didn't see it at first because my pride couldn't take it that he—that this man wasn't another conquest of mine, that he was a plant. But I've been thinking things through, and I see it all now."

Cyrus touched her back lightly. Whatever it cost him, he was charged with giving comfort to the suffering, and Sally Lamar suffered greatly.

She looked up at him. "Hold me, Cyrus."

He patted her shoulder. "You don't have any proof that Wilson did this thing. Perhaps you want to believe he did because it would lessen your own guilt?"

"I wish I could cry. Why can't I cry unless I'm drunk?"

"Because you've shut down what should be natural. In self-defense. You aren't going to risk having Wilson see you're vulnerable. Tears make you vulnerable, so you think."

She nuzzled her face on his chest again. "You are so wise. How'd you get so wise, young Cyrus, who was a kid with me only yesterday. Wasn't that just yesterday?"

"If you want it to be," he told her quietly. "You can turn the clock back, Sally. Be new again. God lets you do that—He wants you to."

"They're going to smash my marriage. I've pretended I was hard, but I'm not. I've been wrong. I'm sorry about that, but I want to keep my husband. Your father is working with Wilson to make that impossible."

"I'll deal with my father," Cyrus said.

She clutched him tighter. "Don't tell them I said anything. Wilson would be so angry."

"I won't. I don't have to." He wasn't happy at the thought of

Celina and Jack getting together, but it would solve more than one problem.

"That man—the one Wilson's using to trap me—he's got evidence against me."

"If you are right about that, let me know and I'll talk to Wilson. I can't promise anything, but perhaps I can soften his heart." And if he couldn't, perhaps he could remind Wilson Lamar that Cyrus was a man with a very long memory, and there were some behaviors an electorate might not swallow too easily.

"You're going to help me, aren't you?" Sally said. Her body had relaxed.

"I'm going to do my best."

"So am I." She sounded breathless. "I'll read the book. I'll read it this very night so we can talk about it tomorrow."

He stared straight over her head. "I'm not sure I can make it tomorrow."

"Oh, please say you can. Just for a little while?"

"Sally . . ." This was getting tougher by the second. "I've got to go."

"I understand." But she didn't release him. "I'm being selfish. You've told me you're a man with a man's needs, and you've suppressed those needs for so long. Does it make it harder when I hold you?"

"I think you know it does," he said quietly.

Sally let out a long, long breath. "Would you just hold me, too? Just this once? I don't know what it's like to be held by a good man, Cyrus. A man who doesn't want something from me."

In his mind he knew he must refuse and break the contact. And that would be another rejection, this one from a person she considered "good."

Cyrus put his arms around Sally and embraced her awkwardly.

"Thank you," she said, and sighed again. "You are the kindest man on earth. Come tomorrow—to this room. I promise I'll have questions about the book."

He hesitated, but said, "All right."

"Same time?"

"Same time," he agreed, and dropped his hands.

Sally touched her brow to his collarbone, took her arms from his waist, and turned aside.

Her left hand brushed over his penis—his erect penis.

He grimaced and felt heat in his face. Their eyes met and he thought he saw pity in hers. He didn't want her pity!

"Good-bye, Sally," he said, and strode to the door.

"Good-bye, dear Cyrus," she told him. "See you tomorrow."

He didn't answer. He wouldn't be there tomorrow, or any other day.

The afternoon had turned even more sultry. Cyrus barely saw where he walked. He had no cause to be ashamed of having natural bodily reactions, yet he felt deeply shamed by allowing himself to react to Sally, and letting her know he'd reacted.

A few large raindrops fell.

He passed the open doors of a club where a single horn sent its sad sounds into the late-afternoon humidity.

Her body had felt so good. He'd come close to disgracing himself entirely.

Another rush of hot blood hit his face and neck. He stopped and faced bars that closed off the courtyard of a café.

He pretended to study a menu attached to the bars.

Inside people chattered over wine beneath a glass canopy where grapevines dripped from webs of twine.

If he decided not to return to see her tomorrow, he'd have to make sure she didn't go either. Her frail ego didn't need another blow.

If he decided not to return. What was happening to him? He could not go. He's already told himself he couldn't.

At a table to the right, a trio caught his attention. Rather the raised voice of the only woman at the table caught his attention because it was familiar. The three were too engrossed in an angry encounter to notice a man in black watching them from outside, where the day was turning dark.

The woman said, "You will regret it."

One of the two men held her wrist against the table and said something Cyrus couldn't hear. The next time the woman spoke, her face was still contorted with anger, but she kept her voice low.

Cyrus drew back, using the angle between himself and the trio as his blind, or he hoped it would work that way.

They knew each other, these three. They hadn't met only days earlier, or by accident this afternoon, and for the first time. There was connection there, and it ran deep.

Finally the younger man stood and threw money onto the table.

He looked down at the other two for several seconds before opening his wallet and extracting a large wad of bills. This he slammed against the other man's chest. He sneered when it was promptly accepted.

Walt Reed quickly pocketed the cash, giving his wife a triumphant smile as he did so.

When Wilson Lamar's young bodyguard stalked from the cafe, he was too angry to notice Cyrus watching from the doorway to which he'd retreated.

Twenty-six

Until Amelia's return to New Orleans, Celina had been increasingly convinced she would, indeed, marry Jack and that it was the right thing to do.

Although she'd wanted to get away sooner, she'd stayed with Amelia until Tilly ventured down from her domain, and then it had been impossible to refuse the woman's evident attempt at making peace by asking Celina to have some tea and cake with them.

Celina was still certain she would marry Jack, but not so certain it wouldn't turn out to be a mistake.

She hadn't intended to stay so long in Chartres Street. Darkness began to close in and she hurried on her way to Royal Street. Despite the slowing down of Dreams's business, she still felt an urgency to keep working. Jack had surprised her by taking his new duties very seriously. He was convinced that at least at present their focus should be on individual needs among children who were no longer hospitalized. To that end Celina had obtained a list of discharged patients from St. Peter's and was in the process of making calls.

She was tempted to make a detour past Les Chats and try to talk to Dwayne privately about Antoine.

But if someone was watching and listening, searching for any sign that Celina or Dwayne knew more that they'd admitted, it would be a mistake for Celina to go to Les Chats.

Celina automatically looked behind her. The evening crowd was revving up. Locals moving with purpose. Tourists laughing and drinking from plastic cups while they gazed through open doors into clubs. Many already carried bags of the obligatory souvenirs—T-shirts, cheap masks and trinkets, incense sticks to ward off evil spirits they'd forget about the instant their visit to The Big Easy was behind them.

The scene was surreal. She paused and drew back against a building, saw the laughing faces and expansive gestures in slow motion. A kernel of panic assailed her, but she took deep breaths and willed herself to be calm. Too much had happened. Too much more was about to happen. Wilson's assault . . . She put a hand on her belly and tried to think of the baby, not of how she had been conceived. Errol's death needed closure. But what could a citizen do if the law wasn't interested—or appeared not to be interested? And Antoine. Tomorrow she would go— No, Rose had specifically begged her not to try to make contact. The woman had promised she'd get back to Celina somehow.

Why hadn't Rose come back to see her yet?

Jack would be angry when he discovered Celina hadn't told him the details of Rose's visit.

"Hey, good lookin'," a man who was barely more than a teenager yelled into her face. "How about you and me goin' dancin'?"

She shook her head. His face was too close to hers. A sun-reddened face. Straw-pale hair. Bloodshot blue eyes that closed slowly and opened slowly. He held a plastic cup of pink slush. A fruit daiquiri from one of the bars that sold nothing else.

Celina turned from him and walked on, swallowing gulps of air. Sweat formed between her shoulder blades and instantly turned cold.

She was going to marry Jack Charbonnet and live with him and his child in Chartres Street. This week she would take that step. What did she really know about him? Only what was public knowledge. And that when they made love he could chase away any doubts.

The kid with the straw hair passed her with several buddies. They called out to her but kept on moving.

A street vendor slapped a disc into his CD player and snapped his fingers, dancing while he straightened rows of cheap jewelry pinned to boards atop a trestle table. Some who walked by clicked their fingers too, and bopped their own dance steps.

The gaudiest city in the world. Celina loved it, or she did when she didn't jump at the slightest sound and panic in crowds.

She walked on, deliberately keeping her pace leisurely. But her heart didn't slow down, and her stomach didn't relax.

An elderly woman sidestepped a tall, emaciated girl on Rollerblades who wore psychedelic elbow and knee pads with her cutoff jeans and halter top. Unfortunately the girl was no expert on the blades. She lost control and walloped into the woman, who dropped a basket overflowing with groceries.

Apples rolled, and oranges. Grapes splatted on the sidewalk, so did a carton of milk. A bottle of vitamins broke, scattering pills in all directions.

The girl yelled, "Watch where you're goin', you old hag," righted herself, and skated away.

Celina hurried forward and went to her knees to help.

"Young people," the woman muttered. "They got no respect no more. Sign says you can't have them things on the sidewalk. Them skates. Do they take notice? Not them. Look at my grapes. And them vitamins cost a bundle."

"It's awful," Celina said, gathering items and returning them to the basket as quickly as possible. The grapes she picked up and began to drop in a garbage can.

"Don't do that!" the woman said. "I gotta take 'em back. They packed 'em in the bottom of the basket, didn't they? Bound to get squashed. The store will have to replace them."

"Yes, ma'am," Celina said, only vaguely shocked. She rounded up the plastic net for the grapes and scooped them inside.

"Look at those apples." The woman tutted and pointed to the bruised fruit. "I'll have to make a pie with 'em."

"I bet it'll be a great pie."

"If there's enough of them left. Where'd they all go?"

Celina searched in all directions and caught sight of both apples and oranges that had rolled into an alley. Despite the darkness, she went after the fruit and began picking up pieces.

The alley was dank. Overhead the walls of the old buildings on either side bulged. Clothes flapped on lines along galleries. If they'd dried at all today, they'd already be wet again because they'd been left out too long.

She felt movement behind her and started to turn around. A blow between her shoulder blades caused her to stumble. Before she could cry out, a length of fabric was jammed into her mouth and her head was forced back against a shoulder.

Celina kicked with her heels. And she jammed her elbows backward and struggled. She tried going limp and dropping her dead weight in the other's arms. She was promptly jerked upright with the gag. It cut into her cheeks and threatened to make her vomit.

She squirmed and tried to scream. Only a muffled squeal emitted. One arm was free, and she reached over her shoulder, scouring about for the man's eyes. His response was to capture that hand too, and anchor it behind her back.

Celina stared down the alley toward the street. Surely the woman had seen what happened. Surely she'd go for help.

People passed the end of the alley. They laughed and jostled. They didn't look into the darkness between the buildings.

There was no sign of the woman or her dropped groceries.

The man behind her spoke not a word. The gag was secured, and he dragged her backward, backward, backward, and against a wall. That was when she saw what she hadn't noticed before. A van, black or some other dark color. It gleamed dully. Celina saw it from the corner of her eye, gradually saw more of it as her assailant pulled her along its side.

Once past its length, she was shoved against the back doors of the vehicle and her hands were lashed together behind her back.

She kicked out again, but the doors of the van swung open and she was pushed, facedown onto the floor inside. With several efficient movements her ankles were also secured.

The van sagged as the man leaped in behind her. Then a bag descended over her head and she saw nothing.

Screaming silently, choking on the gag, she writhed and tried to turn over, but a foot came down in the center of her back and she lay still.

Her baby. She must protect her baby.

A sharp rap sounded. The van's engine turned over and the hard floor vibrated beneath Celina.

He could not expect her to follow his orders as if she were a child or a well-trained dog. Jack jogged through the streets. Tonight he really could describe what people meant by having one's heart in one's throat. Every breath was a struggle.

How had he come to this point with Celina? How could he possibly have changed his mind about her so drastically?

Why had she defied him when he'd specifically told her not to leave Chartres Street?

He shook his head. He'd already covered that. She couldn't be expected to follow his wishes blindly. She'd do what she wanted to do.

And she could have walked directly into the hands of some of Win's depraved hoods.

Jack broke into a run. He banged into a man, spun him around, and yelled, "Sorry," as the other started spewing expletives. It was hot, too damned hot, and another rain squall announced its presence with fat drops that spattered Jack's face.

He'd gone looking for Sonny Clete, but had only managed to track down one of his minor soldiers, a man known as Primrose, for no reason Jack could imagine unless it was a cruel reference to his ears. His ears had frilly lobes and popped from high on the sides of his head. Primrose hung out at a totally nude strip joint on St. Peter Street in the warehouse district. Sonny was known to spend a good deal of time there, too, but he hadn't shown today although Primrose kept insisting he was on his way. Eventually Jack had decided this was an attempt to detain him. He should have left as soon as he discovered Sonny wasn't around.

Sonny was neck-deep in whatever was going on, and something was definitely going on. Win's trouble antenna had been screaming while Jack was with him, and Sonny Clete had been the one to flip the switch to on.

That was much as Jack had planned. He'd set Sonny up to rattle Win. Jack wanted a war, but he hadn't planned for potential reprisals against him that would put Amelia and Celina at risk.

He walked at a more sane pace. According to Tilly, Celina had gone to talk to Cyrus, no doubt to explain Jack's plans for them to marry this week.

At least there were no anxieties about sexual compatibility.

Despite his anxiety, he grinned. No anxieties at all.

Skidding to a halt at the entrance to the courtyard at Errol's place—he'd always think of the Royal Street house as Errol's place—he felt jumpy inside again. He didn't want Celina staying there anymore. In the morning they'd make arrangements for their wedding.

These things were important to women, the trappings of the occasion. He'd like to find a way to dress up what would otherwise seem like a formality, but wasn't sure how to go about it.

He reached the outer staircase, and the door at the top flew open at once. Cyrus emerged onto the steps with Dwayne behind him. They both stared down at him.

Jack's mouth forgot how to make saliva. He swallowed and swallowed, and his throat only grew more dry.

He turned his face up to the other men and said, "Where is she?"

Cyrus closed his eyes and scrubbed a hand over his mouth.

"She isn't with you?" Dwayne said.

"No, goddammit," Jack said, leaping up the rest of the stairs three at a time. "She should be here."

"I was sure you would have found her by now," Cyrus said. "She called from your place to say she was on her way. That was two hours ago. I phoned your place and a woman called Tilly said I should wait here in case she came. I was so sure you would have her with you by the time you showed up."

"We're calling the cops," Jack said, barging into the building. "Not a word from her? Nothing?"

"Nothing," Dwayne said. "Even if she walked backward she'd have been here an hour and a half ago."

"I don't need you to tell me the obvious," Jack snapped, tearing the receiver from a telephone in the hallway. He dialed 911 and asked for the police. "A missing person," he said when he got an answer. "Celina Payne. Last seen? What? Oh, when? About two hours ago."

He swiveled to see Cyrus and Dwayne. Neither of them would meet his eyes. "I don't give a shit about your rules. I don't care if you don't think two hours constitutes being missing . . . What? No, goddammit, we did not have an argument. I don't argue. Fuck you, Officer. My fiancée is missing. She shouldn't have taken longer than twenty minutes to get from my house to hers. I think she's been abducted. What makes me think that? Celina was Errol Petrie's assistant. Does that ring a bell? No? He was murdered only days ago. I'm still not ringing any bells for you? How about there are some very nasty people in this town and I think at least one of them has it in for me. This nasty person is very likely to have decided to get at me through Celina."

He took the phone from his ear and stared at it. The lecture about how long a person had to be missing to warrant some sort of concern on behalf of the police was being rolled out for a second time.

Jack slammed down the receiver. "They won't do anything except tell all cars to keep a watch out for her."

"She couldn't have returned to your place by now, could she?" Cyrus asked. His face resembled damp chalk.

"Tilly would have called at once." Nevertheless Jack punched in his number and waited until Tilly answered. She told him what he had feared she would, and he hung up again.

Dwayne flexed his hands at his sides. "Why would someone hurt Celina, Jack? There's a reason, isn't there? Otherwise you wouldn't be so scared—you wouldn't be so sure she didn't just go shopping on the way."

He thought about that. "And why wouldn't she go shopping? That's a normal thing for a woman to do."

"Antoine isn't around," Dwayne said, eyeing Jack significantly. "I shouldn't have had to come here to find that out. Someone should have told me."

"Things have been kind of hectic." Jack passed the others and went to the office. He rifled through folders, looking for something on Antoine. "I now know Antoine must have found out something that frightened the wrong people. The wrong people evidently had something to do with Errol's death. Antoine came to you to say he saw something, Dwayne."

"But he didn't tell me. He started, but clammed up and took off."

"Okay. But evidently someone saw him with you and they don't believe he changed his mind about talking to you."

"I'm tellin' you—"

"You don't need to tell me, Dwayne. I believed you the first time. These people also think Celina had a chat with Antoine. He came up to talk to her the same day he tried to get to you. What I can't figure out is how they know that."

Both of the other men frowned.

"I guess it doesn't much matter how. They do. And they're rattled. Which means they've got something to be afraid of. Roughly translated, we're close to finding out who killed Errol—or the killers think we are."

"We've got to find Celina," Cyrus said abruptly. "Dear Lord, we must locate my little sister. She's fragile enough without being exposed to this type of horror."

"Yeah," Jack said. His own insides were trying to fold in on themselves.

"What do you mean, yeah?" Cyrus said, grasping Jack's arm. "Celina has suffered greatly. We both know that. And she's pregnant, Jack. I've been concerned about her because she's not as well as she should be. She'd never stand up to harsh treatment."

"Harsh treatment?" Dwayne's voice broke and squeaked upward. "You think someone would treat our Celina harshly? That they'd hurt her? Surely they wouldn't do any such thing." He tottered to one of the chairs in the office and fell into it. "She should never have been allowed to remain in this house after Errol was killed. She should have been taken somewhere absolutely safe and watched over all the time. I should have insisted she come to live with Jean-Claude and me. Oh, my God!"

"Cool it, Dwayne," Jack said, feeling close to being sick. "We're going to work our way logically through this. And while we do that, we'll hope she comes walking through that door."

"I'll rattle her teeth till they fall out!" Dwayne cried. "How dare that girl frighten us all like this because she wants to shop for a few useless baubles."

Jack gave way to a faint smile. "Let it out, Dwayne. It'll help. One of us has to stay here in case she comes back. I've got to search for her."

Dwayne and Cyrus chorused that they were going too.

"Wait a minute," Cyrus said. "Let's think about the route she'd take."

"She'd take the same route I just did," Jack said.

"Unless she's gone shopping somewhere." Dwayne stared at Jack. "I need a drink." He hurried into the parlor and poured liquor into three glasses.

Jack followed reluctantly with Cyrus trailing close behind. They both took the snifters Dwayne offered.

They drank and retreated to chairs, where they sat in silence, sipping at their brandies.

Jack got up to draw the heavy brown drapes over the windows. "There's no point in running around this town with no idea where to look," he said. "I'm waiting another half hour. Then I'm going to the police in person and I'm not leaving until they put out a bulletin."

"I feel as if everything's gone mad around us but we're the only ones who notice," Dwayne said. "Surely they ought to have leads on what happened to Errol by now."

"I talked to O'Leary again," Jack told them. "He said somethin' garbled about wanting to avoid giving the killers any signals. But I think I understand. I did hear from Errol's lawyers. Lowell and Maxwell. Very well thought of. Evidently they'll read the will anytime we're ready. I'd told them we're not ready."

A choking sound escaped Dwayne. He made no attempt to hide the tears that welled in his eyes. "It's all so cold. I miss him so much. He was always there for me. The least judgmental man I ever met."

"Me too," Jack agreed.

Cyrus said, "I never really knew him very well. What I did know, I liked. For Celina to be so fond of him, he had to be a good man."

"I thought the two of them had something going," Jack said, no longer concerned with holding anything back from these two. "I thought Celina had wormed her way into his affections. That she'd played on his weaknesses—at least where women and sex were concerned—to get close to him. I thought she was an opportunist."

"Amazing how stupid an intelligent man can be sometimes," Dwayne said, heading back to the brandy with his empty glass.

"I deserved that," Jack said. "I never gave her a chance, but I couldn't see beyond the beauty pageant title and all that goes with that in my mind."

"None of that was Celina's idea. She did it for my mother."

"I know that now," Jack said, somewhat sheepish. "But I didn't then, and I came to hate her. When Errol died, I thought it was her fault somehow."

Dwayne made a tutting sound. Cyrus remained silent.

"I think I've been as honest as I can be with her about that. I haven't held anything back." Nothing but a great chunk about his activities with Win Giavanelli, and the plans he'd set in motion long before Errol's murder. Those matters were not for any woman to be involved with. "Oh, hell, why doesn't she come back?"

"Could she have gone to her parents?" Dwayne asked, unable to keep a curl from his lips at the mention of the older Paynes.

Cyrus got up and made a call. He didn't ask outright about Celina but talked around the edges. What were his folks up to this evening? Why? Because he cared about them. So did Celina. She had an odd way of showing it. Why was that? Because she refused to do as her parents told her, and cultivate the Lamars. Well, Cyrus couldn't speak for Celina on such matters. She was a big girl who could make up her own mind. Why didn't they speak to her about it the next time they saw her. They intended to do just that.

He hung up. "She's not there."

"Could she be dealing with some business?" Dwayne asked.

"Not at this time of night," Jack told him. "Why did I leave her alone?"

"You can hardly follow her around all the time."

"Follow her, nothin'," he said through his gritted teeth. "I'm goin' to tie that girl to me. Or maybe I'll use handcuffs."

"Look," Dwayne said, "we should sit down and get good and drunk. Then, when she gets back, we can manage a real raging row. What d'you say?"

"Sounds kind of good," Jack told him, but the words felt hollow.

Cyrus gave a forced chuckle. "I hope we've got enough booze. I want to be *really* mad at her."

Jack refilled their glasses, and they perched on chairs, listening for the door and staring at the telephone. He looked at his watch. Nobody laughed anymore.

She smelled the waterfront.

Two men, and she was almost sure there were two, pulled her from the back of the van. They untied her ankles, then each of them held one of her arms and bundled her along roughly enough to cause her to trip repeatedly.

They had driven into a building of some sort. She thought she was right about that because the noises had changed, and when the back doors of the van had opened, she'd heard big doors sliding shut. Like hangar doors. Or warehouse doors.

A warehouse on the waterfront, or near enough to the waterfront for her to smell it, and hear river sounds.

They walked her onward until she cracked her shins on something metal and choked on her own cry. Promptly the two men hauled her off the ground and swung her forward. A door with a high metal threshold.

They said nothing to each other, and nothing to her. Not that she could have responded.

She was released.

The air about her changed subtly as people moved. She listened to their footfalls, and strained to hear anything else that might help when—and if—she got away from here.

Had they brought Antoine here?

She trembled inside.

Was he here now?

Would they do the kinds of things to her that they'd done to him?

Was Antoine dead? She believed he must be. And she'd done wrongly by not trying to get help for him regardless of what Rose had said.

Why didn't they say something?

The hands gripped her arms again, hands that were hard, the fingertips a sharp pressure into her flesh. They moved her inexorably forward. A dank odor rose and permeated the bag over her head. Several times she stumbled, but they held her up and she felt them move her through one area after another.

At last they stopped walking and released her. She made no attempt to move. There was no question of speaking.

To her horror, a length of string or something similar was wrapped around her neck and tied, she presumed to keep the bag in place. She shuddered so violently her teeth drove into the cloth they'd used as a gag, and she retched.

Noises—scuffling, sliding, wood scraping on wood—continued for some time. Then she was lifted again by one man on each side of her. They set her down and she wobbled. Gingerly, she shifted her left foot forward an inch, then backward, and realized she'd been set on top of a stool or short stepladder.

She ached to scream that they were sick, and that she had nothing they wanted, and was no threat to them. Why were they doing this to her?

If she wasn't very careful she'd fall, something she couldn't afford to do, especially now. If she ever got away again, she'd take great care of herself, and of her baby. She'd follow Jack's instructions to the letter.

Jack had insisted that it was dangerous for her to walk about the city alone. Why would he be so certain of that? She'd never had problems before.

A sound like a whip snapping through the air captured her entire attention. A hand descended on her right arm. The man held her steady and shifted her feet a little, making her stance more stable. She'd like to ask him why he was bothering, when he obviously intended to make her suffer.

Another hand ran down her back—and rested on her bottom and squeezed.

Her knees began to buckle. Nausea welled into her throat. They could do whatever they wanted to her.

The hand lingered, then was removed.

One hand settled on the back of her neck, another worked something over her head.

A noose.

She was standing on some sort of narrow stool, or short ladder with a bag over her head and a noose around her neck. Her hands were tied. Only her feet were unfettered, but if she made the slightest move in the wrong direction, she'd fall. . . . She'd fall—and hang.

The noose tightened, and pulled until the back of her neck was forced upward.

Cowards. Filthy cowards. One woman who had been easy to pick off in an alley, and they felt they had to terrify her before they killed her.

When one of her tormenters took each of her nipples between finger and thumb and pinched, she screamed low in her throat and barely managed to right herself.

"Cut it out," a voice said clearly. "Leave her be."

Confusion overwhelmed her. She was to be dependent on one crook with a conscience, while a pervert was determined to take advantage of her helplessness.

"Nod or shake your head." The same voice spoke. "You know a man named Antoine."

She immediately nodded. The more honest she could appear, the better.

"Very well?"

She shook her head.

"But he worked for your boss—Errol Petrie?"

Celina nodded.

"Good. You're doing just fine."

Pressure low on her belly passed downward and between her legs. The silent man cupped her mound. Blackness swirled inside her head. He humiliated and hurt her.

"Let it go," the other man said. "If you're horny, we'll make sure you get something real good before the night's out. I heard of something juicy. Just be patient."

A grunt was all the acknowledgment this announcement received.

"Celina. Did Antoine come to you and tell you about something he thought he saw one morning early? On the morning after Errol Petrie was killed."

She shook her head violently.

"Emphatic. Have you been asked that before?"

She nodded, and tried to steady her stance as much as possible. She detested the notion that these men were looking at her when she couldn't see them, and that she was utterly vulnerable before them.

"Antoine didn't tell you about someone he thought he saw at the Royal Street house on the morning after Errol died?"

She shook her head again.

"Good, good."

"But his wife, Rose, she came to see you?"

What was she to do? She shook her head slightly.

"Well, now, that sure is commendable. Loyalty while under fire. Want to try that answer again?"

A hand slid inside her top and rose to fondle her breasts. He undid her bra and used both hands to squeeze and push her together.

"Want to try again, Celina?" the voice asked. "Rose came to see you."

This time she held absolutely still while the beast she couldn't see handled her with an intimacy that made her feel faint.

"Did Rose tell you Antoine had seen someone that morning?"

She shook her head. The air was cold on her naked breasts, and she realized the one man had lifted her blouse to give his buddy a view.

Please God don't let them rape her.

"Enough!" the voice said. "Give it up *now*."

She was promptly released. Her blouse covered her again.

"Okay, I believe you. But Rose did come to you, and I'm sure she showed you one or two things. Don't bother to deny it. She had instructions about what she was to do. She came to you with some show-and-tell. But you haven't told anyone, have you?"

Celina shook her head no.

"Good, good. My buddy here and I are going to have to give this situation some thought. That will take some time. Meanwhile, you just stand real still, Celina. If you do, and if we decide we can afford to let you go, we'll be back for you. But if you get careless and fall off that step stool, well . . . *c'est la vie*. Isn't that what they say?" He fumbled beneath the hood and removed her gag. "Wouldn't want you choking to death on us. No one will hear you anyway."

Their footsteps retreated.

She swallowed and moistened her chapped lips.

Not a glimmer of light showed through the bag over her head. Her bra had been left undone and rested bunched and uncomfortably taut beneath her breasts. How that kind of man reveled in humiliating people—especially people weaker than himself.

For a long time she heard no sound at all. Then came a sound she wished had stayed away. The scratch and scrabble of rodents. She smelled and felt the dampness. The rodents squealed as they went about their business.

Celina felt the extent of the step with her toes. No bigger than about ten by five inches, and squared off at the edges. Maybe the stepladder was homemade. What if it was weak? What if it broke under her weight . . .

In the distance she heard a clock strike. She couldn't make out what time it was. Her darkness was utter, her fear overwhelming.

Sweat streamed down her body. She braced her feet slightly apart, hoping to steady herself.

Not a single sound in this place. Even the rats had lost interest here and scampered on to more fulfilling real estate.

It was cold, cold as if she was standing in water that turned the air dank and frigid.

She heard water dripping somewhere. There was nothing but the darkness, and the solitary, measured drip. She was tired. She hadn't known how tired until now when, despite her horror, she wanted to close her eyes.

A dog barked in the distance.

The bellow of a horn on the river quickly faded.

The drip continued.

They might never come back. Maybe she didn't want them to. But if she remained where she was, eventually she'd have to sleep. Then would come the fall that went on and on. She would never get up again.

Sing. If she sang, she might keep herself awake. "Didn't he ramble," she sang. "Didn't he ramble Didn't he ramble Didn't he . . . Didn't . . ." If she made too much noise, they'd come after her again. She thought of the one who'd handled her, and shuddered so hard, her teeth chattered.

She hummed and hummed. Tuneless humming. When she'd won the Miss Louisiana contest, she'd danced. Tap-danced. She never could sing, but she really loved dancing.

Celina started to move her feet, then remembered, and steadied herself.

Somewhere in the building a door slammed. In the distance. Probably a metal door. It didn't slam, it clanged. Not that it mattered.

Please don't let them be coming back here.

Please don't let that man touch me again.

"Didn't he ramble Didn't he ramble. Hmmm, hmmm, hmmm. Didn't he ramble." She couldn't breathe and sing. How could that be? "Didn't he ra-am-ble. All around the town. Didn't he, hmm, didn't he, hmm, didn't he?" She wanted to scream and scream and scream until someone came.

"Shh, shh." *Quiet, Celina.* The only ones likely to come were them, the ones who would hurt her.

The beginning of a cramp hit her right instep. She wiggled her toes. Since she'd been pregnant she'd been susceptible to cramps in her legs. Probably because she wasn't getting enough calcium. Babies took a lot of calcium for their bones and teeth. Their teeth were in their gums already before they were born. And they had fingernails and toenails really early. She'd read a book about that.

"Ten tiny fingers, ten tiny toes."

Drip, drip, drip. Were the walls plaster or metal? Or were they brick? The water might run down the brick in rivulets that switchbacked past uneven spots.

Would the brick be red or that yellow color?

If there was dripping, it must be coming through the roof. A one-story building with holes in the roof.

She must keep thinking, keep awake.

A door smashed shut again. This time a closer door.

"Goin' back home. Back home to New Orleans. Home, sweet home." She couldn't remember more of the words. "Back home . . . home, sweet home. Go home, go home." Something about a carnival queen.

The cramp knotted her instep this time. She pressed down on the ball of her foot. Another knot shot out on her calf. It ached to the back of her thigh.

Strength of will could overcome all. Any threat could be ignored.

She sucked in a breath and blew it out, worked her foot, sucked, and blew.

Light-headed. Oh, she couldn't be light-headed. Light-headed and nauseated. Bile rose in her throat. She swallowed and gagged.

Fuzziness closed in around the edges of her brain. A misty picture at the center, a picture of nothing in particular, but framed with thick fog.

"Stay awake. Stay awake, please. You can't go to sleep here. You have to wait till you go home. No sleeping. You're not tired. Oh, no, you're not tired."

She forgot what she was saying and brought her lips together. Inside the darkness of the hood, her eyes closed. A quiet place inside her. Curl in and seek the silence. *Inside you can be where no one can touch you.*

The distant clock chimed again.

Celina sang some more, sang songs she couldn't remember, but it didn't matter. When would they come back for her? "Didn't he ramble." Maybe they would just pull the stool away. Maybe that's what they'd planned from the start. They might try asking her some more questions, but only to give them an excuse to misuse her some more if they decided she was lying.

Drip, drip, drip. What if there were a pipe leaking and the room was filling up with water? Soon she might feel the cold and wet covering her feet. She sniggered. Twice dead, that's what she'd be. Hanged and drowned. Would she hang first or drown first? Maybe it wouldn't matter. Kind of like Errol. She might hang before the water went over her head.

Her eyes wouldn't stay open. Her head ached and didn't do what she wanted it to do. She couldn't hold it up anymore.

Her left foot slipped and she jolted upright. "Didn't he ramble. Didn't he ... Didn't he ... Didn't ..." *Don't fall asleep.*

Just close your eyes. Lock your knees. It's okay. Lock your knees and close your eyes. There, feels good. My head wants to rest somewhere. My neck hurts.

The cramp struck her calf once more. Celina cried out and lifted her foot. She stamped it down, curled up her toes, stamped again, and missed.

Her shoulders were birds' wings. Trembling. Ready to fly. A noose around her neck, like they put a line on a bird's leg when they train it. The rope tightened. She fell. No way to stop the fall. *My baby.* She opened her mouth and yelled *Help,* but no sound came.

Slowly her legs buckled, and then she was on the floor, spread on her belly, her bones hurting, her flesh stinging.

The rope fell about her. She felt it like a long snake killed in midair and left to fall in coils. It hadn't held, hadn't hung her. They would be angry.

Consciousness began to slip away.

Laughter.

"Clumsy girl." The voice of the man who hadn't touched her. "Clumsy, clumsy girl. Good thing you didn't have far to fall, hmm? Sit up, please."

She opened her eyes.

"Sit up, please. *Now.*"

Celina scrambled to do as she was told.

"How was that? Have fun, did you?"

"I don't know what you mean."

He coughed. "I'm askin' if you liked your peace. Everyone needs space. Isn't that what they say? We gave you some space and quiet. What did you fall off for?"

"Tired," she mumbled.

"Time for you to go home, then."

He was teasing her. Torturing her.

"Did you hear what I said? Time to go home."

"Yes, yes, time to go home."

"How about, yes, thank you?"

Celina said, "Yes, thank you. I thought you were going to—"

"Hang you, maybe? Well, we were practicin' this time. Here, you can take this as a memento. Look at it anytime you're tempted to say something you shouldn't say. To someone who doesn't have no business knowing."

A hard object was thrust into her hands, shoved into her ribs.

"You don't say anythin' about Rose, you got that?"

"Yes," Celina said, whispering, feeling what he'd given her. "The top step of the ladder. It broke off."

A high giggle to her right sent shivers over her body. "What?" she asked. "What did I say?"

"You're holdin' your ladder, baby. All of it."

She passed her hands over it again. Anger all but made her throw the piece of wood she held.

"Two inches off the ground," she was told, "and with a rope around your neck that was just draped over a beam with a little bag of potatoes weighting the end. Not tied to anything. Ain't that rich?" He laughed, and his companion joined him. They laughed and snorted and coughed.

Celina dropped the wood on the floor.

The hands she hated hauled her to her feet and she was pushed forward. Her legs hurt so she could scarcely walk.

Through the building again, lifted over high thresholds.

"You're sick!" She shook her arms, tried to dislodge them. "You tried to terrify me to death. Sick!"

Their renewed laughter shattered the last morsel of her composure. One of them held her while the other replaced the gag. She sagged, but they held her up between them and half dragged her until she heard the van doors open again. She landed on the hard bed of the vehicle. Once more the floor sagged as one of the men joined her. Then they drove away.

It seemed a long time before they came to a stop. She waited for the second man to join them in the back, but he didn't. Instead, the man who was with her opened the van, climbed out, and unleashed her ankles. Then he pulled her out.

"Now, you keep quiet, okay? Keep quiet, lean on me, and walk. We're lovers out for a walk in the rain. Nothing unusual about that. It's not far. Nod if you understand."

She nodded

"Good girl. And while we walk, you listen."

They walked. His shoes clattered on stone. Her softer shoes made little sound. "We're almost there," he said. "Now, you've been a good girl. And I'm not talking about tonight. This was necessary for a number of reasons. There are people who have to find out we mean business. You're going to help us make that clear to them."

She let her head fall forward and hung back. She'd pass out at any second.

He shook her gently. "Almost there. Then you'll get some sleep. But listen to me. So far you've kept quiet about Rose's visit. And if Antoine said anything to you, you've kept quiet about that too. I'd prefer to make certain you won't ever be tempted to change that, but for now we need you alive."

For now. They could come for her again. Of course they could.

"So this is what you tell your new friend. The one you're so close to. You don't tell him anything about Rose or Antoine. Got that?"

Yet again she nodded.

"Uh-huh. That's it. That's the way."

He pushed her to her knees, gripped the cloth at the back of her neck, and pressed her face into something soft. "What you do tell Jack Charbonnet is that if we get wind of anything that's against our interests, you'll die. So will that nice little girl of his."

Twenty-seven

Sally let herself into the house through the kitchens. Everything was in darkness. She'd stayed at the hotel until night finally fell, then hailed a cab in the street and told the driver to drop her a block away from the house.

She didn't want to see or talk to anyone.

After Cyrus left her at Maison de Ville, she'd cried. Why hadn't she seen him for what he was before it was too late, and the Church had him. If she'd married Cyrus rather than Wilson, her life would have been different—better.

The book Cyrus had left with her was in her purse. She'd read it at the hotel, but it hadn't made her laugh the way he'd promised. *The Screwtape Letters.* Letters from a lesser devil on the subject of winning humans. Maybe she'd laugh if she didn't see herself in every weakness written about in those pages.

Tomorrow they'd talk about it and he'd make her feel better about herself.

When she reached the vestibule she made no attempt to stop in at any of the main-floor rooms. She wanted to sleep again.

"Took your time gettin' home, didn't you, sweetheart?"

At the sound of Wilson's voice, Sally jumped and spun around. "You're supposed to be at a meetin', aren't you?"

He lounged against the wall just outside his study. "Over a long time ago. And where was the lovely wife who was supposed to be at my side?"

She didn't want a fight. "I'm tired, Wilson."

"I asked you a question." He straightened. "Where have you been?"

He had no right to order her about or to demand. "I've been out." She took the black scarf off her head and looked straight into his face. "I need more time to myself. I'm sick of meetings, and smilin' at people I don't like, and being nice to people who twitter at me, then talk about me behind my back. It's shallow. I'm about fed up to the teeth with shallow people, and shallow talk, and selfishness."

Wilson sauntered toward her. "Why, that was quite a speech. I didn't realize you knew that many words. You'd better be careful. If too many people hear you going on like that, they'll start thinkin' you're not just a pretty face."

"Good night, Wilson."

"You're not going anywhere until I tell you I'm through talkin'."

"I am not your dog," she told him. "Do you understand me?"

"Why are you wearin' that ugly thing? You look like an Italian grandmother in mournin'."

She smiled sweetly. "I wonder what some of your constituents would think if they knew you've got a nasty comment to make about every ethnic group on the planet."

"As long as I'm not with the group in question, what I say about them can only serve me well. My motto, beloved, is Know thine enemies and scorn them when they're not around. In other words, I'm a consummate politician—in all things. And don't you just love me for it?"

"I hate you for it." She stopped with her mouth still partly open. Those were words she'd thought often enough, but never intended to say aloud.

Wilson's smile evaporated. He narrowed his eyes and closed in on her. "Finally you tell the truth. People have suggested that you aren't the faithful, supportive little wife you pretend to be, but I've always defended you. I've been a fool. Get in my study."

She turned away from him and said, "We'll talk tomorrow."

"We'll talk tonight," he told her. He strode beside her and took hold of her hand. "We've got a few things to get straight."

Sally had to run to keep up with him. He rushed her into his study and shut the door.

"Don't manhandle me, Wilson. You forget, bruises show, and you can't afford to have people wondering why the *little* wife looks as if she's been beaten up."

"I'm not into beating women," he told her. "But if I were, there are plenty of places that don't show."

She sat down, but wouldn't let herself look away from him.

"What were you doing at the Hôtel Maison de Ville?"

The breath she took choked her, and she coughed. She kept on coughing and got up to get some water from a carafe. Drinking gave her a chance to regroup.

"Well?" Wilson said.

Clearing her throat, she wiped at her tearing eyes. "I don't know what you're talking about."

"I'll make it plainer. Why did you meet Cyrus Payne, *Father* Cyrus Payne, at a hotel?"

She shook her head.

"What did you tell him?"

"Nothing."

"You always had a soft spot for him. You wanted him when you were a kid. You were always oversexed. I haven't forgotten what you did to him at the prom. He'd die if he knew you told me about that."

"I doubt it."

Wilson fastened a hand on her arm and swept her against him. "I guess you figured the poor, frustrated *father* would be ripe for you to pick, huh? How was it? Was it the ultimate kick for you—fucking a priest?"

"*Stop it.*" With every shred of strength she possessed, Sally fought to free herself. "You wouldn't know a good man if he saved your life. You are the most selfish creature I ever met. And you're sick to say a thing like that about Cyrus."

"Oh, Cyrus, is it? Cyrus, Cyrus. Did he come like a Roman candle? Get it? Roman candle?" He guffawed.

Sally averted her face.

Wilson shook her. "Nothing gets away from me. Nothing that belongs to me, not unless I decide to make a gift of it. I haven't started giving to the Church that I can remember."

"You're wrong," she told him. "There's nothing like that."

"Behave. Do you understand? Behave, or you'll suffer. Now, tell me everything that was said."

"It was private," she told him defiantly. "You knew I was going to seek his counsel. His spiritual counsel."

"Oh, right." Wilson closed his eyes and tipped his head up to the ceiling. "Spiritual counsel. That's the first time I've heard adultery called that."

Arguing with him was pointless.

"What did he say about Celina?"

She stiffened. Now they were getting to what was really on his mind. He didn't give a damn what she did—he only wanted to know if his beloved Celina had been mentioned. "We didn't talk about Celina."

"Liar. What did *you* say about Celina? Did you tell him I think she'd make a great aide."

"Aide?" Sally said. "Unfortunately that isn't the first time I've heard a mistress called that."

He slapped her across the face so hard, her neck hurt. She put her hands over her eyes and willed herself not to cry.

A light tap sounded at the door. Wilson gave her a shove into a chair and said, "Come in."

It was Ben who entered. Sally saw him glance at her, and the sneer that lifted a corner of his mouth. He went directly to Wilson and murmured something in his ear.

"You don't have to whisper in front of me," she said loudly, too loudly.

Wilson gave Ben his entire attention and whispered back.

Ben nodded and Wilson followed him from the room, pausing only to point at Sally and say, "Stay."

"I always knew we should have bought you a doggie," she said, but only felt more out of control.

As soon as the two men had left, she got up and went swiftly to the door. Opening it a fraction, she peered out. Wilson's back was to her, but he held out his hands in welcome to those two horrible preacher people who'd crashed the party the other night.

Ben stood diffidently aside, his hands behind his back. She became increasingly convinced that there was something she didn't know about him. If she could only find out, she'd use it to get rid of him.

"You owe us," the preacher said. "You said if we did what you wanted, we'd never go short of a thing."

"Mr. and Mrs. Reed," Wilson said in his best win-'em-over voice. "Come into the living room and have a drink."

"We don't drink," Mrs. Reed said, drawing up her bosom inside a very ugly brown dress. "Liquor is the devil's tool."

"Come on and let me make you comfortable," Wilson said, unsinkable as ever. "I insist." He strode to throw open the living room door. He held it open until the Reeds, with obvious reluctance, did as he asked.

Before he closed the door, Wilson looked back at Ben and grimaced. He inclined his head and Ben nodded.

Sally closed the door again, very carefully, and hurried to resume her place in the chair.

After several minutes she decided Wilson hadn't done as she feared and sent Ben to guard her. She relaxed. Tomorrow she would ask Cyrus to help her figure out what to do. The difficult part would be to avoid telling him more than he needed to know. More than she wanted to burden him with.

The phone on Wilson's desk rang. Once only. A button remained alight on his intercom panel. The call had been answered elsewhere.

Sally knitted her brow. Wilson wouldn't answer a personal call in front of strangers, especially strangers like the Reeds, whom he clearly detested. There was only one other phone that rang on this line—the cordless in their bedroom.

She got up and went to open the door again.

At first she saw nothing through the crack. Then Opi came downstairs with the cordless phone from the bedroom Sally shared with Wilson. The chubby little man who ran the household went directly to the living room and knocked. Wilson appeared and took the phone. He gestured for Opi to close the Reeds in, which he did.

In a low voice Wilson said, "Neville? Good news, I hope?" He folded one arm on top of the other and paced, his heels clicking on the marble tile in the foyer. "Too bad. Why did you call if you don't have news? I told you I'll take care of you, and I will. If you get me what I want. Your time is running out. I've got my ducks in a row. So far you haven't managed to pull off one thing we agreed to. If I have to do everything myself—including clean up your mess—then I'll consider any debt to you paid. Do we understand each other?"

Sally opened the door slightly wider. What could Wilson be talking to Neville Payne about?

A large hand effectively covered her nose and mouth. Another large hand gently closed the door.

Ben Angel removed his hand from her face and swung her around. He smiled with his mouth. His blue eyes were . . . evil. "I promised you surprises," he said, shaking his head. "I haven't been keeping my promises very well so far."

"I'm going to scream," she told him.

His smile broadened. "And risk having Wilson find out that you're an alley cat who can't keep her claws off any available meat? Hush, chère, and let Ben give you a little surprise, him. Yes? Come with me." He lifted her, then tipped her over his shoulder to carry her.

Wilson had spent a fortune converting what had once been a

spacious buttery between a sitting room and the dining room into his own private bathroom. Ben took her inside and set her down on black granite tiles.

"You had pictures taken of us, didn't you?" she said, winded. "Didn't you?"

"I know nothin' about no photos, me," he told her.

"In the gazebo. You know what I'm talking about. Why did you do that? As if I didn't know you intend to blackmail me with them."

"You're tired," he told her. "I see it. And I see you need to relax and have some fun. The kind of fun you like, huh?" He took off his coat, undid his tie, and slipped it from beneath his collar.

"No," Sally said. "I don't want to."

"But of course you do. Take off that bad dress, *chère*. I got a good surprise for you, me."

She tried to get around him.

He laughed and caught her, closed the door at the same time, and locked it. Holding her arm, he went to the shower and turned it on. "Steam is good, yes? I like steam too. Just like you."

She opened her mouth, but he covered it with his own, and when he raised his head again she could scarcely breathe.

"Scream," he told her. "No sound comes from in here. You didn't know? Mr. Lamar tells me. He sometimes needs a place to be. A place where he can do what he want. A politician needs this. So much public life. You understand?"

"Let me go," she whispered, staring around the room.

He continued removing his clothes.

"I want to go upstairs, please, Ben."

"You don't know what you want. But you will when you get it. Afterward you won't feel like spying on your poor husband anymore. You'll be too tired, you."

She started to protest again, but stopped when he peeled off the last of his clothing.

The man's grin was self-satisfied. "Now," he said. "We have a nice shower."

Twenty-eight

Jack hung up the phone again. NOPD didn't want him to call them. They would call him. Unless he had a matter to discuss other than Errol Petrie's murder, which was under investigation, or the whereabouts of Celina Payne, whom they could not as yet consider missing.

"Still no satisfaction," Cyrus said. "Why does someone have to die before they do anything?"

"Don't," Jack told him. "They said they can't put out a bulletin on Celina yet." He was afraid to leave in case she showed up, and afraid not to leave in case she didn't.

Dwayne shook his head repeatedly from side to side. "We have a right to ask for action."

"They say they're *following leads* on Errol, but they don't have any comments at this time."

"If they won't look for Celina, we're going to have to try ourselves. Where would we start?" Dwayne hitched back a drape and looked out of the window.

Jack pulled him away. "How many times do I have to tell you not to do that?"

"More, apparently," Dwayne said. He set to work with his teeth on his fingernails. The latter were already nonexistent. "I can't stay here doing nothing much longer."

"I don't want you on the streets alone," Jack told him.

Dwayne raised one eyebrow. "Why, Jack, I didn't know you cared."

"Don't mess around," Jack said. If his fears were realized, Win had at least one renegade soldier—unless Win himself had decided to teach "the snot-nosed kid" a lesson. "Antoine spoke to you, Dwayne, and to Celina. I think that's a problem. Until I'm sure it isn t, we analyze every step before it's taken. Don't ask me to elaborate, because I can't yet."

Cyrus clapped Dwayne's shoulder. "We've got enough to worry about. Listen to Jack. He knows what he's sayin'."

"You two stay here," Jack told them. "I want to run over to my place and check on Amelia and Tilly. If Celina doesn't show up—and we don't hear anything by the time I get back, we'll have to figure out how to start searchin' for her."

Dwayne turned his back, but he nodded.

"Call if you do hear something," Jack said to Cyrus. "Leave a message with Tilly if I haven't got there yet."

With a silent prayer that there would be a message by the time he got home, a message saying Celina was fine, he went outside and down the steps.

At the bottom of the steps he stopped. To his right, a figure crawled among the shrubs. "Hey, podner," he said, preferring not to go too near, "if you're looking for a bed, there's a shelter. You want me to make a call?" They'd pick the poor devil up and take him wherever was most appropriate—or expedient.

He made to run back up and use the phone, but a whimper stopped him.

He breathed in, then couldn't exhale. In one swoop, he dragged his "poor devil" from the shrubs and stood her upright. "Celina! My God, Celina. Oh, Celina. Oh, thank God."

A black fabric bag covered her head and was fastened about her neck with string. He fumbled to get the string untied, but his fingers wouldn't move fast enough.

She butted him with a shoulder, made another sound, and turned away.

He hadn't even registered that her hands were tied behind her back. The knots were simple but efficient and he quickly had them untied. Her arms didn't immediately move, and when he brought them forward, she moaned.

Placing her hands under his shirt, against his skin, he guided her head onto his shoulder, worked the small knots in the string, then removed the hood. Underneath, a gag explained why she'd been unable to speak. He removed it quickly and disciplined himself not to hug her. Instead, he took her hands between his and peered at them, at deep grooves where the rope had been. He rubbed her wrists gently, grimaced at her shuddering gasps. As the circulation returned, there would be pain.

"Can you talk?" he asked.

"Yes. My arms hurt. And my hands."

"Who did this to you?"

"If I could tell you, I don't suppose I'd be here, would I?"

She sounded hoarse but very lucid. "You don't know who it was? Strangers? Can you describe them? The police are going to need something to go on."

"No police."

She wasn't lucid. "We'll talk about that. Let's get you upstairs. Dwayne and Cyrus are there. They're as crazed as I've been."

Celina resisted his attempt to shift her. "I said no police," she told him. "Promise me now."

"You aren't—"

"Jack! I'm not a lot of things at the moment. But I'm scared. I am so scared I wish I could hide anywhere that would feel safe. There isn't anywhere safe. They can get me if they want to, I know that now. You must promise not to call the police."

"*Chère*, you know we have to report this."

"You aren't thinking." She began to rub her own hands and wrists. "This wasn't random. This was a setup. I left your place, walked right into a diversion, and got pushed into a van waiting in an alley."

He touched her hair. This had to be a warning aimed at him. Win had all but promised it could happen. But he'd also more or less promised it wouldn't. What had changed his mind? Sonny Clete could have decided to preempt Win's next move and turn rogue.

"Jack." Wincing, Celina settled a hand on each side of his face. "You aren't hearing me. They must have been watching your place. They knew I was there and saw me leave. And they aren't novices at picking people off. Next time it'll be a different setup. I don't want there to be a next time."

"And you think not tellin' the cops is the way to avoid a next time?"

"I think those people are beyond the law. What made them do that to me didn't have anything to do with the world I know. I'm not sure . . . Your father was killed by gangsters. Isn't that what I was told? You must know about that kind of people."

What had made him think it would be easy to make sure she never made connections between him and his father's world? "My parents died when I was a kid. I wasn't involved in the way my father made his money." Stopping her from pursuing this track was imperative.

"Could there be a reason for someone like those people—the people your father knew—could there be a reason for them to be afraid of you?"

No instant answer tripped to Jack's lips. He detested where this was going, but she wasn't likely to stop. "Do you know what you're asking? I don't think I do."

She dropped her hands to his shoulders. In a very small voice she said, "Those men sent you a message."

The hair on the back of his neck prickled. He would wait, let her make all the steps on her own now.

"I don't want Dwayne or Cyrus to know what I'm going to tell you. I don't want them more involved than they already are. Jack, if you do anything those men don't like—anything that will cause them trouble—they will kill me." Her fingertips dug into his muscle. "And they'll kill Amelia."

The night was utterly still.

"Amelia?" No one would touch his little girl, dammit.

Sonny Clete believed you, Jack. Sonny had bought the story that Win was showing favoritism to Jack, and Sonny took that to mean he could be squeezed out as heir apparent to the boss if he didn't protect himself. What Jack hadn't foreseen was that Sonny would move against him rather than against Win. That would have to be changed.

"Jack?"

"Don't worry. I know how to keep you and Amelia safe." He'd better not make any mistakes after this.

"We'll make sure we all stay safe," she told him. "I want to help. Only cowards use women and children to get what they want."

"You are really something, Miss Louisiana. Cool, no matter what."

"I'm not always cool. And I've never been so terrified. But now I'm mad, Jack, and I've never been so mad. Who are these people who think laws aren't made for them? I'm going after them. You watch me. I'm going to hunt them down and make sure there isn't a person in the world who doesn't know their faces. I'll figure out how they can be brought to justice without putting anyone in danger. They aren't going to be able to find a place to hide, never. That's when they get out of jail. They do awful things in jail to men who attack women. I hope they take them apart in there. I—"

"Celina, *chère*—"

"I'm going to launch a campaign to clean up crime in this city. It's time New Orleans grew up. Enough is enough. We shouldn't want to be known as a dangerous place to be. We—"

He kissed her very carefully but very determinedly, and when he paused for breath and looked into her glittering eyes, he saw the tears that all the words had held back. "Cry, love. We'll deal with those turkeys together. But it isn't going to happen overnight. And you aren't going to be running around on your own in the near future. Please let me be in the driver's seat for a while, okay?"

She nodded yes.

His heart pounded. Amelia would have to be watched whenever she left the house. And Celina. He said, "Cyrus and Dwayne are out of their minds, too."

"I'm not out of my mind."

"I didn't say you were," he told her hastily. "I meant we're all pushed to the max and this has been a terrible night. The police wouldn't mount an active search because you hadn't been gone long enough."

She pounded a fist on his chest. "I'm going after them too. I'm going to organize a citywide committee to look into the NOPD. There are things going on here that could bear a close examination. And I'm the woman to do it because I'm *mad*, Jack. Those hoods think they've frightened me into submission, but they're wrong. I'm coming out fighting. Just as soon as I figure out how."

He smothered an irrational desire to laugh. She was incredible. Anger obviously worked very well to carry her through difficult— no, impossible times.

"Let's go up and put your brother and Dwayne out of their misery."

With his arm around her waist, they climbed upward more rapidly than he would have expected. He rested his hand on the side of her belly and spread his fingers. Junior was putting on weight. "This guy is growing," he said. "I'd better get a doctor over to take a look at you and make sure everything's okay."

"It is okay. I've got an appointment tomorrow, and I'll keep it."

"We're going to a wedding on Friday." Even as he said it, he decided the wedding would come to them in Chartres Street.

She halted and looked up at him. "Just like that?"

"I thought it was a cute delivery."

"Oh, yes. Cute. We're going to a wedding on Friday. How do you figure that'll be the date?"

"I've worked it out, and that's when it'll be." He would do anything to take her mind off the terror she'd been through. "You just leave things to me."

He opened the door and took her inside.

Dwayne and Cyrus came into the hallway and Dwayne let out a

whoop. He rushed at Celina, but skidded to a halt just short of grabbing her. He gaped at her. "What's happened? What have they done to you? Who did it?"

"Kidnapped," Celina said, her voice still hoarse. "Tied up. Left in the dark with a bag over my head and made to think I was on top of a stool, when I was really standing on a piece of wood on the ground. Noose around my neck. I thought it was tied to a rafter, when it wasn't. I was afraid to move because I expected to fall and hang. Threatened . . . manhandled. Don't ask. It was horrible, but now I'm so angry I intend to use their disgusting behavior to put them away forever."

"They don't put people away forever," Cyrus said.

His sister responded, "I don't want to listen to reason, so don't bother."

"We'll see they go somewhere forever, sweetcakes," Dwayne said, his eyes hard. "I've got friends—large, dangerous friends. They'd love a righteous excuse to use force."

"Hey," Jack said. "The reprisals will have to wait. I've got to take care of Celina."

"Finish," Dwayne said. "What else?"

"Threatened," Celina went on. "Driven around on my face in a van. And then thrown down under the bushes in the courtyard with a gag on so I couldn't even call for help."

"I'll kill them," Dwayne said. "Slowly."

"They must be brought to justice," Cyrus said. He pushed Dwayne aside and embraced Celina. "Sorry, kid. Not adequate, I know, but I've been scared out of my wits. We all have. You've got to do exactly what Jack says. At least until we can feel you're safe again."

"She's safe now," Jack said, wishing he felt as sure as he sounded. "Until we get satisfaction about Errol—and make sure whoever did this to her is behind bars—Celina isn't going to be out of my sight."

"That's a fine idea," Cyrus said, "but I hardly think it'll be easy to pull off. After all—"

"Yes, it will," Jack said, silencing him. "We're getting married on Friday. Until then Celina will be with us at my place. And after that she'll be with us at my place. When she isn't with me somewhere else."

The expressions on the other men's faces would have made him laugh if he had it in him. "Glad you're both so excited for us."

"Friday?" Dwayne said. "As in *this* Friday?"

"This coming Friday."

Cyrus cleared his throat and didn't say a word.

"Later we'll ask you to bless the marriage," Jack said, proud that he could still think clearly enough to cover all bases. "But there isn't time to get everything done that needs to be done for a church wedding by the end of the week, and we don't want to wait—for obvious reasons."

Cyrus nodded. "I'll be there." He stroked Celina's hair and Jack marveled again that such unlikable people as Bitsy and Neville Payne had raised two great children.

"I need to check on Amelia." He felt an urgent need to see that she was safe. "I'm going to take Celina with me, but I'd like to ask you to stay with Cyrus, Dwayne. Someone needs to be here all the time in case the police decide to make a stab at solving the case. Any problems with that?"

He expected a smart comeback, but Dwayne said, "Whatever you think. I'll call Jean-Claude. In fact, I'll call him right now and ask him to come and take you two home."

"That's not—"

Dwayne waved Celina to silence and placed the call. "He'll be right over," he said when he'd hung up. "Then he'll go back and close."

Celina went to gather some clothes.

Only minutes passed before they heard the roar of Jean-Claude's pride and joy, his vintage red Morgan, right-hand drive and complete with leather straps around the hood—or bonnet, as Jean-Claude insisted it be called.

With Celina wedged in the middle, and her small bag squashed behind the seat, Jean-Claude drove to Jack's place. A quiet, thoughtful man, the only comment he made was, "This is real bad stuff, isn't it?"

Jack said, "Yes. It'll pass—soon, I hope—but we've got to do what the police won't. We've got to look out for Dwayne and Celina. Don't ask me to go into the whole thing now. I don't want Dwayne anywhere he could be isolated and picked off, okay."

"You got it," Jean-Claude said, drawing up in front of the Chartres Street property. "Be in touch, huh?"

Jack assured him he would, and Jean-Claude drove away.

Looking around, searching shadows, and staring at faces under the streetlights, Jack rang the bell on his own door. He and Tilly had an agreement that when she and Amelia were at home but Jack was out, the heavy old bolt would be used.

Soon there were footsteps on the stairs inside and Tilly called out, "Who is it?"

"A mannerless ghost," Jack said, and the bolt slid back.

When she opened the door, Tilly said, "I've been insane with worry about you two," and Jack didn't miss that she'd included Celina in her concern.

"You get in here," she said. "Upstairs with both of you. You look terrible, Miss Payne. You'd better have a shower and go to bed. Maybe some warm bread pudding and cream. Lots of butter and cream are good for women in the family way. Build yourself up, and the baby. Poor—" She paused, and gulped.

Jack and Celina looked at each other.

"I'm sorry," Tilly said, sounding miserable. "I can't think what came over me. Carried away, I guess."

"I thought maybe it wasn't so obvious," Celina said.

"I knew when I first met you," Tilly said. "I've always been good at noticing those things, and it isn't what you think so much as what I see in the face, in the eyes. I thought that was it, and then I took a look elsewhere and knew I was right. But I didn't mean to . . . I'm sorry."

"You don't have to be," Jack said. "We certainly aren't. Where's Amelia?"

Tilly looked bemused. "In bed. Where else would she be at this hour?"

Avoiding Celina's eyes, he said, "She has been known not to stay there."

"I just checked," Tilly said. "Fast asleep with F.P."

"Her frog," Jack said, unsure if Celina remembered. He couldn't keep the fear at bay, but he was going to have to try. "There's going to be a wedding on Friday, Tilly. Think you might like to come?"

Tilly sniffed. "I'll think about it."

"You do that." Jack leaned down until she looked at him. "I'd be very sad if you weren't there."

"In that case I'll come," she said.

"Oh, good," Jack told her. "Do you suppose we should get Celina off the street and inside for all that good, baby-buildin' stuff? She's had a horrible time, Tilly."

Flustered, Tilly turned and rushed upstairs while Jack secured the door and followed with an arm around Celina again. "I'm going to want more details," he told her very quietly. "There may be things that mean nothing to you, but they could give a hint of something to me. We're going to need all the help we can get to make sure we put an end to this." And he would surely be paying Win another visit real soon.

"I don't want to talk about— Some of it wasn't important."

His gut sucked in. In other words, "manhandle" had been code for more intrusive liberties. "We've got lots of time. Forget it for now. Are you sure we shouldn't get a doctor over here to look at you?"

"Sure. Really. I'm jelly between my ears, but I'm strong and I don't feel there's any reason to overreact. But we're going to get them, Jack. And we've got to start right away if we're going to find . . ." Her voice faded away.

He looked at her curiously. "Find?"

She swallowed and made a great deal of running her fingers through her hair. "I want to find them," she said, but it sounded lame.

Now wasn't the appropriate moment to push her on anything. "Excuse me. I'll be right back."

He left the two women and tried not to dash to Amelia's room. Black curls showed between the pink pillow and pink sheet. Jack tiptoed around the bed until he could see her face by the glow from the night light. Her thick lashes moved in sleep. Frog Prince's head rested beside hers on the pillow.

Relief shouldn't be so tainted by dread. Celina couldn't possibly guess how far he'd go to make sure the police weren't involved now. This would be between himself and Win—as long as Win still held the real power.

Leaving the room as quietly as he'd come, Jack closed the door and returned to Celina's side. He felt the intensity of her gaze. She squeezed his forearm and he hoped his smile was careless enough.

"I told you Amelia was asleep," Tilly said, coming out of the kitchen with a steaming mug. "Herbal tea. Drink it down, it'll relax you."

Jack took the mug for Celina and carried it directly to his bedroom. When he got inside and looked back, Celina still stood where she was, at the top of the stairs, with Tilly, who actually smiled benevolently.

He beckoned to Celina, who came slowly toward him, then let him sit her on the couch in his room to drink the tea. Leaving the door open was no accident. He did not want her to feel threatened, and he also wanted her to eat whatever nasty-sounding concoction Tilly intended to offer.

That offering wasn't long in coming. Bustling about, Tilly pulled forward a small table and set a tray on top. A bowl of bread pudding with melted butter and cream floating on top, and scattered with brown sugar, was flanked by another mug, this one filled with steaming milk.

"Thank you," Celina said, and actually looked at the food with anticipation. "I'm really hungry."

"Of course you are. That baby's taking everything, you mark my words." She beamed at Jack with what he realized was something close to grandmotherly pride. "And we want a healthy baby and mother, don't we, Mr. Charbonnet?"

He cleared his throat and said, "We certainly do. Thank you, Tilly."

"Don't you worry about a thing," she said, her hands folded on her middle. "And I suggest you lock this door so our young lady doesn't decide to pay a visit. If she needs anything, I'll take care of it. You both need some time alone, and some sleep. If you want me, call on my line, Mr. Charbonnet."

With another proprietary smile at Celina, she left.

Jack couldn't think of anything sensible to say.

"Not what you expected, hmm?" Celina said, spooning down the food in her bowl with evident relish. "She thinks this is your baby."

He glanced away. "Good. That's what we want people to think." He didn't say that with every moment he spent with Celina, he wished even more that the baby were his. "Tilly's right. You need to sleep. I should get some paperwork done. Do you need anything before I go?"

She set down her spoon and picked up the hot milk. "Could you lock the door, please? I'd like to feel safe."

He frowned. "You want me to lock you in? I'm not sure you'll like that."

"I want you to lock us in. Would you mind, Jack? I'd really appreciate knowing you're here with me tonight."

"Celina—"

"No, don't apologize. I'm the one who is sorry. You're a busy man and I shouldn't take up any more of your time." She set down the milk and got up. "I've turned your life upside down. I have no right to ask for even more consideration."

He ran the tips of his fingers lightly down her arm. "Every day I get a stronger picture of just how brave you are. And how brave you've been. We're in trouble. I'm not going to lie to you about that. But you make it easier because you're strong." He locked the door and returned to move aside the table she'd used. "There's nothing I have to do that can't wait for tomorrow. I wanted to stay, but I didn't want to crowd you."

Her smile turned down and for an instant he thought she would cry, but she blinked back the tears. "Thank you. I'd be lying if I didn't say I'm so scared, I have to block it all out or I'd be paralyzed, but you make me feel safe, Jack. I've dragged you into something that's not your responsibility, but you just keep on backing me."

"That's not a chore, *chère*." There were feelings that should be put into words, but he wasn't sure he was ready to say them yet. He might never be ready. "We got here together because I judged you, and I judged you wrong. But for once, a mistake paid off."

"Which mistake?" She eyed him anxiously.

"Thinking that you were a conniving, evil, manipulative little witch who was out to capitalize on my dead friend's tragedy to further your own ends. And that you were responsible for driving him over the edge and making him fall off the wagon. Have I missed anything?"

She gasped and wrinkled her nose. "That's horrible."

"It was horrible. Past tense. I'd really like it if you'd lie down."

"Would it be okay if I take a shower."

From the look of her, she might pass out at any moment. "If you're sure you're okay to do that. But don't lock the door in there, okay?"

She turned an interesting shade of pink, but said, "Okay."

Bathrooms were really personal.

In the movies they often showed characters poking around in bathrooms, looking for . . . usually they didn't know what they were looking for, except something they had no right to find.

Narcotics?

Birth control pills.

Celina stood under beating hot water in Jack's shower and grinned. She grinned? She found the thought of birth control pills funny? Either she was approaching hysteria, or her sense of humor had taken a sick twist.

She liked being in Jack's shower. It felt intimate, a little forbidden. And the smells were so good, his smells. Soap that was very simple, that came in a large slab and reminded her of walking in a forest— and of him, her bare feet where his stood, her face lifted to the water in exactly the place where he lifted his. Silliness, all of it. Somehow she'd managed to turn a convenience into a romance. But she liked the way this silliness felt.

Looking down, she smoothed her soapy tummy. How could she have thought anyone was likely to be fooled for much longer? How many people must already be whispering, *"Have you seen Celina Payne lately? No? Pregnant, darlin'. I expect we'll be hearin' about the weddin' any day, don't you?"*

If Jack had his way, they'd be hearing about the wedding any day now.

That man who put his hands on her must have been too . . . She bowed her head and let the water pound on the back of her neck. It could be that the other man, the one who had asked the questions, had realized she was pregnant and that's why they hadn't killed her. He had seemed more human than his disgusting companion.

Neither of them was human. She was alive because, unlike Antoine, there were too many people who would raise the alarm if she disappeared—or she'd been taken in the first place only because she'd been elected to warn Jack for some reason.

No relationship could survive dishonesty.

She hadn't been dishonest, wasn't dishonest. Telling Jack or anyone else about Antoine and Rose hadn't been her choice to make.

Had it?

She turned the water off hard and clung to the faucet. Her head felt muzzy. Several deep breaths didn't make her feel better. Bad judgment couldn't be wished away, and when it came to Antoine, it had been a bad call not to at least ask the advice of someone she believed in. Cyrus. Or Dwayne.

Her eyes ached.

She should have asked Jack. She must ask him now. The longer she delayed, the bigger the wedge between them was likely to be in the end.

Tonight was as good a time as any. The towel she'd hung over the shower enclosure slid down the glass. She didn't catch it before one end was soaked.

"It's been that kind of day and that kind of night," she said to herself, and climbed out to walk carefully across the dark tiles to get another towel.

Heaviness in her legs made her weak. She reached the sinks and braced herself on the counter.

The baby. Could something be wrong with the baby?

Stop. Be quiet. Think. It's me, not the baby. I'm sick of thinking. And sick of trying to decide what's best. And I'm tired, darn it, just so tired.

She sat sideways on the lid of the toilet, folded her arms on the counter, and rested her forehead on top. *So very, very tired.*

Water from the shower turned cold on her skin and evaporated, but sweat broke out along her hairline. All she needed to do was dry off and make it to the bed.

Jack would be there.

This was all so strange. Time seemed suspended. Her tummy fluttered inside. Like a little bird flapping fragile wings in there. She loved bread pudding, but it had probably been too heavy after not eating for so long—and suffering a shock that might have thrown her blood sugar into a spin.

Her eyelids didn't want to open.

Little bird flitting in there.

"Celina?" Jack was calling her.

Bird? She sat up and stared at her belly again, and spread her fingers wide—and concentrated.

Wasn't it too early?

The baby moved! Tears welled in Celina's eyes, and her throat tightened. Faint, and unlike anything she'd ever known before, a tiny being moved inside her.

Jack tapped on the door and she looked up. The door opened a fraction and he said, "Celina? Are you all right?"

She remembered she was naked and took a towel from a pile on a hamper beside the toilet. "I'm okay," she said. "Jack!"

He slammed the door wide open. "What is it? You need help?" Dressed only in his white shorts, he was a long, leanly muscular expanse of male.

Celina got to her feet and wrapped the towel around her. "The baby's moving, Jack. I thought it was too early, but it did. Then it did it again—twice. Two times."

"You scared me. You've been in here so long."

"The baby moved."

"He did, huh? That must be really somethin' to feel. Did it hurt or something? You should sit down."

She began to laugh.

"What?"

Celina couldn't get a word out without laughing harder.

"You're hysterical," he said. "Take some deep breaths."

She held her breath, choked, coughed, and laughed some more. "Celina?"

"Yes." More laughter. She'd lost control.

He smiled, but with question in that smile. "Can you get it together enough to tell me what's so funny?"

"I . . . I'm amazed. And happy. I can't stop laughing, but I want to cry."

Jack looked uncertain. "I guess it's an emotional thing, feeling a baby move for the first time." His hand on her back sobered her instantly, and she looked up at him.

"Come on," he said quietly. "I'm taking you to bed and you're going to sleep as long as you can—preferably around the clock."

"It's a miracle, isn't it?" she asked him. "From something so awful, something wonderful happens, and you can't blame that wonderful thing for the way . . . I mean I love this baby. I love her so much, it makes me feel filled up and overflowing. Tears and laughter. All muddled up. I am happy. I am so happy and I thank God for her."

She felt tears on her cheeks but didn't recall crying them. When Jack held out his hands to her, she let him ease her gently against him.

His breath moved the top of her hair. "A man never gets to feel what you're feeling now," he said. "Not in anything like the same way. But he has his own feelings about these things. Mostly he feels . . . a father feels proud and protective. I should speak for myself. I felt that way."

For an instant she felt envy. Envy for a dead woman? "That's a lovely thing to hear you say." No, not envy, wistfulness. But she was privileged to have him share what he'd felt for his own unborn child.

Keeping an arm around her, he gathered the cotton nightgown she'd brought into the bathroom and walked with her into the bedroom again. "Put this on and climb into bed," he told her, starting to walk around to the other side of the bed.

"No, don't leave me yet."

"I'm not leaving you, chère," he said, returning. "You and I are going on together from here. I'm going to get into bed and go to sleep."

"I'm sorry. I'm being selfish. You must be as tired as I was."

"Was? What does that mean?"

She clutched the towel. "How can I be tired? Something just happened to me for the first time."

"Yes, so it did." Slowly he looked from her eyes to her stomach. "I'd like to touch it. They know it's important to do that, for fathers to bond, as they say."

This time Celina felt the tears slip free. "Yes," she whispered.

Spreading the fingers of his left hand, he rested them on top of the towel, pressed carefully, and frowned. He added his right hand, and frowned even deeper.

"I did feel it," she told him. "Like a bird. But I did."

"Hmm."

Celina took hold of his right wrist and moved his hand under the towel. His eyes flickered back to hers, and she saw him swallow. "Do you feel anything now?" she asked.

He shook his head. "I will though. Every time you feel him, tell me and I'll listen."

"Listen?"

"Yes. Sound funny, huh? I just think of it as listening."

She stood still and held her breath. "I feel her."

Jack went to his knees, parted the towel, and pressed his ear to her navel. Celina forgot to clutch her scant modesty. The towel fell to the floor. She stood naked and held Jack's head against her.

"Do you hear?" she asked, breathless.

"I hear," he told her. "Oh, I hear you in there, kiddo. How d'you think the Saints will do this year?"

Celina squeezed her eyes shut and felt her baby moving within her again.

Jack held her thighs and kissed her tummy lightly. "I will protect you," he said. "You, and this child you love."

Twenty-nine

He heard footsteps and got busy with the frying pan, preparing to appear engrossed in cooking breakfast. "Tote that baaarge," he sang. "Lift that baaale." He'd been told he had a pleasant enough baritone, but he caught Amelia's frown, and the sight of her peach-laden spoon suspended on the way to her mouth, and wondered if he'd lost his touch.

Celina pushed open the kitchen door and came in wearing a loose violet-colored cotton shirt over jeans. She hadn't had nearly enough sleep, but she looked fresh and clear-eyed.

"I heard you singing," she said to him, but she smiled at Amelia. "You sounded happy. Didn't he, Amelia?"

He wished he were as happy as he'd like to have been. "Good," he said. He should congratulate himself. He could almost hear a time bomb ticking, and the bomb bore his name and the names of everyone he cared about. "Amelia always tests me when I cook, just to see if she can make me feel inferior to Tilly. I insisted Tilly take the morning off. She looked so tired."

"She's not used to gallivantin'," Amelia said without a trace of a smile. "You two tuckered her out. She told me."

"Did she?" Jack asked.

"No school?" Celina said. "I didn't know this was a holiday."

He'd already prepared his excuse. "Conferences today and tomorrow."

Celina didn't comment, but neither did she look convinced.

His daughter studied Celina. "You slept in Daddy's room."

Rather than do the expected and look to Jack for inspiration, Celina said, "Yes, I did. I expect that makes you feel funny, doesn't it?"

Amelia managed one of her famous frowns. "Why did you? Daddy said you'd sleep in the room next to me when you came here."

"Celina was very tired," Jack said rapidly. "She had a very bad experience yesterday after she left you and Tilly. I want to talk to you about that. She slept in my room so that I could make sure she was all right."

"Like I sleep in your room sometimes if I have bad dreams?"

"A bit like that," Jack said. "Please take F.P. off the chair."

"I can sit over there," Celina said, starting to pass behind Amelia.

Instantly Amelia grabbed her frog and patted the seat of the chair beside her just as Jack did when he wanted Amelia next to him. "Tilly said you must be looked after. Just like when I'm sick and I have to be looked after. She said you need to be quiet and sleep a lot, and eat lots of good food. Tilly said you and Daddy will soon have something very special to tell me."

This time Celina wasn't quick to answer, and she did look at Jack.

"Sit down," he told her. "Do you like French toast?"

"Daddy only knows how to make French toast," Amelia said, sounding smug while she scooped up another canned peach.

"Then I'd love French toast," Celina said, sitting beside Amelia. "Your frog is very handsome."

"He's ugly. But it's just a disguise."

"Because he's really a handsome prince?"

Amelia's disgusted expression made Jack turn away to hide his smile.

"*That's* not our story," she said. "That's a fairy tale everyone knows. Frog Prince is a frog who is a prince. A prince who's really a frog. And he's really ugly. But that's so he knows who to love, because if you love him when he's ugly, it's because you know he's pretty inside. *That's* the disguise. That's right, isn't it, Daddy?"

"Oh, it certainly is." This daughter of his caught every word he spoke and tossed it back. He would have to be more and more careful to weigh what he said.

"Tilly said I couldn't come in your room."

Jack busied himself checking slices of bread to see if they were cooked.

"This is a time for all of us to get used to change," Celina said. "I hope you're going to like having me here with you."

Preoccupied with listening for Amelia's response, he slid toast onto a plate.

Amelia didn't say anything.

He set a plate in front of Celina. "Orange juice?"

"You don't have to wait on me."

"Orange juice?" he repeated.

"Thank you."

"What's the surprise?" Amelia asked. "Are we going on a vacation?"

Jack met Celina's eyes and raised his brows. "Not immediately, squirt."

"Can we go to Disney World?"

It was Jack's turn to frown. "What is this? Blackmail?"

"Jack!" Celina said. "I'd like to go to Disneyland, too. Maybe we can—next year, perhaps?" She glanced at him and he turned up his palms.

"That's a long time," Amelia said, burying her nose in her juice glass. When she came up for air, she said, "So what's the surprise, then?"

"You never let anything go, do you, Miss Charbonnet?" He sometimes regretted assisting her to grow much older so much sooner than she needed to. "This Friday Celina and I will be married. The wedding will be here. We'll have a party. A small party, but it will be nice."

Celina narrowed her eyes, and he didn't blame her for disliking his overbearing attitude, but he had no choice.

"What will I wear?" Amelia asked, moving right along. "Can I have flowers and stuff?"

"Absolutely," he told her, wishing Celina didn't look vaguely sick. "Celina, while you were still asleep I called Dwayne for a recommendation. I thought he might know a good wedding coordinator. He insists you need look no farther than Dwayne LeChat. He wouldn't hear of anyone else getting involved. He says he's going to make this an event to remember. He knows exactly what has to be done."

She laughed, but then, to his horror, her eyes filled with tears.

"Dwayne's going to have some dresses brought over for you and Amelia," he told her rapidly. "Something for Tilly too, but don't tell her, she'll say she doesn't need anything."

"It'll be like in the movies," Amelia said in a hushed voice. "Am I going to be a bridesmaid? I never thought I'd be one, because you don't know anyone, Daddy."

"Of course I do," he said rapidly. "Just because I'm not a social animal doesn't mean I don't know anyone."

"Can I be your bridesmaid, Celina?" Amelia asked in her delightfully guileless manner. At least the thought of a celebration in which she would star was deflecting her from other thoughts.

Celina had located a tissue and dabbed her eyes. "I'd like you to be my bridesmaid," she said. "What kind of dress would you like?"

Amelia looked down at herself as if visualizing. She draped F.P. over her lap and held out her arms. "Yellow. With lots of skirts that stand out."

"I thought you didn't like yellow," Celina said.

"I was being a little toad," Amelia said, matter-of-fact. "That was before I understood that Daddy needs someone for when I get married and go away. Tilly told me, and I know it now. Otherwise he wouldn't have anyone. I like yellow, and it's your favorite."

He hugged his daughter, and bumped heads with Celina, who went for the child from the other side. They held her between them, Celina with her eyes closed while Amelia smiled a wide, satisfied smile. He wouldn't fool himself into thinking there wouldn't be tough days ahead once the glamour of yellow frou-frou was over, but he'd take the break for the moment.

"Today we should invite anyone who ought to be here," Jack said. "It won't be many. Your parents, my mother-in-law—if it's not asking too much of her. Cyrus. Dwayne and Jean-Claude. You parents may want the Lamars here." The idea didn't please him.

"Not them," Celina said at once. "Just family. Dwayne's family— so is Tilly, I'm sure."

"And the baby."

Jack straightened.

So did Celina.

"What did you say?" he asked Amelia.

She swung her feet, moved her plate aside, and sat F.P. on the table. "We may ask Phillymeana if we can take it to the North Pole, and if it's very good, we won't leave it behind when we come home."

Jack looked at Celina over the child's head. She screwed up her face and bit her lower lip.

"Tilly said a lot of little-kid stuff about storks and how sometimes they come fairly soon when people get married." Amelia raised her face to Celina. "You've got a baby in your tummy, haven't you? That happened to Betty Smith at school. Her daddy got married and her new mommy already had a baby in her tummy. Betty told me how you tell." Amelia bowed her head of soft black curls and looked closely at Celina's belly.

"Would you like to feel it?" Celina said, although she gritted her teeth. "I felt it move for the first time yesterday."

Amelia considered, then put a small hand on Celina, and removed it again very quickly. "That's it, hmmm? Doesn't feel like a baby, does it?"

"I guess not," Celina said.

"You'd better have a lot of skirts on your dress for the wedding," Amelia said, and before they could laugh, she bounced her frog and said, "the rude ghost came again last night. He wanted me to look out of the window, but I wouldn't."

"Good for you." The less he encouraged Amelia's retreats into fantasy, the better.

"The man you sent to the school told me I shouldn't worry about things like that."

Jack slid his own plate onto the table very slowly and dropped into a chair. "Man? What man?"

Amelia took off the bow Tilly had tied among her curls and attached it to her frog's leg. "The man at school. Sometimes he comes to talk at break. He's nice. He stands by the wall down at the bottom of the hill, where we roll. But he only talks to me. Not any of the others."

Jack didn't remember feeling so cold. "You've been talking to a man you don't know? A stranger who hangs out by the school?"

"Oh, Daddy." Her look was pure coquette. "Don't be silly. He told me you'd say something like that just to pretend you didn't arrange for him to be there to keep me safe. He said I should just try it and see if he wasn't right. And he said I should tell you he said hi, and he's keeping a real good eye on me. If he had to, he could get me out of there before anyone knew I'd gone."

Dwayne had called and informed Celina that dresses would be delivered later in the day. He just knew she'd be able to make a choice, and there would be a selection for both Tilly and Amelia.

While Jack sat on the couch in his bedroom and cracked his knuckles repeatedly, Celina listened to Dwayne telling her what her wedding cake would look like and who would sing "Ave Maria." He always cried when he heard "Ave Maria," Dwayne said. Jean-Claude would play the accompaniment. The food was all set, and the champagne-apple cider for Celina.

"Are you sure we have to go to so much trouble?" Celina asked.

Dwayne let out a huge sigh. "How many times do you intend to get married?"

"Once."

"We're going to go to trouble. Things you do once should be memorable, darlin'."

"I'm going to arrange home schooling," Jack said to the ceiling. "She's not going back to that school. The bastards. Following a little kid around."

"Dwayne," Celina said. "Someone's been following Amelia at school. A man."

"For God's sake!" Jack leaped to his feet. "For all you know, the phones are bugged."

"We'll talk later, okay?" Celina said, and when Dwayne, sounding subdued, agreed, she hung up and said, "I know you're upset, but please don't speak to me like that."

"I've got too much on my mind."

"We both do. And we aren't alone."

He didn't apologize. He did nod and subside to the couch once more.

The phone rang and he reached for it. "Charbonnet." He scrubbed at his face and rolled his eyes. "Hi, Charmain. No, Cyrus Payne isn't here, why?"

He listened, then said, "How do you know Celina is here?"

The doorbell rang downstairs. Celina was too involved with what Jack was saying to Charmain Bienville to take much notice.

"I'll ask her. Do you mind speaking to Charmain?" He held the receiver to Celina, who took it reluctantly.

"Is that you, Celina darling?" Charmain asked as if they were dear old friends. "You are one hard woman to find."

"You've found me now. How did you do that?"

"Just a hunch. We reporters are famous for our hunches. Without 'em there wouldn't be anything printed in the papers. Have you got a statement?"

Celina blinked, and played with the telephone cord.

"Does the silence mean yes or no?"

"It means I don't have the faintest what you're talking about. A statement about what?"

Jack was on his feet again, standing over her, holding out his hand for the phone.

Celina turned her back on him. She wasn't ready to have any man run her life. "A statement about what, Charmain?"

"Oh, don't play that innocent game with me." She dropped her voice. "What's he like, Celina? Just between you and me. A lot of women would give their eye teeth—and other things—to sleep with Jack Charbonnet."

Celina swallowed but couldn't quite fail to grin—just a little. "Is that what you wanted a statement about?"

"Very funny. Are you telling me you don't know what I'm talking about?"

"I don't know what you're talking about."

In the silence that followed, Celina could hear Charmain tapping her pen on the mouthpiece of her phone. At last she said, "Never mind. I'll get back to you," and the phone went dead.

"What did she want?" Jack asked. "You should have let me deal with her."

One stand for independence was enough for now. "Apart from inside information about your sexual prowess, I don't know what she wanted."

Her statement had the desired and very satisfactory result. Jack stared, and for once he was at a loss for words.

A tap on the door heralded Tilly. "Excuse me," she said. "But your parents are here to see you, Miss Payne."

"Here." Celina felt disoriented. So much in so short a time. "Well— where are they?"

"In the parlor. We don't use it much, but I thought . . ." She looked at Jack, who made an approving sound. "The wedding will be in there, so that Dwayne LeChat told me on the phone. He's coming later to decide on the decorations." If she was delighted, she exhibited enthusiasm in an unusual manner.

"I'm sure Dwayne will make things very pretty," Celina said.

Tilly drew herself up. "I certainly hope so. He's hired a photographer. Amelia's all atwitter about having a new dress and flowers and so on."

"We'd better see your parents," Jack said, steering Celina forward. "Please keep an eye on Amelia, Tilly. Under no circumstances is she to leave this house."

"No, Mr. Charbonnet," Tilly said, and Celina thought the woman turned a little paler. "Should I offer Mr. and Mrs. Payne tea or something?"

"They'll have a drink," Celina said, knowing her father would be well into the drinking hours by now. She dreaded facing whatever his mental state might be.

Very deliberately, Jack took her by the hand and led her down the hall to the parlor, a large, airy room opposite his study. The French windows were open to the gallery over Chartres Street, and sheer white drapes drifted in a slight breeze. Bitsy Payne, in a pale pink knit with military gold braid, hovered beside her husband with her pink purse handle gripped in both hands. In a cream blazer and navy slacks with a fine cream stripe, Neville lounged in a rattan armchair, one white buckskin shoe propped on the opposite knee. Light caught silver streaks in the man's overly long, sandy hair. He was the consummate society dandy, all the way to his diamond pinky ring and the navy and cream polka-dot cravat he wore tucked into the neck of his shirt.

"Hello, Mama, Daddy," Celina said. She held Jack's hand so tightly, she crunched his fingers together. "Who told you I was here?"

He shouldn't like the feel of her skin on his as much as he did, but what the hell, he was sinking into this thing with her all the way up to his neck and he didn't want to climb out anymore.

"We figured it out, girlie," her father said, sniffing, and eyeing the drinks cart. "I could use a drink before we deal with all of this."

"Help yourself," Jack said, and Neville heaved his large frame from the chair and did just as he was told. He didn't ask if anyone else wanted something, and no one made any attempt to follow his example.

"What's going on here, then?" Neville asked, swaying forward and waving his overfull glass of scotch. "Between the two of you. We didn't bring up our girl to be promiscuous, Charbonnet. You might not understand that kind of moral standard, but then, you aren't one of us."

"Daddy," Celina whispered.

"Hush," Jack told her. "It doesn't matter."

"The hell it doesn't," Neville said. "Don't you suggest you don't need to take what I say seriously, you upstart. And you can get your hand away from my daughter now."

Bitsy twisted the handle of her little Chanel bag, but said nothing.

"If you can't be civil, Daddy, I think you should leave," Celina said. "This is Jack's home. He doesn't have to listen to anyone insulting him here."

"It's also Celina's home," Jack said. "We'll be married on Friday. We'd like you to be here, but we'll understand if you can't make it."

"Speak to her, Neville," Bitsy moaned. "She'll be the end of us. Make her understand."

"You can't marry him," Neville said, drinking the pariah's scotch with no apparent ill effect—other than getting drunker by the second. "He's not one of us. I'm not saying we're snobs. We aren't. Far from it. But—"

"You are snobs," Jack said. "But there's more to it than that, isn't there? Why don't you explain it all to us?"

Neville choked on the liquor. Wiping a hand across his mouth, he said, "Don't have to explain a goddamn thing to you, Charbonnet. Father was a hood—a gangster. Not our kind. Keep to your own."

Jack knew an instant of uncertainty. The overdressed fool spoke a degree of truth. Their backgrounds were very different. Jack never wanted to be the cause of trouble for Celina, but they were too enmeshed now. Even if he could make himself let her go, which he doubted, it wouldn't stop his enemies from using her to get at him.

He looked sideways at her. Her cotton shirt rested softly on her breasts, like a coat of violet paint. He sucked in his gut. He'd been somewhere between vaguely tumescent and fully erect ever since he'd discovered what it could mean to be with this woman.

"Jack and I are getting married," Celina said quietly. "At three on Friday afternoon. Will you come?"

"Show her, Bitsy," Neville said. "Go on, show her what we're already having to put up with."

Shaking visibly, Bitsy opened her little bag and removed a piece of newsprint folded very small. She unfolded it, fumbling badly, until she could attempt to smooth the paper and hold it out to Celina.

Jack looked over her shoulder and let out a whistle. "Well, I'm damned. Is that . . . ? It is, isn't it?"

"How can they say stuff like this?" Celina said. "They don't know Cyrus. It wasn't like this."

"You want to say how it was, girlie?" Neville said, even more slurred. "Just how was it?"

"It says—"

"Oh, don't say it out loud," Bitsy said tearfully. "I can't believe it. Imagine the questions we'll have to deal with. The shame of it."

Celina said, "So this is what Charmain was calling about, and wanting me to comment on. She writes this column under a pseudonym. Everyone in town knows she does the gossip."

"Gossip," Bitsy moaned. "That kind of gossip, no less. Where is Cyrus?"

"He's probably at the diocese," Celina said, her patience wearing thin. "He isn't going to be amused by this. But he'll be less amused if he hears your attitude."

"What member of the Catholic Church was seen entering a well-known New Orleans hotel with a well-known senatorial candidate's wife?" Jack read aloud. "Spurious stuff."

"Look at the picture," Neville said. "Tell me if that isn't my son following that slut into the Maison de Ville."

"It could be," Jack agreed. "But I don't see him naked in bed with her, do you? Were you aware that she had asked him to give her spiritual guidance?"

Neville guffawed nastily. "Is that what they call it now? In my time it was catting around."

"Sounds as if you might know, Mr. Payne."

Bitsy turned her back, and Jack regretted his quick tongue. "Look, I'm sorry, but this is classic stuff on a slow day in gossipland. Forget it."

Celina gave him the cutting. A photo showed Cyrus looking back while Sally Lamar held open a door into one of the guest wings of the hotel. Celina's glance into Jack's eyes spoke reams on how damning the shot looked.

"I'll talk to Charmain if you like," Jack said for Celina's sake, not the Paynes'. "One good thing to remember is that she never stays on one topic for long."

"Read on," Neville said. "The suggestion is that because of our son, the Lamars may be heading for a divorce. Says Wilson's devastated, but that he doesn't intend to give up the race."

"Touching," Jack said. "And effective. Should be good for a large female block of support."

Celina was oddly silent, and stiff-lipped.

"Well," Bitsy said. "I must say, you've been kind, Jack. Maybe we misjudge you. Would you forgive us if we stole Celina away from you for a couple of hours? We'd love to have her with us for lunch—for old time's sake. It doesn't look as if there will be any more opportunities for us to be together again before she's married."

Jack stopped himself from remarking that Bitsy made their marriage sound like a death.

"Oh, Mama—"

"Don't disappoint your mother," Neville said. "I've reserved a table for us at Galatoire's. You know how your mother loves it there.

It used to be such a treat for you and Cyrus when you were growing up."

Jack didn't want her out of his sight, but he couldn't risk making too much of a deal in front of the Paynes. Surely she'd be all right with them, and once they'd left, he'd follow at a distance.

Celina was watching him. He felt her looking at him but didn't look at her. This time he'd let her make up her own mind.

"Okay," she said. "But I can't be gone long. I've got too much to do."

"Wonderful!" Bitsy clapped her hands. "Oh, this will be lovely. Quite like old times. We'd better go, Neville, or we'll be late for our reservations, and you know how it can be there."

She needn't have prompted. Nevilie pushed upward from his seat, took a quick step to steady himself, and offered an arm to his wife. Waving Celina ahead of him, he proceeded to leave without another word to Jack, who waited only five minutes—long enough to give Tilly safety instructions, before setting out himself.

Galatoire's was busily elite. Some said it was the best seafood restaurant in the Vieux Carré. The maître d', dapper in black evening dress, bowed graciously and showed Neville and his party to a round table in one of the restaurant's more secluded corners.

On a small table apparently produced for the purpose, a silver vase containing dozens of perfect red roses was flanked by two bottles of champagne iced down in buckets, and several dishes of caviar surrounded by tiny crackers.

In the center of their dinner table, a low crystal bowl displayed a mass of fragrant, floating gardenias.

As Celina and her parents approached, conversation dropped to a mild buzz, and all eyes were upon them.

"Daddy," Celina said quietly. "This is very lovely, but you shouldn't have gone to so much expense." She also wanted to say that it would have been a perfect opportunity to show Jack that they accepted him into their family.

A chair was held for her, and she sat down.

Mama and Daddy took places also. That's when Celina realized there was a fourth place. "Is Cyrus coming?"

Bitsy raised her chin as if determined to be brave. "We won't speak of that now."

"May not be able to avoid it," Neville commented.

The level of conversation rose again excitedly, and Celina looked up to see Wilson Lamar coming into the room—alone. He was beautifully dressed in dark gray with very white linen. His handsome, perfectly tanned face held a remote expression. Of course, he was the wronged husband today. How could she have forgotten?

He crossed the room without making eye contact with any of the many who looked his way. Sympathy etched every face. Celina marveled at the man's ability to work an angle.

It was then that she realized where he was heading.

Wilson arrived at their table and went around to the vacant chair, the chair that allowed a view of him to most restaurant patrons. He smiled wanly at Neville, who said loudly, "My dear fella. Terrible day for you. Terrible day. I can't tell you how responsible we feel. Our son, and so on. Join us, why don't you?"

"You aren't responsible." Wilson shook his head. "But I'm afraid I wouldn't be very good company."

Celina doubted there was a person in the restaurant who wasn't hanging on every word—even if they did have to be repeated for some of the more distantly seated patrons.

"We insist," Mama said severely. "It's at times like this that you need your friends. And we won't believe you don't blame us if you turn us down."

Wilson sighed, managed another weak smile, and sat down. He smiled at Celina and said, "I see this is a celebration for you and your parents. It's nice of you to let me crash."

"Nonsense," Mama said. "You've always been among our dearest friends, hasn't he, Celina?"

She was forced to nod.

A champagne cork popped and glasses were filled. Celina ignored hers, but her parents drank deeply of theirs. Wilson took a sip and set the glass down. Then he bowed his head, and, to Celina's total, sickened disgust, fumbled across the table until he could clasp her hand in his and thread their fingers together.

"We think of you as a member of the family," Neville said. "You can always turn to us."

Celina was helpless to stop Wilson from taking her hand to his mouth and kissing her knuckles. "Thank you," he said in a voice loaded with emotion. "You have been the sister I never had, Celina. I shall never be able to thank you and your parents enough for being there whenever I needed you."

With his free hand he pushed his napkin aside, pushed it toward

Neville, who slid it into his lap with as much nonchalance as he could muster.

After an interval, Celina saw her father fumbling below the table. His lips moved. He was counting. Then elation made his eyes glitter. He pushed a bulky envelope into the inside pocket of his jacket.

Thirty

Wilson Lamar's chauffeur, Jack thought he'd heard Lamar call him Ben, clicked off his cell phone and dropped it into his pocket. The man drew back into a doorway not far from the entrance to Galatoire's, and remained there until he saw what he'd obviously been waiting for: Neville and Bitsy Payne hurried onto the sidewalk and immediately entered a waiting taxi.

When the taxi had pulled away, the chauffeur started toward Lamar's silver Mercedes parked at the curb. Jack, with his head behind a newspaper and feeling like a character in a bad movie, prepared to go to the restaurant. He'd known Celina was already there, and he'd seen Lamar enter. There was no doubt that she didn't like the wanna-be senator, yet Jack would wager a good deal that the man had gone to Galatoire's to seek out the Paynes.

A dark-haired woman, more running than walking, hurried to cut Lamar's chauffeur off from entering the Mercedes. Jack had a better angle on the woman than on Ben, but there was no mistaking that the man's body tensed, and muscles in his jaw jerked.

The woman gripped his arm and clung on despite his efforts to dislodge her. "Did you think if you ignored us we'd just go away?" she said, her voice carrying clearly over the few feet that separated her from Jack. He leaned against the side of the building and kept the paper high. "You are just like your dreadful daddy."

"Go home," was the terse response. "And take that man you live with. And *don't* come back. You've already gotten more out of this than you had coming."

"If it hadn't been for us, you wouldn't be here. We gave you your opportunities."

"I was in the right place at the right time and I *took* my opportunities."

"If that man hadn't come snoopin' around, tryin' to find out some dirt about Errol, you'd still be passin' the basket in Baton Rouge." The words were issued on a hiss.

"Keep your voice down," Ben said. "This isn't the place for this."

Jack noted that the man's voice had lost its Cajun inflection.

"Don't you tell me what to do. You came back to me because you couldn't make it on your own. Just like that no-good daddy of yours."

"Whatever happened to him, Mama? Was he another step to your success—such as it is? Gettin' rid of someone never did bother you, did it? Not as long as someone else did it for you."

"Shut your mouth, boy," the woman said, sounding close to hysteria. "You don't know what you're talkin' about. We got a lot comin', Walt and me, and you're goin' to make sure we get it."

"Or?" Ben said calmly. "What will you do if I don't?"

Jack turned a page and risked looking at the pair. He raised the paper again immediately. Mrs. Reed. Mrs. Reed with dark hair graying at the temples and pulled back into a band at her nape. He should have known the blond do was a wig, only he hadn't taken much notice. She was Ben's mother. And Ben was Lamar's chauffeur. And the Reeds had been Errol's supposed guides to salvation. And Mrs. Reed was waiting not only for the reading of Errol's will, but for some sort of payoff from Ben. Who did she mean when she said someone had gone to Baton Rouge looking for information on Errol?

"Wilson Lamar's got the most to lose," Joan Reed said. "What d'you think the newspapers would make of a man who took a fancy to a boy half his age, then brought him to New Orleans and pretended he didn't know him?"

Wilson Lamar.

"Mama, shut your mouth."

"You won't hit me here, boy. What would the people who vote make of the candidate arranging for a pretty boy to work in his house, to be his constant companion? Are you helpin' him get over his wife carryin' on with that pagan priest? And then there's the dead man who led your sugar daddy, Lamar, to us in the first place. There's a lot here that's worth good money, boy, and we're gonna get us that money."

"You," Ben said, his voice so flat that Jack looked at them again, "you will do nothing I don't tell you to do. You understand?"

The big, too smoothly handsome boy "held" his mother's hand.

Her face contorted and Jack was certain that if he stood closer, he'd hear bones grind together.

"Do you understand?" Ben repeated.

She had the guts to raise her chin defiantly. "If we go down, you go down with us, Ben *Angel*."

"If I go down the way you mean," Ben said, his voice husky and menacing, "they'll need a mass grave for the victims, but I won't be one of them. I've got myself a woman who can hardly wait to help me bury the rest of you."

Thirty-one

"Eat," Wilson said. "You're too pale, darlin'."

Celina kept her eyes on the door, waiting for her parents to come back. They'd been called to the phone but if, as they'd promised, they were going to return, they should have come by now.

"I'm talkin' to you, Celina," Wilson said. "People are bound to look at us. Let's not give them anythin' to gossip about—not anythin' I haven't planned on."

She gave him her full attention. "What exactly did you plan on?"

"I'm just pavin' the way. Makes sense, doesn't it? You are my rock in difficult times. You stand by me and become my aide, my hostess when my wife cheats on me at the time I need her most. The sooner people start to see how you're standin' by me, and how I'm turnin' to you despite the fact that it's your brother, the priest, who cuckolded me, well, you can see how that's goin' to play out. I'm a forgivin' man with a big heart, and you're a strong woman ready to face criticism of your beloved brother to try to make things right.

"It's perfect, honey. You're exactly what I've always needed. Beautiful, naturally sexy but demure, one hundred percent on my team. We're goin' to be invincible, Celina baby, and you're never goin' to regret seein' things my way."

Not a single word would reach her tongue, not a word that made any sense. The man was mad. Deluded, and crazed by his ego and ambition.

"Do you like the roses?"

She looked at them. "Red roses," she said, feeling foolish.

"They're for you. A sign of what I feel for you. And the gardenias." He took one from the bowl, shook off the moisture, and put it into his buttonhole. "That night—you know the night I mean. That night your skin smelled like gardenias. Ever since I've kept gardenias around the house to remind me of you. Your skin is soft like this too." He caressed the flower he wore on his lapel. "Soft and dewy. Velvet ready to open for the right man—for me."

Nausea overwhelmed Celina. She made to get up, but his hand on hers kept her seated.

"Sally was never right for me. Too obvious. Too oversexed. She could never be satisfied with one man, even a man every woman wanted. You'll never have to doubt me, Celina. I'm going to be faithful to you. Of course, we'll have to be discreet for a while, but soon enough—when I've finished with Sally—the people will be ready and willing to see me with you at my side permanently."

"Please let me go."

"She can't have children," he said. "Sally. She never got pregnant, and it wasn't for lack of tryin'." His smile lifted his upper lip and his eyelids lowered a fraction. This was his fiction and he'd come to believe it all absolutely.

"My parents will be back any moment. I don't think we should continue this conversation." She dared not risk making him lose his temper when she had no idea what he might do. "You have a lot of contacts. Have you heard anything new about Errol?"

"No. Put that out of your mind." He laughed. "You know Bitsy and Neville aren't comin' back here, Celina. You're too smart not to know. I gave your daddy a little spendin' money, enough to keep the two of them busy for a few days anyway."

She'd known Wilson had given her father money. "What was the money for?" she whispered.

He trapped her hand again, composed his face into a tragic mask, and said, "Why, for deliverin' you, of course. Somethin' biblical in that, don't you think? Well, perhaps not. But your mama and daddy have earned their livin' for years by providin' what other people want and can't get without them. They're good at it. I wanted you today, and it wouldn't have been nearly as easy if I hadn't had dear Neville and Bitsy to bring you here."

She felt wild. Her own mother and stepfather had taken money to get her here? The anger must be controlled or it would destroy her. If she weren't so angry, she'd be sad. "Wilson, the first thing I want you to understand is that my brother is not having an affair with Sally. Sally asked him to help her because she's troubled. He went to meet her at the Maison de Ville. I will back him up—I'll back both of them up on that story if necessary. I will not allow you to drag my brother's good name—his *pure* name—through the mud."

Wilson compressed his lips.

"The second thing I want is for you to allow me to leave this restaurant. Quietly and with a minimum of fuss. I can't afford scandal any more than you can. I'll deal with my parents later."

"You aren't goin' anywhere unless you go there with me."

"Let me go."

"I'm divorcin' Sally. I want you to marry me."

Her eyes felt filled with sand and as if the lids were too short to close.

"Not immediately, you understand, but as soon as seems prudent. I'll be good for you, Celina. And you are goin' to be so good for me. We already know that, don't we?" His eyes flickered to her breasts, and back to her mouth. "We are very good. The best sex I ever had was with you."

Rape. The best sex he'd ever had was rape.

"I love you, Celina. I've loved you for years. When you were in those contests I hated it that other men looked at you, but that was your mother, not you. It was her fault, her ambition, and it's over. You're all mine now."

"Wilson, I have to go."

"Not now, Celina. We've got plans to make. And the beauty of it is that we're makin' them right here in front of the cream of New Orleans society. They're pityin' me, and thinkin' what a kind woman you are. We're goin' to travel together. I want to do an old-fashioned whistle-stop tour through the state with you in the background. You'll make sure everythin' runs like silk. And at the end of the day you're goin' to be silk in my arms, honey, and silk between my legs."

"*Stop* it," she hissed. "Stop it now, before you disgrace yourself in front of everyone."

He laughed, but quickly covered his mouth. "You think I can't control myself better than that? It's been a very long time since I jacked off if I didn't want to, baby."

"I'm leaving."

"Not until we know when you're comin' to me. Oh, Celina, we're goin' to have it all. Give it six months and we'll get married. After the elections. But that doesn't mean we've got to be on a diet in the meantime. Baby girl, I've relived that night again and again, and I can't wait any longer to take you like that again."

"You raped me." She fell back in her chair, staring, her vision blurring.

His face came toward her across the table. He frowned. "No such thing. What happened was what you asked for. You wanted to be taken by force and I obliged. You loved it, Celina. You're that kind of woman. Cool on the outside and running, hot cream on the inside. Oh, baby, I want to lap up that cream."

"You disgust me." She got up. "Don't try to contact me again— ever."

Wilson smiled up at her. "Sit down, sweetheart. Maybe I came on a bit strong, but you are like a drug in my blood, and I haven't had a fix for a very long time."

"Good-bye."

"Good-bye? *Sit down.*" As if he'd forgotten his audience, he caught her forearm and jerked her down into the chair again. "You can't afford to do anythin' I don't want you t'do. Do you understand? I made you mine that night. I bound you to me. Try to get away and I tell the world that little Miss Louisiana tried to advance herself by hitchin' her wagon to a future senator, then tried to capitalize by comin' on to him when his wife started playin' around on him."

She closed her eyes and stroked her stomach. This little one was no part of this man other than through the small accident of his sperm. She would never let her child know who her father was. No, she would make her baby all her own, and Wilson Lamar could say what he liked about her.

Slowly a pool of silence formed around her, and she grew calmer. Opening her eyes, she reached for some water and drank deeply, and met Wilson's blue eyes, his hard and horrified blue eyes.

Celina set down her glass.

He settled an unyielding hand on her wrist. Very, very softly, his voice like thin steel, he said, "You're pregnant."

She felt the color drain from her face.

"My God. You little fool. You're pregnant. You got pregnant by me and you didn't do anything about it. What the hell are you trying to do—ruin me?"

Her mind scrambled. "Ruin you? Why would my pregnancy ruin you? It's nothing to do with you."

"It's my baby, isn't it? I always knew it was Sally's fault we never had children. I always thought there were children who had my blood in their veins but I never knew about them. That's my baby, isn't it? *Isn't it?*"

"No. *No.*"

"Don't lie to me, you little slut."

She gasped, and the tears that seemed part of her condition sprang into her eyes. "This is *my* baby, Wilson, not yours. Understand that? My baby."

"Oh, surely. Your baby. How interesting that it must have been conceived around the time I took you. Oh, no, my dear, you're going to do exactly as I tell you. I've made a lot of plans for us, and you're not going to ruin them now. I've taken risks because of you. I have to have you, and no brat is going to spoil that until I'm ready to trot out the obligatory offspring. The time is wrong, all wrong."

"Stop it, please. You're frightening me."

"Good." He pasted on a smile and poured more champagne into her still-full glass. "Pick that up and smile at me before you drink."

She ignored him.

His fingers dug into her wrist. "Pick it up."

"You can twist my hand off, Wilson." She felt suddenly calm again. "Pregnant women aren't supposed to drink and, as you've noted, I'm a pregnant woman. What risks have you taken because of me?"

"Forget that. You have to have an abortion." He spoke so softly, she had to strain to hear, and what he'd just said rendered her speechless. "I know about a clinic. Out of the state. Very discreet. No problem made about what month you're in. I can't risk going with you myself, but Ben will do it. I own him. He'll do whatever I tell him to do."

She opened her mouth in an attempt to get more air into her lungs.

"First thing in the morning you'll go. The arrangements will be made just as soon as I get back to my office."

"Well, I found you, Celina."

Jack's voice flowed over her like a sweet, cooling wind. She looked up into his face, into his clear green eyes, and saw him frown.

"As I live and breathe," Wilson Lamar said. "Jack Charbonnet. This is a private party, Charbonnet, and you aren't invited."

"Jack," she said faintly.

He pulled a chair close beside her and sat down. Ignoring Lamar, he studied her face. "Something's wrong, Celina. What's happenin' here?"

"Either you leave, or I have you thrown out," Wilson babbled. "I don't know why they let your kind in here."

"Possibly because they like to encourage gentlemen," Jack said. "Celina?"

"I'm okay, but I'd like to leave now." She looked at Wilson's hand on her wrist.

Jack looked too and said, "Get your fingers off my fiancée, Lamar, or I'll take them off and you may never use them again."

"Celina and I are having a discussion and—" Wilson stopped talking but his mouth opened and closed soundlessly.

"Not anymore," Jack said. "We're getting married on Friday, and we're very busy makin' our arrangements, so, if you'll excuse us."

"The hell I will," Wilson ground out. "I suppose you're going to tell me she's carryin' your baby. Or are you just so damned desperate to marry your way to respectability that you don't care if she makes a fool of you with another man's child."

Jack's fist drew back.

Celina threw her free arm across him, knocking a full glass to the floor. "Oh, my, would you look what I've done." She leaped up. "I am just so clumsy sometimes. I'll get someone to clean that up, Wilson. You just go right ahead and finish your meal. It's been so nice to visit with you."

Jack was also on his feet. He went to Wilson's side and bent so that only the man and Celina could hear him. "You are going to pay for insultin' this woman," he said. "My future wife. Just think about that."

"Oh, I will," Wilson said, the flare in his eyes suggestive of madness. "I will think about it, and while I do, you think about how she egged me on. How she forced sex on me when I was drunk. You won't be so quick to marry her then. And just in case you don't know, that baby you're goin' to pretend is yours is mine, Jacko. It has to be, unless she found some other schmuck to play her rough sex games at just about the right time."

Jack grabbed Wilson by the collar and yanked him to his feet. "*You?*" he said. "It was *you?*"

"Don't," Celina begged. "Not here, please. Let him go, Jack."

Wilson's face had lost all color. He grappled with Jack's hand at his neck.

Celina backed from the table and Jack didn't try to stop her. His eyes lost all expression, and he shoved the other man away.

"I thought I could make you see things my way, Jacko," Wilson said, dropping into his chair again and straightening his tie. Conversation had faded at nearby tables and he looked self-consciously around. He cleared his throat and said in low tones, "In case you haven't already found it out, the *lady's* an animal."

Jack rallied and said coldly, "Watch your mouth, Lamar. Celina will become my wife on Friday."

Wilson pushed to his feet and smiled in all directions. He passed Jack and Celina, offering them similar smiles. Scarcely moving his lips, he said, "I have other plans for the *lady*. She won't be any other man's wife if I have my way."

Thirty-two

Jack and Celina looked through the grimy windows that separated Detective O'Leary's office from a room filled with police officers—male and female—clerks, and a variety of civilians either looking for help, or trying to convince a member of the NOPD that a horrible mistake had been made.

He felt Celina. Without touching her, he felt her and the sensation bound him to her even more tightly. For hours he'd watched her—and tried not to let his feelings show. And he'd stuffed the sick rage down inside until it threatened to choke him.

Wilson Lamar was her baby's father.

Yet again Jack's stomach clenched, and the muscles in his back and thighs. If Celina hadn't been there, he'd have dragged Lamar from the restaurant and beaten him to a bloody pulp. Thank God she'd been there. When he went for Lamar it wouldn't be in front of an audience.

That slime had raped Celina.

The tension in Jack's spine hurt. His head hurt more. Regardless of how her baby had been conceived, he had passed beyond the point of wondering if he could come to love it. He already did. She carried the child and no part of her could be other than lovable. That would be his salvation, that he loved Celina and she would become his, everything that she was would become his. She was both woman, and woman with an unborn child in her womb. He wanted the entire package for himself.

"Celina."

"What?"

He hadn't meant to speak her name aloud. "Nothing. I want you to get some rest as quickly as possible. This has been some day."

She smiled at him, a smile that lingered while she studied his eyes. Then she returned her attention to the room beyond the windows.

For her he could be, or do anything. Tough, cool Jack Charbonnet had done the unimaginable; he'd lost himself to a woman and he loved being lost as much as he loved her. Almost.

Immediately after leaving the restaurant, while his head pulsed with fury and he struggled not to go after Lamar again, he had told Celina what he'd overheard between Ben Angel and Mrs. Reed. They'd driven to Baton Rouge then, to the area where they understood the Reeds lived, looking for answers about Errol, and on the way they'd talked about Wilson Lamar, and about the way the Paynes had been willing to take money to get Celina alone with him.

Jack studied her some more. A brave woman with the kind of inner strength that could make a man feel very humble. Tiredness made her ethereal, and so lovely to him. She'd been loyal to her parents, too loyal. But for their own ends they'd offered her up to a man they knew she hated and she was finally angry enough to want to keep her distance from them.

His own problem would continue to be an urge to kill Wilson Lamar.

"I had no idea it was like this," Celina said. She sat in a wooden chair with one leg shorter than the others, and looked startled each time she moved and the chair lurched. "How can they have time to deal with anything properly?"

"They can deal properly with anything they care about."

"We're just going to ask about Errol, aren't we, Jack?"

He crossed his arms. "Probably. If we mention Wilson Lamar, we'd better tread very lightly, if that's what you mean. Here comes O'Leary. Let me take the lead, if that's okay?"

She didn't have time to answer him before O'Leary pushed open the door and smashed it shut behind him. He tossed his hat at a hook behind his desk. The hat missed and fell on the floor. O'Leary left it there.

Balding, gray-faced, and apparently exhausted, he turned dull eyes on Celina and Jack. "Yeah?"

"Celina Payne and Jack Charbonnet. Errol Petrie was—"

"I know who Errol Petrie was." He threw a pack of Camels and a Bic on his desk. "And I know who you are. I asked what you want here."

Jack rose. "I want action. And I want *answers,* O'Leary. Errol's been dead long enough for you to at least be able to give us a full autopsy report."

O'Lear shrugged. "Petrie drowned."

"We know that." Jack stuck his hands in his pockets. They were safer there than in O'Leary's bored face. "How long was he dead before we found him?"

"I'm not at liberty to disclose that. Could compromise the case."

"Compromise is a big word with you, isn't it?" Celina said.

"I'm just doing my job, ma'am."

"We have a right to know more," Jack said. "The day he died you asked if I'd turned Errol over. Why?" He heard Celina's indrawn breath but concentrated on watching O'Leary.

The man shrugged again. "No reason you can't know. He went into the water facefirst. Never had a chance. Whoever did it to him was big enough to make sure he took in enough water not to be able to fight back fast enough. There were bruises on the back of his neck and between his shoulder blades, and his toenails had bled where he kicked the bottom of the tub."

"Oh," Celina said, and Jack turned to her. She screwed up her eyes. "Oh, Jack. Poor Errol."

"What we don't have," O'Leary said, "is a suspect. Possible motives, but no suspects. The man had a past. He'd been a drunk who liked women too much. He still liked women when he died, not that it's a crime. But he could have made some husband or boyfriend angry enough to kill him. Do you have any ideas you'd like to share on that?"

Jack hated that after the hours they'd just spent asking questions in Baton Rouge, Celina had to go through this too. She'd refused to go home without him, so there had been no choice but to let her come. "Errol lived a good life," he told O'Leary. "He committed himself to serving terminally ill children. You're right about his past. That isn't a revelation. He'd kicked his problems, but you're also right that there's something we're all missing. And I don't think it's an angry boyfriend or husband. We stopped by to mention a possible lead you might want to take a look at."

"Oh, good," O'Leary said, flopping into his chair and hauling his big, dusty shoes onto his battered desk. He closed his eyes and let his head loll back. "So why don't you two experts set this amateur on the right track?"

"You're a touchy man, O'Leary," Jack said. "We're as tired as you are, and maybe as jaded about now. But we lost a friend and no one seems to give a . . . no one seems to care a whole lot. Celina and I went to Baton Rouge to ask some questions this afternoon. Then we came straight back here to see you. Errol had been going there to some prayer meetings. For some time, only we didn't know about it. Evidently it brought him some peace."

"Different strokes," the detective said without opening his eyes. "Learn to play a tambourine or somethin', did he? Speak in tongues?"

"It's a cheap shot to poke fun at what matters to other people," Celina said, effectively silencing Jack and snapping O'Leary's eyes open. She continued. "What you think about the way people choose to worship isn't the issue here. Errol spending a lot of time in Baton Rouge is. Would you like to know what we found out today? Or should we leave and see what we can do with the information ourselves?"

Jack almost laughed. She should have been a diplomat.

"Spill it," O'Leary said, uncrossing and recrossing his dirty black laceups. "And cut any detours if you don't mind, ma'am. It's been a long day."

"It's been a long day for us too," she said. "Errol Petrie started attending prayer meetings just out of Baton Rouge. That seems to have been about six months ago. The people who were the ministers are called Joan and Walt Reed. They showed up here in New Orleans shortly after Errol's death. They said Errol had told them he'd make sure they never wanted for anything. Evidently Errol had even replaced their tent. According to them, they saved his spirit and that gave them the right to ask about his will."

She paused and looked at Jack. O'Leary's eyes were closed again.

"We asked around the area. The Reeds' place is closed up—which isn't surprising since they're here in New Orleans like a couple of buzzards waiting to pick the bones."

"What did you find out?" O'Leary asked.

Jack didn't care if the man listened, or attempted to do anything with what they told him. He just didn't want to be accused of concealing information. "Errol took a liking to Mrs. Reed's son, Ben, by her former marriage to a man called Angel. Mr. Angel dropped out of the picture some years back and Mrs. Reed remarried. But what's interesting to us is that Errol Petrie was kind to Ben—who is bright—and encouraged him to go back to school."

"Admirable," O'Leary muttered.

Celina raised a hand, signifying she wanted to carry on. "Errol lost his own son. That may have played a part in the way he wanted to help this young man. Anyway, Ben helped out at the prayer meetings. Collecting donations and so on. We don't know if he ever went back to school, but he's been seen here in New Orleans. Another man went to ask questions about Errol Petrie and what he was doing on all his visits to Baton Rouge. This man was looking for dirt, according to the people we spoke to. They didn't know his name. But they said he liked Ben Angel, and one night there was an argument between Ben and his folks and Ben took off with this man."

"Is this going anywhere?" O'Leary said, jerking his feet to the floor and leaning across his desk. His eyes were bloodshot. "If it's going to take a while, I'd like to get some of the stuff that passes for coffee around here." He tapped a smashed Camel from the pack and lit up. Smoke curled, making him close one eye.

"Ben Angel is here in New Orleans," Jack said. "I saw him around lunchtime today outside a restaurant. I also saw Mrs. Reed talking to him. That was just before Celina and I took a run to Baton Rouge. Would you check something out for us, please?"

O'Leary spread his arms. "My time is your time. I'm a public servant, and you're the public." Stuck between his moving lips, the cigarette bobbed up and down when he talked.

Jack didn't find O'Leary amusing. "You people were called to a fund-raising party held at the home of Mr. and Mrs. Wilson Lamar. There'd been an attempted robbery and the suspect was apprehended by the pool. Would you look up that incident, please?"

For an instant Jack thought O'Leary would refuse, but he pushed to his feet and left the room. Ten minutes later he returned with a computer printout in his hand. "Is this it?" He pushed the paper at Jack, who scanned it quickly and handed it back.

"Well?" O'Leary asked.

"That would be it. Where's the rest of it?"

"That's the lot. Lamar let the kid go. We don't take kindly to being called out, only to be told there aren't any charges and we wasted our time."

Celina shifted to the edge of her seat. "No charges? They didn't—"

"Uh-uh." O'Leary opened a penknife and cleaned his fingernails with the tip of the blade. "Evidently the kid didn't get a chance to take anything, so Lamar waited until we got him in the car and downtown, then came in and told us there weren't any charges. The end. Not a thing we could do."

In other words, Wilson had used the elaborate piece of drama Celina had described to justify his decision to employ Ben Angel, the aquarium man who never saw an aquarium before he saw the ones someone else had already put in for his new boss. The biggie was why? There were a lot of whys. Unless Wilson had a thing for boys, Jack couldn't come up with a reason.

"We came to pass all this along in case it's of any use," Jack said. "The man who brought Ben back to New Orleans was Wilson Lamar. Ben is now his bodyguard and chauffeur. Nothing against that, but Wilson did go to Baton Rouge several weeks ago asking questions about Errol and what he was doing there." He felt Celina shift and realized he'd just violated his own earlier statement, and all but accused Wilson of playing a part in some plot.

O'Leary tossed the printout on his desk. "Is that it?"

Celina and Jack looked at each other and stood up in unison. "That's it," Celina said. "Just checking in."

"Well, we certainly do thank you. Don't hesitate to come by with any other brilliant pieces of detective work. I'm always lookin' for ways to sharpen my skills." The man shook his head. "Maybe I'll take the pair of you along on a bust. Budding pair of sleuths like you shouldn't be wasted."

Jack held his temper—just. "There is something else you might do if you've got a spare hour. Errol had a man who worked for him for years. His name was Antoine. I don't know his last name. But he's gone. He left Royal Street some days after Errol was killed and never came back. That was several days ago now. I wouldn't have said he was the kind of guy to abandon a sinking ship, which makes me wonder if he's afraid of something."

"*Now* are we finished?" O'Leary said.

"Yes, sir," Jack told him. He put an arm around Celina's board-stiff shoulders and walked her out to the street without another word to a member of the force.

On the sidewalk she said, "What made you mention Antoine?"

"I've been thinking about him. I like the guy and I can't figure out why he's dropped from sight."

Celina didn't say anything and he looked at her curiously. She was serious, but then smiled suddenly and warmed him as only she seemed to warm him these days.

"Going to O'Leary was a waste of time," he muttered.

Celina said, "No, it wasn't. Now we know that whole thing with the boy who supposedly robbed guests at the Lamars' was engineered to explain why Wilson hired Ben."

"Only it doesn't," Jack told her, walking toward Les Chats. They needed to check in with Dwayne. "What it proves is that good ol' Wilson felt he had to have some sort of cover for hiring the kid. But we still don't know why he hired him."

"You are just too sharp for yourself," Celina said, smiling up at him. "And now we're going to have to find out that little piece of information for ourselves."

Dwayne hadn't been at Les Chats. A worried Jean-Claude spoke of some man who came to talk to Dwayne and how Dwayne left immediately afterward, saying he was going to Royal Street to talk with Cyrus, whom he'd evidently come to trust. Jean-Claude had smiled at that and said, "I swear that boy is feelin' guilty 'bout somethin'. Nobody does guilt like a good Catholic boy. I guess your brother has become his confessor, Celina. Now, there's a priest even I might be able to get excited about." He smiled, but it was a deliberately lascivious smile, and they all laughed.

They found Dwayne stretched full-length on the bright yellow sofa in the parlor at Royal Street. He took one look at Jack and Celina and put an arm over his face.

"Is Cyrus here?" Celina asked. "He said he would be."

"The good Father has gone to counsel his nemesis. Mrs. Wilson Lamar. I told him he has a death wish, but he reminded me that he has a responsibility to God's children. That brother of yours is just too good, Celina, but I like him. A decent man can be hard to find, and he's decent."

"Yes, he is," she agreed. "Thank you."

"Your daddy called," Dwayne said. He looked uncomfortable. "I know I'm not supposed to say a bad word about someone else's parents, but that man surely does think he should be able to control his children. And he does not want his little girl getting married to a man he hasn't chosen."

Celina sighed. "My folks can't understand that their children don't care about the same things that matter so much to them." She was too tired to dwell on just how disgusted she was with her parents.

"I'd say you understand them very well." Dwayne spoke to Celina, but his eyes were on Jack. "Your daddy wanted to know where you were, girl. You and Cyrus. I couldn't give him any information on you because I didn't know."

"Thank you, Dwayne. You couldn't do anything else."

She waited for Jack to say something, but when he didn't, she said, "Jean-Claude said a man came to see you and you were upset afterward. D'you want to talk about it?"

"Do I want to talk about how I was told not to talk? Short conversation. Really short when you consider I never got to hear what it is I'm not to talk about."

Jack surprised Celina by sitting in an armchair and pulling her to sit on his lap. He did it as easily as if they'd been doing similar things for years. "I take it you're talking about when Antoine came to see you at the club. Someone came by to warn you not to talk about it?"

"Yeah. He bruised my arm." Dwayne unbuttoned the cuff of a loose sleeve and rolled it up to reveal multiple purple bruises. "Wretch. Pickin' on a pacifist."

"He might not know you're a pacifist," Celina couldn't help saying. She earned herself a baleful stare.

"Could you pick out the guy?" Jack asked.

Dwayne gave him a pitying look. "A man tries to unscrew my arm and you think I might not remember his face? He had ears so high on his head, the wind would have to go under his hat."

Jack didn't comment.

"I told the man Antoine didn't say a thing," Dwayne went on. "He came in wearing that ridiculous hat and shifted from foot to foot, lookin' around like he was afraid he was about to lose his virginity."

Jack smiled at Celina but quickly looked away.

"Where's Antoine?" Dwayne asked. "I've known him for years, and he isn't the type to run away from some trouble. Especially not trouble that involved Errol. He loved Errol. I would not say this if we weren't in up to our necks, but Antoine's illegal. Errol found him and his wife and kids—they were babies at the time—down in Florida and took a shine to them the way he was always taking a shine to the underdog. He brought them back here and put Antoine to work. He paid him enough to live okay. Antoine wouldn't disappear at a time like this."

"Unless he's afraid of being deported," Jack said grimly.

"That wouldn't stop him," Dwayne insisted.

"Jack told the police he hasn't seen him," Celina said. Her head thumped.

"The detective—he's the one who's in charge of Errol's case—he didn't seem interested. People come and go in menial jobs around here all the time. It would be tough to get the police interested."

Could it be so tough if she told about the T-shirt and the broken front tooth? Celina asked herself.

"Anybody home?" came Jean-Claude's voice as the door to the hallway opened and slammed shut again. "Do I have something for you. Oooh, boy, there's trouble in River City and a certain person's in the middle of it. Cyrus!"

"Get in here, JC," Dwayne called. "And keep your voice down, darlin', we aren't deaf yet."

Looking cool in a beige linen suit, Jean-Claude appeared in the doorway. "Where's Cyrus?"

"With Sally Lamar," Celina said promptly. The less hedging, the better. "He doesn't take kindly to liars and gossips."

"I guess he isn't gonna want to give Charmain Bienville a hickey, huh?" Jean-Claude said.

"JC," Dwayne said severely. "Not in front of Celina."

Jean-Claude actually turned a little pink. He said, "Sorry. I forgot. You sure that's where Cyrus is?"

"Absolutely," Celina said. "He made arrangements to meet her again today, and he said he refused to let some small-minded gossip-mongers stand in the way of his counseling a needy soul. He thinks Sally is sincere in wanting to make her peace with God."

"Difficult to believe," Dwayne said. "But I'd never argue with Cyrus if the subject was God."

They all laughed and the atmosphere lightened. Jack asked, "Where are they meeting?" but Celina shook her head and said she didn't know. The less she shared Cyrus's plans for claiming Sally's soul for the Lord, the better.

"Do stop flitting about," Dwayne said. "All of you. We've got a wedding in three days. I have a lot to do and I need the cooperation of the happy family."

"I thought we wouldn't have to do anything," Jack said. "Dwayne the expert is taking care of every detail."

"As long as you agree to everything I've arranged, you don't have to do anything. I've looked at your parlor several times, Jack. It's going to be a fairy tale by the time I've finished. I rendered a design and there'll be a lowered ceiling like a striped big top made of silk streamers with painted flowers twining up the streamers. The painted flowers will be echoed with the real thing. There will be urns standing in every corner of the room, in the windows, everywhere we can put a stone urn. I've been promised I can do roses and have plenty to choose from, so it will be roses. I thought pale pink and cream. Celina?"

"Very pretty." She couldn't imagine preparing for a wedding, least of all her own.

A knock at the door silenced them all and Jean-Claude went to look. He came back with a tall, clearly very expensive crystal vase filled with long-stemmed red roses.

When the delivery boy had left, Jack asked if he could see who Celina's secret admirer might be, and she told him to go ahead. She couldn't stop him indefinitely anyway.

A card said, *Forgive me, please,* but wasn't signed.

"A secret admirer no less," Dwayne said. "How romantic." He caught Jack's eyes and said, "Sorry."

"Not so secret," Jack said, his lip curling.

Celina let the comment pass.

"I didn't want to bring this here, but I've got to," Jean-Claude said, pulling a folded sheet from an inside pocket of his jacket and handing it to Jack. "By tomorrow this is going to be all over the city. Cyrus's name will be dragged back into it. See if it isn't. He's going to need some advice."

Jack took the sheet from one of the city's sensationalist rags. Celina looked over his shoulder. She sat upright on his lap so abruptly, she butted his jaw with her brow, and he grunted.

A lurid photograph on an inside page showed a woman apparently in the throes of sexual ecstasy. The back of a man covered much of her, but one breast—slightly fuzzed out of focus but crowned with what appeared to be a blossom—was revealed. She clung to some sort of bars and her legs were wrapped around the man. No imagination at all was required to visualize what couldn't be seen.

"Hell," Jack muttered. "Seems like taking freedom of the press a bit far."

"That's Sally Lamar," Jean-Claude said. "Some employee of Lamar's talked out of school to a reporter. I've got a hunch he probably also arranged to have that shot taken. I bet the little creep cleaned up. Her friend in the picture is *unnamed.* Now ain't that justice?"

"Insatiable Senator's Wife," Jack read the headline aloud. "Senator's bodyguard speaks out about victimization by his boss's wife. He told the reporter, 'She made it clear that she expected sexual favors, and if she didn't get them, you were likely to lose your job.' Bull. I don't like Sally Lamar, but I don't think she'd have to stoop to this."

Celina didn't analyze that statement too deeply. Sally was a lovely, desirable woman, and Jack was a sexual animal himself.

"So," Dwayne said, "what's the punch line?"

Jack read on and suddenly crumpled the paper in his lap.

"What?" Dwayne and Celina asked in unison.

"According to this, Sally Lamar says she's been trying to find peace in other men's arms, men other than Errol's since he died. She says she's going to give Wilson an amicable divorce because he deserves it."

Celina bowed her head.

"Jeesh," Dwayne said, his eyes huge. "What d'you suppose is going on there?"

Jack shook out the paper and read again. "Mrs. Lamar tearfully admitted to having sex with dozens of men, influential, well known men in New Orleans. She says she's insatiable and will seek treatment, but that it isn't fair to burden her husband with her troubles at a time when he's seeking election."

He looked up and around the room. "She says she hopes he'll find someone else to marry, someone who'll be the helpmate she couldn't be. And the parting shot is that she's going to offer herself to the police for questioning because she believes she was the last to see Errol Petrie alive. That was while they were having sex in his bath."

Thirty-three

It was all over now. Sally walked rapidly down an aisle in the dark church until she reached a small side-chapel lit by guttering candles suspended on heavy chains. There was a smell of old incense, and it sickened her, but she had known the only way to get Cyrus out to see her at this time of night would be to meet him on the kind of turf he understood best.

It was all over unless Cyrus could come up with a way to help her.

She entered the chapel and wasn't surprised to see a tall man in clerical garb seated to one side of three kneelers. In the flickering gold light from the candles, he was painfully handsome.

"Cyrus," she said, her voice breaking. "Thank you for coming."

"Come and sit down. We must be careful we're not seen or heard. No one followed you?"

"No one. I was very careful. I left a party when no one was looking and took a very circuitous route here."

He indicated another chair, and she moved it close to him.

Cyrus said nothing, but she felt him draw back inside himself. Her sexuality frightened him, but then, it always had. "I wanted to see you as soon as that horrible picture came out in the paper," she told him.

"Yes. Fortunately, although my superiors are displeased with the publicity, they choose to accept my version of what happened. And since my job is to aid the troubled, I cannot be chastised for trying to do so."

She sat down so close their knees touched. "Did you see what was in the paper about me today?"

"I was shown by my archbishop."

Sally shuddered with genuine horror. "How awful. It was a setup, you know."

"That isn't any affair of mine. Do you want absolution?"

"No! No, thank you." She wanted to scream at him to be a man just this once, and react with a man's emotions. "It says in the paper that I've agreed to divorce Wilson."

"Have you?"

She slid from her chair and went to her knees beside his thighs. "I don't believe in divorce." Careful to make no sudden moves, she stroked his hard thigh, then rested her head there. "Please make me feel better, Cyrus. Comfort me. I'm so alone. He made me say those things because he was angry. Tell me what I should do to save my marriage? Should I bring Wilson down if it will keep us together? I can do that, you know. I'm not stupid. All the tricks he's played are obvious to me. He set me up because there's another woman he wants, but he's got to have public sympathy before he can get rid of me without losing enough votes to finish him."

"Why are you telling me all of this?"

"Because you're involved in a way. It's your sister Wilson wants. He's always wanted her. And if he can get rid of me and have the world think I've done him some terrible wrongs, they'll rally around him when he marries your gorgeous, squeaky-clean sister."

"Sally, my sister isn't interested in your husband."

She sighed and brushed her cheek back and forth on his leg. "You are a wonderful man, Cyrus. But you don't understand some things. You could be right and Celina may not want Wilson—yet. But she could change her mind when the chance comes along and she sees what it could mean for her in the future.

"I'm sure you're wrong about that."

Sally sighed again, and said, "You've got so much more wisdom than I do. You're probably right."

Cyrus shifted in a way that assured her he was reacting to her touch. Sally maneuvered herself between his thighs and sat on her haunches, looking beseechingly up at him. "Will you help me?"

"I'd like to," he said, and she felt his sincerity. "I'm just not sure what I can do."

"You can speak to Wilson. Warn him that if he persists with his attack on my reputation, I'll give him away. I know how Ben Angel got into our house. It's all so clear now. I found out Ben never had anything to do with servicing aquariums or installing them. That's what he told me he'd been doing at the house. But someone else did it. That was another of Wilson's covers to get someone into the house in a so-called legitimate manner."

Cyrus leaned forward. "Why wouldn't he just employ the man? Why go to such lengths?"

"To flaunt him before me. He knows I've been, well, horny. Forgive me, Cyrus, but I don't know how else to say it. I told you Wilson hasn't touched me for a long time, but he knows my taste in men, and when he saw this boy he must have known I'd take one look at him and want him, so he made sure that's what happened. He planned it all, right down to having Ben Angel have pictures taken of us, and then talk to the papers and tell a bunch of lies. Wilson's always wanted Celina. Now he thinks he's going to get her."

"I'll talk to Celina," Cyrus said. "But I know she's going to be amazed at the suggestion."

"I don't really care if she sleeps with Wilson," Sally told him. "I want to stay married to him, but I don't *want* him anymore."

Cyrus looked at her without comprehension.

"You know what I want. I want you. I made a mistake years ago when I pushed myself at you. But I'm older and wiser now." And the perfect way to push mud in Wilson's and Celina's faces would be to knock Celina's brother off his ivory perch. Also, Sally wanted him. It was as simple as that—and she wanted to bring Wilson down.

How sweet it would be to have their set rallying behind her instead of her prick of a husband.

"Please stand by me when I make an announcement to the papers about the kind of things Wilson's done. He's an addict, you know. Cocaine."

"Please," Cyrus said. "That's for him to deal with."

"Not if he's making a play for Celina, surely."

"Celina's getting married."

Sally stared at him in the gloom. "You're kidding."

"On Friday. To Jack Charbonnet."

Laughter bubbled up inside her. Poor, stupid Wilson would be furious. "Why, that's wonderful news," she managed to say. "I'm glad for Celina. Did you know Wilson was insanely jealous of Errol?"

"I can't say I did."

"Well, he was. Partly because he knew Errol and I were lovers. But he also hated it that Errol found it so easy to gather people's sympathy. *And* he thought Errol was having an affair with Celina and he intended to stop it at any price. Do you understand what I'm telling you? Wilson would pay anything to get Errol out of Celina's life permanently—including the cost of hiring someone to kill him."

"No, Sally. This isn't right."

"We aren't in a confessional. I haven't asked you for absolution. I'm talking to you as an old friend."

He averted his head.

Gently, Sally slipped a hand over his cheek and eased his face back until he looked at her again. "I made love with Errol the night he died. When I left he was still alive and feelin' fine. It wasn't until after I left that he supposedly went into cardiac arrest and had an accident in the bath, or whatever they're saying happened to him."

"Do you expect me to listen to you talking about committing adultery, and not react."

"I expect you to react to the fact that I know what happened to Errol." She rose to her knees and held his face between both hands.

He didn't flinch or try to pull away.

Sally kissed Cyrus. She tried to deepen the contact, to part his lips, but he held as still as stone until she was panting with the effort to make him respond.

"I'm in love with you," she whispered.

"No. But we won't argue. Please sit on the chair."

Rather than do as he asked, she kissed him again and ran her hands into his hair. And once more he sat, wooden and unresponsive.

"What's the matter with you," she hissed. "Aren't you a man anymore?"

He smiled. "Oh, I'm a man—a man who takes the vows he made seriously. I'll help you if I can, but I don't want this."

She sat on the cold stone floor and pulled her skirts around her knees. And she sulked.

Cyrus leaned forward and tilted up her chin. "You've got your whole life ahead of you, Sally. Use it for something worthwhile. If you can help with what happened to Errol, do it. You'll be doing a lot of people a service."

She made up her mind rapidly. If nothing else, she'd get back at Wilson. "He knew I was sleeping with Errol," she said. "He didn't want to sleep with me himself, but he never has liked it if someone else got part of me. Like I told you, Errol was alive when I left him. And he wasn't in the bathroom. We'd been in the bath, but we moved to the bed, and that's where he was when I left him.

"Errol knew something about Wilson. He said as much. He told me I should put distance between Wilson and me because there was going to be a lot of unpleasantness.

"Cyrus, Errol said he would be seeing Wilson later that night. He said someone else had arranged the interview and that Wilson would be withdrawing his senatorial candidacy afterward. He also said he was afraid for his life, but couldn't step back from what he intended to do.

"Find a way to tell the police—some trustworthy police. Get them to question Wilson about that night. I think Wilson waited until I left Errol. Then he killed him."

Sally left the church and walked rapidly toward the side street where she'd left her car. Wilson had tried to destroy her, and he'd probably succeeded. But she was going to take him down with her.

Moonlight slid in and out behind swags of thin, yellow-tinged pewter cloud. One moment there was an eerie light on the scene, the next, near darkness.

Her heels echoed on the sidewalk.

Since Ben Angel was so quick to tell lies to some scandal rag, why shouldn't he be just as quick to demonstrate some of the behavior he'd told them she foisted on him.

She'd find Ben and demand a "surprise."

Cyrus's strength to deny her warmed her in an odd way. He must be the last honorable man left alive. She'd chosen her ally well. He'd make sure Celina had nothing to do with Wilson.

In a building to her right, a lone horn played. It wept in the night and turned her heart. She loved this city, every facet of it. It was sometimes almost prayerful in its spirituality, sometimes so steeped in sin, it smelled of rot.

Her car was on the next corner. She speeded her step and fished her keys from a pocket in her skirt, selecting the one to open her door as she went.

Once beside the Mercedes, she aimed the key and remotely unlocked the combination that also turned on an interior light. She smiled. There were so many things Wilson would have to do without soon. After all, she was the one with the money.

Sally reached to open the car door. She didn't see the hands shoot from beneath the front end of the car. They closed on her ankles and yanked, bringing her crashing down in the gutter and smashing her head on the curb.

The horn drowned her scream.

She did see the yellow moon on the blade of the knife, and opened her mouth to scream again, but a hand, pushed into her mouth, cut off the sound.

Weight thrown on top of her knocked the wind from her body. A sweating face leered down. How well she knew that face.

The pain, when it came, shot from the point of her chin to her crotch. The gurgle from her throat was blood escaping through a wound on the outside. Then the stabbing began.

Thirty-four

La Murèna didn't draw suburban couples looking for late-night dining after a show and before returning to the kiddies.

Jack entered the windowless front door with only a glance at the inch-high red neon name above a bell to the left.

He was jumpy, which meant he was a wise man—or at least that his basic instincts were good. This was not a good place for him to be, but what he needed couldn't be found anywhere else. He had to get Win to call off his watchdogs. It no longer mattered if the man paid for the death of Jack's parents, not in the way Jack had originally visualized. Win Giavanelli was old and sick, and his power was dwindling. Jack just wanted out; he wanted to turn his back on the past and protect those he loved.

He wasn't a fool. These people didn't take kindly to good-byes. His task was to sever all connections without appearing to sever them at all.

"Slummin', Jackie boy?"

Sonny Clete got off his bar stool the moment he saw Jack.

Jack affected a bored countenance. "One of those nights, Sonny. You know what I mean. The ones when you know you need sleep but can't get any."

A martini in one hand, Sonny sauntered up to Jack. "Sleep like a baby whenever I need to myself." He talked around a toothpick clamped between his teeth. "Guess that comes from knowin' the rules of the game and stickin' to them. Avoidin' steppin' on toes that could make me real miserable."

No translation of Sonny's message was needed. "I envy a man who sees life in black and white," Jack said. "There isn't a shade of gray on your horizon, is there, Sonny?"

Moving the toothpick from one side of his mouth to the other and back again, Sonny thought about that.

Jack's hands were in his pockets, and he realized his palms were wet.

"Know what I think about gray?" Sonny said. "I think I don't like it. Never did. It threatens the order of things—that nice black and white you said back then—I believe in that, and I get rid of gray just as fast as I can. Why don't you go home and try to get some sleep?"

"I came to see Win."

"Like I said, why don't you go home and try to get some sleep?"

Jack decided he had nothing to lose by trying a very direct approach with this man. "I'm not a made man, y'know, Sonny," he said, watching the other's expression carefully. "Maybe it was out of respect for my mother, who didn't approve of any of this, but Win never invited me into the family—not the way he asked you. D'you understand?"

The toothpick made another round trip. "I got it. But you want to be invited, don't you? You want to be made, and then you want to be the fastest rising star that ever entered the ranks. You want what some of us spent a lifetime workin' for, and you want it as a gift. But even if you got that, you'd be a boss without no army. Ain't no good to be a boss if all your soldiers turn deserter."

"You aren't hearin' me," Jack said. "I don't want any part of your action. I've got my own thing and it doesn't . . . Sonny, I respect that you will be Win's eventual replacement. Now, I need to talk to the man."

"Why?" Sonny's move was subtle, but it was aggressive and it cut off Jack's path to Win's private room.

"Personal," Jack told him, losing his smile. "I've got some personal business with Win. If he wants to tell you about it afterward, that's his business. I'll say good-bye before I leave."

He walked very deliberately around Sonny and headed for "The Room" as it was called. The stiffness between his shoulder blades didn't feel good, but he made sure he sauntered rather than hurried to knock on the carved mahogany panels.

"Yeah?" Win's voice was loud and hoarse.

"It's Jack."

After a slight pause, Win called, "Get in here," and Jack did as he was told. Once inside, with the door closed on Sonny's angry eyes, he relaxed, but not much.

"You eaten?" Win asked.

"Yes, thank you. I need a few minutes of your time, if you can spare them." He wondered, not for the first time, when Win slept or showered or did all the things he obviously did do without ever seeming to leave this room.

Win spread his beefy, beringed hands. "My time is your time. Always has been. Sit down."

Jack took a chair facing Win and saw the other man frown. He was a side-by-side guy. Looking someone in the eye didn't come easily.

"I've been having some problems," Jack said baldly. "You always told me that if I had problems I was to come straight to you. The last time you invited me here, you made a real point of it. So I'm here."

"What kind of problems?"

"I think Sonny's edgy around me. When you mentioned the idea, I didn't take it seriously, but now I do. I think he's afraid I want his spot, and that you want me to have his spot. I think he's makin' moves to ensure that doesn't happen, and I don't like the way he's doin' that."

Win hefted his tumbler of red wine and drank deeply, never taking his eyes off Jack.

"The woman I'm going to marry got severely roughed up. And some goon's been following my daughter around. I'm getting threats, Win, and I'm here to ask if you could find it in your heart to do something about that."

Several more swallows of wine, and Win set down his glass. He flattened his palms on the table and leaned toward Jack. "You got too much of your father in you. He thought he could call the shots, too."

"My father was a member of the family. I'm not."

"Not the way he was. But you're close to me, and that means a lot of people are going to make assumptions—unless you go out of your way to show they don't got any need to make those assumptions."

"How would I go about doing that, Win?"

"Easy. I know it would hurt, but pay a little homage to Sonny. Let him know you respect him."

Jack's stomach hated that idea. "Can't you make him lay off?"

"Maybe." Win waggled his head. "But you gotta help me. You gotta play it my way. I've got troubles of my own. There's a lot of talk about how I'm losin' my grip. People are linin' up, pushin' for where they want to be when I'm gone, that kind of thing."

"You aren't going anywhere." Jack's jovial laugh didn't ring true in his own ears. "You're a rock, Win. Rocks outlive the world."

A faint smile crossed Win's full features. "The rock's wearin' a bit smooth. It started wearin' smooth a long time ago." He leaned even farther across the table and beckoned for Jack to do the same. "I gotta tell you somethin' in case there isn't another chance."

Jack was aware of an unpleasant thudding in his chest. He bent close to Win and didn't flinch when Win caught hold of his hands. "I gotta look after my own first, you understand?"

Jack nodded.

"I got family. You know what I mean. Blood family. My wife and kids, and their kids. I got five great-grandchildren. I owe it to all of them to look out for their future."

"I'd do the same thing."

"But I want you to be okay. For that to happen, you gotta follow orders. Don't do it for me, do it in your mother's memory."

Jack did flinch then.

"I never told you the truth about your mother. Now I got to do that. I loved her, Jack. I wanted to marry her."

Revulsion turned Jack's stomach. "I didn't know that, Win." He did know that Win was at least twenty years older than the woman he was talking about.

"She was a good woman. She was too good for your father, but she wouldn't listen to me. She married him. I wanted her, but she would have your father."

Jack didn't remind Win that he must have been a married man with kids when he was trying to stand between Jack's parents.

"You coulda been mine." Win's hands tightened on Jack's. "I always think of that. That's why I've taken care of you. If things had gone my way, you'd have been mine."

And illegitimate. "What does this have to do with now?" Jack asked.

"Nothin'," Win roared suddenly. "I'm just explainin' why I had to look after you all these years, and why I gotta let you look after yourself now. I gotta take care of my own business. Sonny's restless. He wants me to step down. I ain't ready to do that, but I gotta handle things real delicate. I can't allow you to mess things up for me on account of my own family needs me where I am for the present.

"Let me finish. Your mama wasn't supposed to die. They got carried away. Leastwise, that's what I was told."

Jack believed, as he had always believed, that Win had advance knowledge of exactly what was going to happen at the home of Pierre and Mary Charbonnet on a sunny afternoon by the pool. Too terrified to leave, Jack had been watching through the pool-house window when Win arrived at the scene of the carnage. He'd come with the assurance of a man who knew what he expected to find. He'd shown no surprise. That could be only because he'd ordered it. Jack had also seen Win pull Mary Charbonnet gently from the pool and carry her to a chaise, where he covered her with a towel. That hadn't made sense until now, but it didn't make Jack hate him less or hurt less. Win hadn't shed any tears over Jack's father.

"Will you do something for me?" Win asked. "Will you be respectful to Sonny? Maybe you could ask him to call around at the *Lucky Lady* for a little present, say once a month. Tell him it was my idea. Tell him that and make it a meaningful present, Jack. Then I think you'll be okay."

He couldn't let the rage he felt show. After so many years of feeling he had these unwelcome connections under control, and that he'd eventually punish Win Giavanelli, Jack saw it all slipping away, and he hated it. "You think that's what it'll take to make sure no one decides to have any more private chats with the woman I'm going to marry, or with my daughter?"

Win fell back in his chair. He appeared gray with exhaustion. "That's what I think. But you know you always gotta be careful."

"I know that Win." Jack stood up. "I'll consider your suggestions. And I'll do what I have to do." Whatever that might be.

"And you understand that I say these things for your own good? Because I think of you like another of my sons?"

Only with difficulty did Jack choke out a yes.

Back in the bar and already dreaming of the fresh air outside, Jack's progress was halted by Sonny, who stepped in front of him again.

Jack nodded. "Time to go home, I guess, Sonny."

"Is that all you got to say to me?"

He wasn't going to offer him "presents." "No. I want to say something else, and I hope you'll take it in the spirit it's meant. Quit worrying, Sonny. You're safe. Understand?"

Sonny's pasty face turned purplish. "You arrogant son of a bitch. You think you get to say what happens in the family?"

"Not at all. It's just that you seem to think I'm some sort of threat. I'm trying to put your mind at ease."

Sonny took hold of a lapel on Jack's leather jacket. "That's good of you. Let me make a suggestion to you, Jack. Things can start being talked about. Things you don't think will ever be mentioned, especially after five years or so."

"Like what?" Jack was genuinely puzzled.

Sonny's smirk wasn't a pretty sight. "Like something a man might not want his daughter to know. Like how he was in the car his wife drove into a swamp. That he got out and she didn't."

Jack reached for the back of a chair and held on.

The action didn't escape Sonny's notice, and he puffed up with satisfaction. "I see I'm hitting a nerve here. I don't suppose the man would want his kid to know how some said he should have been able to get his wife out of that car too."

Jack shook his head. "I tried. I couldn't."

"So you say. But word has it you sat on the bank a long time before you went for help. In fact, you went for help only when someone you knew came along unexpected."

Wilson Lamar. Wilson had been coming from a whorehouse tucked away beside a bayou on the banks of the Atchafalaya. Wilson, the respected lawyer who already had big political aspirations which Jack had been vocal in opposing. That night Wilson had made sure Jack understood that no one could prove he'd been coming from a whorehouse when he found Jack, but the fact that Elise was dead inside a car in the swamp was concrete. No official suggestion had ever been made that Elise's death was anything but a suicide, and Jack didn't want Amelia to know that her mother hadn't been alone in the car. Elise had insisted upon driving and had begged him to let her go alone. He'd refused, and she'd sent them both into the slimy water.

"I see I've got you thinkin', Jackie," Sonny said. "I like that. A thinkin' man. Get in my way and some little birds will start chirpin'."

Jack stood tall, which was considerably taller than soft Sonny. "I've got a warning of my own to hand out," he said. "Stay out of my way and I'll stay out of yours. That means stay away from anyone connected to me. We aren't a threat to you. Got it?"

"Maybe." Sonny still chewed his toothpick. "And maybe I can make sure you're never tempted to step over the line onto my side of the turf. In case you haven't noticed, the papers have been real useful to some lately. I can't think of a better way to spread bad news. Bad news for some. I think some folks must have an in with a reporter or somethin', what do you think?"

Jack watched and waited. He wasn't expected to respond.

"Yeah, well, I thought you'd agree. The last thing I'd want to see would be a hint that your poor little dead wife wasn't the one driving the car that night after all—that you could have been behind the wheel. It would be a real shame if the rest of your life got messed up like that."

Thirty-five

"Cyrus?" Celina gripped the arms of her chair and strained to hear. "Cyrus, is that you?" She rose from the couch in the parlor but didn't attempt to leave the room.

"It's me," Cyrus called out. "I'll be right there. Would you like some iced tea?"

Iced tea? She hadn't thought of eating or drinking for hours, certainly not since Jack left, angry because she'd insisted on remaining to wait for Cyrus to come home. "Yes, please," she said after opening the door. "Sounds good."

Every nerve twitched. Every muscle jumped. Why was there still no word from Jack? She'd spoken with Tilly, who said she and Amelia were fine, but that she hadn't heard from Jack since he'd checked on them before leaving Celina. Tilly had added that Celina should be in Chartres Street, too.

Cyrus came with two tall glasses of iced tea. He looked pale and withdrawn. His eyes had the sunken appearance of a man who hadn't slept for too long.

"Are you all right?" Celina asked him, taking the glass of tea.

"What are you doing alone?" It wasn't Cyrus's way to answer a question with a question.

"Jack had to see someone. Dwayne and Jean-Claude went back to the club."

"You shouldn't be here on your own. Or anywhere else."

Under siege.

Celina touched the cold glass to each of her cheeks, then rested it against her forehead.

"Celina?" Cyrus said tentatively. "What is it? Something new?"

"No!" she shouted, and then couldn't believe she'd raised her voice to her brother. "No, Cyrus. Not something new, just something that I should have told you—and Jack—a long time ago. Now I don't know if I can tell you at all. And if I do, I don't know what you'll want to do about it. I'm so scared about everything, and so confused. And I'm not the kind of woman who gives in to pressure."

He studied her for so long that she put shaky fingers to her mouth, afraid of what he'd say next.

"You're too strong," he told her at last. "That's the problem. Would you please tell me everything that's on your mind? I promise you I won't repeat a word you don't want repeated, and I'll help you, Celina. You know I'll help you even if there doesn't seem to be a way."

"I know," she said, nodding. "How was it with Sally Lamar?"

He made lines on his sweating glass with a fingernail. "Difficult. She's a very complex woman, and she's in trouble. But we all know that. Talk about you, please."

She sat down, and immediately got up again. The baby made a fluttery little movement, and Celina put a hand over the spot.

"You aren't in pain, are you?" Cyrus asked, coming to her at once.

Celina smiled at him. "No. The baby moves a little now. You're going to be angry when I tell you what's on my mind. And some of that anger's going to be directed at me. Jack's going to be angry, too." She didn't want to say aloud that she feared he might not want anything more to do with her.

With a gentle touch Cyrus held her arm and urged her back onto the couch. He sat beside her. "I am not going to be angry with you. I can't speak for Jack, but I can tell you that he's a good man. You know I'm uncertain about this marriage, but I still believe he's honorable, and that he cares about you. At first I thought you'd worked out some sort of compromise for reasons I didn't know—"

"We had." She must lay it all before him now.

"But that's changed, hasn't it? You feel something for him?"

Leaning against his arm, she gave him her glass to set down and said, "I've fallen in love with him."

"Ah" was all Cyrus said.

"I haven't told him the truth. I haven't lied, I just haven't told him things he ought to know. He could have helped me make the right decisions, but I didn't trust him. Cyrus, this is Wilson Lamar's baby. Jack does know that now—since yesterday. We talked about it all the way to Baton Rouge, and he tried to convince me he could handle it calmly, but I'm scared he might decide to go get Wilson alone. If he does, I can only guess at what might happen."

The quality of the following silence was like ice on Celina's skin. With her leaning against him, Cyrus remained utterly still.

"Jack deserved to know that from the beginning, but I wouldn't tell him because I've been afraid of what Wilson might do to Mama and Daddy."

"He threatened to punish them because you're carrying his child?"

"Until yesterday—at lunch—he didn't know I was pregnant at all. He noticed, made the assumption that it was his child, and told me I had to have an abortion."

"You led me to believe you'd been raped. But you had an affair with a married man?"

"I *was* raped."

Cyrus made white-knuckled fists on his knees.

"Afterward I stopped working for Wilson's campaign. I was doing some work for him, remember? He threatened me. He said that if I told anyone what had happened, he'd say I was ambitious and I encouraged him because I wanted to use him. Then he'd make Mama and Daddy look like fools, he wouldn't use them in his campaign the way he has, and they'd be ostracized by the people who matter most to them."

"So you let him get away with it?"

Her scalp prickled. "It sounds so . . . I sound so weak when I say it aloud, but I didn't know what to do or who to talk to. Errol was the only one I thought I could trust, so he got elected. Wilson had started trying to begin a relationship with me. He came here one day when I was alone, and I thought I was going to pass out, it scared me so badly. I knew then that I couldn't get through this whole thing alone. When I finally told Errol, he wanted to go to Wilson immediately. Then, when I begged him not to, he asked me to marry him."

Cyrus looked at her and guided her face against his shoulder. "Poor kid. Errol was such a good man. I suppose you turned him down."

"I told him I'd think about it. But then he was killed."

Someone else came into the house, and Cyrus got up. "Who is it?" he asked loudly.

"It's Jack. I'll be right there." Determined footsteps followed, and a vaguely windswept-looking Jack appeared. "Cyrus. Boy, am I glad to see you here. Where's Dwayne?"

"He had to go back to the club with Jean-Claude," Celina said, relieved to see Jack but praying he wouldn't press to know whether or not she'd been there alone. "Jack, I just told Cyrus something I've been keeping to myself. I thought it was for the best, but I may have been wrong. Now I've got to have help deciding how to deal with it." If Jack was going to be angry because she'd already told her brother what she'd been unable to voluntarily tell the man she was going to marry, so be it. They didn't exactly have a long, intimate . . . they didn't have a long history.

With no attempt at embellishment or justification, she told Jack about Wilson Lamar—about the threats against her parents, and Celina's fears for them. She finished by saying that she was worried because Jack hadn't mentioned the revelation that had been made at Galatoire's since he and Celina left the place.

Jack turned so white, she feared he might be ill, but she quickly recognized signs of deep anger rather than sickness. He took off the leather jacket he wore and balled it in his hands.

"I've wanted to bring the subject up again," Celina said. "But I haven't known how. You've seen me trying to keep an even relationship with the Lamars. I don't think you could ever have thought I liked them, not unless I'm a better actress than I think I am. And after you found out what that man did to me, you must have assumed—correctly—that it was for my parents' sake that I kept quiet about him. He's so arrogant, he doesn't believe he'll ever be accountable for doing wrong. You saw how he was at the restaurant yesterday."

Jack muttered something unintelligible under his breath.

Celina felt an irrational urge to cry. What a pointless exercise that would be. But what was Jack thinking? She almost laughed aloud. Why should she expect to have any idea what he was thinking? That kind of thing took time to develop, and they hadn't had that time.

"Why don't you share what's on your mind?" Cyrus asked. "We're in this together. I had quite an interview with poor Sally Lamar tonight. We've got trouble all around, and we're going to have to move forward together."

"What's on my mind?" Jack showed his teeth, but not in a smile. He threw his jacket toward the nearest chair, and missed. "What's on my mind is that there is so much that's rotten, in every direction I look, that I'm not sure where to start trying to dig us out. But, by God, I will dig us out."

Celina trembled inwardly. This cold anger was something she hadn't witnessed in him before. "Where do we start?" she asked.

He spread his arms, then let them fall to his side.

She turned on her heel and walked around the couch to pull back one of the sheer draperies at the windows.

"Get away from there," Jack said.

She ignored him. "I'm going to start. Don't interrupt me, please."

"Celina—"

"If I want to stand by the window, I'll stand by the window. Get over it, please.

"When Antoine's wife came to see me, she did have something to talk to me about. Her name is Rose, Cyrus. A straightforward, decent woman. They have two boys and they're working very hard to give them a chance in life. Now that I know they don't have legal status in this country, I fully understand that poor woman's fear.

"She came to beg me not to talk about anything Antoine might have told me regarding the hours around Errol's death. I told her I didn't know anything, and that Antoine hadn't had a chance to tell me, although he'd tried to. She just kept telling me that I mustn't say anything, because if I did, she and her boys would suffer. She already had cigarette burns."

"What?" Jack reached her side so quickly, she took a backward step. He took her by the shoulders and kept her walking until she was well away from the windows. "What did you just say?"

"Antoine's wife came to me with cigarette burns on her arms. A man had waited for her in their apartment. He had something over his head so she wouldn't be able to identify him. And he threatened her. He told her to come and warn me to keep my mouth shut or he'd make sure I did."

"And you didn't tell me? Even after you went through that nightmare yourself? You must have assumed the two events were connected. But even if you hadn't, why didn't you *tell* me?"

She pushed him, but he didn't release her.

"Answer me, Celina."

"You're angry with me. I knew you would be."

"You bet I am. What would possess you not to talk to me about a thing like this? Was I a fool to think we'd reached a place where we were being honest with each other?"

Cyrus arrived beside Celina and put an arm around her shoulders. "It's okay. We're all stretched too far. Let's try to keep calm."

"My God," Jack said under his breath. "What is Antoine doing about all this?"

"That's it," Celina told him, her voice rising. "That's why I didn't know what to do. They've got Antoine. Or they had him. Now I don't know how to find Rose again. They took him and hurt him. They gave Rose evidence of it to show me. Rose brought his shirt here, his T-shirt, and it was covered with blood. And one of his teeth. They were a warning to prove what they're capable of. Rose begged me not to tell anyone."

Jack's face froze. All expression gradually slid away into blank confusion. Cyrus held her even tighter.

"His *tooth*," Jack finally said. "His wife brought you one of his teeth?"

"Part of one. With gold on it. Oh . . . oh, I don't know what to do about anything. I don't want to be here anymore. I want— No, no, I am not going to fall apart. I refuse to let those people do that to me or to anyone I love."

"And you didn't have anyone you dared to ask for help," Jack said, his eyes on hers. His laugh was short and bitter. "I can't blame you, I suppose. We've all been spinning out of control. But we're going to have to take that control now. Apparently it won't be easy, because it takes longer than we've had to learn to believe in someone else. Or it does for some of us."

No matter what she said, he wouldn't understand how she'd gradually slipped further and further from being able to confide in him about Antoine. "I'm sorry" was the best she could do.

"I don't think that's going to help Antoine much," he told her. "By the time they had him, it was probably too late to help, but it might not have been. I want your agreement that you're not going to hold anything back from me again."

Cyrus left Celina and gathered up the two used glasses.

"Celina," Jack prompted.

She felt such a failure. "I'm sorry," she repeated.

"I should let you two talk alone." Cyrus turned toward the door.

"Please don't go," Jack said. "I can't imagine a more awkward moment for this, but I've already waited too long. Can I say something I've wanted to say to you, Celina? Would you mind if I said something personal in front of Cyrus?"

"I'll go outside," Cyrus said rapidly.

"Please don't go away," Celina told him. To Jack, she said, "I don't mind."

He ran a hand over her tousled curls, rested the backs of his fingers on her cheek, touched the tip of a forefinger to her mouth—put his other hand on her stomach. "You've cut the ground from beneath me tonight. I thought we'd come much further than we have. That scares me, but I love you. I hope you feel something similar for me. And I hope that with this marriage we aren't getting into something we'll both regret."

She looked back at him for as long as she could before she bowed her head to hide her tears.

Jack rested both of his hands gently on her belly. "Any sane person would look at what's happened to the two of us, and to the people around us, and say fate is really mad at us, but it would be a lie. If I could bring Errol back, I would. You know I would. But I can't be sorry that you and I got together. And I'm not sorry about this baby. Now, let's go home."

Thirty-six

Jack heard gunshots before he saw the swirling lights of police vehicles. He swung Celina behind him, kept hold of one of her hands, and slid along the wall until he could peer around the corner into Chartres Street.

Someone on a bullhorn yelled unintelligible orders toward the house opposite his own. Searchlights turned the facade of that building blinding white. A crowd, held back by barricades, had gathered at either side of the house.

"Jack?"

"Hold still," he told Celina. "It's not our place. Appears to be something in the old ladies' house across the street." The house Amelia had insisted was inhabited by ghosts and goblins.

"Those were guns being fired."

"Just do as I ask, *chère*, and stay put. I need to listen."

Minutes passed. Jack was too far removed to see faces, but two men were brought from the building in handcuffs and shoved into a police wagon.

Next to appear in the doorway was a frail-looking figure borne in the arms of a brawny police officer. Jack assumed this to be one of the old ladies. She was placed in a waiting aid car. Another woman, this one leaning on a stick but stomping along under her own steam and exuding ire even at a distance, followed her companion into the waiting vehicle, which promptly drove away. The wagon had already left.

Instructions for the crowd to disperse came over the bullhorn.

"Time to go home," Jack muttered, and they walked against the reluctant tide of departing thrill-seekers until they got close enough to approach a cop.

"Clear the area, please, sir," the man said. Ridiculously young, his chest swelled with importance. "No more to see here tonight."

"We're returning home," Jack said, proud of his patience. "We live there." He pointed toward windows where there were suspicious gaps between curtains. Two pale shapes behind the dark glass in Jack's study needed no identification.

"You go along home, then," the police officer said. "Everything's over now."

"What happened?" He could hope the cop was young and green enough to enjoy expounding.

Taking off his cap and wiping a forearm across his brow, the boy—and he seemed little more than a boy—said, "Afraid I can't say much, sir. Mob related evidently. They were using the house to observe someone they intended to take out."

Jack affected a suitably horrified expression and nodded.

"Seems they tricked the two old ladies into letting one of them in to check out the gas or some such thing. Then they kept them prisoner in a back room for weeks. The one woman is a bit weak and wobbly, but the other's more mad than anything, from what I hear. We've got the hoods though. Must be because of the Giavanelli thing. The whole family's turned upside down, so they say. Those two got careless, and the feisty old lady took a cell phone from one of them and called us."

Jack wondered what the officer would reveal if he could say much.

"Do you know who they were, er, staking out?" Celina said hesitantly.

"Some dude by the name of Chardonnay. Never heard of him myself. Not that it matters now."

Jack decided he wasn't offended. "Something happened with the Giavanellis, you said?" Keeping his tone impersonal wasn't easy.

"The man—Win Giavanelli—he got taken out by his second in command. Then someone tried to take that guy out. Then, well, I guess there was quite a mess by the time they finished shootin'. It was in some restaurant called the Marina."

"Could that have been La Muèna?" Jack asked, although he was on automatic pilot now.

"Yeah, yeah. Something to do with Italian fish, I know that."

"I think I've heard of it," Jack said. "Did the other guy, the second in command—did he make it?"

"The way I heard it, he's in the hospital. In pretty bad shape."

But Win was dead. So why didn't he feel elated? Jack wondered. Why did he feel flat and as if he'd just encountered the biggest anticlimax of his life? He looked at the woman beside him. She was real. She was important. And he hadn't tried hard enough to let her know he'd come to think of her that way.

The cop cleared his throat and put his cap on again. "Well, you go carefully now."

"Thanks, Officer," Jack said. "You're a credit to the force. I guess we'll do as you suggest and go home."

With Celina's hand tucked against his body, he made sure the young policeman didn't see where they were going, and went to ring his doorbell. The door opened as if Tilly had been waiting on the other side. She stood back and tugged on Celina's sleeve to hurry her inside, then urged Jack in and whipped the door shut again.

"It's over, Tilly," he said. "Win Giavanelli's dead."

He felt Celina's stare, but accepted Tilly's hug and let his own eyes close.

"Now you can let it rest," Tilly said. "Your poor mother's been dead a long time. With that man gone, you can let her rest at last."

"Yes," he agreed. "Thanks, Tilly. Somehow, now that it's over, it doesn't seem so important."

"That's the way it is," she told him, letting him go and stepping back, smoothing down her apron. "We make things important by building them up. Then, when they're over, they don't matter a hill of beans. We've had excitement around here tonight."

"We know. We just got the scoop outside." He followed Celina and Tilly upstairs, filling Tilly in on the details from across the street as they went.

"I told you I saw someone watching, Daddy."

He spun around to see Amelia and Frog Prince in the hall. Amelia, her feet bare as usual, wore her favorite pink checked nightie. "You're supposed to be in bed asleep, young lady."

"With men firing guns, and all those lights?" she asked, all prim disbelief. "I told you I saw funny red lights over there, and someone watching out the window."

"You said you saw ghosts over there."

She turned up a small hand. "So I got it a bit wrong. They were just bad people who lock up old ladies and spy out of their front windows. They were spying on this house, weren't they, Tilly?"

"Yes," Tilly said. "A police officer came and spoke to me, too."

"So you'll listen to me next time, won't you, Daddy?"

He looked at his daughter, and the rush of love he felt for her rocked him. He swept her up and hugged her until she cried, "Ouch!" and he nuzzled his face into her shoulder before setting her down.

"I'll go to bed if you come and tuck me in and tell me some more about Phillymeana," Amelia said.

"Philomena." It wasn't all over, not everything, but at least he could hope his child and the woman who would be his wife would be safe.

"If you want to, you can come too." Her face very serious, Amelia spoke to Celina. "But you have to be quiet while Daddy tells me a story, or he stops right in the middle of everything."

"I'll be quiet," Celina said. She still looked shocked and withdrawn. And they still had to decide how to deal with what they knew about Antoine and finding him . . . dead or alive.

"Okay, then." Amelia gave Celina an appraising look. "I don't think you're very well yet, are you?"

"I'm fine, thank you."

"No, I don't think so. You're one of those brave people who doesn't make fusses. Like me. When Daddy finishes telling my story, you'd better sleep in his room so he can make sure you're all right."

In the darkness, with Celina breathing softly and evenly beside him, Jack lay awake, his thoughts turning over all that had happened, and all that might yet happen.

Before they'd left Cyrus, he'd explained Sally Lamar's desperate telling of her theories about her husband, and he'd explained what the woman wanted, and how she hoped to get it. Jack found it hard to find sympathy for Sally, but nevertheless he found her pathetic, a wounded creature who would probably never be healed.

He was convinced that the failure to find out what Antoine had wanted to say had been the biggest mistake made. But it was too late for that now. Whoever had taken him had proven the depth of their depraved determination to preserve themselves. It had rocked his confidence badly to discover that Celina had kept what Rose said to herself, but, again, he had to try to understand her reticence.

The phone by the bed rang.

He snatched up the receiver, holding his breath while he hoped Celina wouldn't awaken. She turned toward him and curled against his side. Jack smiled and murmured, "Yes," into the phone.

"Mr. Charbonnet?"

He hesitated. The hoarse voice wasn't one he recognized. "Who wants to know?"

"Is that Mr. Charbonnet? I need to talk to him."

Jack frowned and held the phone closer. "This is Jack Charbonnet. Who wants him?"

"I'm in a hospital, me. They no know who I am. Mr. Errol, he trust you. You always good to me, too."

It couldn't be. He couldn't get this lucky, not just when he didn't know what to do next. "Antoine?"

"I hear that name, me," the man said. "I hit my head. They don't know who I am. You understand? No one here know who I am. That mean no one who want me find me. That Antoine, him had lots of trouble. Him afraid for his people, his woman and boys. But he alive."

"The police—"

The phone was hung up on the other end.

"*Merde,*" Jack muttered. Slowly he put down his own receiver. The caller had been Antoine, who was obviously terrified and hiding out. Now all that could be hoped was that he'd call again. Next time, if there was a next time, Jack would examine every word before he spoke it.

Antoine had to make contact again.

The phone rang again. He switched on the light and was too tense to feel remorse at the sight of Celina opening sleepy eyes and blinking with confusion.

He put a finger to his lips.

She pulled herself to sit up and nodded, her face too pale, and her eyes too dark. His T-shirt—that fell off one slender shoulder—didn't help the waiflike impression.

The phone bell went off again, and he answered this time. "This is Jack Charbonnet."

"Is Celina Payne with you?"

He gritted his teeth. Now was not the time to lose his temper. "If you want anything out of me, friend, you'll identify yourself."

"I'm calling on behalf of Mr. Wilson Lamar."

"I don't care if you're calling on behalf of the President. Who the . . . who are you?"

"Who I am doesn't matter. I'm Mr. Lamar's employee. He's too upset to make his own calls, but he thought he should try to get a message to Miss Payne. Since she and her family may be drawn into what's going on."

"You could be talkin' another language. I'll give you one more chance. Keep it simple, sweetheart, or I'm hangin' up and unplugging this phone."

"Because of something that happened last night, Miss Payne's brother is bound to be taken in for questioning by the police. Her parents have already been contacted and they aren't taking it well. Mr. Lamar asked me to let her know that. She isn't at her Royal Street address, so I was instructed to see if you can get a message to her."

Celina bent forward. Her head rested on her knees. Jack stroked her back and rubbed her neck. "I can do that for you."

"Thanks. Mr. Lamar's wife went to meet with Father Cyrus Payne this evening. Shortly afterward she was found stabbed to death beside her car."

Thirty-seven

How much had the bitch told Cyrus Payne? Wilson wasn't a praying man, but he decided he'd pray now that Father Cyrus would feel he had to keep whatever Sally had said to himself.

He'd unplugged the phone in his suite, but he could hear the intermittent drone of ringing elsewhere in the house. Wilson intended to use his "bereavement" to best advantage for as long as possible. After all, a man distraught over the violent killing of his wife couldn't be expected to attend to business too soon after the event. And while he was in seclusion, he'd be thinking his way through the maze his life had become. Or he would when he *was* finally in seclusion.

Charmain came out of the bathroom nude. He watched her with a mixture of irritation and arousal. They had been sleeping together for years, but this was the first time in this house. He'd never planned for them to do so, ever, but she'd arrived around midnight, minutes after the police had delivered their bombshell about Sally and then left. Charmain had intercepted police radio messages and was, as ever, ready to offer Wilson "comfort."

"I'd better blow," she said, putting on her diamond watch before grinning at him. "Of course, there's more than one way to blow, isn't there, lover? I'm ready, willin', and available. Might cheer you up."

"Thank you," he said tightly. "But I think you about wore us both out for now. You'd better go out down the back stairs." A horrifying thought struck him. "Where did you leave your car?"

She giggled and ran her hands through her short hair, still spiky and wet from the shower. "On a side street, silly. Would I park in the driveway at a time like this?"

Very slowly, too slowly to please Wilson, she stepped into a lavender-colored satin teddy and pulled it up her long, lithe body and over hard little breasts that came to sharp points. Every inch of Charmain was erogenous, and she moaned softly even at her own touch.

Wilson knew better than to hurry her. Rather he watched and offered the appreciative smile he knew she craved.

"You always did enjoy a little reverse striptease, Wilson," she said. "You should have taught Sally more about how to turn you on. She never did get it. She was too obvious."

His stomach turned. "Let's leave Sally out of this."

"Oh, my"—she pulled on black stockings with lace tops and slipped a little black dress over her head—"you'll have to forgive me for forgetting the niceties. Respect for the dead, here I come."

Affecting a deeply serious expression, he levered himself off the bed, where he'd been stretched out fully dressed, and went to her. He kissed her the way she liked it, hard, biting her lips, then picked up her purse and handed it to her. "Thank you, darlin'. You were a lifesaver. But then, you always have been. I'll make sure it's okay, then you go out down the back stairs and through the garden. It's quiet there. Everyone's watching the front. This is the first time I haven't entertained any member of the press who showed."

Charmain pushed a hand between his legs. "That's because you were entertainin' this member of the press, sweetie."

Wilson removed her hand and cautiously opened the door. The balcony was empty, and he waved Charmain forward. She gave his rear a last sharp pinch and tripped away toward the back of the house with her high-heeled sandals trailing from one hand.

The instant she was out of sight, Wilson closed himself in and leaned on the door. He and Charmain went back a long way—it could be that it was too long.

When he'd been to a window that allowed him to see Charmain disappear from the property, he called for Ben Angel and started mulling over the next moves that needed to be made.

He couldn't pretend he mourned Sally's death, but he had to be certain there was nothing about it that could affect him negatively.

Ben came into the room carrying a tray of coffee and some sandwiches. Wilson motioned for the door to be closed. "I'm not going to be able to put the police off much longer," he said. "Somethin' tells me there may be a few things you'd like to talk to me about first."

Ben slid the tray on top of the dresser and turned to his boss. He didn't waste valuable time on innocent shock. "I didn't have anything to do with your wife's death, if that's what you mean."

"Murder," Wilson said. "It was murder, Ben. Let's not invent pretty words for ugly things."

"I didn't murder Mrs. Lamar," Ben said, his face devoid of expression now. "I've done everything you've asked me to do. That wasn't one of them."

"Very admirable," Wilson told him. "And you weren't startin' to feel a little nervous after the pretty picture appeared in the paper—and your honest little quote about the lady of the house expectin' sexual favors from members of the staff? You didn't worry that she might try to defend herself and raise some questions about you, implicate you in some things that could get you into serious trouble? The big question is who gave the picture to the paper? It wasn't supposed to be for anythin' but scarin' Sally, was it?"

Ben swallowed loudly. "All I did was what I was told to do. I sure did not give that photo to anyone, did I? Why would I. Never saw it till it was in print."

"Well, somebody gave it to somebody, Ben. If it wasn't you—and like you say, that wouldn't make any sense—well then, I can't think who it would be other than the photographer. I was the photographer, so I know it wasn't me. The idea of setting up that little tableau was to scare the shit out of Sally and make it easier to get rid of her, nothin' more. Things are plain out of hand now."

"Where's the film?"

For an instant Wilson's mind went blank. Then he went into the closet and tore aside suits hanging along one bar. "Shee-it, where is my mind? Of course I should have checked the goddamn film. I should have destroyed it—only I thought it might be useful for somethin' sometime." Like making sure Ben Angel stayed in line. Wilson dragged out a sport bag, unzipped it, and took out a camera.

"That shoots my last hope," Wilson said, holding the empty film compartment open. "Someone else could have been taking shots too—only they weren't. Who the fuck would know anything about it in the first place?"

"As soon as you saw the paper you must have known the film was gone . . . sir. You—"

"Yeah, yeah. I wasn't thinking straight. This has been a difficult time." He didn't meet Ben's eyes. Then an ugly realization dawned. "Someone in this house. Someone else in this house knows what we've been doing. They're going to hold me up for megabucks." He narrowed his eyes at Ben. "You little bastard. It was you, wasn't it? You think you're going to get even more out of me."

Ben's dark blue eyes flashed. "Have you heard me askin' you for money?"

"No."

"I'm not going to, me. And I didn't have nothing to do with what happened to your wife last night."

"That isn't going to be easy to convince the police of—not after you set yourself up as a suspect by talkin' too much."

"What about you? You think I would be silent, me. You think I stay silent about you if the police come for me?"

Wiison grew still. The kid had balls. "Maybe we'd better do some talking about the questions the police might ask, and what kind of answers they ought to get."

"The only talkin' we need to do is to agree that we don't know anythin' about takin' photographs. The end."

Wilson snorted. "You blew that when you gave your sob story about Sally's unquenchable appetites."

"There's no proof of anythin' else, not about me." Ben squared his stance. "But there's proof about you. There's the negative for that photograph, and there's whoever got their hands on it and knows where they found it."

A gentle tap on the door jarred Wilson to his feet. "Who is it?"

"It's Opi, sir."

"Whatever it is can wait. I'm not up to talkin' right now."

Wilson waited for sounds that the man was leaving. They didn't come. Another tap did.

"Go away!" Panic welled within him. He stared at Ben and quaked at what he saw in the younger man's demeanor. Ben Angel, upstart and opportunist, pitied Wilson Lamar. He took a calming breath and said, "Come in, Opi."

The door opened slowly and Opi's bald head appeared. He glanced at Wilson, but turned his full attention on Ben. "I don't know what's happenin' around here, no, I surely don't. You got to go down to the police, Ben Angel. Someone want to see you down there."

Wilson stepped forward and beckoned Opi into the room. "Don't talk loud, man. We aren't all friends here."

Opi looked behind him, but showed no anxiety. He did do as Wilson asked. "You got parents?" he said to Ben.

Ben's supercilious assurance had fled. He bounced on his toes. "Most people have parents, old man."

"They come here, right? Mr. and Mrs. Reed. They come to a party, right? And they come to see Mr. Lamar another time."

"Will you get to the point?" Ben balled and flexed his hands, then pounded a fist into a palm.

"They your parents?"

"She's my mother. He's my stepfather. What of it?"

"They been taken in for questionin' and they askin' for you. They call for you, not a lawyer. They say you gonna take care of things for them."

"What are you talkin' about?" Ben yelled.

Opi backed away and reached behind him for the door handle. "They bein' asked questions about the mistress's death. Mrs. Lamar's death. I guess the police think your mama and stepdaddy killed her."

Thirty-eight

"You never asked me why I did it, Celina."

She finished taking her shoes from their box and gave Cyrus her complete attention. "Do you mean why you went into the priesthood? I assumed you had a calling—whatever that is. Sometimes I've envied you because you've seemed so sure of the decision you made."

With his hands in the pockets of his black suit trousers, he braced his feet apart on the rug in Jack's bedroom and fixed his eyes on something only he saw. "Most of the time, I'm sure. I'm always sure I've got a job to do for God, and most of the time I like doing it."

"You make it sound a bit like making circuit boards."

He continued to stare into the distance, but smiled faintly. "Not such a bad analogy. Maybe like making sure all the parts are there. For me it's always been that faith had to be part of the equation or the whole didn't work. But that doesn't mean every day is easy, or that I don't struggle with being a man."

She looked at him curiously. Cyrus had never talked about himself this way. "It's because of Sally, isn't it? The shock's making you question everything. It's very raw, it's bound to be."

"What happened to her wasn't God's doing. You can't believe in free will and still blame some higher being for the terrible things men do to each other."

These were waters that threatened to rise over her head very quickly. "Did you hear they've got the Reeds in custody?"

He lowered his heavy lashes. "Yes. Because their car was seen parked on the street where Sally died."

"More than that, Cyrus. Someone looking out a window saw a

man leaning over something. Then he ran to a car. He was leaning over Sally. Walt Reed doesn't deny it was him, but he insists he and his wife saw Sally fall, but nothing else."

"Poor Sally. Maybe if she'd married someone other than Wilson she'd have had a chance."

Celina gave him a long look. He raised his eyebrows and shook his head faintly.

Today was her wedding day. Because this was the date that had been set and the appointed hour approached, they would go ahead with the ceremony, but it felt wrong to celebrate anything with Sally Lamar lying dead. And it was even harder while Errol's murder went unsolved.

Cyrus was beside her before Celina was aware he'd moved. "Don't think about it anymore now. You look so beautiful. A really beautiful bride." He kissed her brow and looked at her tummy. "I must be a most unconventional priest, but there's something even more beautiful about the presence of the child. Innocent creature. Love him or her well—I know you will, and I believe Jack will, too. I look forward to being an uncle."

On cue, tears blurred her vision. "I'd better do some fast talking or I'll mess up my makeup." She gave a watery laugh. "I'll ask the question. Why did you become a priest, Cyrus?"

"To escape," he said promptly, and half turned from her. His throat moved sharply. "Now I'd better talk fast—and not to save my makeup."

She punched him playfully.

"I wish she'd asked for absolution."

Celina inclined her head and frowned in question.

Cyrus glanced at her. "Sally. I asked her if she wanted reconciliation, but she refused. Maybe if I'd pressed a little, she'd have changed her mind. Celina, I struggle with my sexuality. I don't mean I'm not sure of my sexuality. I . . . you don't want to listen to this."

"I want to know everything about you. And I'm honored if you want to tell me." Her heart beat fast. There had always been a chasm between them. Cyrus's goodness had been there, a presence she felt but didn't dare approach or try to breach.

"When Sally Lamar came to me . . . Just the night before last—I can't believe she's dead. She was so alive. She . . . she wanted me to react to her. I . . . oh, God help me, but I wanted her. I'd wanted her that night when we were teenagers too, and . . . I wanted her then, but the two things were at war inside me. The desire to serve God and the desire to be fully a man with a woman. Then there was a recoiling from the world the way it is. It made me feel helpless, and desperate to feel less vulnerable."

Celina went to her brother and took him in her arms. At first he held his body rigid, but then he embraced her convulsively, held her close, and rubbed her back. The baby chose that moment to make the strongest shift Celina had felt so far, but she doubted Cyrus would notice.

He stood quite still except for stroking her back and shoulders very slowly. "That is really somethin'," he said. "The baby. How does that feel inside you?"

She pressed her lips together for an instant, then said, "Incredible. I love it."

"Does it make you feel closer to God?"

For a moment she didn't understand, then she realized that he would wonder exactly that. "Because a baby is such a miracle? No. But it is a lovely idea. Cyrus, are you trying to tell me you might be changing your mind about the priesthood?"

"No. No. I'm just trying to make you understand a little more about me. I'm not holy. I'm just a man who struggles with his humanness and sometimes wishes he didn't have to win or quit, that's all. Enough of that." He put her at arms' length and said, "This is your day. And I should be counselling you, but I don't quite feel up to it. I'm just going to tell you to be happy, and to love a lot—love as much as you can."

Without warning the door swung open and their mother came in. She ignored Cyrus and glared at Celina. "I can't believe you'd even consider going ahead with this marriage. Neither can your daddy."

"If you'd rather not be here, I understand," Celina told Bitsy.

"You do not look good in that color. It washes you out. What is it? *Bisque?*"

"Mama," Cyrus said, but Celina shook her head at him.

She gave a disinterested downward glance at the calf-length gown Dwayne had finally chosen when she'd refused to choose anything herself. "Dwayne says it's called candlelight. And I like it." Tier upon tier of lace dipped to points tipped by a single pearl drop. It was a spectacular thing. She would do her best to be happy wearing it while she did what she wanted to do very much: become Jack's wife.

"We both know about it, Celina." Bitsy, in beige shantung with matching hat, dabbed a handkerchief to the corner of each eye. "Did you think you could keep it a secret forever?"

Her pregnancy. "The only thing that surprises me is that you haven't mentioned the baby before this afternoon."

"*Hush!*" Glancing behind her, then at Cyrus, Bitsy turned very red. "How can you speak of such things aloud like that. Someone might hear."

"It's about time," Celina said, slipping on her low-heeled pumps and checking her makeup and hair.

Bitsy went to the door and opened it. Neville Payne promptly came into the bedroom Celina would soon be sharing with Jack. Jack was getting dressed in the next room.

"We've got a car outside," Neville said, including Cyrus in his frown. His face appeared bloated and purplish. Celina had become accustomed to thinking of him as having flecks of silver in his hair, but today there seemed many more. He waved her toward him. "You're coming away with us right now. Whatever's gotten into you doesn't matter. We're goin' to put it behind us before it's too late."

Celina rarely looked at Neville and thought of him as anything but her father, her daddy, but she was suddenly and forcefully reminded that they were not related by blood. Would her real father have been so insensitive today?

"I'm going to check on Amelia," she said. "Tilly's getting her dressed and she's so excited she'll be hard to handle. Tilly may need some help."

"Takin' on a man like this," Neville said. "And his child. Even *thinkin'* about takin' them on means your mind isn't balanced. It's because of—" He waved in the general direction of her now very obvious pregnancy. "I suppose it's Errol's. We never wanted you livin' in that house. Well, don't go through with this marriage. Not just to give a child a name."

The words hurt. "Why ever not, Daddy?"

"Because I know you can have Wilson Lamar, that's why. He wants you. And you owe it to us."

Cyrus waved a hand in front of his face. "How can you suggest something like that after what's just happened? The man's wife just died. And this isn't Errol's baby. You say his name as if he weren't dead, and as if some of us weren't desperate to find out who killed him and see justice done."

Celina couldn't bear to continue this conversation. "I'm going to my wedding now. You can come, Mama—Daddy. Or you can leave. Please yourselves."

"Celina."

She didn't respond to her mother or look at her father when she passed them and went into the hall. Jack was ahead of her and turned back. Behind him, hopping up and down in a frothy yellow organza dress, Amelia spread her arms and did whirligigs.

"Hi," Jack said, coming toward Celina. "Ready to go to a wedding?"

He wore a beautifully cut tuxedo, a simple tuck-fronted white dress shirt, black tie, and cummerbund. And he made Celina's knees weak.

His hand was outstretched, and she took it. "You surely know how to take a man's breath away," he told her. "You're gorgeous."

Side by side they went toward the parlor where Dwayne was popping in and out of the door, watching their progress.

The instant they arrived at the entrance to the room, applause broke out. Gathered beneath the silken bower Dwayne had promised, and crowded together, was a crush of familiar faces from clubs on Bourbon and shops on Royal. The burlesque cast from Les Chats had turned out in their fabulous finery.

Jean-Claude, amazing as always, played Pachelbel's Canon on a keyboard, and the sound constricted Celina's throat.

She took the bouquet of cream orchids Dwayne handed her, accepted his kiss on her cheek, and went forward with Jack to agree to be his wife.

When they exchanged rings she'd never seen before, and held hands, and looked into each other's eyes to make promises she intended to keep, she prayed that God would smile on them.

They were pronounced husband and wife, and Jack leaned to whisper into her ear. "We're strong, you and I. We will make this work."

She nodded and said, "Thank you," and turned to face the assembly.

Standing together, Jean-Claude and Dwayne sang "Ave Maria." Their fine voices rose in marvelous harmony.

Celina's tears for the beauty of the words ran unchecked.

She felt Jack's hand on top of hers on his arm. They walked from the room and would return in a short while to mingle with the guests for a "celebration."

When they stood in the bedroom, face-to-face but without a word to say to each other, she felt a bitter certainty that without a miracle, theirs could be a tragic alliance.

Jack studied her so very seriously and said, "I know, Celina, I know. You're as afraid as I am. But we have more than so many couples have when they take this step. I love you very much. More every moment, if that's possible."

She nodded. "Forgive me if I'm trite, but I love you, too."

Thirty-nine

He couldn't quite shake the sensation that if he closed his eyes for too long, he'd open them and Celina would be gone. She shouldn't be there at all. They shouldn't be there—together. The events leading to this evening were more than fantastically improbable, yet they'd happened.

Jack didn't believe in premonitions, and he refused to continue playing with any notions that he could just wake up tomorrow and discover Celina had realized her mistake and left.

"This is a special night, isn't it, Daddy," Amelia said. Still bedecked in yellow, and still wearing yellow lace-edged socks and white patent Mary Janes, she sat at the table in the dining room they rarely used and ate the beignets Celina had suddenly decided were the perfect late-night wedding meal. Amelia's bedraggled frog sported a yellow ribbon around his neck.

"A very special night," Jack agreed. His little girl had fallen in love with the idea of having a mother. If he'd acted irresponsibly, she would suffer—they would both suffer.

Celina said, "Beignets and hot chocolate. What could be more special? You do know that pregnant women sometimes have strange cravings—for food—don't you, Amelia?"

Jack's daughter licked her fingers and frowned. "Cravings? That's like things you want a real lot. Do you want liver and icky stuff like that?"

She looked aggrieved when Jack and Celina laughed.

The three of them—Tilly had pleaded exhaustion and excused herself—sat at the colonial-style table with its highly polished surface, and scattered powdered sugar over fine white linen place mats.

The laughter softened the tension, and Jack breathed a little more deeply. He'd dispensed with the tuxedo in favor of gray chinos and a navy-blue shirt. Celina wore a bright red cotton sweatsuit and managed to appear exotic. The orchids she'd carried that afternoon were arranged in the center of the table, and she'd put one of the flowers in her hair, and another in Amelia's.

He smiled from one of them to the other.

They would make it work because they wanted to so much. His self-assurances were starting to sound like mantras.

The sound he'd come to dread interrupted his thoughts. The phone ringing in the hall.

"Don't answer it, Daddy," Amelia said.

She'd never know how badly he'd like to follow her instruction. Feeling Celina watching him, he left the dining room and lifted the receiver. "Charbonnet here."

"I read the paper. Errol help me read better, and I read the paper. And I see photographs. I know that man—the one in hospital. Sonny. Him almost dead, it say."

Antoine. Jack closed his eyes, held his breath, and willed himself to be calm. "I called every hospital for miles around looking for you. Nothing. You hid yourself well. I've waited for you to call back."

"I was afraid, me. Bad things happen."

"I know. It's all right now though. We can get everything worked out."

"My woman hurt. Burned."

Jack rested his brow against the wall.

"They come and threaten. Use cigarettes on her. One man. She tell me. She don't see his face, but I know him, me. She tell me she talk to Miss Celina, too. She like Miss Celina."

"Okay," Jack said. "Listen carefully and please don't hang up. You're going to be safe. I promise you that I'll keep you safe. Where are you?"

"My woman and boys, they safe now. They away from the Quarter. I'm nearby, me."

"Will you come to us here? In Chartres Street?"

There was silence, and Jack feared Antoine would hang up again, but he didn't press the man.

"I want to tell the things I know, but I'm not sure. I want that man to be punish for Rose. He very bad."

"If I promise to keep you safe, will you come with me and identify him for the police." At last Errol would get some justice, even though in death.

Another pause followed before Antoine said, "You go to the hospital, you. If I can, I meet you there."

Jack had argued, threatened, pleaded with her to stay behind, but Celina had refused. She wanted to see Antoine with her own eyes, and she did not want to take her eyes off Jack.

Police officers, seated on chairs outside the door to his glass-walled cubicle, guarded Sonny Clete.

Celina didn't think she'd seen the man before. His head was swathed in bandages and his open eyes moved incessantly above swollen pouches of bloodfilled skin. His fingers twitched, the nails scrabbling ineffectually at the thin white coverlet. Tubes and wires attached his body to machines that pumped, or beeped. Leads ran incessantly across screens.

Celina and Jack had stood there for half an hour, but there was no sign of Antoine. "He isn't going to come," Celina whispered.

"We can't be sure."

"Have a seat, ma'am," one of the cops said, getting up. When she tried to decline, he insisted, and she felt obliged to sit down.

"Don't say his name out loud," Jack said, his voice low. "He's coming now."

Celina couldn't stop herself from looking up, and along the corridor.

Balanced awkwardly on crutches, one leg in a cast to the knee, one arm in a sling, Antoine came toward them. His hair looked more white, and his shoulders weren't as massive. He had, in fact, lost a considerable amount of weight. When he drew near and raised his head, Celina had to swallow a cry. His face bore signs of a terrible beating. Sutures showed through clear dressings, and bruises stained almost every inch of skin. He was missing half a front tooth.

"Hello, my friend," Jack said.

Celina got up and went to Antoine. She rested a hand along his jaw. "Thank God, you're here," she said, and they exchanged a look that let her know he understood that she was giving thanks for his life.

"We have permission to go in," Jack said. "He looks worse than he is. He's pretty bad, but expected to live."

The policeman who had stood up said, "The door stays open."

The second officer added, "Here come the law," and referred to a nurse whose rubber-soled shoes squished officiously on the pale yellow linoleum.

She held up a silencing finger and went into Sonny's cubicle to do the things Celina assumed she did on a regular basis. Then the woman came out again. She looked skeptically at Antoine. "I take it this is the person you were waiting for. No more than five minutes in there, mind. And you look as if you belong in a bed yourself, sir." A sympathetic smile softened her scrubbed face before she returned to her station.

"Ready?" Jack asked.

Antoine didn't respond, but neither did he hesitate to go to the injured man's bedside. "Shot you, did they?" he asked, looking down at Sonny. "I read that, me. You prettier in your picture in the paper. You a true mess, yes, sir. The man who burn my Rose, he the man who do all this to me, right? He tie me up and beat me, right? Brave man, him."

Only Sonny's eyes moved. He swallowed and, in a dry whisper, said, "I didn't have no part of it."

"You there when he do it," Antoine said. "You the man who sit behind me. I know your voice. I hear it before—when you go to Mr. Errol. I see you there too."

"I didn't touch you, old man."

"You let the other one touch me. And him touch my Rose, and threaten my boys."

"Nobody stops Primrose." Sonny swallowed and his throat clicked. "He's dead now. Died with Win."

"You mean you killed him when you killed Win?" Jack said.

Celina expected someone to stop them and throw them out at any moment.

"It wasn't that way. I didn't mean to shoot Win. It was an accident. Then Win's personal triggerman did this to me. And he killed Primrose. I never saw the rest of it."

Antoine let out a breath. "Dead," he said. "They leave me to die. But Antoine strong. It take me hours, but I crawl out of that place, and they take me to hospital. I pretend my head too bad for me to remember nothing. Not my name. That way no one find me."

"Including your friends," Jack muttered.

"I think I live to kill that Primrose. A man call Primrose?" Antoine shook his head.

Celina heard the squeak of returning nurse's shoes.

"Antoine," Jack said urgently, "this is the man you wanted to tell Dwayne about, isn't it? And Celina? You saw him leaving Errol's place after he was killed."

"Yes."

Celina put her hands to her mouth.

"You wanted to say you'd seen him because he was the only one who could have killed Errol."

Antoine looked at Sonny. "He the last one."

"I went to get the money," Sonny said. "Errol liked to give me money because I watched out for you, Jack. I went to pick it up that morning—it was almost light. But poor Errol was dead, so I went away again."

Celina headed off the nurse at the door and whispered, "Please give us just two more minutes? I promise we'll leave then."

The woman looked dubious, but said, "Two minutes."

"You were taking payoffs from Errol?" Jack said.

"Just a few times. And real recent. He was concerned about you."

"Damn you," Jack said. "You extorted money from Errol."

"Keep your voice down," Celina warned him. "They'll kick us out. That explains the money Errol took out of the Dreams account."

"You gonna be put away for what you did to my wife," Antoine said.

"I didn't—"

"You were part of it. You let it happen, and you helped that Primrose with what he did to me. I tell the police so."

Jack's agitation grew visible. "And you'll tell the police about seeing Sonny leave Errol's. He must have killed him."

Antoine frowned. "The woman there too. The one who come sometimes in the night. When I work late I see her sometimes. She there that night, but she leave before. Later this one come."

"I tell you, Errol was dead when I got there," Sonny said, his voice growing weaker. "On the bathroom floor. But I saw him." He narrowed his eyes at Antoine. "That's why we had to teach this one some lessons. He was too dangerous. He could have fingered me for somethin' I didn't do. I don't like injustice."

Celina almost laughed aloud. "And then you and your friend grabbed me. I didn't see either of you, but from what was said, I'm sure it was you. Did you take me and scare me almost to death because you're such a justice freak?"

Sonny ignored her and kept on looking at Antoine. "He was dead when I got there, I tell you. That's why I had to lean on you. You coulda fingered me for somethin' I didn't have nothin' to do with."

"Well," Jack said. "Would you know the woman, Antoine?"

"Mrs. Sally Lamar," he said without hesitation.

Jack scrubbed at his face. "Do you think that woman could have held Errol under the water until he drowned, then hauled him out onto the floor."

Antoine shook his head. "Not her. But the man, maybe."

"Sonny? Yeah, I surely believe that too."

"Could be," Antoine said, "or the other one, the man who come there before this Sonny."

With Antoine between them, Jack and Celina stood in the driveway of the hospital.

"I got me a room," Antoine said. "Nice boardinghouse. Ms. Simmons. On Rampart Street. I go there, me. You let me know—"

"Miss Payne! Miss Payne! Wait, please."

The nurse from the ICU puffed up to them. "Thank goodness I caught you. There's an emergency at home and they need you there."

Jack bit back the temptation to tell the nurse that Miss Payne, was Mrs. Charbonnet. "Do you mean her present home?"

"The message was from a Mrs. Bitsy Payne."

The woman left at a trot, and Jack tried to read Celina's expression.

"You better go there," Antoine said. "Only trouble call this time of night."

"Thanks a lot," Celina said sharply, and looked abashed. "Sorry. This has been a long day. Jack and I were married this afternoon."

Antoine stared at her, then at Jack—and he grinned his gappy grin. "Well, that good news. Mr. Errol would smile. He love you. Both of you."

"And we loved him," Jack said. "We're going to make sure whoever killed him pays for it." He hailed a cab idling at the curb and insisted Antoine come with them.

"I want you, too," Celina said. "You shouldn't be on your own. Not even at nice Ms. Simmons's. We'll deal with whatever my parents want, then you can use a spare bedroom at our place."

Jack couldn't hold back his broad smile. He couldn't ignore his pleasure at hearing her refer to her new home so naturally.

With Antoine a reluctant third passenger, they rode into the Garden District, to Neville and Bitsy Payne's slightly shabby Italianate cottage on Chestnut Street.

Jack paid the cabbie and took his card, extracting a promise that the man would return when called.

A figure approached along the sidewalk, and Cyrus was illuminated beneath a streetlight.

"Gathering of the clan," Celina said to her brother when he joined them.

They went in a pack up the uneven front path. The gardens weren't as well-kept as they must once have been but they were still beautiful. A tangle of lush palms and vines cut out much of the moon's glow. White paint around the arched dormer window did gleam. So did stone parapets along the base of the roof.

The only light that showed inside the house was through glass panels in the front door. Jack hesitated. Should he have sent Celina back to Chartres Street?

She went ahead and tried the front door. It was unlocked and she stepped into a wide, stone-tiled hall. Finely molded ceilings soared above walls covered with russet silk.

Bitsy erupted from a darkened corridor, but before Jack could do more than register her disheveled appearance, he saw Charmain Bienville behind her.

"There you are at last," Bitsy shrieked. "I have waited and waited for you two, and what do you do? You bring strangers with you." The glower she aimed at Jack paled beside the one she gave Antoine.

Cyrus said, "Celina brought her husband and their good friend. What is it, Mama? Why the frantic summons?" He looked at Charmain. "And this is?"

"Oh, you know perfectly well," Charmain said. "Cyrus Payne, you've met me many times."

He made a politely disinterested sound.

"It's your father," Bitsy said, crossing her arms tightly. "He's locked himself in his study and won't come out. Wilson's been trying to talk to him, but Neville just tells him to go away. Cyrus, your daddy says he wants to *end* it all. He says his life is ruined. I can lay this at the feet of our children. You've brought us so low. Now it's up to you to save the man who adopted you and has given his life to you."

For once Wilson Lamar chose the right time to put in an appearance. As soon as he saw them all, he had eyes only for Celina. Jack felt an insane desire to punch the man's nose.

"I'm going to talk to Daddy," Celina said. "He's probably had too much to drink. This isn't the first time he's locked himself away and made threats about killing himself."

"Oh, how can you?" Bitsy wailed. "We've never been on the brink of such disaster before. You know how bad it is, don't you, Charmain? You talked to him before you came over."

"You do have a way of showing up before the bad news hits, Charmain," Wilson said, his mouth turned down. "I'm starting to wonder what comes first, you or the bad news. Or perhaps you *are* the bad news."

"What does that mean?" She faced him. "Just what does that mean, Wilson?"

"You got to my house to commiserate with me about Sally's death almost before the police left. How do you explain that?"

"Damn you," she said. "I . . . I heard it on the radio."

"It wasn't on the radio yet," Wilson pointed out.

"Police radio," Charmain said. "Reporters live with them, in case you've forgotten."

"Always around," Wilson said vaguely. "Always . . . close. You took it, didn't you?"

"Shut up, you fool," Charmain hissed. "We can talk later."

"Why didn't I think about you taking it. You were at the party. You probably followed me, then took the film out of my closet."

"*Shut up.*"

"I'm going to Daddy," Celina said, and pushed passed the pair. Jack followed her to a door where a line of light showed at the bottom.

"It's Celina," she called out, tapping. "Can I come in, Daddy?"

"Are you alone?"

She glanced at Jack, who nodded and drew back.

"Yes."

"I'm goin' to end it all, girlie. It's all goin' to come out, and I can't face the talk."

Jack had started to edge away, but now he held his ground.

"Hush," Celina said. "It can't be as bad as that."

"It's worse, baby. Your daddy thought he could do what was best for you—best for all of us. But I made a mess of it."

"Let me in." Panic loaded her voice. "Open the door, please. I want to come in."

"I never want you to see ugliness because of me," Neville Payne said. "I'm just goin' to finish it. Then they can send in the professionals. They know how to deal with these things. You look after your mama. She isn't strong. She's not used to dealin' with difficult things. Above all, you shelter her from the talk there's goin' to be, hear?"

"I hear," Celina said quietly. She bowed her head and leaned on the doorjamb. "We can work this out. Whatever it is, we'll work it out. Don't do something silly, please. We need you."

"If you needed me, you wouldn't have married that gangster. You'd have stayed with your own kind and married the one man who could have given us all back the life we used to have. He's clever. And he wants you so much. He'd have found a way to keep all this quiet, but now it'll come out, and I can't take that."

Jack wanted to ask what the hell the man was talking about, but knew better than to interfere now.

"You shouldn't have told Errol about Wilson, baby. That was stupid. People like us stick together. And Wilson didn't mean to hurt you. He wanted you real bad—he always wanted you real bad. And he was getting rid of that wife of his when everything went completely wrong. He would soon have had all the evidence he needed to divorce her without hurting his campaign, and marry you."

"I'm not carrying on a conversation through this door anymore," Celina told Neville. "Either open up, or I'm leaving. You aren't making any sense."

"You told Errol Petrie that Wilson had . . . Well, you told him, and Errol came to me expectin' me to take action against Wilson. I couldn't do that. I told Wilson. He told me what I already knew. Errol had to go. Your fault, baby, for not keepin' your own counsel the way you were taught."

Jack saw when Celina held her breath.

"I had to wait for Wilson's own wife to get out of Errol's bed before I could go in there. She was an animal, a sex-crazed animal. Tied him up and everythin'. I was afraid she wouldn't leave while there was still time before mornin'. I did it. I did it good, but Wilson talked too much and that Bienville bitch knows and she'll use the story. She came and told me she would."

When Celina raised her face, Jack was appalled at her pallor. She settled her dark eyes on him for an instant, then pummeled the door to Neville's study and yelled, "Let me in! You killed Errol? My God, you're mad. Let me in now!"

An explosive sound of breaking glass galvanized Jack. He threw himself at Celina, knocking her to the ground and covering her with his body.

A man's voice raised in screaming sobs shook him. He inched along, away from the door, with Celina beside him.

"Stay where you are."

He looked up and over his shoulder at a cop with gun drawn. A gun aimed directly at Jack's head.

"I'm not going anywhere," Jack said. "Would you like me to raise my hands?"

"Don't raise anythin'." The gun wavered slightly, and Jack figured this was not a seasoned member of the force. All the more reason to lie quite still.

Running feet seemed to close in from all sides. A woman shrieked. Another shouted—this one easily identifiable as Charmain Bienville, who was certain the police "couldn't possibly know who they were pushin' around." Wilson Lamar blustered loudly, but evidently these officers were not easily impressed by personalities.

The cop with his piece trained on Jack spoke into a walkie-talkie and promptly told Jack to get up slowly, take "the lady" with him, and to go into the study.

Within moments Jack, with an arm around Celina, stood in Neville's mahogany and leather domain, together with Bitsy, Charmain, Cyrus, Wilson, and Antoine. Antoine was promptly helped into a chair.

Glass from a broken French door littered the desk and the floor. Neville's hands were cuffed behind him, and the man who held his arm was Detective O'Leary, whose expression was more than a little satisfied.

The detective parroted rights in all directions.

Bitsy crept into a chair and stared at the floor.

"I don't need a lawyer," Charmain said. "God, what a mess. I need the phone. My paper expects me to check in."

"You'll be checking in," O'Leary said. "We'll take you in person and you'll check in at a place we got in mind. You won't be writing any stories about it."

"I only came to try to help my old friends, the Paynes," Wilson said. "If you'll excuse me, I'm still in shock and I'd like to get home to bed."

"We'd all like to get home to bed." O'Leary's glance took in the six police officers ranged around the room. "And we will. But some things can't be hurried. I told you we would let you know when we had what we needed, Mr. Charbonnet."

Jack struggled with what he'd learned. "You killed Errol, Neville? Because you wanted to protect Wilson and then wait until he was free to marry Celina?"

"Shut up," Wilson snapped. "All of you. Don't say another word."

"You've got that wrong," Charmain said. "Wilson and I go back a long way. We've got an understanding, haven't we, love?"

"Cuff her," O'Leary said brusquely.

The officer who followed that instruction had to deal with a spirited scuffle, but he accomplished his aim. When he finally held her in front of him, O'Leary approached and said, "You've already been read your rights. You're sure you don't want a lawyer present?"

"I've already said I don't need one. Now, get these things off me."

"We have witnesses, Miss Bienville."

She grew still. "You're trying to make me say something that'll make me sound guilty. I haven't done anything."

"Mr. and Mrs. Reed were taken into custody. They were found in the vicinity of the car where Mrs. Lamar was murdered. They say they saw the crime committed by a woman with a knife who stabbed the victim repeatedly."

Charmain renewed her efforts to struggle free. "Let me go now, or I'll sue your asses."

"Charmain Bienville, I'm arresting you for the murder of—"

"I didn't do it!" Charmain screamed until she retched. Gagging, gulping for breath, she whispered, "Those Jesus freaks did it. They followed her because they were afraid she might say something damning about their darling son. Something that would ruin their chances to clean up."

"Who exactly did they follow?" O'Leary asked, almost disinterestedly.

"Sally, of course. Wilson knew that bitch inside out. He saw that Ben and knew he'd found what he needed. Ben's the type Sally went for. Wilson figured she wouldn't rest until she got him inside her pants. And he was right. And it was all working. No one would have blamed him for divorcing her after the way she shamed him. Then we'd have been together. But she had to start shooting her mouth off to the priest." She avoided looking at Cyrus.

"Mr. Angel told us all about it," O'Leary said. "I must admit it sounded a bit fantastic, but ambition drives people to desperate measures, so I've discovered."

Charmain's face crumpled. "I love Wilson. I'm not ambitious, I just love him. I'd do anything for him." A police officer caught her as she passed out.

"Including murder," O'Leary said.

Forty

"Philomena wrapped the cape of stars around her and kissed the Dragon Prince. The cape wasn't cold, but warm, very warm. And it sparkled. Philomena had always been partial to a little sparkle.

"Ahead, at the very top of the world, lay the North Pole. Philomena was disappointed to see that it was a bit frayed, and stuck together with Mickey Mouse Band-Aids in places."

Celina smiled at Jack and adored him for his patience. They'd arrived back from the most gruelling experience of her life to find Amelia too excited to sleep, and he'd found the patience to tell her the requested story.

"The very top of the pole was missing altogether, and Santa's toy makers were chipping another one out of a block of wood in the workshops."

Cyrus had insisted they leave Chestnut Street, and that he would remain with Bitsy, who was sedated and unlikely to awaken for hours anyway. They must, Cyrus told them, have at least some of their wedding night alone together.

Amelia snuggled against Celina, and they were both propped against the little girl's pink pillows. Amelia said, "The North Pole's broken because the elves keep bumping into it when they're taking flying lessons. Santa takes their licenses away, but as soon as he gives them back, up they go again, and *bam*."

"Who's telling this story?" Jack asked.

Amelia wiggled until she could see Celina's face. "I told you he's bossy," she said.

Choosing diplomacy that might prove ultimately dangerous, Celina said, "You did. And he is."

Jack's green eyes grew narrow in the way she'd come to know as a warning. Fortunately she expected to enjoy any punishment he meted out.

"Go on, Daddy," Amelia said. "Just a little bit more. *Please.*"

"The Dragon Prince led the way, and Philomena walked in his footsteps because she didn't want to get her satin slippers wet in the snow if she could help it."

"Her slippers are green," Amelia said. "Lily-pad green with magic water lilies on them that open when Phillymeana's really happy. And they light up to show the way and everything."

"Wonderful," Celina said, watching Jack. Such a complex man, and each layer yielded something else she hugged to her with a sense of having found another treasure. She had started to feel she could belong here, that he wanted truly her.

"That's when Nobby Gnome came swooshing down the hill on his sleigh pulled by fifteen Jack Russell Terriers."

"*Jack Russell Terriers?*" Celina said before she could contain herself.

"They're very well suited to the job," Amelia said. "Daddy told me. It's because they've got lots of energy and they like to run around. So Nobby can't wear them out. He's always rushing somewhere, see."

"Nobby Gnome swooshed down the hill on his sleigh pulled by fifteen Jack Russell Terriers," Jack said in an ominous tone. "He swirled to a stop near Philomena and the Dragon Prince, opened the fur blankets at his feet, and lifted out the most beautiful elf baby they'd ever seen. 'This one is placed in your care,' he said. 'Because you've proved that you consider love the most important gift of all, you shall take him home and if, when we meet again, this baby is strong and happy in an appropriate home you have found for him, then I shall ask you to serve me again.' "

"No!" Amelia said, popping to sit up again. "That's wrong. Nobby gave the elf baby to Phillymeana and the Dragon Prince to take care of in their home, so they took the baby home and he grew strong and happy and they *still* got another one later on."

Celina hugged Amelia, who put her face on Celina's stomach and patted it at the same time.

Quiet, watching them thoughtfully, Jack sat still on the edge of the bed. Celina met his gaze over Amelia's head.

Very soon Amelia closed her eyes. Celina eased her down into the bed, tucked F.P. close beside her, and pulled up the covers.

Jack stood and waited for her to come to him. He took her to their bedroom, where he locked the door.

"What a day," he said.

"Unbelievable. There's so much to get used to and deal with."

"For both of us. Look, I'm going to say what needs to be said right now. When I had just asked you to marry me, I told myself I was protecting Errol's image. That was part of it. I already wanted you—the baby was a great excuse to do something about it."

She pulled the bedraggled orchid from her hair and twirled it in her fingers.

"You aren't going to make this any easier, I see," Jack said. "Okay, I can handle it. You are my wife and I want you. I want you in my life. You make me complete and I didn't even know I wasn't complete until I wanted you.

"Do you think you want to make this work? I mean, do you think you'll want to stay with me even after the baby's been born?"

The words she wanted to say were a jumble. "Yes," she told him. "Thank you."

He turned up his palms and frowned. "Yes, thank you? That's it? You don't feel more strongly about it than that?"

Celina rested a hand on her tummy and said, "I feel so strongly I can't put it into words. You are already my life. You, the baby, Amelia. And what you just said is too much. I hoped we could make something out of what we feel for each other, but I didn't dare hope for this much."

Jack lowered his hands. He let out a noisy breath. "That means you want it to work as much as I do."

"At least as much."

He laughed, sobered, laughed again—and paced and shook his head. "Good. Great. Yes, great. Oh, *yes*, great. Absolutely great." He closed the drapes before shedding his clothes.

She could look at him forever. Tall and straight, and strong, with green eyes that were narrowed yet again, he did things to her that made her wonder if she wasn't a nymphomaniac.

Totally comfortable with his nakedness, he came to Celina and pulled her shirt over her head.

Promptly she attempted to cover her belly.

"Don't," Jack said, moving her arms and taking off the rest of her clothes. "I've been waiting to do this for hours. Making love to a pregnant lady who happens to be your wife is . . . oh, it's so sexy."

Celina wrinkled up her face. "The most difficult day of . . . well, at least of *my* life, and you tell me the only thing you've had on your mind is sex?"

"I'm a man. You know how base we are. And in case you've forgotten, this was our wedding day."

"That was a good bit."

Jack ran his hands over her breasts, traced pale veins with the tip of a finger. He kissed her and walked her to the bed. The backs of her knees connected with the mattress, and she toppled onto the bed. With a hand braced on either side of her shoulders, Jack leaned over her. "The wedding was a very good bit. Now comes the *really* good bit."